FACING EVIL

Sally

Enjoy

FACING EVIL

CL HART

Cavalier Press
2005

FACING EVIL

ISBN 0-9765664-2-7

0 9 8 7 6 5 4 3 2 1

Cover Design by Michelle M. De La Rosa

Published by Cavalier Press, LLP
P.O. Box 6437, Falls Church, VA 22040
Web site http://www.cavalierpress.com

Printed and bound in the United States of America

Acknowledgements

With great respect and admiration, I would like to say thank you to those people without whom this novel would never have come into being: to Dr. Marco Terwiel for your medical knowledge and input; to everyone at Cavalier Press – quite simply – thank you; to my parents, whose love and support has guided me uphill and always forward; and to Meredith, my Angel – it is your love that makes me believe that I can fly.

In memory of
My Nana and My Chappy
R.I.P.

PROLOGUE

The shrill ringing pulled her mind from a distant nightmare. She reached for the phone with one hand and fumbled at the bedside lamp with the other. An empty liquor bottle fell to the floor.

"Sarah?" Her heart ached when she recalled where she was and why. She sat up in bed and rubbed her gritty eyes as she listened to the voice on the other end of the line. "Sorry, Lincoln. Say that again?" She tried to focus as the voice spoke.

"Okay. Hang on." She reached for the pen and notepad sitting on the nightstand. "Why are you calling me? Okay. Who's at the crime scene? All right, I'll be there, but it'll still take me a bit."

Minutes later, Abby Stanfield emerged from the bedroom tucking the folded paper into her jeans. Walking silently, she slipped her borrowed cell phone and the black wallet containing her gold shield into the pocket of her leather jacket.

She reached for her keys and as an after-thought grabbed a bagel to eat on the way. Hearing the pounding of the rain, she turned back and snatched a new ball cap that read POLICE. With the bagel still in her mouth, she quickly pulled her hair through the cap and headed out into the miserable gray of the early morning.

☯

The flashing lights of the gathered police cars directed Abby to her destination. She approached a uniformed officer, lowered the window of her Jeep and showed her ID.

"Park it over there. Quinn's down that path. You can't miss him." The officer raised the yellow tape, allowing Abby to wheel alongside a patrol car.

She climbed slowly out of her vehicle. She was tired and sore and it showed. Slipping a piece of gum in her mouth, she headed for her partner.

"Abby. Down here." She raised her hand in acknowledgment and made her way towards a man holding an umbrella. Even in the pouring rain at a murder scene, she could see his tie and white pressed collar under his dark raincoat.

"Morning, Linc."

"Morning. Thought I better get you out here before you heard about it from somewhere else. Down here." He motioned down the path.

"Heard what?" Abby stopped and stood nose to nose with the black man holding the umbrella.

Lincoln Quinn was one of the few people Abby literally looked up to. At six feet one inch, most people were unable to look her straight in the eye, but Lincoln Quinn topped her by several inches. They were more than partners; they were friends. He had taken her under his wing when she had first arrived in the department with her new, gold shield.

"You're not even supposed to be here, so I'll make this quick." He noted the tired look in her eyes and the faint smell of alcohol, but he didn't blame her. She had good reason. He wondered how much sleep she had had over the last few days.

"Lincoln," Abby interrupted his thoughts. "Show me the body."

Lincoln pointed over his shoulder. "It's over here."

They made their way through the tall trees of the park. A winding asphalt path took them down toward the handful of men scouring the crime scene. The rain had stopped, but the sounds of incessant dripping echoed loudly as they made their way toward a small bridge. The creek running beneath was engorged with rainwater, turning its color murky brown.

"Abby—wait."

It took her a moment to realize Lincoln was no longer beside her. Turning back, she looked at her partner.

"What?"

"Abby, before you go down there …"

She turned from the concerned features of her friend to the men below them who had stopped working at her approach.

"Abby, wait!"

Ignoring him, she took the last steps down the path.

There were half a dozen men performing various crime scene investigation procedures, but they all stopped working as she approached. They wanted to see her reaction.

"Goddamn it, Abby, would you wait?" Lincoln caught up to her and grabbed her by the arm. "Look at me."

Her eyes moved slowly over the men and fell onto the stained white sheet draped over a motionless mound next to the creek. The noise of the swollen stream made it hard for her to make out what Lincoln was saying. Through her thick jacket, she felt his grasp on her arm tighten, as he gently shook her.

"What?" Her own deep voice sounded distant as she turned to look at Lincoln. "What?"

Lincoln released his hold.

"It's Ward."

"What?"

"It's Billy Ward." Abby followed him as he bent down and pulled back the white sheet to reveal a face.

Abby looked down at the victim. Past emotions pulled at her. *It was unreal; it was untrue; it couldn't be …* and then Lincoln's words finally hit her. It was Ward. The reality of it felt distant, but at the same time the pain was so close that it almost overwhelmed her.

The man at her feet had short black hair, wet from the rain. His face was battered and bruised, frozen in a grossly distorted mask of death. Something was in his mouth, but Abby didn't look at it closely. She swallowed hard, but refused to look away. "You fucking bastard—you had it coming," she whispered hoarsely, "you had it coming."

"And they made sure he got it," Lincoln said as he lifted the sheet higher.

There were multitudes of stab wounds, dark and deep; cuts and slices opened the flesh with wide gaping wounds. Large abrasions and small scrapes covered what was left of his exposed, bruised body. Abby's eyes went down his mutilated and beaten body, but they stopped at his bloody butchered groin. "Jesus Christ," she said quietly as she looked back to his mouth, where his penis had become his gag.

☯

An older woman in a late model sedan wheeled up to the closed gate of the park.

"Morning, lieutenant." The young patrol officer nodded at the woman.

"Is Detective Stanfield on site?" Lieutenant Banks asked.

The officer suddenly looked uneasy.

"Officer … Barker is it? Is Detective Stanfield on site or not?"

"Yes, ma'am," he admitted.

"Thank you." She watched as the gate opened. "Keep that press back. Way back. Understood?"

Officer Barker nodded.

Lieutenant Mary Banks seldom left her desk, but the torture and execution of the city's infamous murderer and rapist was enough to bring her out, even on this miserable morning.

William Daniel Ward was the lowest form of animal, one who preyed on young innocent women. He had a demented reverence for high school girls; he loved them but he hated them. Using a sap from a dieffenbachia plant, he made a paste that would numb their vocal chords, rendering them silent so that he could brutally and repeatedly rape and sodomize them, knowing no one would ever hear their desperate screams. When he was finally through with them, he'd cut and dismember them. They died a slow and extremely painful death. Every law enforcement officer in the city was involved in one aspect or another of the case, but Detectives Stanfield and Quinn were the primary investigators. Abby and Lincoln had worked hard, but they couldn't seem to catch a break. Then chance threw them a name; William Daniel Ward. A spark of possibility grew to a flicker of probability. Abby became fixated on the case, working like one possessed, but Billy Ward had covered his tracks well. Then his thumbprint showed up on a soda can found in the last victim's car. Abby finally had a chance to bring about the end of the fear that held a stranglehold on the city. It wasn't much, but it was enough for a warrant. She made sure she and Lincoln checked every step, crossed every "t" and dotted every "i" before they left for Ward's farmhouse on the edge of town.

The two served the warrant. All the evidence they needed was there for them to find. The room he had kept his victims in, the knives he had used, the clothes he had left behind and all the blood that would forever stain the basement of the house on Elderberry Lane.

Abby and Lincoln had him, without question, without doubt. The evidence had given them all they needed. They were confident and the prosecution was satisfied they had the right man. The victims' mute voices and the extensive evidence found in that basement, had led them to an arrest in the most gruesome case the city had ever seen. The case was about to be delivered to a judge on a silver platter and then it fell apart. A first year law student stumbled across a major malfeasance in the evidence that crumbled the foundation of the prosecution case. The warrant had listed the house, not the basement. The defense argued the basement was a detached dwelling because it had a separate entrance and the judge agreed. He threw out all the evidence and William Daniel Ward had walked out of the courtroom a free man.

Abby and Lincoln left Billy's corpse to the forensic team and had headed towards the parking lot. A simple statement on Lincoln's part had started a heated conversation, and now they stood face-to-face, oblivious to those around them.

"Not all of it has to make it into a police report!"

"Goddamn it, Abby, Banks needs to know! They're part of the investigation."

"No, they're not!"

Her patience and emotions were riding on her sleeve. She was exhausted and he could see the events of her life clearly on her tired face. "It's her name …"

"Don't! I mean it!" Abby's temper flared and she got up in his face. "Just back off!"

"Abby, you need to learn to trust people."

"What the fuck is that supposed to mean?" Abby fired at her partner as a set of headlights flashed over them.

"It means exactly what it means. You don't trust me!" A car door slammed and Lincoln and Abby looked over to see Lieutenant Banks heading straight for them.

I don't fucking need this right now. Abby ran her fingers through her hair.

Lieutenant Banks approached them. "Lincoln," she said nodding. "Abby—we won't go into why you shouldn't be here."

"It was my idea …" Lincoln started.

"She's a big girl, Lincoln, she knows she isn't supposed to be here. That aside, tell me the two of you are not standing here arguing while evidence is being trampled and lost."

"No, what evidence there is has been collected," Lincoln replied as his brown eyes shifted to Abby.

"What do you mean, what evidence?" Banks demanded. "Elaborate."

"What there is wouldn't fill a shoe box. It's like Ward fell from the sky. There's nothing, not a footprint, a tire track, nothing. Ward didn't die down there," Lincoln stated.

"Show me." All three turned and headed for the location of the dead man.

Lieutenant Banks was quiet as she examined the crime scene for herself. She had yet to look at the body. Whatever evidence was there for the human eye to see wasn't going anywhere, and any secrets the scene held were for forensics to find.

Abby excused herself for a moment and walked over to the detectives who were doing the measurements.

Lieutenant Banks watched Abby. "She can't be here."

"I had to call her."

"She's not a part of this. I want her out of here. Understood?" Lincoln nodded. There was a long pause before she spoke again. "On a personal note … how is she?"

Detective Quinn kept his eyes on his partner as she conferred with one of the investigators. "I don't think it's hit her yet. I mean, I wasn't expecting her to shed tears, but …" Lincoln's voice trailed off.

Neither spoke for a while, each lost in their own concerns. Abby wasn't the only female in Lieutenant Bank's squad, and though she tried not to play favorites, sometimes she knew she did. There was something special about Abby. She was a dark shadow of mystery hiding behind a wall few got past.

"I don't want this coming back to bite us in the ass, Lincoln."

"I know, lieutenant."

"There's going to be a lot of people looking in the wrong direction over this. By the numbers and by the book. Got it?"

"You have my word," he promised and then returned to the job at hand.

Lieutenant Banks waved for Abby to join her. She walked to the creek bridge and waited at the weathered handrail as Abby approached.

"The body wasn't dumped from up here," Abby stated firmly. "With all the rain we've had in the last few days, the ground down there is very soft and would have shown some sign of that amount of weight landing even from this small height."

The lieutenant nodded as she looked up to see the mortician coming down the trail with Lincoln.

"Abby, after everything …"

Abby held up her hand. "I know."

"The press is out there in full force and I don't want this to become a media circus. If your name shows up in any more headlines …"

"It won't."

"It can't."

The two women studied each other. "My hands are tied, Abby. I'm sorry." Lieutenant Banks turned to leave, but then turned back to face Abby. "This case has been your main focus for so long … and once before I had to force you to take a step back and take a leave of absence. Don't make me do it again."

Abby's eyes drifted down to the swollen creek rushing below her, but she made no sign that she heard her lieutenant's words.

"Abby, he's dead, and no matter what happens, he can never touch another girl again."

Abby remained silent as the water churned beneath her.

"Abby, I'm sorry about Sarah."

Abby's memories swirled with the water below and it took her back to another time—before it all started—to a time when it should have all ended.

PART I

CHAPTER I

The courtroom was out of control, but Abby sat calmly in the last row. The judge banged his gavel, but soon gave up and left for the sanctuary of his chambers. The assistant district attorney threw his papers into his briefcase, his face a mixture of disbelief and anger. Some of the victims' parents cried as they struggled to understand what had happened and why the man who had murdered their children was about to walk free. Members of the press fell over themselves to be the first to get the news out to the public.

"Abby? Abby …" She could hear Lincoln's voice, but she couldn't pull her eyes off Billy Ward. The alleged murderer turned from his lawyer and his intense blue eyes fell on Abby's solemn face. He held up his wrists to indicate they were no longer in cuffs.

You animal! I have seen what you have done with those hands. Those innocent people who should be alive right now … Abby's mind swirled as her anger boiled below the surface.

"Abby, let's go. Come on." Lincoln's words permeated her hatred as she watched Billy Ward smile a crooked teasing smile as he dared to wink at her. Detective Quinn saw the exchange between the cocky criminal and the silent woman next to him, and he realized he had to get her out of there. Rising, he grabbed a fistful of her leather jacket and pulled her to her feet.

"Come on!"

She rose at his command, but she had yet to break the stare. In the mass exodus from the courtroom, Lincoln attempted to steer Abby away, but in the press of bodies, they were forced closer to the man she loathed.

"Abby, does this mean we aren't going to be having our little conversations any more? 'Cause I'll miss that, just like I'll miss you—calling out my name in your sleep," Billy laughed.

Lincoln saw the hatred in Abby's eyes. "Abby, forget it. Let's go!" Lincoln warned.

"Mister Ward, how does it feel to be a free man, even though most of the people of this city believe you are guilty of all those charges?" A young reporter pushed a microphone into Billy's face, but Billy kept his eyes on Abby.

"I'm a free man because I'm an innocent man, who was wrongly accused. I'm not a murderer or a rapist, but I am a man, and I do love beautiful young women." He laughed. Some people in the crowd cringed at the sadistic sound.

Lincoln had his hands full, desperately trying to get his partner out of the hallway outside of the courtroom and away from Billy. Realizing that it was almost impossible with the mob, he pinned her up against the cold marble and wood wall. "Goddamn it, Abby, stop it before you do something stupid."

Abby pulled her eyes away from Billy and focused them on Lincoln. "We can't do a thing Lincoln … not a fucking thing until that animal rapes and murders someone else and then disappears into whatever hole he lives in. We have nothing, because everything there was just got thrown out." She clenched her teeth. "He's a murdering bastard who gets pleasure out of raping and torturing girls …"

At that moment, Billy and his entourage of lawyers and reporters walked by Abby and Lincoln. The throng of moving bodies jostled the detectives just as Billy leaned into Abby. "Thanks for everything, sweetie. Until we meet again." He smiled and kissed her.

All hell erupted as Abby broke from Lincoln's hold as if he wasn't even there. "I'll fuckin' kill you!" Abby roared. Her first punch broke Billy's nose; the second cracked a few teeth.

Flash bulbs popped off in every direction as the ruckus drew the television cameras from outside into the mêlée. Free from Lincoln's grasp, Abby was uncontrollable as she let loose a flurry of powerful punches. Parents of some of the dead women got close enough to join in. People were pushing and shoving, some trying to get away, others trying to get closer. It was chaos.

It took the police and the court officers forever to get control of the situation. Realizing what the scene was going to mean for Abby, Lincoln grabbed her by the back of her jacket and with the help of two other officers dragged her to the rear of the crowd.

"Get her out of here, detective," one of the uniformed officers said. Winded, all Lincoln could do was nod as he dragged his disheveled partner towards the stairs. They said nothing as they clambered down the cement stairwell, every movement echoing in their ears. They reached the door that read *Parking Garage. Authorized Personal Only* without running into anyone.

When the heavy fire door slammed shut behind them, Lincoln turned Abby around to face him. "Are you out of your mind?"

"He had it coming!" Abby yelled back at him. "We had him dead to rights and because of some …" Her breath came in gulps as her anger festered. "Technicality …" She spat.

"We screwed up."

"We didn't screw up, Lincoln, the law did. There isn't a sane person out there who doesn't know he did it." Her head was pounding as she struggled to get the words out. "That … that animal is going to prey on someone else."

"And we will be there to catch him."

"I'm not going to stand around and wait for someone else to become a statistic." Abby's adrenaline pumped wildly through her body as she shook a fist at him. "He's killed too many already."

"So you put your entire career on the line and go after him. Jesus, Abby, the whole press gallery saw you split the man's face open as you threatened to kill him."

"Do I look like I give a damn?" she yelled back at him.

"Abby, you're one of the best cops I know, and I'm not going to stand around and watch *you* throw your life out the goddamn window because of some filth like Ward!" he yelled back at her, his own anger exploding. "He won this time, and you let him get to you. He won. You lost." The statement sent Abby over the edge. She collected Lincoln's shirt in her hand, then cocked back with a closed fist.

"Go ahead and hit me, if it'll make you feel better." He watched her eyes and he knew she wasn't going to hit him. "Abby, you're like a sister to me. I don't want to see you throw everything away. Not like this."

She still held him by the front of his shirt, but slowly her grip loosened and she dropped her head.

"It's been a shitty day. Let's just get out of here and go have a drink somewhere," he said as her right fist finally relented and fell to her side. It was then he saw her knuckles.

"Abby, look at what you did. You need to get that …" He looked down at her left hand and saw the blood. "You're a mess."

Abby looked down at her bloody hands. They still shook from the rush of adrenaline. From deep inside her jacket came the distinctive warble of her cell phone. "Shit," she said with a dejected sigh.

"Want me to answer it?" he questioned.

She shook her head. "Let it ring."

"You know who it's going to be," he said looking at her and she nodded. "You okay?" he asked as the cell phone rang a few more times and then went silent. When Abby did not answer him, Lincoln looked at his battered and bruised partner. He still had one question. "Abby, what were you thinking about, going after him like that?"

"You want to know what I was thinking about?" She did not attempt to hide her frustration as she turned to face him. "I'll tell you what I was thinking about. I was thinking about all the girls we've let down. I was thinking about Cheryl Lawrence, Traci Stempler, Anita …" The names continued but she no longer had a voice to say them. Abby went quiet for a moment before she continued. "I'm sick of him. I'm sick of having to clean up after him." Abby finally lifted her head. "I wanted this to be over." Lincoln was surprised at the growing shimmer in her eyes in the dim light of the underground garage. It was rare to see her cry.

"Abby …" he started, but she stopped him.

"Let's just get out of here," she said as she attempted to hide her tears of frustration.

"The only place you're going is the hospital," Lincoln said as he opened the car door for her.

Abby slid in without a word.

☯

"Abby? You okay?" Lincoln asked with concern as they came out of the hospital.

Her mood was dark and somber as she looked down at the blue fiberglass cast on one hand and the bandages wrapped around the other. "I can't reach my cigarettes," she said with frustration as he opened the car door for her.

Lincoln smiled. "Don't look to me to help you. Maybe it's a perfect time to quit," he said with a chuckle as he closed the door.

Walking around the car, he slid into the driver's seat with a smile still on his face.

Abby looked over with a glare. "Yeah, well. Keep on laughing, 'cause I won't be able to do any of the typing for the reports either."

His smile faded from his face as he realized the truth of her comment.

"I want to swing past my place before we hit the station," Abby said as she stared out the window. "I need to change my shirt."

Lincoln said nothing as he glanced over at the crumpled and bloody shirt she was wearing. He didn't mind. The drive into the canyon was out of the way, but it delayed their return to the station.

Pulling into the gravel and dirt driveway, they heard the deep bark of Abby's dog.

"I'll only be a sec," she said, sliding from the car.

"I'll wait out here."

"Hey, Buck." Abby greeted her dog as she fumbled with the gate. The huge dog was a wolf husky hybrid they had recovered from a crime scene a few years back, part of a litter of seven that needed homes. Most went to people within the department, but for some reason, no one wanted the pup with a floppy ear, Buck. Abby thought she was only going to take him in until someone else stepped forward, but no one ever did. She hadn't fooled anyone. They knew he had found his way into her heart.

Lincoln opened the gate and reached down to ruffle the immense dog's head. "Your mommy was a bad girl today, Buck. She has gotten us into a lot of trouble," Lincoln said in a playful tone, to which the dog responded with a small howl. "Yes, again, but don't be too hard on her. She only did what I would've done if I could've reached the bastard first," Lincoln explained quietly as he scratched Buck's head and looked up to the top deck and the windows of Abby's bedroom. "You be good to her right now, Buck. She's having a rough time." He leaned back and waited for her to return.

It was a long time before he saw movement in the kitchen window. Abby opened the back door and stood with her black bra showing from under her open denim shirt. "I can't get the buttons," she said in dejected annoyance.

Lincoln smiled at her dilemma as he walked over to help.

"Say one word of this and I'll whack you up the side of the head with my cast."

"Who'd believe me anyhow?" Lincoln retorted as he did up the last button.

CHAPTER 2

Lieutenant Banks barely looked up when Lincoln knocked and the two partners entered. She held out her hand for their reports as she picked up her glasses sitting on the desk. "Turn on the TV and have a seat."

Lincoln turned the channel until he found one of the news stations. With the volume turned low, they sat and waited as the lieutenant scanned their reports.

When the news came on, Lieutenant Banks reached for the remote and turned up the volume. The newscast showed some of Billy Ward's victims before it started to show what had transpired at the courthouse earlier.

"I'll fuckin' kill you!" Abby launched herself at Billy Ward. The news anchor's voice began to commentate on the action on screen.

"The woman you see savagely attacking Mr. William Ward is none other than Detective Abby …"

"Savagely attacking?" Abby protested.

"Detective!" Lieutenant Banks warned.

"… the case against Mr. Ward, dismissed earlier. We will show this once again. Since the unprovoked attack came from out of nowhere, it may be difficult to see. If you look to the left of your screen …"

Abby jumped up. "Lieutenant, I'm not saying what I did was right, but they're showing a very slanted view."

"Detective, I'm aware of what happened. We—and by *we* I mean the Captain, Superintendent Gilmer and myself—saw the raw footage. And I'm unhappy with the way they're airing this, but …" Lieutenant Banks stopped talking when Billy Ward came on the screen.

He sat in a wheelchair with his nose heavily taped, his right eye swollen shut, and a row of black stitches along the right corner of his mouth. Beneath it all, a keen eye could see his leering smirk.

Playing the audience for all he could, Billy Ward cleared his throat with a grimace.

> *"What happened today at the courthouse ... was unfortunate." He paused and carefully licked his lips. "Detective Stanfield has a tendency to be overly emotional and a little out of control regarding this case because she has been working so hard on it. My heart and concern go out to her for having exhausted herself while hunting me and making my life so ... so unlivable." He looked up and stared into the camera. "I hope she never has to experience that kind of ... frustrating loss of personal privacy."*

"I think I'm going to puke," Lincoln said in revulsion.

> *"I hold no ill will toward anyone, especially Detective Stanfield. And against the recommendation of my lawyer, I do not intend to pursue any charges against the police department or any of its members. I do hope ... this issue between Detective Stanfield and I ... can be resolved. And I hope," Billy leaned forward just slightly and looked straight into the camera, "she gets the help she needs ..."*

"You fucking little ..." Abby's eyes were wild, her face red with rage.

"Detective!" Lieutenant Banks ordered, "Enough. It's over. Be glad he isn't suing."

"Glad? That's what he wants. He's playing with us. Just like he has all along."

"Then let him play, because sooner or later he's going to make a mistake and we'll be there waiting." The lieutenant dropped her head and looked down at the paperwork on her desk. "Abby," she looked up reluctantly, "you did what we all wanted to do but that doesn't make it right. You're supposed to uphold the law—not break it. I hate to do this, but you've left me little choice—"

"Are you firing me?" Abby looked desperately at her partner.

Lincoln looked at his superior. "Lieutenant, that's not right. If the roles had been reversed, it could've been me taking that swing at Ward."

"But it wasn't you Lincoln. It was Abby."

Lieutenant Banks turned back to Abby as the tall detective sank into her chair. "You're not fired Abby. I want to make that perfectly clear. But Ward was right about one thing. You're too close to this. You need to back away before it consumes you. This is a case, a gruesome one, but it's still just a case, and I should've done something about it long time ago." The lieutenant took a breath. "You've six weeks of banked vacation time and the doctor recommended at least six weeks medical leave …"

"You've got to be kidding me? Twelve weeks off just for punching that piece of shit? I can see the six weeks until the cast comes off, but come on, lieutenant, twelve weeks?"

There was a long and dreadful pause before Lieutenant Banks looked up to face Abby. The detective shut her mouth when she saw her boss was not finished. Lieutenant Banks continued reluctantly. "And another twelve weeks in exchange for keeping your badge for that scuffle at the courthouse."

The air in the office grew heavy as Lieutenant Banks and Lincoln looked at Abby. They waited and watched as her mouth opened and closed several times. Lincoln knew his partner and he held his breath waiting for an explosion, but Abby remained silent.

She rose to her feet and moved to the window to look down to the flurry of traffic below. "For a grand total of six months," she finally said softly.

"They wanted your badge, Abby, but I wouldn't give it to them. The only reason we even got Billy Ward in front of a judge was because of your hard work and tenacity. I refused to let you go, Abby. You're too good of a cop."

"But six months," Abby said as she turned from the window. Her face showed disbelief, but her dark eyes danced with anger. "Six months. Those sniveling, pencil pushing bastards are trying to make me the scapegoat because he walked. They're hoping I'll quit, aren't they?"

"Abby, you need a break," Lincoln said. "Take it. Take what they're offering. Give yourself time to heal. Put this behind you."

Abby showed no sign of hearing Lincoln's words. "They want me to quit because I had the balls to do what everyone else only dreamed of doing. We watched while he went from girl to girl, raping and murdering. We did nothing! He was laughing at us then and he is laughing at us now. Six months! They're hoping I'll quietly walk away. Well, you can tell them I don't do anything quietly!" She ripped back her jacket and with a grimace of pain pulled her gun from her shoulder harness. She slammed the gun down on desk, followed by her badge. "I quit!"

Abby stalked out of the office, slamming the glass door that read *Lieutenant M. Banks* so hard the glass exploded and cascaded loudly to the floor. She walked away without blinking an eye.

Lincoln stood stunned as he watched the last of the glass trickle to the ground, and then turned to his boss.

"Don't worry, detective. I've no intention of keeping her badge or her gun. I spent half the day fighting for her to keep it." Lieutenant Banks picked up Abby's gun and badge and held them out to Lincoln. "She's got a temper. That's no secret, but she's wound too tight right now for her own good and we both know it."

"Yes, ma'am."

"Go talk to her. Convince her this is a good thing."

Lincoln nodded as he pulled open the remains of the door.

"Detective." Lincoln looked back at his boss when she spoke. "I don't want her hanging around here, is that understood? I want her out of town and not at home talking to you on the phone every hour. I want her gone. Away from Ward, away from the media, away from here."

"Yes, ma'am." He stepped over the glass and started to close the door.

"Why bother?" Lieutenant Banks said sarcastically.

Lincoln nodded and backed away from the mess.

The lieutenant hollered after him. "Tell her she owes me a new door!"

☯

Abby reached down with her right hand to open the door to the roof of the police station, the thin white line around her lips evidence of the pain she felt. Stepping back, she put her boot on the handle and kicked open the door. The heavy steel swung open with a bang.

Clouds darkened the afternoon skies, but the solemn detective took no notice as she made her way down the three stairs to the small covered deck the officers used when they wanted a smoke or just a break in their day. She stood there motionless, except for her long hair waving in the wind. Abby stepped up onto one of the wooden deck chairs and sat down on the back of it, huddling herself deeper into her leather jacket.

She knew her anger had gotten the better of her in Banks' office just as it had at the courthouse. Billy was a free man and she had just handed in her badge. No matter how she looked at it, the day made no sense. She hated how she had handled herself. Abby looked down at the cast that went from her forearm to the tips of her fingers. With a grimace, she managed to wiggle just the end of her index finger.

It had been a long day. With a heavy sigh, she reached into the inside pocket of her jacket with her right hand. A slice of pain went through her hand, telling her it was unhappy with the way she continued to treat it.

With a loud hiss, she pulled her hand back and looked at the bandage. It was all she could do to pull out the pack and remove a cigarette with her teeth. She left the cigarette dangling from her mouth as she pulled out her lighter with a groan. After several attempts, she only managed to get a spark.

"To hell with it!" She tossed the lighter and cigarette to the ground in frustration.

"I could've helped you with that." The deep voice of her partner instantly curbed her rising temper.

"I've been meaning to quit anyways."

"Smoking or your job?"

"Both." Her voice echoed her disappointment. "How am I gonna afford to smoke without a job?"

"Oh, cut the shit. We both know your parents left you so much money you never have to work another day in your life."

"Lincoln," she warned.

"Fine, be a hard ass. But I'm not packing this around for the next six months." Lincoln pulled her gun and badge out of his pocket. "Come on, take it. Banks said she didn't spend all day fighting for it so you could leave it behind."

She looked at her weapon and shield for a long moment before she finally reached for them. "What the hell am I suppose to do for six months?"

"Learn a second language?" Lincoln offered with a small smile.

"Oh, you're funny." She gave him an icy stare.

"How about a nice vacation? Dance on a table in Greece or go cuddle a koala?"

"What exactly are you trying to say?"

"Banks says you can't stick around here."

"I got that part."

"I don't mean 'here' as in the police station. I mean 'here' as in the city. You have to leave town."

"Oh, for the love of …" Abby climbed off the chair and walked across the rooftop. "I feel like I'm being run out of Dodge before sundown."

"Come on, Abby, give it a chance. Go away somewhere. Sleep in, get fat, fall in love. I don't care so long as you take a break and come back as the woman I used to know. Abby, you're too young to be burning out this fast."

Back and forth she paced, her long strides digging deep into the roofing gravel as the wind blew her hair. Light rain began to fall but she paid it no attention.

"Will you stop and talk to me? It's starting to rain."

"Do I look like I give a shit? I've got months to do nothing. Maybe I'll catch a cold and die!"

Lincoln shook his head as the rain speckled the wooden walkway and the gravel. "Why can't you just look at it like a rest?"

"Because, you big, dumb bastard, no one takes a *rest* for six months."

"You could get pregnant and take a year off on maternity."

Abby stopped her pacing and turned to look at him as raindrops fell onto her face. "Is your tie on too tight? I don't want *more* time off!" She threw her arms up in exasperation and returned to her pacing. "Men! How the hell you ended up running the freakin' world is beyond me. Jesus Lincoln, you don't think me being gay might make getting pregnant a little difficult?"

Her sharp mind and quick tongue were part of what he loved about her. He stood up and put his hands on his hips to show his seriousness. "Look, I talked to Carla and we'll look after Buck and your place for you."

She stopped again and turned to look Lincoln in the eye. Even from this distance he could see he had said the wrong thing. "I don't care where I'm going, but wherever it is … I'm taking my dog with me!"

Lincoln held his hands up in mock surrender. "Okay, okay, all right. Far be it from me to come between a girl and her wolf."

"He's not a wolf, he's a hybrid. Part wolf. Buck's a great dog and would never hurt a fly, you know that."

"Yeah, I know. He's a big puppy with big teeth," Lincoln said with a small smile.

"And he'd eat you anyhow." Abby looked up at her partner in despair. "What am I going to do and where am I going to do it?"

"Why don't you head to that retreat you sent Carla and me to on our honeymoon? It was a great place, Abby, with fishing, hiking and horseback riding." He could see that his words were sinking in. He threw his arm around her shoulder as she gave him a playful jab to the ribs with her elbow.

"You can be such a moron. The proverbial missing link."

"Fine, but I'm a missing link who's surrounded by beautiful and stubborn women. Come on, Carla has dinner on and she'll kill me if I don't bring you home."

CHAPTER 3

Taking her hand off the steering wheel, Abby flexed her fingers the best she could. The long drive had felt good, except for her hands and her butt. The mountains around her had become high and rugged, and the evergreens thick and tall. It had been a long time since she had been to the Gold Creek Resort, but her memories of it were as clear as if it was yesterday.

Gold Creek Resort was where she had spent most of her summers when she was a child. The secluded resort was on the edge of a small lake nestled between three mountain ranges. The towering peaks were always capped by snow and their rugged terrain carpeted with a thousand different hues of green. The lake was stocked with rainbow trout for fishing. Its pristine waters were great for canoeing, and each small cabin positioned on the shore had its own dock. There were trails for hiking or horseback riding, tennis courts and even a small restaurant. The memories brought a smile to Abby's face. She hadn't told Lincoln and Carla that she had been there before, because it seemed like a lifetime ago. The lifetime of a happy child long since buried by the brutality of the real world.

Abby saw the sign for Gold Creek Resort hanging off the massive timbers that framed the entrance. Pushed off to one side was a gate that had never been closed. A dirt road led to the resort. Slowing down, she prepared herself for an onslaught of memories. Following the road along the lake edge, she noticed a few changes since she had been there last.

"I guess twenty years will change just about everything," she said aloud. The small cabins along the lake looked bigger and more secluded—and the lodge, once built out of post and beam, was now a long, log structure. The main building was tall with a high peak roof, and the gables were filled with windows facing the snow-capped mountains.

Pulling into a parking spot in front, Abby barely had the Jeep's motor turned off when the front screen door opened.

"Abigail!" An elderly woman quickly made her way toward the vehicle. "Twenty years or not, I would know those eyes anywhere."

"Helga, it's so great to see you." It took Abby a moment to get the door to the Jeep open and even longer to pull her cramped and tired body out of her seat. The woman, who had known Abby as a child, wrapped her arms around the tall detective. "You are much taller now, Abigail, you promised you would not grow taller than me," she said in a Scandinavian accent, followed by a wink.

"Actually, it's just Abby now," she whispered into Helga's ear as she relished the moment and the hug. Although Abby had not returned to the resort in twenty years, she talked to Helga and her husband, Günter, regularly by phone.

"Whatever you say, dear. Let me look at you, child." Helga said as she pulled out of the heartfelt embrace for a better look. "It has been long time, but I see little Abigail. The years have been good to you. I have heard it, but now I see it. Though the cast and bandages are new, yes?"

Abby nodded with a smile as Helga continued her running evaluation. "I still see the pain in those beautiful eyes of yours."

The detective tried to ignore the comment.

"What you need is love. You need love in your life, child. You need to let it all go and learn to love. Let the dead rest in peace." Seeing the effect of her words. Helga quickly changed the subject, her round face filled with a smile. "So this must be the young man in your life?"

Buck's tail wagged happily as he noticed the two faces looking at him. His powerful front legs hung out the window as he waited for his owner's command to release him from the Jeep. "You were right, he is a big and handsome boy, but it's not enough. You need a pretty girl to make those eyes sparkle again."

Not wanting to get into that conversation, Abby called on her companion to change the subject. "Buck, come." She barely got the dog's name out before he came through the open driver's door and landed in a sitting position at Abby's feet. He wiggled and squirmed like a child wanting attention, his tail beating the hard packed dirt.

"I had a hybrid back in the old country. Most are good. Some are not, but I can tell he is good puppy, *ya*?"

"Yes, but this *puppy* is four years old and about one hundred pounds too heavy to be a lap dog," Abby commented as Buck enjoyed all the attention he was getting.

"Günter will love him. Come child, there are so many things I want to show you. Changes we have made, but first I will show you where you are staying." Before Abby could say a word, Helga had Buck back in the

Jeep and she was getting in behind the wheel. The tall detective smiled as she walked around to get in the passenger side of her own vehicle.

Helga took them on a slow tour of the resort, pointing out changes along the way. Abby listened, but kept her eyes on the winding trails they drove. One was barely wide enough for her Jeep. The large tires made little sounds as they compressed thousands of pinecones littering the trail. The wild flowers rising up on either side of the trail were so close to the side of the Jeep Abby was tempted to reach out and pick some. The rays of the afternoon sun shot through the trees in contrast to the shade of the thick branches.

"Here you are, dear, the last cabin on the lake. The best for you." Helga turned down a narrow lane and pulled in beside a small log cabin. Abby noted the driveway, lined with recently stacked firewood, had fresh rake marks where someone had just cleaned off the debris deposited by the forest. Abby looked over her new accommodations as her Jeep came to a stop.

Four wooden steps led up to a beautiful L-shaped cedar sundeck that went along the side of the cabin and around the front. Tall evergreen and alder trees surrounded them, giving Abby all the privacy that Helga had promised on the phone. Stepping out of the Jeep, Abby was a little surprised to see smoke coming from the river-rock chimney protruding from the tin roof. As she held open her car door, Abby gave a small nod to Buck to let him know he was free from the confines of the vehicle.

"I will get your bags, dear; you have no hands to help. You look around; make acquaintance with the mountains again."

Abby gave a short whistle and Buck bounded to her side as she began wandering down to the dock. She took a deep breath and the aroma of nature instantly recharged her tired body and revitalized her memories. The air was clean and crisp as it blew off the high white peaks and a slight breeze rippled the water of the lake. Abby's boots echoed on the wooden dock as Buck walked next to her, his eyes and ears registering all that was new to him. Abby sat down on the bench at the end of the dock and Buck quickly sat next to her feet.

Abby's dark eyes took in all that hadn't changed in twenty years and for the first time in a long time she felt connected to her surroundings. She always had a keen understanding of life and nature and knew a person's time on earth meant nothing to a mountain that would stand unchanged for a million years. The ripples of the lake constantly licked at the underbelly of the wooden dock; the floating moss-like algae clung to the submerged pilings and would until time eroded what man had built. She recalled with a sad smile the image of her father in the lake, the water up to his chest, and Günter by his side as they built a dock for each cabin.

Buck's head snapped around and his ears twitched, alerting her to someone's presence. Turning around, she saw Günter coming out from the cabin and a smile spread across her face. "Easy boy, he's one of the good guys," Abby said to her dog as she got to her feet and headed back down the dock.

"Ah, my little angel has all grown to be a tall beauty."

"Günter, you and Helga are good for a girl's ego." They held out their arms and hugged each other tightly. His hair was completely white now, but other than that he hadn't changed since she had seen him last.

"You are so tall now, Abby," he said. "You have your father's eyes, my dear … And the smile of your mother."

Abby smiled as she gently put her fingertips against his lips. "Please."

He understood without saying a word as his tanned and leathered face clouded with concern. Günter reached for her battered and broken hands. "You are right and we have much to catch up on when you feel you want to. But some I already know," he said with a wink.

Putting an arm around her waist, he directed her to the cabin. "Come, I have left you a treat in the cupboard in your cabin; a bottle of the best aquavit," he said in a whisper He looked back and waved at Helga. "I know you enjoy the bottles I send at Christmas, and after what I saw … You might need it for medicinal purposes." He turned back and smiled at her. "You have the best left hook of anyone I know." He gently patted her cast as he guided her to the stairs at the front of the cabin and the wide double front doors.

"You saw that? Even up here?"

"We may be out in the country here, but we are not in the old country."

The inside of the cabin was simple but showcased Günter's Scandinavian craftsmanship. One bedroom opened out onto the deck via a sliding glass door. A full bathroom included an antique tub. There was a countertop with a small sink next to a wooden table with four chairs, and then finally a sofa and a rocking chair in front of the river-rock fireplace.

Helga had both doors into the cabin wide open.

"The box arrived this morning. You have people who care for you, yes?" she asked.

Abby nodded as she walked over to a large box sitting on the counter behind the table.

"There is a card here." Helga pulled it out and handed it to Abby.

Abby,

I thought I should make sure you had everything you needed to keep your ass in the mountains and away from here. Relax and enjoy.

Linc

Günter lifted out a brand new tackle box, holding it out for Abby to see, but she held up her damaged hands and smiled. "That is going to have to wait for a bit," she said.

In the bottom of the box were several small wrapped boxes. "And three boxes of chocolates and three cases of beer." Abby turned to Günter's chuckle. "I think I'll need one of the fridges."

"I will bring you one," Günter said.

"Come now, Günter. I think Abby needs some rest and some time alone." Helga took her husband's hand. "Let us know if you need anything, my child."

"I will. I can't thank you both enough for everything you've done here …" Abby motioned to her surroundings.

"We are just glad to have you back," Helga said with an adoring smile.

After a quick but loving hug from both of them, Abby finally was alone. She stood on the deck watching them until they turned onto the trail and headed back to the main lodge walking hand-in-hand.

The silence around her was deafening as she sat down on the bench on the deck, but soon nature began to talk to her and she felt her body relaxing. Hoping to help it out a little, Abby went back inside and searched for the bottle of aquavit. Günter had been true to his word and the bottle of nearly pure grain alcohol was where he said it would be. She poured herself a small cup of the golden amber and then sat down on the sofa.

"Now what?" she asked aloud to no one. It was a question she didn't have an answer for as she took a long drink of the potent alcohol. Looking around the empty cabin, Abby wondered if she would still have her mind in six months.

The fire crackled, its flame drawing her stare hypnotically. Feeling the warmth of the alcohol in her system, Abby leaned back and closed her eyes. Her life had been running at top speed for so long the sudden change of pace was almost more than she could handle. Restless and irritated, the detective paced the small log cabin. She moved back and forth, her long legs striding in no direction as she continuously sipped at her glass of aquavit. Soon the sun disappeared, taking with it the outside light and Abby's world began to change. The log walls closed in and the silence screamed as visions and memories cried out in her mind.

She opened the double doors leading out onto her deck, hoping the cool night air would refresh her thoughts, but it was no use. Pouring another glass of aquavit, Abby laid her tired body down on the lounge chair on the deck. Sometime in the night, as the fire's embers glowed red in the ashes, Abby's empty glass slid silently from her hand as she passed into a world of no pain.

CHAPTER 4

The loud chirping of morning birds crashed through her alcohol-induced fog. Abby squinted and blinked hard as she tried to recall where she was. One look at the mirrored surface of Lake Alouette and all the realities of her life came back to her. She pulled herself up into a sitting position and closed her eyes with a deep groan, only to open them again when she heard the steady thumping of Buck's tail.

"What are you so happy about?" she asked as Buck leaned forward and licked the side of her face.

"Stop it. What's your—Oh my God! I forgot to feed you. I'm sorry. I bet you're hungry?" The large dog replied with a small howl.

"All right, all right. Give me a sec, will ya?"

After she fed her dog, Abby went to the coffee maker, filled it with water and heaped the dark coffee into a filter. Then impatiently she stood over the carafe and waited.

"Hello?" a voice in the distance called out.

"Come on in, Günter," she offered gently through her hangover.

"Good morning, you sleep good?" the tall white haired Scandinavian asked as he walked in carrying a small bar fridge.

Stopping to look Abby in the eye, Günter's expression told her she wasn't fooling anyone.

"You know, grains are good for breakfast, but not the liquid kind." Abby heard the care and concern in his voice and held her tongue.

"You are all grown up now Abby, and you have had your share of things to deal with …"

"I'm a big girl, Günter."

"Yes you are, so I don't have to tell you, alcohol will only mask the problem and then it will make it bigger." He watched her for a moment before deciding what to say. "Abby, you have time on your hands and that can be a good thing or a bad thing. You need to look and see what is around here. It is yours to take when you decide to take it. You have seen so much for one so young, Abigail, but there is a lot of life left in you—life to live."

Standing on the threshold of the front doors, Abby listened to Günter's words as she sipped her coffee and looked over the beautiful view before her. She heard him approach her from behind, but she said nothing as he placed a hand on her shoulder. She turned and offered a small smile and Günter knew she had no response for him.

"Helga will be looking for you for lunch," he said as he made his way across the deck and down the stairs.

"Tell her not wait, I won't be there." Abby never saw the look of disappointment on his face as she turned back into her cabin.

She hadn't meant to be rude or disrespectful, but she hadn't come here to be lectured or doted on by either of them.

By mid morning, Abby had pulled out a puzzle and left its pieces scattered on the table. She had started a novel but only read the first few pages. She had pulled out her fishing gear, but left it leaning against the wall next to the fireplace. Finally, after a fitful morning, Abby decided maybe a nap would do her good, but then again maybe not. Sleeping was something she didn't look forward to. It left her mind open and vulnerable to nightmares, taking her down dark and shadowy paths. They were far away from the comforting dreams others found in their sleep.

Abby's nightmares concerned murdered girls who had been raped and tortured. Beautiful young girls who had been cut and carved on while they were still alive, silenced by a paste made from the leaves of the dieffenbachia plant stuffed into their mouths. Abby saw them whenever she closed her eyes—each one of them—before, during and after their murders. She knew their names, their birth dates, and in maddening detail, their brutal deaths. Their silent screams begging for someone to help them. They would pull at her, their outstretched bloody hands grabbing at her arms, scratching and tearing at her. Their voices cried out her name, pleading for someone to stop their pain as a long thin knife cut deep into their flesh. Abby could hear the sound of the blade as it carved down to the bone; see the gloved fingers around the handle tightening to saw harder. Then came the laughter; his deep demented laughter. And he was laughing at her.

Billy Ward's face came out of the shadows, laughing and taunting her as his knife continued to cut away at the flesh of the young girls.

"You can't help them, Abby." He brought up his knife and drove it into Abby's breast. "You can't! You can't! You can't!" With each chant, Billy brought out the knife and plunged it in again. "You can't save them and you can't stop me."

Abby dove at him, her hands aimed at his throat.

The flash of fire in her fist immediately awoke her from her nightmare. A thin sheen of sweat glistened over her muscular body, matting her hair to her face and forehead. Her breathing came in gulps as she looked at her right hand and the dots of blood cracking through the scabs of her stitches.

Going into the bathroom, she ran cold water over her hand then mopped her face with a towel. Looking into the mirror, Abby had a hard time looking at her own reflection; there was guilt in her eyes, in her features, darkening her soul. Shaking the excess water off her hand, she left the bathroom and headed for the bottle of aquavit. She quickly tossed the first splash into the glass and down her throat. After pouring another, she put the cap back on the bottle and walked outside. Standing on the edge of the deck, her gaze fell on the waters of Lake Alouette. Draining her second drink, she went back inside to pour another and to fetch herself a cold beer from her fridge.

"Come on, Buck." The big husky followed her on to the dock. Carefully, she juggled the bottle and the glass until she made it out to the bench. Stretching out her long legs, she sat and looked over the lake. She watched a few people out on the water in their canoes while she sipped on the potent alcohol. A flock of ducks flew overhead and loudly made their descent down to the water, causing Buck's head to tilt back and forth as he watched their progress.

The slow afternoon mixed with the power of the aquavit and soon Abby found herself laying on the dock in a warm relaxed stupor. The sun was slowly making its way towards the rugged mountaintops, but she gave it no mind or thought. Lying on her back, with her knees up and her eyes closed, Abby placed her empty glass on the wooden dock. Feeling around with her right hand, she reached for her beer. It was warm now, but she was too comfortable to go and get a cold one.

Picking the bottle up with the only two fingers working, Abby placed it on her stomach. When she reached with her left hand to hold it, her heavy fiberglass cast clinked against the glass. She opened one eye and looked at the bottle. The cast on her hand made it impossible for her to grasp the slick glass. Realizing the problem, she switched hands and held the bottle with her right as she attempted to open it with her left, but there wasn't enough of her left fingers sticking out for her to touch the bottle cap, never mind grasp it. Abby lifted her head and glared at the bottle.

"Well, this is annoying," she said as she sat up and placed the bottle between her knees. Whatever she had done to her knuckles in her nightmare had made them swell and the tightness of the stitches on her right hand made it impossible for her to get a hold of the cap. Her growing anger and frustration quickly began to wash away the warmth and relaxation she had found in the sun. She had no idea how long she battled the bottle, but as she lifted it to her teeth, she noticed Buck was looking behind her. Abby, with the beer bottle cap between her teeth, turned to see a beautiful red-haired woman walking down the dock towards her.

"Please don't do that," the woman said politely motioning towards the bottle in Abby's mouth.

The detective froze. With the sinking sun behind her, the woman looked radiant if not angelic. Abby was speechless as she sat and stared. The beautiful stranger stood on the dock with two bottles of beer in one hand and an opener in the other.

"I come with an opener." The smile that brightened the young fresh face caused Abby's heart to skip a beat. The woman motioned towards Buck. "Please tell me he's friendly."

"Huh?" was all the detective could muster.

"Your dog? Is he friendly? That mountain of hair is a dog, isn't it?"

"Huh? Oh yes, Buck … Leave it," Abby commanded and the husky's shoulders relaxed. But he kept an attentive eye on the stranger.

"I'm sorry. I didn't mean to intrude, but I couldn't help but notice your situation." The woman turned and pointed with her bottle opener at the cabin next to Abby's. "I could see … We're neighbors … I wasn't being nosy or anything … well, maybe just a little. I mean, I'm not normally a nosy person, but with all the activity around your cabin the last couple days … I mean, both Helga and Günter were cleaning up around the place … not that the place was messy or anything. I mean, they keep all of the cabins and the resort neat and all … well, I was wondering if it was someone famous coming in …"

Abby sat and listened to her neighbor's nervous ramblings as her own dark eyebrows knitted in question and confusion. Suddenly, the woman realized she was doing all the talking and she stopped with an embarrassed flush to her cheeks.

"I'm sorry, I didn't mean to intrude. If you'd rather I left …" Her cheeks reddened further.

"Huh? What? No. I … ah, no. Please." Abby finally regained the power of speech and motioned for the woman to sit. "Sorry. I didn't mean to be rude. It's just that I wasn't expecting anyone."

"If you would rather be alone, I understand. A lot of people come up here for time alone. You know, to relax and get back to nature and all. Well, if that's what you want. I'll just open your beer … actually, have one of mine. It will at least be colder than yours. I'll just open this up for you." She put one of her beer bottles down and then flipped off the cap of the other with an ease that made Abby smile.

"You know, that's not as easy as you would think. Don't go. Please, sit."

The woman hesitated as if deciding whether to accept the offer, but then sat down with a smile. She offered the opened beer to the detective.

"My name is Sarah," she said with an easy smile.

"Abby. Thanks," the detective said as she accepted the offered beer and took a long drink.

Sarah drank from her own bottle and then wiped her lips with the back of her hand.

Abby's gaze drifted over Sarah's face and the detective thought that she had never seen such a friendly smile on such an innocent face. Her eyes were alive and alert as she looked down at Abby's hands. Such a beautiful face on such a young woman, a young innocent woman very much like one of those in Abby's nightmares. The ones calling out for justice against the evil …

"So what's the other guy look like?" Sarah's question pulled Abby away from the grizzly path her mind was traveling down.

"What's that suppose to mean?" Abby snapped back without thinking. She hadn't meant for her tone to be so harsh, but the question caught her off guard.

"I'm sorry. I just meant … I didn't mean to insinuate anything. I just wondered what happened to your hands. But it's none of my business."

Abby silently cursed herself for responding like a cop with an attitude. "No, it should be me apologizing. I didn't mean to snap at you. It's just that … Well, it's a subject I'd rather not discuss. Sorry," Abby said.

Feeling more than a little uncomfortable, both smiled politely at each other before looking away and taking long silent pulls from their beers.

Looking out of the corner of her eyes, Sarah was more than a little impressed with the gorgeous woman next to her. Her dark hair and dark eyes contrasted with the white teeth displayed in that brief smile. Sarah had watched her arrival with interest and curiosity, and when she had seen Abby emerge from her cabin, Sarah had been mesmerized by the long easy strides of the woman as she walked out on to her dock, her large dog by her side. And as she had watched Abby struggle to open her beer, Sarah knew this was the woman she wanted to meet. Now, sitting so close to her, she could feel the woman's intensity just under the surface, like a fire smoldering on the brink of igniting.

Lost in her thoughts, Sarah looked down at Abby's fingers as she picked at the label of her beer.

Feeling eyes upon her, Abby turned to meet Sarah's gaze.

"So, is this your first time?" the detective blurted out.

"Pardon?" The question startled Sarah.

"Is this your first time here at Gold Creek?" Abby felt the thickness of the alcohol in her tongue, but she knew it was the attention of such a pretty young woman that was giving her communication difficulties.

"Ah, yes, yes it is, though you probably wouldn't know it. I enjoy the country, not much of a city girl actually. It's beautiful here isn't it?"

"Mmm hmm," Abby agreed as she took another drink of her beer. "This was nice of you. Günter brought me a fridge this morning, but I didn't want to go back into the cabin to get a cold one."

"You obviously know them well, Günter and Helga, I mean, for them to fuss over your cabin and your arrival like that."

"Yeah, very well," was all Abby offered.

"So this isn't your first time I take it?"

"Not hardly." Abby found herself struggling to maintain a pleasant civilized conversation. She was too used to being the one to ask the probing questions.

Has it been so long since I've talked to another woman on a purely personal basis that I can't even be civil?

"Well, it sure is nice here. I just got here myself. I didn't know there was fishing here or I would have brought my own gear," Sarah said as she looked out over the still lake.

"Günter has equipment you can rent," Abby offered. "Or there's a small gas station with a store about four miles down the road a bit, Flanagan's. They have equipment."

"I was going to make a call today, but believe it or not there are no public phones here. Can you imagine that in this day and age? And my cell phone is totally useless," Sarah said, changing the subject.

"Helga only got her phone up here about five years ago, but other than that the only phone service is at Flanagan's."

"I brought up my lap top but I guess the Internet is out of the question," Sarah said with a chuckle and a smile. "It's like turning back the hands of time, coming up here."

"Yeah, but that's part of its charm."

"So you're here for a week?" Sarah's question was innocent enough, but she saw a dark shadow flicker on Abby's face.

"I wish," Abby said. The detective's eyes scanned the distant mountain as if looking for an answer. "I've got some time to kill, so I'll be here for a few months," she added bitterly.

"Wow, a few months. Don't you work?"

"Yes, I work."

If Sarah heard the animosity, she chose to ignore it. "What do you do?"

Abby paused for a brief moment. "I, ah, I work for the city." Abby didn't see the hesitation on Sarah's face as she changed the subject. "So where are you from, Sarah?"

"Me? The east coast originally."

"And now?"

"My suitcase," Sarah laughed at her own answer, but Abby remained solemn.

"Why's that?" Abby was unaware her tone was changing and her questions were starting to sound like an interrogation.

"I move around a lot."

"Why?"

"I guess I have a natural curiosity—for beautiful things."

"Really. You just go wherever you want?"

"Not always, sometimes something or someone has to guide me," Sarah paused, feeling a little uneasy with her answer. "Or sometimes I just go wherever the winds take me."

"And why did the wind bring you here?"

"I had a calling, a friend actually. She recommended the place," Sarah said with a smile, hoping to lighten the darkening mood. "She said that I'd like the view here."

"And do you?" Abby's questions kept coming and she missed the flirtations coming from the friendly little red head. Her bitterness at being away from work, mixed with all the alcohol she had consumed in the last twenty-four hours, brought out an ugliness Sarah did not like.

"Do I?" she asked as she pulled on her bottom lip and then looked away from the dark shadows in Abby's eyes. "Yeah, I think the view is breathtaking." Sarah threw out the line but came up empty as Abby continued to fire off questions.

"What is it that you do for a living?" The probing tone of the question was unmistakable, but Abby showed no signs of realizing it.

"I, ah, I work for myself," Sarah said vaguely, more than a little taken aback by the apparent cross-examination she was being subjected to.

"Doing?"

"What is this? Twenty questions? Look, I was just trying to be nice and neighborly, but I can see you'd prefer to be alone. Enjoy the view." Sarah rose to her feet quickly.

"Wait, look I'm sorry, I didn't mean to come off like that. I …"

"Well, you did! Enjoy the beer. You can keep the opener." Sarah marched off the dock without looking back.

"Sarah, I'm sorry. I didn't …" Abby could see Sarah had no intentions of stopping as she walked up the stairs and into her own cabin. Abby sat down with a loud audible groan.

"Well, I came off like a super bitch, didn't I? I can't even carry on a conversation with a decent person anymore." Abby was utterly disgusted with herself as she spoke to her faithful canine companion. "What the hell have I become? Don't answer that." After several long self-analyzing moments, Abby looked down at her dog. "I guess a bit of a break wouldn't hurt, huh? If you say one word about Linc and the lieutenant being right … I'll … I'll neuter you. Again!"

Buck tilted his head to the side, but remained silent as he watched her tip back her beer to drain the last of it. Picking up her empty glass and the other full bottle of beer, she went back to her cabin.

Abby spent the remains of the afternoon and evening out at the end of her dock, returning to her cabin only to refill her glass with aquavit. One by one she watched as each cabin's lights went out for the night, though most of her attention was on the dimly lit cabin next to hers. Hidden by the cover of darkness, she had watched Sarah leave and return from dinner at the lodge. Then Sarah's bright lights went dim as she lit candles and a fire, but soon the flickering light of a computer screen replaced the orange glow.

The detective watched through the window with interest as Sarah sat at her table, her delicate fingers flying over the keyboard of her laptop. The redhead had sparked something in her hardened heart, something Abby hadn't been expecting. Pulling her knees up to her chest, she rested her chin and made no attempt to wipe the goofy grin off her face. It wasn't the alcohol that made her smile, though she did find it amusing that Sarah held a pencil in her teeth the entire time her attention was on her computer. No, the smile was there because Sarah had done what no one else could. For a brief moment, Sarah had taken Abby's mind off her life and the evil turmoil Billy Ward had created in it.

It had been a long time since Abby had been in a relationship. Though a strict disciplinarian when it came to her schoolwork, Abby had come alive in college. She stopped denying that women turned her head. And when the women on campus found out, the line at her door only seemed to grow. She dated but only on her terms, revealing little about herself and always keeping her relationships from getting too serious. It made her quite mysterious, and that combined with her dark good looks earned her the reputation as being the catch of the campus. Abby kept her personal life to herself, refusing to reveal anything about her parents or her family. It had been a conscious decision; no one could hurt her if she didn't let anyone in, and that was the armor she had taken with her into adulthood. Most of the time she was happy with that—until this afternoon.

Abby brought her focus back to the movement in Sarah's cabin. The woman had finished what she had been doing and folded down her computer. Rising from her chair, she walked over to the window and looked out in Abby's direction. Though she couldn't see her, Abby felt Sarah's eyes searching for something or *someone* in the dark.

CHAPTER 5

Leaning against the glass of the phone booth, Abby adjusted her sunglasses as she listened to the second ring of the phone. Her head was pounding; she had woken up with an epic hangover.

Bloody aquavit, she thought as she ran her hand through hair that seemed to hurt.

"Detective Quinn." Lincoln's deep voice rumbled painfully through her head, but she still smiled.

"Linc, it's me."

"Hi, me, you're not supposed to be phoning here," Lincoln said in a light-hearted tone.

"Oh, come on. You miss me and you know it."

"Have you just gone mad? If …" Lincoln paused and scanned the squad room. "If I get caught talking to you, I'll be joining you."

"Oh, come on. Just throw me a bone or something. Please, you owe me." A devious smile spread across Abby's face.

"I owe you? How thin is *your* air up there? I owe you? You're certifiable," he sputtered into the phone. Abby chuckled even though she yearned to be at her desk across from his.

"Seriously, Linc, just fill me in." Hearing the plea in her voice, the working detective knew he couldn't resist.

"All right look, can I call you back?" he asked as he looked at see where his lieutenant was.

"No, I'm at the pay phone at Flanagan's. You know cell phones don't work up here."

"Okay, give me, say twenty minutes and phone me back? It'll give me time to get out of here. I swear Banks has my desk bugged."

"Okay, twenty minutes. Thanks, Lincoln."

Leaving the phone booth, Abby strolled over to and up the stairs into the general store.

Instinctively she ducked at the sound of the bell on the door above her head. Looking up at the bell, Abby pushed back the rush of childhood memories and continued into the store. The worn and stained wooden floor echoed under her boots as she strolled casually down each aisle, her eyes scanning the assortment of items on the shelves. She recalled with a small smile that, as a child she hadn't been able to see over the shelves; now she towered over them, giving her a view of the entire store. Just like years ago, if there was something that you needed, odds were Flanagan's would have it. From fruits and vegetables to auto parts, they had it all, because they had to.

As she made her way up and down the aisles, a rack of postcards caught Abby's eyes. With a devilish smile, she decided to purchase one for Lieutenant Banks. Most had pictures of the resort, the lake or the mountains, but she looked through them all until a card with an old picture of Flanagan's storefront caught her attention. For several long minutes her eyes scanned over what her memory had forgotten before she returned the card to the rack. Shaking off the effects of the black and white photo, Abby selected a postcard with a picture of Gold Creek's new lodge on it and then made her way up to the counter.

The young red-haired man who stood behind it had been watching her as she made her way around the store. When she stopped next to the postcard display, his eyes took in every inch of her, from her cowboy boots to her long hair. He knew she was a visitor because he knew all the locals, but she moved with a familiarity that told him she had been here before. Twice he saw her look at her watch and he wondered if she was meeting someone.

As Abby approached the counter, she tried to ignore his teenage staring; he was harmless and she knew it. Glancing up at the clock on the wall, she realized she still had a good ten minutes before she could call Lincoln. Looking around the store again, her eyes fell on the fishing gear off to the side. *Sarah.* That single word awoke something inside her—something she had kept hidden for a long time.

The corner of Abby's mouth lifted into a smile. "Can I leave this here?" she asked him as she laid the postcard down on the counter.

"Su … su … sure," Sean Flanagan stuttered, grinning broadly as he watched her walk over to the fishing rods.

"I can hel … hel … help you," he added quickly, coming around the counter.

Abby gave the impression of listening with her full attention as he gave her his best sales pitch, but her mind wasn't on fishing. It was on a certain redhead back at the resort. When she had decided on her purchases, Sean carried them up to the counter and then eventually out to her Jeep.

"Holy shit! That's the b … b … biggest, I mean, wow." Sean quickly corrected himself. "That's the biggest d … d … dog I've ever seen."

"Easy there, Buck. Careful," Abby cautioned. "He doesn't like people rushing up to him."

"He's friendly, r … r … ight? Can I … I … I pet him?" Sean asked as he placed her things in the back of the Jeep.

"His name's Buck," she chuckled. "Go ahead. I have to make a call." Sean raised his hand in acknowledgement but said nothing.

Abby watched the two as she listened to the phone ring. When Lincoln answered, she closed the phone booth door. "Hi, it's me again."

"Okay, before I say anything, I want your word that you won't be calling me everyday, deal?"

"Deal. What's going on?"

"Not so fast there, I'm serious Abby. Banks is watching me like a hawk."

"Okay," Abby said in a more serious tone. "Just bring me up to date."

"Fine … Let's see. The press is looking everywhere for you; it's still a close race as to those who want to give you a medal and those who think you need to be medicated."

"Funny."

"And you are all the press can talk about."

"Great." All her career she had kept her personal life private. She sighed heavily and hoped she could ride out the storm.

"We're watching Ward's every movement; so far, not much. On a different note, the families are filing a class-action against him."

"That doesn't help us."

"No, but they can use the evidence we couldn't and as long as he is tied up in court, he can't go anywhere. Hey, how are you anyhow?"

"Bored, I'm seriously thinking about becoming an alcoholic …" she let her voice trail off, thinking about what had transpired yesterday on the dock with Sarah.

"Hey, I thought about it, and I think Japanese."

"For what?"

"The language you should learn, I think it should be Japanese. You never know, it could come in handy."

"You're killing me here."

"I know. Take care, Abby. Say hi to Günter and Helga for me."

"I will," Abby said before she hung up the phone.

Turning around in the phone booth, she stood for a moment and watched the young boy still playing with her dog. Sensing his master's attention, Buck stopped and turned.

"He su … su … sure is a nice dog, lady."

"Call me Abby," she said as she walked over to the front steps.

"My name is Se … Sean." He stood up on the steps, almost eye-to-eye with her, and smiled.

"Well, thanks for your help, Sean," Abby said as she walked toward her Jeep. The husky leaped into the back seat and then turned to howl at his new friend.

Sean waved as Abby pulled away from the store.

☯

The sound of the Jeep leaving next door pulled Sarah's attention from her computer. Walking across the hardwood floor of her small cabin, she saw only a glimpse of Abby and her dog leaving.

"Where are you off to so early this morning, Abby Stanfield?" Sarah said aloud to no one as she stood at the window.

Once the Jeep disappeared down the trail, her gaze turned toward the lake and the distant mountains. She had to admit, this was one of the most gorgeous places she had ever been to in all her travels. Sarah always had liked the west, but for some reason had never put down roots anywhere. The clock and the hustle of the city ran her world, not the lone call of a loon making its way through the morning mist. She did love the country, but it was the city that paid her bills.

Looking back at her laptop, Sarah realized she had lost interest in what she had been working on. She sat in front of the screen lost in thought. She knew she had things to do, but her mind kept going back to yesterday afternoon and the anger and pain she had seen in Abby's dark eyes.

Crossing over from the side window, Sarah stopped in front of the glass doors. Yesterday's run-in with Abby had shaken her and she was not used to that kind of reaction. She prided herself on her instinctive ability to separate her personal emotions from her professional ones, but yesterday afternoon she had failed—miserably. Almost from the moment she had set eyes on Abby, strolling casually down her dock, Sarah had found herself drawn to the turmoil in the other woman's life and the secrecy surrounding her past. There was something so mesmerizing about the way she moved, almost cat-like, her long legs striding without effort as she glided along. Then when Sarah finally got a chance to talk to her, she had felt tongue-tied and nervous, like a naïve young schoolgirl. But it wasn't nervousness making her feel that way; it was excitement. She felt drawn like a moth to a flame. She knew she was putting herself in danger the closer she got to Abby. *If she was to find out who I am and why I'm here* … The thought bothered her, but it didn't matter; she still couldn't seem to stop. Sarah knew before they exchanged a single word that there was a fiercely independent streak in Abby Stanfield. Her do-or-die mentality drove her to succeed where others would have failed.

Watching Abby struggle with her bottle of beer had been amusing at first, but that soon changed. Before she gave it another thought, Sarah had grabbed the bottle opener and a couple of beers. But she hadn't been ready for what she saw when she got close enough to look into Abby's eyes. Something so powerfully entrancing it made her forget why she was there, something dark and mysterious as it moved like a shadow, deep in her eyes.

Sarah had no idea how long she stood there looking out the window thinking about Abby. When she did come to her senses, she knew she had to get out of her cabin. Maybe something to eat would take her mind off things. She saved what little she had done on her laptop and then headed to the lodge for breakfast.

☯

Balancing a tray of pancakes, fruit and tea, Sarah made her way outside to enjoy her breakfast on the deck. There were several tables empty, so she opted for one next to the railing.

"Good morning to you, Sarah. How are you enjoying your stay?" Helga said as she approached her.

Sarah found her host's smile contagious. "It's absolutely beautiful here, Helga, everything is … is perfect."

"Good, good, that is what I like to hear." It was hard not to feel the energy vibrating off the Scandinavian woman who obviously loved her job and her life.

"Actually I was wondering—would it be possible for me to extend my stay?" Sarah asked.

Helga paused, closing her eyes as if to study her internal booking schedule. "Yes, I do not see that as a problem."

"In the same cabin?"

"Ah, you like your cabin there?"

"Yes, yes I do. It has a very nice view."

"Dear, all the cabins have a nice view," Helga said as she reached over and patted Sarah on the shoulder. Then she winked. "But not all have a neighbor like Abby."

Sarah choked at the comment, her eyes opening wide in disbelief. Had her unprofessional feelings been that obvious?

"I watch, I see. Abby is a beautiful woman, on the inside and the outside. And like a daughter to me, so I watch." Helga turned to leave, but paused. "Your cabin is short one bottle opener, no?"

Sarah's open mouth curled slowly into a smile, it was obvious her neighborly hospitality had been seen. "Yes. Yes, it is."

"Yes, I think so. You be good to her, she is not as tough as you might think." With a wink, Helga was gone on to the next table.

☯

Sarah's walk between her cabin and the lodge should only have taken her about five minutes but on this bright morning it took her much longer. Energized and refreshed, she bounded up the stairs onto her deck, but stopped in her tracks as she came around the corner. There, leaning up against her cabin, was a brand new fishing pole with a white flag tied to the end of it. Sarah smiled at the peace-making gesture, knowing all too well who had left it. With a smile, she collected the pole and opened her front door. Pausing on the threshold, her eyes went from the pole in her hand to the laptop waiting for her on the table. It only took her a fraction of a second to decide that her computer and her work could wait.

☯

Abby stretched out on a lounge chair, her dark glasses hiding her bloodshot eyes. The moment Sarah came through the trees, Buck announced her arrival with a low ominous growl. The detective's head turned at the sound and a pleased smile crossed her face when she saw Sarah walking toward the cabin, the white flag of surrender still waving on the fishing pole.

Though Abby had a book on her lap, something told Sarah she wasn't reading. "Hi there," Sarah said as she approached the stairs to the deck.

Abby said something under her breath and Buck backed away to lie down next to her chair.

"Would he really eat me?" she asked, keeping her eyes on the large husky.

"Probably not, but I wouldn't put it past him."

"I'll keep that in mind." Sarah was almost positive Abby was joking.

"Come on up," Abby offered as she put her book down and stood up from her chair. Sarah was surprised to see the title *Japanese for Beginners*.

"That's a mighty task," Sarah said, pointing her fishing pole at the book. "Learning Japanese?"

Abby chuckled. "Getting even with a friend, and who knows, it may come in handy for ordering sushi."

"Oh, one of my favorites," Sarah beamed. "And speaking of raw fish." She held up the rod and flag.

Abby pulled off her sunglasses and placed them on her head.

It's her eyes, it's all in her eyes, Sarah thought as she tried not to stare.

"Sarah, I'm not very good with words or with apologies, but I'm truly sorry for my behavior yesterday. And, well, I was at Flanagan's this morning and when I saw the rod, and you'd said you'd forgotten yours …" Abby looked down and picked at the fiberglass of her cast, before she spoke again. "Part of the reason I'm up here is because I … well, need to learn to relax. Jesus, I'm shitty at this. Sarah, I'm sorry and I was hoping you'd let me make it up to you … maybe take you fishing or something."

The sheepish look on her face melted Sarah's heart right there as she thought about the *or something* that Abby offered.

"Hey, we've all had bad days. Why don't we just start over?" Sarah said with a smile as she leaned her pole against the cabin, then extended her hand.

"My name is Sarah and I'm staying in the cabin next door."

You excite me, Sarah-from-the-cabin-next-door, and I'm not sure how to deal with that Abby bit down on her lip before she broke into a full smile, "Abby." There was an immediate connection as they shook hands and looked into each other's eyes.

"Can I make you a coffee, Sarah?"

"Sure, if you make it a tea," Sarah responded with a bright smile.

☯

They spent the morning in polite conversation and, though it took a bit of time, Abby actually started to relax. Sarah's easygoing nature had the somber detective smiling and laughing on several occasions. They found they had numerous things in common from fishing and hiking to a love of music and the theater.

"*Les Mis* was still incredible; the music was so moving, and that little boy …" Abby said as she gazed over the rim of her coffee cup.

"But nothing can compare to the music of the night; *Phantom* is by far my favorite," Sarah said as she crossed her knees and pulled them up to her chest. It was a simple motion, but it tugged on something inside Abby.

"The last person I dated thought the theater was where you ate popcorn," Sarah said with a small laugh. "I mean, don't get me wrong, I love the movies too, but it's not the theater."

"I know what you mean. Most of the guys I work with would never be caught dead going to the theater."

They both chuckled at the comment.

"So do you work in an office or what exactly do you do for the city?"

The smile slowly slid from Abby's face as she felt the burden of her earlier untruth.

Sarah watched with interest as her new friend's gaze fell to the cedar deck. *She is a gorgeous woman—but there's something that she's hiding. And what wouldn't I give to find out what it is?*

Looking up, Abby bit at her lips as she wished for the delaying tactic of lighting a cigarette. Realizing the question was still hanging, Abby decided to relieve her conscience and to tell the truth.

"Actually Sarah, I don't work for the city. Well, I do but … I'm a cop." Abby saw the look of confusion. "I'm sorry. I didn't mean to mislead you but I don't usually tell people what I do. I mean, I'm proud to be a cop, but … well … Sometimes it seems like everyone has a speeding ticket they don't agree with or a case they want to argue about. So most people don't even know what I do. Mind you, apart from my dog and the kid at the video store, I don't talk to a lot of people outside of work. It … well, it wasn't something I wanted to get into."

"I understand. Actually, I don't—but that's okay. You have your reasons and I can respect that. But something tells me that's where those came from," she said as she gestured toward Abby's cast and stitches.

"These? I guess you could say they're part of the reason why I'm here."

"Part?" Sarah asked cautiously, not wanting to push too hard.

"I've been working a little too hard and it's affected my judgment. I was given the ultimatum of an extended break or a permanent one."

Sarah was listening intently. "Wow. So what'd you do?"

"I did something no one else had the balls to do."

"What was that?" The question sounded innocent enough but it was more than Abby was comfortable with revealing to a stranger.

"Hey, I've had enough coffee for now. Can I get you something else?" Standing up she reached for her cup as she looked at Sarah for an answer.

"Ah … wow, look at the time. It's lunch already. I should get out of your hair."

"Trust me; you're not in my hair. You wanna go and grab something at the lodge?" Abby didn't want the morning to end. She could not explain it but she had found a comfort she wasn't ready to let go of.

Sarah thought about the invitation before she finally answered with a smile. "Sure, why not?"

Leaving Buck happily laying on the deck, Sarah and Abby headed for the lodge.

☯

On her hands and knees in the warm dirt, Helga saw them coming down the path toward the lodge. Leaving her container of marigolds for a moment, she leaned back on her heels and watched them. Even from this distance, she could see they were in conversation.

"Good afternoon, girls."

"Afternoon, Helga," Sarah brightly answered back.

Abby held open the door for Sarah to walk through and then she leaned back to whisper to Helga. "Stop grinning. We're only having lunch."

"Oh, I know my child—but it has to start somewhere."

☯

Two empty sandwich plates were pushed off to the side as Abby and Sarah continued their conversation, oblivious to the outside world. Time had lost all meaning as they wallowed in a growing comfort neither had felt before. The lunchtime crowd came and went and they had no idea they were the only ones left in the restaurant.

"As I'm walking up to the car I'd pulled over, I realize I'm holding an ice cream cone—not exactly part of the protocol we're supposed to follow."

"So what did you do?"

"I proceed to the vehicle and I'm talking to the driver, trying my best to appear like I'm not holding an ice cream cone, and he's just staring at me. Finally, I ask him what the problem was and he said to me, with the most sincere look on his face, 'Sorry officer, but you have ice cream on your cheek.'"

Sarah burst out laughing at the visual of Abby trying to keep her professional demeanor with ice cream on her face.

"What'da do?"

"What any good cop would do. I wiped it off with my sleeve." With that comment, Abby joined in with Sarah's delightful laughter. *She is so easy to talk to … so easy to look at.* It was a thought that had entered Abby's mind many times that afternoon.

"So, after all that did you still give the guy a ticket?" Sarah asked before she took a sip of her white wine.

"No, I didn't."

"Didn't have the heart to?"

"No … I didn't have any place to put my ice cream cone." Abby shook her head in amusement as she reached for her beer. "I was just glad no one saw me and that it never got back to my captain."

Their laughter died down and Sarah took a sip of her drink before asking, "Abby, how long have you been a detective?"

"Long enough to know I like it … a lot."

"I bet you've more amusing stories."

"Not really, there isn't a lot to laugh about." The light mood changed, as did the brightness in Abby's eyes. "The only time you laugh is when you need to forget—when the tension becomes so thick you either bend with it or you'll break. Police officers and other emergency personnel tend to have a very morbid and vulgar sense of humor; most people never understand why."

Abby looked down at the beer bottle in her hand as if looking for an answer on the label. Over the years she had made many crude and improper comments about some of the victims they had found and, like her colleagues, she only said them to numb the pain she felt in her heart.

Sarah felt uncomfortable as she watched the dark shadows cross over her new friend's face. It made her feel she was intruding on something very private and painful. She didn't know Abby well enough to be privy to what tormented the detective's mind and suddenly she felt guilty for wanting to. *I want to comfort her, to hold her and make her pain go away.*

Sarah quickly reached out for her wine glass and the sudden movement pulled Abby back from her thoughts. She realized with regret that she had said too much and it had bothered the innocent woman across from her.

"I'm sorry, Sarah. I didn't mean to bring down our lovely afternoon."

"You didn't, Abby. I just never thought about what people like you must see on a daily basis," her voice trailed off.

"Hey, we've spent most of the afternoon talking about me; what about you?"

Sarah smiled as she took another sip from her wine glass. "Me," she swallowed her wine with an uncomfortable smile. *I'd rather not—I don't want to have to lie to you.*

"Yeah, you. You said you're originally from the east coast, but I don't hear an east coast accent." This time the tone of the question was one of interest not of interrogation.

"Okay, I guess I'm busted. I was born on the east coast, but I grew up in Montana. I hate saying that I'm from there because people always assume the only things in Montana are cows and cowboys."

"Well, from where I'm sitting, there's more than cows and cowboys coming out of Montana," Abby said with a smile as she watched the pink rise in Sarah's cheeks.

"And just what is it that you do, Miss … I don't even know your last name?" Abby sounded surprised.

"Well, touché, because I don't even know yours," Sarah said with an easy laugh, knowing all too well that she knew more about Abby then she was admitting.

"Stanfield," Abby answered as she leaned back in her chair and crossed her boots before putting them on the table. "And what is your line of work Miss …"

"McMurphy … Sarah Jolene McMurphy," she tipped her head down in a bow as she raised her glass. "At your service."

"Abigail, get your feet off the table!" Helga bellowed as she swatted at her feet. "Your mother would be appalled."

"Don't you have something better to do than to hang around spying on us?" Abby asked as she sat up in her chair.

"Yes, my dear, I have a resort to run, which is why I am here." Helga crossed her arms and looked back and forth at them. "The kitchen staff needs to get ready for dinner and they can't do it with you two in here." Abby looked from Helga's face to several sets of eyes peering from behind the swinging doors into the kitchen.

"Oh my God! Look at the time," Sarah exclaimed with a start as she looked down at her watch. "It's almost five." She glanced over at Abby.

"Well, I hate to disturb you, but we do need to get the dining room ready."

"All right, all right, we're going," Abby said. Helga left them alone as Abby stood up and Sarah quickly followed suit.

"I had fun this afternoon."

"I enjoyed myself today." Both chuckled lightly at their faux pas.

"It was nice to get to know you, Abby," Sarah said. She found herself flustered as she looked into her dark eyes.

"Same here," Abby said with a smile as they slowly headed for the door. *And I've never wanted to get to know someone more.*

Once outside, they stood awkwardly for a moment, neither wanting to break the spell that had come over their afternoon.

"We'll have to do this again."

"I'm free for lunch tomorrow." Sarah offered at she watched Abby pick at her fiberglass cast. She was thankful for the distraction because she did not want Abby to see her face if the beautiful detective said no.

"I'd like that very much, Sarah J. McMurphy."

"Then it's a date," Sarah said.

Abby quickly nodded in agreement not wanting to think about the connotation of the word *date. Or do I?* With smiles and waves they finally departed, each lost in thought.

Sarah's face beamed as she turned and headed back to her cabin. Tomorrow was a whole day away and she was already looking forward to it.

Something fluttered inside Abby as she watched Sarah's small frame disappear into the trees; it was a feeling she hadn't felt in a long time. *What are you doing to me, Sarah McMurphy?* Leaning back against the porch handrail, she kept her eyes on Sarah as she made her way homeward along the rocky trail. It had been a while since someone had uttered the word *date* to her, and it had been even longer since she had cared if they had. Abby had no idea if Sarah knew she was gay or if that was even how she had meant the word to come out. Either way it didn't matter, because tomorrow she was going to spend the day looking into Sarah's eyes and for now that was enough.

CHAPTER 6

For Abby, the days seemed to pass so quickly. Never before had she been so happy or so confused. She knew she was falling in love and no matter what, she couldn't seem to stop it. Not that she wanted to. She was learning about new feelings and new emotions. The spunky woman in the cabin next to hers had brought out a side of her Abby never knew existed. The hard and confusing part was that she did not know if Sarah knew she was gay, and, if she did, was she interested in her romantically?

As each afternoon wore on, Abby found it harder and harder not to look at Sarah and wonder how she could approach the subject. This was new for her. Never before had she feared someone's reaction to her sexuality. She was having a hard time dealing with the possibility of Sarah's rejection.

Other things were changing too. She found herself learning to enjoy the quiet and the solitude of the mountain resort. Most of her childhood had been spent here, but she hadn't returned since. Looking around, Abby realized it wasn't the resort that had stopped her coming back, but the memories of that day. As an adult, things looked different and she had to admit she had missed coming here and was enjoying her stay. Every morning, with Buck at her side, Abby would lie on her back at the end of the dock where she would lose herself in the lonely sounds of the loons calling to each other over the lake. As the weeks passed, she found herself thinking less and less about the things that had been destroying her life and more and more about what was missing from it.

☯

Sarah stared at her computer screen, but all she could see in her mind's eye was Abby. She couldn't keep her mind off her. Abby was what she was supposed to be thinking about, but not in the manner she was doing it. Those mesmerizing dark eyes had taken Sarah's heart from the beginning. She had seen something so sad inside them, yet whenever she looked closely, Abby turned away. Just what was the detective hiding behind those long strands of black hair—hair she wanted to run her fingers through? She wanted to hold that beautiful face in her hands, look deep into Abby's eyes and tell her that she was falling in love with her.

Sarah pulled the pencil from her mouth and flung it across the room in frustration. Pushing herself back from the table, she stood up and started pacing. She had not come to Gold Creek to fall in love, especially not with this woman. She was here to do a job, period—not to get involved with someone.

Breathing out a deep frustrated sigh, she ran her fingers through her hair as she leaned against the doorframe. Sarah looked out to the changing light of the approaching morning and was about to turn to put the kettle on for tea when she saw Abby walking down her dock with Buck. A wave of desire swept over her as she watched Abby say something to Buck. The husky looked up, wagging his tail with delight.

The two women enjoyed the morning as the sun broke over the mountains. It became a ritual they shared, but only one of them knew it. Every morning Sarah would be at the window to watch Abby stroll down to the dock, with her dog by her side.

CHAPTER 7

The morning found Abby out on the dock as usual, her eyes closed to the bright sun. The lapping of the water against the wooden cribbing beneath her lulled the detective into a warm, dozy state, but she lifted her head when she heard a door close. Shielding her eyes from the sun with her hand, she saw Sarah climbing into her black Honda. When the car pulled away, Abby closed her eyes again and rested her head back on the dock as she mildly wondered where her friend was going.

A couple of hours later, Abby heard Sarah's car return and, soon after, she made her way through the trees to Abby's cabin.

"Good morning," the detective offered as Sarah climbed the stairs.

"Morning," Sarah said as she took a seat in one of the chairs on the deck.

"How about a horseback ride or a walk today?"

The trained detective inside Abby saw a change in Sarah's features this morning. Wherever she had gone or whatever she had done weighed heavily on her normally cheerful appearance.

"You okay?" Abby asked.

Sarah nodded but Abby wasn't buying it. "I was thinking about trying out that new fishing rod I got you," Abby suggested as she looked out over the lake.

There was a moment's hesitation, but then Sarah agreed. Half an hour later, the two were out in the middle of the lake, their fishing lines cast into the water.

Sarah glanced back at the mound of fur sitting on Abby's dock, waiting for his owner to return. "Buck sure is a handsome dog, what is he … Husky? He looks like some sort of mix?"

"He's what they call a hybrid, a wolf mix. He's husky and northern timber wolf."

"Wow, he's a great dog, though. Very protective of you."

"Yeah, he thinks I'm his mother. I got him when he was only about four weeks old. I had to bottle-feed him because he was so young, and no one would take him because he was part wolf. I was just gonna keep him long enough 'til I found a home for him and, well …" Abby turned back toward her cabin and smiled when she saw Buck laying in wait. "He's a great dog—smart as a whip—but he's a sneaky little bugger, too."

Their conversation naturally died away, and soon the only sound was the water gently slapping against the hull of the canoe. Abby watched Sarah from behind her dark sunglasses, taking the opportunity to study her without her knowledge. With her sunglasses pushed up on her head, Sarah held her rod under her arm as she worked on her tackle. Abby liked the small crease on her nose as she concentrated on the task, squinting at the rigging in her hands.

"Did you fish here as a kid?" Sarah asked without lifting her head.

The question was innocent enough, but when there was no immediate response, Sarah looked up. The change in Abby's features was as obvious as the tension in her body language. The lazy smile that had been on her face had slipped away, making Sarah wonder what was going on behind those sunglasses. Not wanting to push the issue, Sarah returned her attention to her lure, though she was watching Abby closely out of the corner of her eye.

Abby looked across the lake and then up at the mountains before she finally turned to answer the question.

"Yes. I fished a lot here with my dad."

It wasn't the answer that puzzled Sarah, but the total lack of emotion in Abby's voice. She could almost hear a door slam shut and she wondered what Abby was hiding.

"I didn't mean to pry."

"You weren't prying. It was a simple question," Abby said, her voice once again relaxed and casual as she offered a broad smile.

Sarah was confused by Abby's pensiveness, but she tried not to let it show as she threw out her line. Watching from the corner of her eye, she could tell that, although Abby's eyes were on the water, her mind was definitely elsewhere. Neither spoke for a long while as they relaxed in the warmth of the afternoon sun, swaying lazily with the movement of the canoe. Suddenly, Abby began to talk. "We came out here quite a bit when I was younger. Some of the best memories I have are of us fishing out here in the mornings. There'd be a light haze over the water and the lake would be so still and calm. Sometimes it would scare me, especially when those damn loons … but Dad would be there and … that was a long time ago."

Abby grew quiet and Sarah watched her struggle with her emotions. She found herself wanting to reach out but thought better of it.

"You spoke in the past tense. I take it your father has passed away?" Sarah asked quietly.

"Yes, they … they passed away a long time ago." Abby lifted her head and looked at the mountains before she looked at Sarah. She offered a small, polite smile but her sunglasses hid her eyes.

"I'm truly sorry to hear that, Abby. Both of my parents are alive, or they were the last time I heard from them. They're on their way to Morocco and then on to … Monaco or Moldova … hmm, I can't remember. Either way, it doesn't matter. I haven't set eyes on them in, oh, six, seven years."

"Really? That's a shame. If my parents were still alive …" Abby looked at the shoreline before she finished, "… my life would be so much different." This time the pain in her voice was clear and Sarah felt an overwhelming need to reach out to her.

"Why's that, Abby? What would be so different?"

Abby didn't answer right away; instead she looked down at her broken hand, her glasses hiding her eyes.

"I … I don't know, but I know it'd be different."

Without warning, Sarah's fishing reel began to spin as a fish took the line. Both women looked up just as the rod bent sharply down toward the surface of the lake.

"Hang on to it!" Abby yelled as Sarah gripped her rod. "Let me get my line in." Abby started reeling as fast as she could manage with her injured hands.

"Oh, man, it's a big one!" Sarah's voice bubbled with laughter and excitement.

"Don't lose him, I almost have … Okay, my line is in." Abby secured her hook, then carefully put her rod down next to her. Turning around to face Sarah, she felt a smile spread across her face as she watched her spunky new friend fight for her catch.

"Slow it down, play him out a bit or you'll break your line."

"I got 'im," she laughed aloud as she pulled and reeled. "He's a feisty one," Sarah said with a grin.

"He's not the only one," Abby said under her breath.

"Yee hee, did you see that?" Sarah let go of her fishing rod with one hand so she could point out the rings left behind where her catch had just broken the surface.

Abby saw the rings but she saw the powerful flex on the rod more. "Sarah, hang on …"

The detective leaned forward for the bouncing rod but just as she got close enough, the line snapped, sending Sarah's hand into Abby's face.

"Ah!" Abby cried out in pain, as her eyes automatically shut.

"Oh my God! Abby!" Sarah dropped her rod and reached for the grimacing detective. "I'm so sorry, Abby. I didn't realize how close you were. Abby, are you okay?"

"Ahhh," Abby groaned in frustration at the sting.

Pulling Abby's hand away from her face, Sarah winced at the sight of the red welt already under her left eye. "Oh, Abby," Sarah said, reaching out as she started to kneel on the bottom of the canoe.

"Sarah … your rod!"

The warning came too late as Sarah's knee came down on the fiberglass rod. The resounding crack sent Sarah back on her heels, and the movement tipped the canoe wildly. Reaching out to steady herself, the only thing within reach was Abby's blue fiberglass cast. Not wanting to hurt her any further, Sarah searched desperately for an alternative, but realized too late that there wasn't one.

"Abby!" she cried out in panic as she tumbled backwards.

"Sarah!" Abby lunged but could do nothing except watch as Sarah toppled into the lake.

The whole situation was quite comical and Abby would have been laughing if not for the ache of her damaged face as she waited for Sarah to resurface. Seconds ticked by before she finally saw Sarah emerge, spitting and sputtering, her arms flailing about erratically. "Ab … by … Ab … I can't swi … " Sarah disappeared from sight again.

Without a thought, Abby dove into the lake. Her heart pounded in her ears as she spun in circles under the water. Resurfacing, she gasped for air as she looked around but saw nothing. Down she went again. It seemed like forever before she finally spotted Sarah. Reaching out, she grasped her hand and pushed hard for the surface, her lungs burning. She felt Sarah's grip tighten as they broke from the water.

"Sarah!" Abby gasped for air as she called out. "Sarah, are you all right? Sarah!" The woman's eyes remained closed as they floated in the water and a concerned Abby reached around to check for a pulse as she continued to call her name. "Sarah! Come on, Sarah!"

She felt Sarah's body move as she held it tight against her own. Her muscles were reacting and Abby knew that was a good sign. "Come on, Sarah, open your eyes!" the detective demanded. Sarah began to cough and sputter.

"That's it, come on, Sarah." The coughs came harder as Sarah forced herself to push the water from her lungs.

Holding on to Sarah and kicking to keep them afloat, Abby looked down into the face inches from her own just as Sarah took a deep breath and opened her eyes.

"You're okay, I've got ya," Abby said. She tried to sound calm, hoping Sarah wouldn't panic. She knew that if Sarah began thrashing about she wouldn't be able to hold her with her injured hands. "Look at me, Sarah. Look at me. You're okay." Sarah's eyes were open wide in terror as she looked from the surface of the lake to the woman holding her so tightly.

Abby saw the fear in her face as she strengthened her grip. "Sarah, you are okay," she repeated, keeping her tone firm and steady.

"Oh my God," Sarah cried out. "Don't let me go! Please! I can't swim."

"I know … I know, I got ya," the detective murmured. She felt some of the tension leaving Sarah's body.

"Okay, we're just going to swim over to the canoe—," Fear flashed in Sarah's eyes when she felt Abby's body move. She began to panic again.

"Wh … whoa! Okay, okay." Sarah's arms wrapped around Abby's neck and they went under as Sarah fought against the terror of the water.

Abby kicked hard to the surface, aware of her own waning strength. "Sarah! Stop it! Sarah! Look at me. I'm not gonna let you go, I promise." She meant every word, but Abby knew she had to do something quickly. The cast meant she only one arm with which to hold on to Sarah as her legs kicked to keep them afloat. The canoe was now a good thirty feet away and moving in the opposite direction, so that was no use. Holding tightly onto Sarah's shivering body, Abby scanned the shore and the lake for help, but there was no one to be seen. Looking back at her dock, Abby guessed that it was almost a hundred yards away, a distance she wasn't sure she could make. Then the answer came into focus as Buck howled from the dock.

"Buck, come!" The moment the dog heard her voice he launched himself from the dock with a splash. "Just hang on, Sarah," Abby whispered into her friend's wet hair as she placed a gentle kiss on the top of her head.

"Ab … by!" The name came in a quivering whisper. Abby watched her dog paddling hard toward them.

"I'm here Sarah, I'm here." Abby leaned back and started to move in the direction of her dog.

"Sarah, I need you to help me."

"I hit y … you in the face, d … didn't I?" Her voice was faint and her teeth were chattering. Abby knew that shock was taking its toll.

"Sarah I need you to trust me, okay? Buck's going to help pull us in, but you have to remain calm. Can you do that for me?" There was no answer.

"Come on, Buck, hurry up," Abby whispered under her breath. Her legs were burning under the strain as she continued to kick towards shore. She heard Buck and knew he was close as she turned to see his head almost within reach.

"Easy, Buck." She reached for his thick leather collar. "Steady, boy. Sarah, just hang on and let us pull you." Abby felt Sarah's hands tighten around her neck in response.

"Okay, Buck, pull! Pull, boy." His instincts were true and he did what was commanded of him. His large paws powered them through the water as Abby assisted with her legs as best she could. She had spent last summer training him for competition in sled and power pulling, never thinking the training would be used to save a life.

Abby held on to Sarah as they slowly but steadily moved through the water. Buck showed no sign that he felt the weight of the women as he paddled to shore.

"We're almost there, Sarah," Abby said as she looked back over her shoulder and saw they were only yards from her dock. "Easy, Buck, slow … slow." She reached out for the dock. The change of movement frightened Sarah and instantly her grip tightened. Thankfully, Abby could feel the sandy bottom of the lake under her feet.

"Sarah, come on. The dock is right here." Abby peeled one finger at a time from around her neck. "Reach out, come on." The moment Sarah's hand touched wood, Abby felt her body relax in relief. Standing behind her, Abby guided her hands and feet up the ladder. Once she cleared the top rung, Sarah collapsed into a ball on the dock.

Ignoring the pain in her hand and face, Abby quickly made her way up the ladder, although her legs trembled with exhaustion. She reached down to scoop up her small companion and took her up to the closest cabin, her own. Once inside, Abby carried her straight into the bedroom and placed her gently on the bed, but when she went to get an extra blanket, Sarah gripped her arm.

"Please don't go," Sarah whispered. Her voice cracked as she started to cry. It broke Abby's hardened heart to hear the pain in Sarah's sobs and she reached out and wrapped both arms around her. Sarah clung to her tightly as Abby nervously did her best to soothe her shattered and shaking friend. She had no idea how long they stayed like that, but when she felt Sarah's shivers growing she knew she had to get her warm and dry.

"Sarah, I need to get some towels and I want to check on Buck." There was no response but the tight hold around Abby's neck released.

"I'll be right back, I promise," she said as she leaned down and kissed the top of Sarah's wet hair. Stepping silently from the room, Abby was not surprised to see Buck lying patiently in the threshold of the doorway with his tail wagging, oblivious to what he had done. Abby knelt down and buried her face into his wet fur.

"Thanks, buddy. You're a good boy, Buck, a good boy." Abby didn't realize she had been crying until Buck lifted his head to lick her tears. "Yeah, I know ... you like her too."

CHAPTER 8

There was nothing but water—deep, dark, murky water—and it was cold. She couldn't breathe. The weight against her chest tightened. Sharp fingers clawed at her burning her lungs. Frantically she searched with her hands for a way out or a way up, but there was nothing. Her thick jacket was pulling her deeper into the water and she didn't have the strength to fight it any longer, so she relaxed and floated freely with the weeds. It was peaceful and quiet as she gazed at the rays of sunlight that were swallowed in the depths.

Then someone grabbed at the back of her jacket and pulled her quickly to the surface.

Sarah wasn't scared, so she felt no need to cry out when her Aunt Patricia pulled her from the lake. She heard people yelling her name as they ran down the dock she had walked off.

"Is she breathing?" She heard the screams of her mother in the distance as she looked up at her aunt's face.

"Sarah, sweetie … Sarah, it's Aunt Patty, sweetheart, talk to me." She loved her Aunt Patty, the youngest of her mother's sisters. She had blue eyes and the reddest hair of anyone she had ever seen. Quietly, Sarah lay there, watching all that was going on around her, but saying nothing. She felt the wooden dock shaking from the running footsteps of people coming to help as she looked from her aunt to her mother.

"Patricia, what happened?"

The fear in her mother's voice was not something she heard often, but she still did not feel the need to say anything as she continued to stare up into her aunt's blue eyes.

"She was walking down the dock and … and she didn't stop. She … she just kept on walking. Thank God it's … only a few feet deep there and … and I could reach her." Pat's words came in gasps as she looked over her young niece.

"Why weren't you watching her? You were supposed to be watching her. She is only four years old, Pat, you have to watch her!"

"I was watching her!"

"Obviously not enough, she almost drowned!"

"Maggie, enough!" Sarah heard her father's voice and instantly her mother's accusations ceased. "Pat, is the child all right or should we call for medical help?" As always, his tone held authority but no emotion. He rarely called his child by name.

"I think so, she seems alert enough. Sarah, you have to talk to me. Are you okay?" Sarah looked into the eyes above her and all she could think about was the icy bite of the water.

"Sarah, come on … say something." Sarah tried but she kept feeling the water, cold and bottomless, as it reached out to draw her down. Its long fingers held her feet as it dragged her farther and farther into the deep and dark …

"Sarah, it's okay, you're safe now." She fought to breathe, pushing hard against the relentless pull, but the chill of death was brushing against her skin. Fighting for her life and for her survival, she kicked and clawed against the heavy weight pinning her arms and legs.

"Sarah!" With a last burst of energy, Sarah pushed with all she had.

"Sarah!" She opened her eyes as she desperately sucked in as much air as she could.

Abby grabbed Sarah by the shoulders and yanked her into a sitting position. Sarah's face was pale, her eyes wide with fright as she struggled to keep her tears at bay.

"Look at me, Sarah. You're okay." Abby held on to her as Sarah's eyes darted around the room. Still gasping for breath, she looked back to Abby, her lower lip trembling uncontrollably.

"Hey, it's okay … it's okay … " The soothing words of care and concern crumbled Sarah's last morsel of resilience and she collapsed into Abby's strong arms. Rocking her back and forth, Abby whispered words of comfort as she rubbed Sarah's back. The shaking stopped, but Abby made no motion to let go. She never wanted to let go of Sarah again. The fear of loss had been a constant in her childhood and this afternoon had reminded her of just how painful that was. *I never want to feel that again. If you need to be held, then I will hold you—for as long as you need–for as long as you want, but I will never let you go!*

Sarah rested her ear against Abby's chest and she let the steady rhythm of Abby's heart lull her into a relaxed state. She swallowed several times before she finally found her words.

"My family had gone to visit my grandparents—they had a cabin on the lake. I know it wasn't summer because I was wearing my winter coat. Everyone was inside, but I—I don't know, I guess I wanted to go outside, so my Aunt Patty took me. We played on the shore for a while and then I walked down the dock, and for some reason I didn't stop walking even when I ran out of dock to walk on. I was young, and, I don't know, maybe I thought I could walk on water." Sarah sighed. "Thank God my aunt was right there. She grabbed the hood of my jacket before I could even touch bottom. I still remember looking at the rays of sunlight in the water and not being overly concerned until I tried to breathe and couldn't."

Abby held her tightly, waiting for her to continue. "My mother freaked. She started blaming my aunt and eventually my grandparents. She said they should have had a gate on the dock. Can you believe that?" She shook her head. "My mother was never the same after that. It was like she was afraid of anything or even anyone hurting me, so no one was allowed near me. At the same time, she was so afraid to get too close to me either. My life became a steady stream of nannies who weren't allowed to hold me and a mother who didn't want to touch me. I only saw my grandparents a few times after that and I never saw my Aunt Patty again."

"Sarah, I … I don't know what to say," Abby replied as Sarah leaned into her embrace. "I'm sorry." Abby gently kissed the top of Sarah's head.

Closing her eyes, Sarah reveled in the moment. "Don't be sorry, Abby; you had no way of knowing. I eventually got over my fear of water, but I never learned to swim."

Pulling Sarah away from her chest, Abby lowered her head to look the other woman in the eyes.

"Why didn't you tell me?"

"It didn't seem to be … Oh my God, Abby! Look at your eye!" Abby had all but forgotten the incident preceding Sarah's plunge, but she recalled it quickly when Sarah tenderly brushed her fingers over the darkening skin.

Abby felt the soft fingertips touching her cheek, sending a wave of excitement through her body. Now it was Abby who was swallowing hard trying to find the words through her emotions.

"It's … I'm sure it's not as bad as you think." She tried to smile reassuringly at Sarah, but the movement of her cheek muscle caused her to grimace, which only deepened the pained look on Sarah's face.

"I'm so sorry, Abby. I didn't mean to. The line broke and then I knelt down on the rod and I lost my balance," Sarah said. Abby tried to hide the smirk growing on her face as she watched Sarah ramble on. It was something she did when she was nervous. "And … and when I tried to grab for something, all that was there was … you dove in after me with your cast on."

Abby looked down at the blue fiberglass, "Yeah. It got a little wet inside, but it's fiberglass."

"I know that, but still, it had to hurt." This time Sarah's hand came up and she held Abby's chin while she turned her face to see the side of her eye and cheek.

"That's going to be nasty. I wish there was something I could do to make it better." Sarah caught the look on Abby's face and turned her chin to look in her eyes once more.

The room was suddenly thick with silence in a new atmosphere laden with unspoken desires. Never before had Abby been so drawn to someone, a woman she knew very little about, yet wanted to. Many thoughts rushed through her mind, but there was one screaming louder than all the others. *What if she's not* … echoed repeatedly in Abby's head as she looked long and hard into Sarah's eyes.

"Sarah, I think there's something I had better tell you," the detective said, almost whispering. Abby knew she couldn't hide who she was any longer, any more than she could hide her anxiety over the 'what ifs' going around in her head. *What if Sarah isn't? What if she hates gays and lesbians? Or worse, what if she's with someone—male or female?* The questions flashed so fast through Abby's conscious. She had to tell Sarah and then hold her breath as she waited for a response.

But she knew telling someone you were gay was one of the hardest things to do. It was a gamble no matter how confident you were. She knew of parents who had disowned children, brothers who had walked away from sisters, and friends who had disappeared faster than a mother's hopes of a big white wedding and grandchildren. People said '*If they love you, it won't matter*' and in a perfect world that would be true, but the world Abby lived in wasn't perfect. In her world, people judged without knowledge and hated without reason. When you met someone, inevitably the time would come when you would have to decide; do you tell or don't you? You weigh the risk against the desire for honesty. Do you tell friends? Do you tell colleagues? Who do you tell and when? She knew it was a risk—it always was when you had to tell someone something so private and personal—but it was worse if you didn't tell and they found out.

"Abby?" The sound of her name pulled the detective from her thoughts. Looking into Sarah's face, Abby suddenly lost the courage. The price of losing her friendship was too high.

"I, ah …" Abby let her eyes drift downward, though she was fully aware of the soft touch of Sarah's fingers still on her chin.

"You, ah …" Sarah said as she once again lifted the detective's chin. "You saved my life and for that I am and always will be …" Sarah leaned forward placing a soft and gentle kiss on Abby's cheek, "… grateful."

Abby closed her eyes and wallowed in the moment. She leaned forward aching for acceptance. She wanted another kiss, this time one of passion—on the lips. She was certain Sarah wanted it, too, as she looked down at the other woman's mouth, inches away from her own. *Kiss me like you want me. I know you want me, I can sense it. Sarah wants me, and I want her. I want her lips, her—*

"Abby! Sarah!" The sound of Günter's panicked voice pulled them apart as they stared at each other. There were questions and reactions but no words as Günter's voice boomed, "Abby, are you in there?" His heavy steps pounded across her deck.

Looking into Sarah's eyes, Abby couldn't find the words she wanted to say as her gaze drifted downward to Sarah's lips again.

"Abby!"

"You better answer him," Sarah whispered as she looked away.

Is she embarrassed, ashamed? Look at me, Sarah. But Günter wouldn't be ignored.

"We're in here, Günter!" Abby hollered to the ceiling, then observed the rising pink of Sarah's cheeks.

"Are you two all right? Another guest told us you got into trouble out on the lake."

They locked eyes again as Günter's words preceded his presence in the bedroom. Standing in the doorway his gaze took in their proximity and their wet appearance before he finally saw the color on Sarah's cheeks.

"Are you two okay? I saw the canoe still out on the lake. I was …" Abby rose off the bed as he approached her.

"We had a bit of a problem but we're all right," Abby said reassuringly but Günter was looking over her eye.

"All right, you say …" He reached out and turned her head to get a better look at her cheek and then he focused on Sarah. "And you, young lady, are you all right?"

"Yes, thank you, Günter. I fell out of the canoe and Abby saved me."

"Well, that would explain why you are wet, but where did you get the shiner?" he asked Abby.

"Günter, we are both fine and we thank you for your concern, but I think Sarah needs some rest."

"All right, Abby. I'll trust you know what you are doing."

"She's a life saver," Sarah said with a tired smile.

"She's more than that. I don't know what we'd do with this place without Abby …"

"Günter?" Abby quickly cut him off. "If you would you be a dear … the canoe is still out there floating around. Thanks, Günter."

Sarah watched him disappear from the bedroom. *Without Abby, what did he mean?* She shifted her attention back to Abby and forgot the thought as Abby's dark eyes turned to meet hers. Sarah could feel the heat on her cheeks as Abby's gaze intensified.

Slowly the detective moved in closer. She remembered the feeling of Sarah's lips on her cheek and she wanted nothing more than to—

"Abby … wait," Sarah held up her hand. *I have to tell her, I want to kiss her but I have to tell her the truth.*

"Abby! Sarah, hello!"

The detective's head dropped to her chest with a groan, as Sarah covered her grin with her hand.

"Abby!"

Sarah watched the expression on Abby's face as they heard Helga's concerned voice. "You better answer her."

"In here, Helga," Abby admitted reluctantly.

"Oh my, we got word your canoe had capsized and …" she came around the corner and stopped at the sight of the two damp women. If Helga noticed the red cheeks, she gave no sign of it as she scurried over to Sarah's side.

"You need warm soup and dry towels. Abby, get out of those wet clothes and fetch me another blanket from the closet," Helga commanded.

"Helga, we're fine."

"Nonsense, you could catch your death in those wet clothes. Now scurry, get what I asked." Abby knew there was no stopping the motherly demands of the elderly woman as she glanced at Sarah with a shrug of her shoulders.

"Come on, change into dry clothes, and go lay on the sofa. Dr. Enderby will be here shortly."

"What? Wait; whoa. You called Dr. Enderby? We're both fine."

"That is for him to say, my child, not for you. Shooting and arresting bad guys you know, looking after someone's health he knows."

"Helga, there's no need to have him come all this way. The man has to be 102 years old."

"You do what you know and I will do what I know. Now go and change."

"But, Helga …"

Most of the time, Helga avoided confrontation, never understanding why people would fight for anything other than the freedom to live. But every once in awhile, when someone pushed the wrong way, she hunkered down and fought back. Turning around, Helga stood her ground over the much taller detective. "This time the doctor is coming."

Without so much as a word, Abby turned on her heels and left the room. Helga looked at the floor for a moment, took a deep breath, then turned to Sarah as though nothing had happened.

Sarah said little as Helga fluttered around her. No matter how many times she tried to tell Helga she felt fine, the older woman smiled and pulled up her blanket. A short while later, true to her word, she brought in a bowl of steaming soup. Sarah began to eat the soup, but Helga showed no signs of leaving. "Helga, you've known Abby a long time, haven't you?"

"Hmm."

"What happened to her parents?"

Helga held the smile on her face. "I think you should ask her that question."

"I didn't mean to pry."

"I know, child. Curiosity is in us all."

"Helga, when Günter was here …" Sarah searched for the right words. "He made a comment about the resort needing Abby. I mean, not that it's any of my business, but are things okay around here?" Seeing the humor in her caregiver's eyes, Sarah was even more confused. "What? What did I say?"

"My dear girl, you need to have a few more conversations with Abby."

"I don't understand."

Helga reached out to pull up Sarah's blanket again. "The resort needs Abby, my dear, because she owns it."

CHAPTER 9

Dr. Enderby arrived and, after he examined Sarah in the bedroom, he returned to the living room to look at Abby, who was waiting impatiently.

"Little Abigail. Haven't you grown into a beautiful young woman."

"Dr. Enderby."

"Your little friend in there is lucky to have you around."

"How is she?"

"She's fine, Abigail. I gave her something to sleep."

"Actually, it's Abby now."

"Of course. Now let me see what you've done here."

He removed her stitches but informed her that her cast needed to be replaced. There was no arguing with the elderly doctor and she knew it. Wanting to check on Sarah before she left, she silently opened the bedroom door. The movement made Helga turn. Seeing who it was, she put a finger to her lips and motioned Abby out the door.

"I have to follow Dr. Enderby back to the clinic. He needs to replace my cast."

"She will be fine, Abby. She will be here when you get back." Helga held out her arms and the two women hugged. "She has questions, that little one does. Questions you need to answer." Helga pulled out of the embrace. "I spoke something and I wonder now if I should not have."

"What? What did you tell her?"

"I told her that the resort belongs to you."

"What?"

"I did not think it would matter." Helga watched with regret as Abby turned away and looked out the front window. "Why, child? Why do you wish this to be a secret from everyone? It has been so long, surely it can no longer matter?"

Helga waited but no answer came as Abby stood looking out over her lake. Her tall body and broad shoulders had carried a weight few knew and Helga wondered how long she would bear the burden alone.

Without turning around, the somber detective walked out of the room.

☯

The long drive to the doctor's clinic in Dexton was exactly what Abby needed—and exactly what she didn't need. Time to think. Her mind was a whirl of questions and her body was a mass of emotional reactions. This morning she had pulled Sarah from the deep waters of the lake, and then there was the kiss—a simple kiss that had taken her breath away.

What is happening to you, Stanfield? Pull it together; it was only a kiss. One kiss and you're falling into a schoolgirl crush. But it's not a crush and it wasn't just a kiss. Or was it? That question was without answer as Abby powered her Jeep along the winding road leading away from Gold Creek. Her thoughts jumped back and forth between want and fear, desire and apprehension. Sarah now knew what only a handful of people did—that she was the owner of the resort. Günter and Helga had run the resort for her father, and they were happy to continue to do so for her.

It had been hard not to tell Lincoln and Carla when she had sent them here on their honeymoon. Günter and Helga had respected her wishes then. *So why had Helga told Sarah now?*

Abby knew why. Sarah had a way about her, a way that made you want to open up. To tell her things you hadn't spoken about in years, to look into her eyes and release the ghosts that haunted your past. To say goodbye to the nightmares with a wave and a kiss—

A kiss. Had it been a kiss or a thank you? The question flew back into her head. Abby knew she needed an answer—and if she couldn't get one, maybe she needed a new train of thought.

A small gas station was coming into view and when she spotted the phone booth, Abby geared down her Jeep. Dexton wasn't that far away; so good old Doc Enderby could wait.

Quickly she dialed a familiar number on the payphone. "Detective Quinn."

"Hey there, big guy."

"Abby? Holy shit, I thought you'd died. How the hell are you?"

"I'm good."

"Good? Did you say you were good? Okay, what's her name?"

"Sarah." Abby knew she was smiling but she couldn't help it.

Lincoln laughed, but his playfulness quickly sobered. "You're serious, aren't you?"

"Yeah."

"Holy shit. You're in the middle of nowhere and you meet someone?"

"I met her at the resort. She's in the cabin next to me."

"Great, all we had was some guy with a hairy back who spent all day out on his dock in a Speedo. Ugh. And what do you get? Some babe, in a bikini I bet. Sarah, huh? Well, she must be something."

"She's something special … really special."

"She sounds great."

"So what's happening?"

"Well, let's see. I don't think anyone has mentioned your name on the news for a while so that's a good thing. Banks got a new door, so she is no longer on the war path."

"Cut to it, Lincoln."

"Billy Ward has been behaving himself, nothing out of the ordinary. Consequently, the lieutenant is fighting to keep surveillance on him."

"Fighting to keep watching him, are you kidding me? He kills how many, and they want us to substantiate why he needs watching?"

"We need proof, Abby."

☯

By the time she pulled back into her driveway, it was well after midnight. There were no lights on in her cabin as she turned off the motor, but the moon was full and the sight of a wagging tail near the door told her she had been missed.

"Hey Buck," she greeted him as she climbed from her Jeep. With a pat to Buck's head, she slipped quietly into her soundless cabin. Looking around in the pale moonlight, she tiptoed over to her bedroom door. She silently turned the handle and peeked inside. There on the bed, bathed in the dim light and looking small and fragile, was the woman who was stealing her heart. Leaning her head against the doorframe, Abby noted the steady rise and fall of Sarah's chest as she studied the peaceful, angelic features. The detective had to fight the temptation to walk over and brush aside her fallen bangs. In the quiet of the night, in the shadow of her former self, the solemn and single detective had to admit that she was finding a warm comfort in this new companionship; it felt strange but good.

"Good night, Sarah," Abby whispered as she closed the door and headed for the sofa.

CHAPTER 10

The twittering of the early birds woke Sarah from her heavy sleep. Looking around the strange yet vaguely familiar room, she wondered for only a moment where she was. When she had told Abby that she lived most of her life from a suitcase, she hadn't lied. She was used to waking up in unfamiliar places. She recalled where she was—Abby's cabin—as well as the why.

Yesterday's nightmarish incident screamed back into her mind as her body shuddered with the memory. Every muscle ached as she recalled her fight for life in the water. Looking up at the ceiling, she forced herself to forget her physical pain but she couldn't ignore what was going on in her heart. The inner battles she had been having over her feelings for Abby were nothing compared to the guilt and fear of discovery she now was experiencing.

Pulling back the covers, Sarah swung her legs around as she sat on the edge of the bed. Stiff and sore, she looked down at the wood floor and sighed heavily as she rubbed her hands against her face. This was not what she had bargained for. *I am falling in love with her!*

Sarah's interest in Abby was more than professional. Falling in love with her subject was bad enough, but now that same woman had saved her life and that put a different spin on everything. The argument she had on the phone just yesterday morning tugged at her conscience, as she reviewed the events that had happened since.

Reaching for the clothes that Helga had brought over from her cabin, Sarah dressed quickly. She'd made up her mind and she knew she had to act before she lost her courage. Soundlessly, she backed out of the bedroom, pulling the door closed behind her. As she turned to leave, she stopped when she saw Abby asleep on the sofa. Stepping quietly forward, she looked down at the detective and longed to wake her—to tell her the truth and let the chips fall where they may. *I didn't plan on this—but who could have?*

It was strange to see Abby's normally intense features so relaxed as Sarah listened to her light snoring. Sarah felt her conscience grating on her mind, battling hard against her inner aching desires. But the constant questioning of her ethics and morals pressed on, but Sarah wasn't ready to answer them. This woman had only offered her friendship and maybe a chance for something more. Sarah took one last look at the dark features of the sleeping beauty. "I'm sorry, Abby," she whispered tenderly. "I can't do this … I just can't." Sarah turned and dashed out the front door.

Abby's eyes fluttered open. She was certain that she had heard a voice. "Sarah?" Abby sat up as she heard the sound of departing footsteps out on the deck. Pulling her blanket around her bare shoulders, Abby ran after the darting figure, but she knew she was too late as she heard Sarah's Honda leaving. Standing alone on the deck, Abby could only watch the dust the car had left behind.

"Can't do what?" Abby cried out as she stood alone on the deck.

☯

By the time her Honda hit the blacktop, hot tears streamed freely down Sarah's face. The guilt she felt dug harder into her soul as the pain of her betrayal weighed heavily on her. She hadn't gone fishing to fall in the lake, but it had happened and there was nothing she could do about it. She hadn't come to Gold Creek to fall in love and there was nothing she could do about that, either. But she had come to Gold Creek for a reason and there was something she could do about that. Wiping away her tears, Sarah thought about her options.

She pulled up in front of the phone booth at Flanagan's—the only phone for miles—and walked silently past the young redheaded boy on the steps. She lifted the receiver and turned her back on her audience.

Sean watched her for a moment, then decided Sarah probably wanted some privacy.

Sarah tapped her fingernails against the glass as she waited. "Daniels," the voice on the other end of the phone answered gruffly.

"It's Murphy."

"What?" He was not one to waste words.

"I'm not doing this. I can't." She hoped he didn't hear the shaking in her voice. "Did you hear me? I'm done, get someone else."

"Didn't we do this yesterday? I thought I had made it perfectly clear. You're doing it, and you'll finish it."

"Forget it, there's no story here."

"I give the orders around here, Murphy, not you. That mouthy bitch is a walking front page and a guaranteed 2 percent increase in sales. I want to know who she's eating breakfast with and who she's fucking sleeping with. Abby is news and that's all I care about, the story. So get the goddamn story!"

Sarah closed her eyes and contemplated her decision. It had taken her years to get this kind of job and she was about to throw it away. "Well, I'm not doing it! I quit!"

"Am I supposed to care? Because I don't. You're there to work, not lay around on a company expense account! So quit if you want. It'll take you a year to pay back what you've already spent there and, in the meantime, you'll never sell another story or write another byline again. Do you hear me?"

"You wouldn't dare." Sarah felt her stomach drop at the threat. Quitting was one thing, destroying her entire career she had worked so hard for—that she hadn't counted on. She physically cringed at the enjoyment in his normally curt voice.

"Wouldn't I? You're not that big, Sarah Murphy. You've got a cute smile and a nice ass and you can string a few sentences together, but if you decide to fuck with me, I'll bury you. When I'm done you won't even be able to write the classified ads for the Iowa Farm Report! You're a little peon and in this business that's yesterday's news wrapped around a dead fish. I chose you to get her to give you the story, Murphy. Get the story!"

He slammed the phone down and Sarah hung her head in defeat. She had nothing but her job and she had been willing to give it up, but this wasn't just her job. Daniels was threatening her career.

Sarah went back to her car and dug around in her purse until she had her notebook. When she found what she was looking for she picked up the phone and dialed. She held a conversation for about five minutes and then she hung up and looked down at the figure she had written; $127.65, the grand total of her life savings.

CHAPTER 11

Every time she heard a sound, Abby wondered if it was Sarah returning, but there was still no sign of her. The longer she waited, the wilder her imaginings became as to where the redhead had gone and why.

Rising from her deck chair, Abby went back into her cabin for another cup of coffee. She took a sip as she glanced at her watch. Aimlessly she wandered back outside and back to the nagging questions. Fifteen minutes later, her cup was empty and her patience had run out.

"Stay here, Buck," she ordered as she made her way down her steps and then through the trees to Sarah's cabin. The layout of the deck and the cabin were similar to Abby's, just a little smaller. Walking across the deck, she felt a little strange as she glanced into the darkened cabin.

"I'm not snooping, I'm just concerned," she whispered to herself as she came around to stand in front of the doors. Leaning in, she cupped her hands on the glass to block the bright sun as she peered inside. Sarah's laptop was sitting open on the table and it relieved some of Abby's concern. "Okay, so you didn't leave."

Turning away from the cabin, Abby glanced over the lake. "Where the hell have you gone, Sarah?" There were not many places to go and even fewer reasons to rush out. Glancing over her shoulder, Abby looked at the open laptop.

"Forget it, Stanfield. You're out of your jurisdiction and way out of line," Abby muttered under her breath. Walking away from the temptation, she reached up to her breast pocket, but stopped when she remembered she no longer smoked. She put her foot up on the railing and struggled with her desire to peek at the computer on which Sarah always seemed to be writing.

Just a quick look, she thought as she walked back to the front door, *but only if the door is open.* Abby reached out for the handle, but stopped before she touched it.

"What am I doing?" she asked herself aloud, but the moment of question passed and she grabbed the handle and walked into Sarah's cabin.

Abby could smell a hint of Sarah's perfume in the warm, cooped-up air as she moved farther into the cabin. Her dark eyes went from the laptop on the table to the open bedroom door.

"Sarah?" Abby called out. Leaning into the bedroom, she scanned over the discarded clothes and the empty suitcase. There was nothing there to tell her where Sarah might have gone. She looked once more at the inviting computer sitting on the table. With hesitant steps, she made her way over until she was looking down at the dark screen. *Just what is it that you are always writing?* Abby crossed her arms, as if hoping the gesture would stop her urge to push the power button.

"Ah, what could it hurt?" she said aloud as she reached to turn the computer on.

Buck's howl almost stopped her heart and her hand froze in mid-air. A car was approaching, its tires crunching on the gravel. Like a child with her hand caught in the cookie jar, Abby felt her face grow hot as she realized where she was and what she had almost done. Not only had she betrayed Sarah's trust, but she had invaded her privacy.

With three long strides, Abby was across the room and out the door before she heard the motor turn off in between Buck's urgent barking. It was only when she looked around the edge of the cabin that she realized, with great relief, that the vehicle she had heard was in her driveway, not Sarah's. Once she came around the backside of the log structure, she recognized the Honda immediately.

"Buck, cease!" she called out as she came through the trees.

"He's scary when you're not around," Sarah said with a nervous smile as she stood next to her car.

"I was just over at your place waiting for you. You left so quickly this morning, I never had a chance to …" *To what, Stanfield? Think about what you're about to say. Chance to what— kiss you good morning? Tell you that I think I am falling in love with you? Chance to what?* Abby's scattered thoughts shut down her comment before she had a chance to finish it.

"I, ah, I need to apologize for that. I guess I should've waited for you to … umm … to wake up." Sarah stumbled over her words, not wanting to explain why she felt the need to leave at the crack of dawn.

Abby, on the other hand, was too busy trying to cover up the fact that she had heard Sarah's departing words this morning, and was uncertain if she wanted to know their true meaning.

"No, that's okay, I was just surprised that you left, and I, ah … I wanted to make sure you were all right. That was a scary day yesterday."

Finding her proverbial feet back on solid ground, Abby decided not to push Sarah's reason for her early departure.

"I'm okay—a little stiff and sore, but that's all," Sarah said with a smile. But as Abby took a closer look she noticed a change in Sarah's normally sunny disposition.

"I'm glad to hear that," Abby said as she walked around the end of the Honda and got a little closer. Now that they were only a few feet apart, Abby could see the redness of Sarah's eyes.

Standing next to her open car door, Sarah felt Abby's gaze and knew she couldn't withstand the intense woman's close scrutiny, so she bent down to hide her face.

"It seems that young boy at Flanagan's remembered selling you one of these," she said as she pulled out a brand new fishing rod.

Abby laughed. "I guess they're making their money off of us this season."

"Looks like it."

"How about trying it out? You know what they say about getting back on the horse that bucked you off."

Sarah looked at the still surface of the lake. "Yes, I do, but I think I'd rather have a nap."

"Are you sure?" Abby did her best to hide her disappointment but she could tell Sarah was tired.

"I just wanted to come over to thank you again and to let you know I had replaced the fishing rod."

"The rod was yours, it was gift. Maybe tomorrow?"

"Maybe," Sarah offered, but somehow Abby wasn't certain she was sincere.

☯

The weekend passed with a few greetings and the odd wave, but nothing more and that was the way Sarah wanted it. There were always judgment calls that a reporter had to make—what was part of the story and what was not, what was a betrayal of confidence and what was good journalism—and as Sarah stared at the blinking cursor, she knew she no longer had any clue about any of it.

CHAPTER 12

Abby woke up with an unreachable itch under her cast and an unquenchable thirst for information. She looked down at her sleeping dog. "All right, I admit it, I miss her," she said.

Buck opened one eye and looked at his owner.

"But what am I supposed to do? I mean, was it the kiss?" A long and drawn out yawn was the only answer Buck had.

"She's been avoiding me, Buck, I know she has. I just can't sit here and pretend nothing happened." Buck lifted his head and blinked at her. "Well, what am I suppose to do?" He stared back at her before he lowered his head and then went back to sleep with a huff.

"Okay, then I *will* do something about it!" She marched with determination across her deck, through the trees and up Sarah's driveway. Much to her surprise, the redhead was sitting outside on her deck.

"All right, what'd I do wrong?" she said stopping at the bottom of the stairs with her hand on her jean-covered hip.

Sarah looked up in surprise. "Pardon?"

"Have you been avoiding me?"

"No."

Looking at Abby after not seeing her for a few days made Sarah's stomach flutter. One side of Abby's long black hair was flipped back over her shoulder, while the other side was tucked behind her ear. Her fiberglass cast hung out of a most appealing soft denim shirt. This was one beautiful but highly agitated woman.

"Well, you haven't been out of your cabin since we talked the other day."

"I'm sorry, Abby, I've had things on my mind and I'm just trying to get them straightened out." *Because I'm afraid to be near you.*

"Is there anything I can do to help? I've got connections, you know."

"Thanks, but this is something I have to figure out myself." *Like do I destroy my career for a beautiful, troubled woman with a dark and mysterious past? A woman I want to get to know, but I'm afraid to?*

"May I?" Abby motioned to the deck.

"Please, come on up." *And sit next to me, close enough to drive me insane—Abby do you know what you do to me?*

Abby took a seat across from Sarah. "This doesn't have anything to do with what happened in the canoe, does it?"

"No, of course not." *But it does have something do to with how much I would like to kiss you right now.* The thought slipped through her mind before Sarah even had a chance to steel herself against it. She gazed at Abby's lips.

"Could I persuade you to go for a ride then?" Abby did not want to leave without some assurance that she would be seeing Sarah again.

You would be surprised at what you could persuade me to do. Sarah's thoughts were out of control.

"Or would you rather not?" Abby asked with a raised eyebrow.

"I'd love to go for a ride with you," she said with a wide bright smile, finally quieting her inner discourse.

They agreed to meet at the corral in half an hour.

☯

They rode in silence along the trails that wound around the large evergreen trees. Sarah watched the ease of Abby's body as she moved fluidly with each step of her black stallion. The gentle rolling of her hips and the relaxed hold she had on the reins told Sarah that Abby had spent more than a few hours on the back of a horse.

The young reporter hadn't realized how high they had climbed until they broke from the trees into a rolling meadow of green. The tall grass moved with the light breeze off the mountains, swaying like waves on the ocean as it rolled.

Abby reined in her stallion and waited for Sarah to catch up. As she moved her horse alongside her, Sarah knew her mouth was hanging open in awe at the scenery around her.

"This has got to be one of the most beautiful places."

"And it gets better." Abby motioned forward and once more Sarah followed as she led her through the meadow and back into the cover of the dark forest. It took a few moments for her eyes to adjust, but even when they did, she still couldn't make out any trail.

"Where are you taking me?" Sarah called out.

"To the top of the world," Abby hollered back.

I'm already on top of the world, Abby, and I'm going through hell because of it, Sarah thought as she gazed at the seductive sway of the woman in front of her.

With nothing else to do but think and watch, Sarah found herself wondering more and more about her mysterious companion and exactly where it was that she was being taken. After all the time they had spent together, Sarah knew nothing more about Abby than before she had arrived. It was supposed to be so easy. Get in, get close and get out, but as she observed the woman in front of her all she wanted to do was to get close and then get comfortable. To snuggle deep into her strong arms, to look endlessly into those dark eyes as she traced her fingertips over the fresh scars on Abby's knuckles, to brush back her hair …

"Sarah!" The sound of her name pulled her back from the very unprofessional place her mind had drifted. She smiled at Abby, who had turned around in her saddle.

"You okay?" Abby looked concerned, as her horse continued forward.

"Yeah."

As they broke free of the cool cover of the trees, Sarah's eyes opened in amazement at the vista before her. The bright blue of the sky was a sharp contrast to snow-capped mountains, and down below the green of the forest ran right to the edge of the clear blue waters of Lake Alouette.

"My God, it's breathtaking." Sarah stood up in her saddle for a clear view of the tiny log lodge and cabins below.

"Pretty nice, isn't it?" Abby almost sounded proud, as she looked down at the view that hadn't changed since she was a child.

"Nice? No, this isn't nice, this is incredible," Sarah exclaimed as she got down from her horse.

Already on her feet, Abby watched Sarah move closer to the edge of the grass.

"Watch it, there's a helluva drop there," Abby warned as she reached for a blanket from behind her saddle.

Sarah crept closer to see the dizzying distance to the rocky bottom of the cliff. "Now that'd hurt."

Abby smiled at the understatement as she laid out the blanket.

Sarah tried to fight the questions exploding in her mind, but she couldn't. "Abby, why didn't you tell me you owned the resort?" Though the sun was bright, Sarah saw a dark cloud roll across Abby's face. Her eyes narrowed into a squint as she looked down at the back of her hand and at the red ribbon of scars crisscrossing her knuckles.

There was no reply as they silently began their lunch. Their sandwiches were soon finished and they sat sipping beers and nibbling on potato chips. Sarah did not notice the deep state of concentration on Abby's face until the somber detective spoke. Her voice seemed distant as she tried to remember something from her past that she had made great efforts to forget.

"I came up here a lot when I was a child. You know, to think about things. This had to be one of my favorite places in the whole world."

Sarah caught the look in Abby's eyes and she didn't like what she saw. "You don't have to tell me any of this. It's your business, not mine."

"I'd like to, and in some ways, I think I need to." Abby paused. "The resort was owned by my parents, but for their own reasons they had Günter and Helga run it. People assumed it was theirs and, when my parents died, I never told anyone different."

"I don't understand," Sarah said quietly, not wanting to intrude on the memories Abby was reliving.

"There were things happening within my family, things I didn't understand. I wasn't old enough." Abby stopped for a moment to look at the view before she carried on. "My mother was a beautiful woman. She always reminded me of a movie star from the old days, with her exotic looks. I remember her black hair was covered with one of those flowery scarves."

Sarah felt a stillness in the air, prickling the hairs on her body as she watched Abby slowly let go of some of her past and the pain she had kept hidden.

Keeping her eyes on the blue water of the lake far below, Abby relived her painful past in her mind. Sarah reached out and gently placed her hand on the arm of the normally stoic woman. She was there as a friend and nothing more, she told herself as she listened quietly to Abby's soft words.

"My father—we had the same eyes, him and me—and he had this big smile, he always did … and just like that … they were gone." Abby stopped talking, but Sarah could feel her trembling with emotion. With her one good hand, the detective wiped back tears as she reached for her beer.

There were no words to say as Sarah watched Abby drain the bottle.

Wiping her lips, Abby looked up to the sky and to whatever lay beyond.

"My Uncle Nate came and looked after things. He took me away from here—far away, and I never came back. Until now. It's been Günter and Helga who've looked after the place. Most everyone around these parts still think they own it and that's fine with me."

"Abby, I … I'm sorry. I'm sorry I made you bring it up. I had no idea," Sarah said as she reached to wipe away a straggling tear.

"You had no way of knowing."

The feel of Sarah's hand on her cheek was so good that Abby pressed her face into the touch. Lifting her eyes, she looked into the comfort of Sarah's compassionate face. There was something in her emerald green eyes that Abby felt in her heart. It was as though Sarah was reaching out to her, wanting to get to know her in a way no one had ever done before.

"I don't talk about it, I never have," she said.

Why the hell did you trust me? Sarah thought as she smiled back at Abby.

"There's just something about you … I don't know, but I'm glad I told you."

"I'm not sure what to say to that kind of compliment. That was a compliment, wasn't it?"

"Yeah, you could say that," Abby said with a chuckle as she sniffed away her uncharacteristic show of emotion. "You know, even my partner doesn't know the whole truth."

"Your partner?" The mere mention brought a chill of realization to Sarah's heart. *Partner, what partner? Oh my God, she's with someone. Why wouldn't she have a partner?*

"Yes, I never knew where to start," Abby said as she took a deep cleansing breath.

Sarah's face flushed as she looked down at the blades of grass just off the edge of the blanket. *God! It had never dawned on me that Abby might be in a relationship, but then again why shouldn't she be? The woman's gorgeous! Those eyes, those legs, all that and brains too! She has the complete package, so why shouldn't she have someone too?*

"Sarah, you okay?"

"Huh? Yes, thank you," she said with a smile, trying to hide her own lies. *Please don't tell me anything else—I can't take this. I'm crushed beyond words. I'm listening to you opening up, trusting me, and every second word I'm saying to you feels like a lie.*

"I'm sorry, I didn't mean to dump this on you. I asked you to come for a ride and then …" *Look at her, she is totally freaked, I should've just kept my mouth shut!* Abby watched the change come over Sarah.

"Please, Abby, don't apologize. I'm glad you trusted me enough to open up." *No shit, you lying piece of reporter sludge.* Sarah's mind screamed at her for daring to use the word *trust.*

"There's something else I wanted to talk to you about before we head back."

Oh please, don't tell me anything more, was all Sarah could think.

"What happened the other day, between you and me," the words felt so awkward in her mouth, Abby wasn't sure if she could get them out. "I, ah …" she stumbled more and then laughed nervously.

Sarah completely forgot her own troubles and tribulations. "What?" Sarah reached over and picked up Abby's hand in a gesture of encouragement.

"There's something I should've told you … about myself when we first met, but it's one of those awkward things that you don't find the need to tell a stranger, but once you get to know someone, then its …" Abby looked down at the soft skin of Sarah's hand on top of hers. The velvety smooth skin of someone who had never raised a hand in …

"Abby?" The detective's expression changed from inner struggle to one of want and desire, which only confused Sarah more.

"Sarah, I like you … a lot, and I need for you to know that. I like you no matter how you look at me."

"No matter how I look at you?" *Are you kidding me? I adore you, Abby*, she confessed in her mind.

Suddenly, the light bulb in Sarah's mind went on as she realized with amusement what it was that Abby was trying so badly to say. As much as she wanted to help her out, she couldn't stop the smirk from spreading across her face, but then the reality hit her … hard. Abby was about to tell her something she wasn't sure she could handle. Everything in her heart and soul told her to walk away, to leave this before it got more complicated than it already was. Abby was supposed to be her story, not someone for her to fall in love with. And Abby was already in a relationship. There was absolutely no way this could work. So then why couldn't she take her eyes off Abby's lips? Because she knew Abby was speaking the truth, something she couldn't bear to do.

"I know this is a different world we live in, a world filled with all kinds of different relationships, old and young as well as … ah, to hell with it. Sarah, I'm gay," Abby blurted out. Then she lifted her eyes to look deep into Sarah's.

"I know."

"You did? You do?" It wasn't the question she wanted to ask.

"Yes." The young reporter was in a quandary. "But you said you had a partner— "

"Yes, and a pretty good one too. Married, but then again all the good ones are."

"But, but …" *Married?* Sarah made no effort to hide the surprised look on her face. This was more truth, than she could handle.

"Yeah, has been for awhile now. I actually sent him and his wife, Carla, here for their honeymoon. She knows about me and that makes my relationship with Lincoln all that much easier."

Abby was involved with *a married man—but she just said she was gay!* Sarah's world just became more complicated and her decisions a lot more confusing. *Abby's sleeping with a married—man!* The information hit her like a rock from the sky. She couldn't help but turn away from Abby's happy expression. The revelation that she was sleeping with a married man and that his wife knew about it took the wind right out of Sarah's sails. She couldn't get her mind around Abby's immoral confession.

They sat in silence, each lost in her own world, neither noticing that the other had become quiet. Sarah's conscience was tapping loudly on her shoulder. All she wanted was to get off the mountain and get back to the comfort of her private cabin.

"We should be getting back, don't you think?" Sarah said as she started to collect the trash from their lunch.

"If that's what you'd like, I'll go and get the horses." Abby rose to her feet and walked to where she had left their rides.

Sarah watched her the entire way, feeling a mix of desire and remorse. The ride back, just like the ride to the clearing, was not disturbed with conversation, which suited Sarah just fine. Her thoughts mirrored the back and forth movement of each step of the horse beneath her. She was a reporter and Abby was the story, but she was more than a story; she was a woman with a dark and painful past who was in need of a friend.

A lot of people believe reporters lacked a certain moral and ethical standard and the truth of it was, most of the time Sarah agreed with them. After all, she hadn't met Abby by accident.

Maybe, Abby felt that being a cop gave her special …" The obvious truth stopped Sarah in her tracks. "Oh my God!" she said aloud as she pulled up on the reins. *Where was my mind, how could I have thought …?*

Turning her mount around, Abby came back to see why Sarah had stopped. "What's wrong?"

"I'm so stupid. Lincoln's your partner," she said in a bold statement that only confused Abby. "Lincoln's your partner, he's a cop."

Her eyebrows furrowed. "Yes."

"I've never felt so stupid. Where was my head? You said to me that Lincoln was your partner and I thought …"

"You thought Lincoln was … that Linc and I …" Abby chuckled at the thought. "Now that's funny. A picture I don't want to think of, but still funny."

Feeling the heat of embarrassment in her face, Sarah dipped her head. "Abby, I'm truly sorry. I didn't mean anything by it. I just—when you said partner … well, to me that meant *partner*. You know."

"Sarah, it's okay, really." Abby reached over and patted her hands. "I think it's funny. Carla, his wife, might even agree with me."

Sarah could only nod her agreement as they urged their horses onward. The smile on her face was genuine as she thought what she had almost assumed about Abby. But now that she knew the truth it made her heart's desire that much more difficult to bear and her smile slowly disappeared.

☯

The stables were barely in view when Abby noticed there were more than a few people milling around. Being a typical cop, things out of the ordinary caught her attention.

"Abby?" Günter rushed towards her.

"What's going on?"

"I was just getting ready to send someone out to find you," he said as Abby slid to the ground. "You got a phone call today."

"A phone call—here?" Abby's voice dropped in tone and, for the first time, Sarah saw *Detective* Abby Stanfield.

"Yes, from Lincoln."

"Sarah," Abby turned to her companion.

"Go—go, I'll be fine." Sarah felt her own rush of adrenaline as she watched Abby sprint in the direction of the lodge.

☯

"How many times … has he called?" Abby gasped as Helga directed her towards the phone.

"Three times, and there were two other calls as well." She held out a small stack of papers as Abby picked up the receiver.

"Lincoln just said to call. A Lieutenant Banks left a message and said to call."

Abby glanced down at the pieces of paper in her hands as she listened to the first ring of the phone.

"Detective Quinn," Lincoln said plainly.

"Linc, it's Abby," she said trying to regain her breath.

"We've got another one." She heard the pain and regret in his tired voice.

Abby closed her eyes.

"She went missing last week, but her parents didn't file a missing persons until Saturday. They thought she was with friends."

"Same MO?"

"Yeah, but— " Lincoln cleared his throat.

"Jesus Christ—what do we have?"

"Abby. It wasn't Ward."

"What the hell are you talking about?"

"Abby, listen to me. It's not him!" Reluctantly he told her what no one had wanted to tell her, not even Banks. "Ward has an air-tight alibi."

"Bullshit. It's him, who else could it be?" she said angrily into the phone.

"We've had him on a 24/7 surveillance. There is no way it was him."

"It was him, we just don't know how. I'm coming back—they have to lift my suspension now."

"No, they don't. Look, I'll keep you in the loop, but that's it, understood? Can I call you at this number?"

"Yeah. You okay, partner?"

"It was bad, Abby. I didn't think they could get worse … He's one sick bastard."

"Don't let it get to you, Linc. It will eat you up inside. Call one of the support officers and talk it out."

"Are you hearing your own words, Abby?"

Abby's mouth was open but she closed it without a comment.

"I sleep at night, do you?" Lincoln asked. The question was a direct hit and he knew it, but she gave no response. Abby looked down at her scarred knuckles as she rolled her fingers into a fist of frustration.

"I'm sleeping just fine, Linc. When the initials are done, I'd like a copy delivered here."

"You got it. Look Abby, I gotta run, Banks is waving at me. I'll get that stuff for you."

Abby hung up, but sat for several moments with her hand still on the receiver. Another murder, another innocent girl wasn't going home again, and this time Billy Ward had the best alibi possible—the cops themselves.

Rubbing her face with her hands in frustration, Abby crumpled up the phone messages Helga had handed to her. Looking down at the ball of wadded paper, she was about to toss it into the garbage can when something caught her eye.

Ever so carefully, Abby pulled the ball apart until she had five separate pieces of paper. She placed Lincoln's messages on the counter, and then the lieutenant's, until she was left with only one.

Abby's blood ran cold as she looked down at the words written in Helga's handwriting.

"Helga!" she shouted as she reached for the phone again. "This message," she said, holding up the piece of crumbled paper, "tell me about this message."

"Which one is that, dear?"

"This one. Is this exactly what he said? When did it come in?"

"Oh, that one. I believe … yes, just after lunch. Lincoln called, then your lieutenant."

"He called first!" She felt her stomach tighten as she quickly dialed Lincoln again.

"Detective Quinn." Lincoln answered on the first ring.

"Billy did it!" Abby said into the phone. The realization chilled her as she looked again at the message in her hand. "He called here and left a message!" Abby looked down at the crumpled note in her hand.

THAT IS FIVE NOW, ABBY.

CHAPTER 13

Sarah paced her cabin, waiting impatiently for Abby's return. Her mind was racing with hundreds of thoughts since the detective's sprint from the stables.

Sitting back down at her laptop, she stared at the few words she had written. Dropping her head, she repeatedly ran her fingers through her hair; she knew her conscience wouldn't let her write what she had recently discovered. Frustrated, she rose and walked to the front doors and looked out over the moonlit lake. Soft ripples lapped gently against the wooden docks, distorting the reflection of the lights coming from the cabins. Strolling out onto her deck, she took a deep breath of warm night air as she sat down on one of the chairs.

The sound of heavy footsteps on gravel interrupted the silence and Sarah saw the lights come on next door. Abby was home, but it sounded like she was not alone as the low hum of voices drifted through the air.

Deciding to investigate, Sarah stepped through the trees as she heard Buck's low howl. Climbing the steps onto the deck, Sarah could see inside the cabin as Abby tossed back a drink. A quick glance to the counter confirmed it was the same stuff she had been drinking a few weeks back. Sarah paused, wondering if she should venture any farther, but when she saw the look in Abby's eyes, she knew she had to. Sarah entered the cabin through the open front doors, just as the glass Abby had been drinking from flew through the air and smashed against the fireplace.

"You fucking bastard!" Abby yelled out as the glass shattered into a thousand pieces. Sarah stopped in her tracks. The angry detective saw movement out of the corner of her eye.

"Sarah, I'm sorry, I didn't see you." Abby said, immediately embarrassed by her outburst.

Sarah smiled hesitantly, her eyes searching for the other occupants, but there was only Buck. "Are you okay? I thought I heard voices and …"

"No, it's just me." Abby was angry, very angry and it showed in the glowing red of her cheeks.

"I … I don't think I should be here," Sarah stammered as she started to back away.

"No, please stay." Abby said. "I'll just clean this up. Please? I'd like you to stay." The thought of being alone suddenly unnerved Abby, but she didn't stop long enough to think about what that meant.

Looking from the open bottle of alcohol to the remains of the glass, Sarah pondered the invitation for only a moment. "All right," she said softly. *But please don't tell me anything.*

"I can help with that," Sarah offered as she knelt down next to Abby, while wondering whatever had upset the somber detective. "So what did it do?"

"Pardon?" Abby asked with a raised eyebrow.

"The glass … what did it do?" Sarah questioned with an uneasy grin.

"Oh," Abby attempted to smile, but only shrugged. "Nothing, it was just the first thing within reach."

"Remind me to stand farther away from your reach." Sarah rose to her feet, her hands cupped carefully around the broken glass. "I'll grab a garbage can."

Coming out of the bathroom after washing her hands, Abby turned to Sarah. "You want a beer, or a tea—how about a shot of aquavit?"

"A beer would be fine. What exactly is that stuff anyhow?" Sarah said pointing at the near empty bottle.

"Aquavit. It's pure poison from Norway. It doesn't have much of a smell and it tastes like … well it has it's own taste. Günter got me hooked on it. He sends me a bottle every year for Christmas. Either way, it will knock the stuffing out of whatever ails you." Abby said as she reached for another glass. Pouring about an inch, she held it up to Sarah.

"Try some."

"No thanks, I like my stuffing inside me. I'll stick to beer."

"Your choice. Cheers." Abby swallowed down a large mouthful.

Sarah took a seat in the rocking chair and Buck happily curled up at her feet.

"How about a fire?" Abby asked.

"You don't have to."

"Every cabin needs a fire," Abby said. She took a drink and placed the glass on the coffee table.

Sarah watched with gnawing interest as Abby went to work lighting a fire. She kept telling herself she wanted to know why Abby was upset out of support for her friend, but the voice in the back of her head knew the truth.

Sitting back on her haunches, Abby stared into the growing fire. It didn't matter where she looked, all she could see was her past burning brightly in the dancing orange and red light. Another girl was dead and Abby felt the guilt and responsibility weighing on her conscience. She had let them down, all of them, and there didn't seem to be anything she could do to stop him.

"Are you okay?" Sarah's concerned words came in a low whisper. She wasn't sure if Abby had heard her, so she leaned forward in her rocking chair. "Abby?"

The voice of the innocent was calling out to her and when the troubled detective finally heard it, she turned away from the fire and from Sarah's questioning eyes. Her gaze went to the black of the night just beyond the window. Many voices cried out to her, desperate pleas she could no longer silence.

"Do you know who Billy Ward is?" Abby finally asked.

There it was. A simple question. This was what she had been sent to write. The question hung heavily in the air, awaiting her answer. Sarah wanted time to stop—she needed time to stop—so she could make a decision. She needed to weigh her integrity, to decide on her honesty and to figure out which principles were going to determine the choice she was going to make. Looking back at Abby, she realized she was about to find out who she really was.

When no answer came, Abby looked back over her shoulder. The flickering flames reflected off Sarah's flawless, innocent face as she stared down at the hardwood floor. It wasn't just the beauty Abby was admiring in her features, but the pensive look that had taken over her face.

"Do you?"

Sarah looked up into Abby's inquiring eyes.

"Do you know who Billy Ward is?"

"I've heard of him, yes."

"Billy Ward is ..." Abby looked out the window and there was a long pause before she continued. "It *was* my job to stop him." She reached for her glass on the table and looked hard and long at the golden liquid before she tossed back a large mouthful.

"I should've stopped him, but I didn't." There was a long pause before she continued. "Each crime scene I went to, the victims he raped and mutilated ... I'd hear them calling my name. I should have stopped him but I couldn't."

"But wasn't he released for lack of evidence?"

Abby's glass paused in mid air as she stared at Sarah. "Are you kidding me?"

"Innocent until proven guilty, isn't that how the law's suppose to work?" she asked naively.

"Innocent until proven … he murdered and tortured young girls. He is *not* innocent and the only reason he's free is because of a piece of paper. A piece of fucking paper!"

Sarah unconsciously leaned back in her chair as she watched the veins and tendons flare in Abby's neck.

"It was a fucking technicality. He did it, believe me. Billy did things to those girls that made the mortician want to puke, and because of human error he was set free to …" Abby couldn't finish her statement, but that didn't stop her from finishing the remaining alcohol in her glass. Silently, she stood, shaking in anger and frustration. She had no words to explain how she truly felt. Realizing that she was losing control again, Abby took a deep steadying breath before she walked over to pour herself yet another drink.

"I don't think that's helping any."

Abby looked up as she finished pouring. "It sure as hell isn't hurtin' any." She didn't mean to sound so harsh, but the alcohol had loosened her tongue and buried her manners.

Feeling more than a little uncomfortable, Sarah looked down at her hands. Rubbing the inside of her palm, she thought about a lot of things but said nothing.

"I'm sorry Sarah, I didn't mean to fly off like that but I … well there's no excuse," Abby said as she screwed the lid back on the bottle. "Those girls went through hell before they finally found peace in death, and I do mean hell. No one deserves that; death shouldn't be a welcomed relief—especially for ones so young." The anger inside her seemed to dissipate as she spoke in a low tone of deep thought.

Sarah looked up as Abby took a seat on the sofa across from the fire. Swirling her drink around in her glass, Abby glanced again at the flames dancing in the fireplace.

"We're born innocent, you know. Our souls are empty vessels without love or hatred. We're like sponges, learning and absorbing all the things around us." Abby hesitated for a moment and then continued. "But I think some people are born mean. Their minds are so diseased and sick that even their most basic thoughts and dreams revolve around other's pain. Their desires are atrocities most people cannot even begin to fathom." She stopped talking to take another drink. "Billy is like that. He has no conscience or guilt about what he's doing or what he's done. To him … to him it's a game—an evil game; a pitiful, desperate attempt for attention. Those young innocent girls are just pawns on a very warped chessboard. Something to amuse him, their pain and anguish give him …" Abby searched for the right word. "Power … it gives him power and pleasure."

Leaning forward, Abby put her elbows on her knees and buried her face in her hands. Sarah saw the thin red lines left behind by the anger Billy had brought out in Abby, the scars that would forever mar her long fingers and powerful hands. The reporter in Sarah was gone. All that remained was a woman starting to see the pain hidden behind a pair of scarred hands, a tortured anguish buried deep in the woman she was falling in love with.

"We thought we finally had him," Abby said as she pulled her head away and wiped hard at the tears she couldn't stop. "I thought we'd finally put a stop to his … we had found everything—his knives scattered amongst the blood-stained bricks of his basement where he had tortured them. The shackles he used to bolt them to the walls." Abby stopped talking for a moment as she stared into her mind at what she could not forget. "Facing evil is what I do—but this … this was different. They couldn't scream, you know. He had made this paste out of the juice of a plant and it numbed their vocal chords. That way he didn't have to worry about anyone hearing them. Not that anyone could have. That basement was like a tomb, cold and damp … it was a horrible place to die." Abby closed her eyes, but she couldn't stop the images. "I had him … I thought it was finally over, but—but it'll never be over."

The words and visions finally broke her down and the unshakable Abby Stanfield fell apart. The emotions she had buried for so long burst to the surface in a tormented sob that she tried to cover up with her only good hand. It was more than Sarah could take and she jumped from her chair to be at Abby's side.

"Hey," Sarah murmured, putting a protective arm around Abby.

"I should've stopped him, but I didn't and now …" Sarah felt Abby's powerful body shaking with emotion.

"Come on Abby, you can't be blaming yourself."

"But I should've and I didn't. And now, he did it again." The anguished cry announcing another death tore at Sarah's heart as she listened in disbelief. "Billy Ward killed another girl."

"Oh my God," was the only thing Sarah could think to say as she held Abby tightly, trying to sooth away the pain. "It was him?" the redhead asked fearfully.

"We know it was him. The MO was the same, but this time he has the perfect alibi … Billy's been under twenty-four hour surveillance. No one saw him leave."

"Then how could it be him? I mean … Abby, maybe you do have the wrong guy?" It was a question Sarah didn't want to ask.

The warm glow of the alcohol and the fire had dulled Abby's senses enough so that she barely reacted to the comment. "Because he told me he did it," she said as she reached into her pocket, and pulled out the crumpled piece of paper, and then gave it to Sarah. She unfolded it and read the words slowly.

"It's a game to him. It's nothing to do with human life or suffering, only whether he's having fun, but he has to win—at all cost," Abby said softly as she snuggled further into the comforting arm around her.

Sarah folded the paper and placed it on the table. Closing her eyes, she gently pulled Abby in closer against her.

"Shhh," she whispered into her dark hair.

"Thank you, Sarah," Abby muttered quietly as she felt herself drifting off into a world of soft comfort.

"For what?" she asked quietly, not wanting to disturb Abby's slide toward sleep.

"For being you … and for being here."

"I wouldn't want to be anywhere else," Sarah said as she kissed the top of Abby's head. Silently, she prayed that Abby would never find out the reason she had come to the resort.

CHAPTER 14

The fire had burned down to embers when Sarah felt the first twitch of Abby's body. She opened her eyes as the heavy weight against her shuddered and jerked and Abby mumbled under her breath. Then the detective's entire body trembled violently, taking Sarah by surprise.

With her hand on Abby's shoulder, Sarah felt the tensed muscles. "Abby—Abby, wake up." Abby continued to mumble incoherent words. Sarah grew concerned as she tried again to awaken Abby from her bad dream.

"Come on Abby, wake up," she orderly sternly as she pushed the detective's dead weight off her small frame.

"I don't think so," Abby snarled, her eyes still closed as she struck out at the demons in her mind.

"Abby!" Sarah called out as the detective shoved her back against the arm of the sofa. Her arms were like hardened steel, unbending as they held Sarah in place. She tried to slap away Abby's fingers as they reached for her throat. For the first time in her life, she felt true fear, as she clawed at the vice-like grip around her throat. Finally, she got two fingers in between Abby's thumb and fingers. It was enough to suck in some desperately needed air.

"*Abby*!" This time the panic in Sarah's voice broke though the horrors of Abby's nightmare and her dark eyes opened.

"Oh my God, Sarah," Abby released her hold and the young reporter immediately began to cough. "Sarah … Sarah, are you okay?" Abby pleaded as she knelt in front of her.

Sarah could only nod as she felt the rush of air burn into her lungs.

Abby was horrified at what she had done and she reached out and collected Sarah in her arms. Holding her tightly, she continued to whisper apologies until Sarah could stand it no more. Pulling back from the embrace, she lifted her chin and looked into Abby's remorseful face.

"I knew it wasn't me who you were fighting."

"But I could have hurt you—or worse."

"But you didn't." Sarah smiled, looking directly into Abby's eyes. "It was a nightmare Abby. A nightmare of things you've seen, things I can't even begin to comprehend. You've got a serial killer playing games with you and the stakes are human lives."

Abby tried to look away but Sarah would have none of it. "No, look at me. Abby, I can't imagine what you've gone through or what you've seen, but I can see what it's doing to you."

Reaching up, Sarah cupped both hands around Abby's face. "You need help, Abby. Just tell me one thing; why? Why keep doing it? Why not just walk away?"

Abby looked down, searching for the words she needed. "Because I need to do this. I have to put him behind bars."

"And if you can't?" Sarah paused. "You're so wrapped up in this case, I don't think even you realize what it's doing to you."

"What it's doing to me? I'm alive and breathing. Billy's victims are not."

"Are you?" Sarah asked quietly. "Are you alive, Abby? Are you really living? Because it looks to me as though your life is totally consumed by this case and that's not healthy. You are out of control, in a dark world of—of evil."

"No, I'm not. I'm in complete control," Abby said with full confidence, but she heard the whisper of truth deep in her mind. She was far from in control. All her emotions were dancing on the edge. The question was which one was going to fall first. Staring at the woman in front of her, Abby brought her mind back to the present and to what Sarah was saying to her.

"You need to let go. When was the last time you did something just for you, just because you wanted to? When did you last do something spontaneous just for fun, something to make you happy?"

Without warning, Abby leaned forward and kissed her. Sarah pulled back, startled. There was no question in her mind whether she liked what had just happened, but rather whether she should.

"You said to be spontaneous and to do what makes me happy," Abby said, the edges of her mouth curling upwards in a mischievous smile. When Sarah didn't return the smile, Abby felt a rising doubt.

Seeing what her hesitation had done, Sarah responded with her heart and not her head. She closed her eyes and leaned forward to kiss Abby's tender lips, but this time it was a statement of desire, not a question of response.

The intensity of the kiss grew, as did their passion and their want. Their lips pressed tightly together and Sarah felt her heart rate quicken when she heard a soft moan come from deep within Abby's throat. The sound ignited a fire that wouldn't be stopped no matter how loud the voices in her head got.

Abby reacted without any hesitation. Everything about Sarah drove her insane with desire. She wanted more—so much more—and she wanted it now. Using her tongue, she parted Sarah's lips, provoking an immediate reaction. Turning her body, Abby reached out with her right hand, gently cupping a handful of red hair as she pulled Sarah closer toward her. A series of prying and pressing kisses left them both gasping for breath. The need for air pulled them apart but it did not stop their explorations as Abby kissed her way to Sarah's neck.

Sarah leaned her head back, giving Abby the room and permission she needed. Now that Abby had a taste of what she wanted, nothing was going to stop her as she trailed her lips downward. The tender skin just below Sarah's collarbone was so soft that she couldn't help but nuzzle her cheek against it. The friction caused Sarah to arch her back, pressing her small, firm breast against Abby's throat. With a slow and caring hand, Abby unbuttoned Sarah's shirt. Once freed of the binding material, she reached in with her other hand to caress the bra-covered breast.

Sarah's sensual moan brought a pulsating warmth between Abby's legs. Stroking the fabric that covered Sarah's nipples, Abby felt Sarah's fingers in her hair pushing her head and mouth harder onto her breast. She reached around the young woman's back with her one good hand and pulled her closer. Sarah responded, wanting more and giving more. Abby felt alive; her skin tingled, her stomach felt tight with anticipation as her lips moved over Sarah's hard nipple.

The availability of two good hands gave Sarah the definite advantage as she lifted Abby's head and pulled her back up for a deep and passionate kiss. As their desires grew stronger, Sarah quickly undid Abby's buttons, revealing the detective's naked chest. She didn't hear the sound that came from her lips, but Abby did. Her want bubbled over as she watched Sarah's hand work up from the center of her stomach. Her firm breast felt Sarah's touch, and her nipples hardened as she pressed her hips into Sarah's.

Abby's good hand was now holding her balanced over Sarah's body as she moved to caress Sarah's breast only to have the fiberglass of her cast scrape across the redhead's tender skin.

With a hiss, Sarah's eyes flashed open at the sting. Flashing lights and sirens went off in her head as she gazed into Abby's warm, dark eyes. *What the hell am I doing?* Sarah's brain screamed into her consciousness.

"This isn't right," she said quickly as she squirmed out from under the breathless and startled detective.

"What? What's not right?" Abby's heart was racing in the grip a mixture of emotion and unbridled passion. "Sarah?" she asked in disbelief she watched her refasten her shirt.

Sarah glanced up at the astonished look on Abby's face and her inviting naked chest, and for a brief moment she wavered in her decision. She pulled her eyes off Abby's athletic bronze body. "I can't do this," she said holding up her arms in surrender.

"Can't do what?" Abby said. "Are we going too fast?" Abby stood up. "Whatever you want, Sarah, just tell me." She desperately wanted to understand. "What the hell just happened? Sarah!"

"I can't—I want to, but I—I can't." Sarah turned and hurried out the door and back to the haven of her own cabin before Abby had to a chance to understand.

"Sarah?" Frustrated, Abby went outside as well and collapsed into the swinging bench on the deck. The cool night air danced over her open shirt as she reached to do up the buttons. Everything in her told her that she hadn't been wrong about the feeling Sarah had for her. She saw it in Sarah's eyes and felt it in her touch. Looking up at the stars, Abby lightly touched her lips with the tips of her fingers. The detective in her knew that people could learn to lie about many things, but the woman in her knew—you couldn't lie about a kiss.

CHAPTER 15

The first thing Abby thought of when she woke the next morning was Sarah. Pulling her jeans on, she walked barefoot through her cabin with her flannel shirt unbuttoned. She stopped only long enough to pull on her boots before she left for Sarah's. Buck's head came up from the porch as the front doors opened and his tail wagged in greeting, only to stop when Abby walked past him trying to tuck in her shirt.

"Come on, then." She slapped the side of her leg, as she ducked beneath some of the low hanging cedar boughs. Abby stopped when she saw that Sarah's Honda was not in the driveway.

"Abby?" She looked up to see Helga coming towards her with a package in her hands.

"This came for you," she said, indicating the box.

It had to be the evidence Lincoln had promised her and she gladly took it from Helga.

"Looking for Sarah were you?"

"Yeah, but I gather she's not here."

"She left early this morning." Helga said as she started back up the driveway. "Is there a problem?"

"Huh? No, I just—thanks for bringing this." Abby held up her hand and waved before Helga could ask anything further.

☯

With a cup of fresh coffee in her hand, Abby became engrossed in the evidence Lincoln had sent. Stopping only to brew a new pot of coffee, she completely lost track of time.

She heard solid footsteps on the deck and looked up to see Helga going past the side window. Abby moved quickly to the door, hoping to stop the elderly woman from coming into the cabin. There were too many things lying about that might upset her.

"Helga," Abby said with a smile. She was about to ask her what she was doing, but the tray of food she was carrying gave it away.

"Well, my child. I figured if Mohammed will not go to the mountain to eat, then the mountain must go to Mohammed with food." She held up the tray as if to show what she meant.

"I wasn't hungry for lunch; that was why I didn't stop."

"That is fine, but this is supper. Lunch was hours ago." Abby looked down at her watch and was startled to see the time.

"Oh my God, it's after six! I was only going to look at this stuff for a bit," she said as she gestured to the papers on her table. "I wanted to go over and talk to Sarah, but I wanted a cup of coffee first. That was … hours ago," she smiled almost apologetically to Helga. "She's back, isn't she?"

"Oh yes, but she has not been into the restaurant all day either." Helga pulled back the colorful towel covering the food. "There is enough here for two."

"Helga, do you ever get tired of playing match-maker?" Abby reached for the tray.

"Never," the elderly woman said over her shoulder.

Coming down the driveway, Abby noted that Sarah was in her usual spot, sitting in front of her computer. But as the detective got closer, she could see that Sarah wasn't typing—just staring at the monitor.

"Hello inside," Abby hollered as she stepped onto the deck. Sarah heard her voice and reached to fold down her laptop. If Abby found her reaction strange, she showed no sign of it.

"I come bearing food." She held up the tray with a smile, hoping she would be welcomed.

Sarah didn't disappoint Abby as a smile spread across her pretty face. "Hi," she shyly answered as she opened the door to her cabin for both Abby and Buck.

"I was informed by Helga that you haven't eaten all day." Abby uncomfortably recalled how they had parted. "I hope you didn't stay away from the restaurant because of what happened last night?"

"No, it wasn't. It was … I just had to … I … ah … got busy … " Sarah turned and indicated her laptop but didn't finish her statement.

Feeling the change in the atmosphere, Abby put down the tray of food and walked over to put her hands on Sarah's shoulders. Looking down at her, Abby noticed the slight discoloration around her neck and guilt and shame came crashing down on her. Without uttering a word, Abby reached out and lightly ran her fingertips over the bruises.

"Sarah, I'm sorry. I can't apologize enough. I didn't mean to push and I didn't mean to assume …" Her words were cut short by Sarah's fingers on her lips.

"You didn't push and you didn't assume."

"Then what?" Abby wanted nothing more than to continue from where they had left off last night.

Sarah paused. "Just—just know you didn't assume and leave it at that for now, please."

Abby studied her face and knew she had no choice but to comply with Sarah's wishes.

"So what did Helga bring up for dinner?" Sarah asked.

Polite small talk continued through the meal and after. Abby looked over at Sarah and could see that something was still nagging at her even though she tried to hide it.

"You're a million miles away, Sarah." Abby paused. "Is this about last night?"

"No," Sarah shook her head. "No, it's more complicated than that." She examined the lines on her palms intently.

Sarah's world was closing in on her—the walls of truth and honor were pushing her from all sides. She hadn't counted on falling in love and now, with Abby only inches away, Sarah felt the fear of discovery tapping on her shoulder. The truth of who she was had to come from her, because she knew if Abby found out from someone else there would be no explanation worthy of the betrayal she was sure to feel. But if she told her now, would there be any chance that Abby would look past it? Could there be a chance?

"Complicated things don't scare me, Sarah, but silence does."

Sarah refused to look up. She knew those haunting dark eyes were watching her every move. Reaching over towards Buck, Sarah kept her eyes and hands busy as she scratched at the side of his jaw, much to the massive dog's delight. "Abby, I ..." The moment she looked up, her courage fell by the wayside. "I ... I just need some more time."

The agonizing expression on her face tore at Abby's heart. She looked so lost and vulnerable that all Abby wanted to do was to gather her up in her arms and protect her.

"So this doesn't have anything to do with what happened last night?"

"No ... well, yes. But not in the way you think. Abby, please—just a few days to finish this."

"If that's what you need then you take all the time in the world. When you're ready, I'll be here waiting for you."

"Promise?" Sarah asked as she bit at her lower lip.

"Promise," Abby said with a reassuring smile.

There was a long pause as they stared into each other's eyes.

"Abby," Sarah said, almost enjoying the squirming of the tall detective. She leaned forward and pecked a quick kiss on her lips. "A couple of days and I'll tell you everything."

"I'll be waiting," Abby said as she turned and left with her dog.

CHAPTER 16

Helga could see Abby stretched out on the sofa but the long body of the tall detective didn't move when she tapped on the glass.

"Abby, wake up, dear." She peered into the cabin and watched as the woman stretched awake. Lifting her head off the arm of the sofa, Abby waved her in.

"Since when do you do wake-up calls?" the detective muttered as she swung her legs around onto the floor.

"Your Lincoln is on the phone and he wants to talk to you now."

"Lincoln is on the phone?" Abby looked up at the elderly woman.

"Yes, he was quite agitated. Barely even said 'hi' to me."

"My Lincoln. Hmm, that's twice someone has referred to him as mine. I wonder how Carla would respond to that," Abby mumbled to herself as she pulled on her cowboy boots, and then followed Helga out the cabin door. The detective was still wiping the sleep from her eyes and the slumber from her face when they passed Sarah's empty driveway. Abby's long strides slowed for a moment when she pondered the absence of Sarah once again. But with Helga urging her on, Abby left the question as she headed towards the waiting phone.

☯

"Lincoln?" she said into the receiver.

"Partner, huh?" His tone was angry and harsh. "I've known you for how long and I have to find out by this morning's paper that you own that entire resort!"

"What?" Abby closed her eyes and sighed deeply. "It was in the paper?" she asked quietly.

"Yeah, front page, right next to the picture of you and Billy. I'm here fending off allegations about our shoddy police work and you—"

Abby cut him off. "A picture!" There was a change in her voice and attitude.

"Yeah, they have a favorite one of you with your fist in his face! The entire resort, Abby! I mean I knew you had money, but I had no idea … but then again how could I?"

"Linc, I can explain," Abby pleaded into the phone.

"I'm sure you can, but right now I don't care to hear it. The press is all over us about this case and about you. It seems someone leaked the information that Billy has been under our surveillance and since there was no way he could have killed this Reanichi girl, then maybe he was innocent all along!"

"What? We both know that he is guilty as sin!"

"Do we? I'm starting to wonder just what I know and what I've been told."

"Lincoln, I'm sorry that I never told you that I owned the resort. I had my reasons, besides … but I didn't just keep it from you, I kept it from everyone."

"Well, obviously not from everyone. Look, we dropped the ball on this one, Abby, and now it's blowing up in our faces. I just thought I should warn you. Lieutenant Banks was on the rampage but she's upstairs right now. When she gets back, I'm sure you'll be on her hit list. And I'm sure once everyone finds Gold Creek on a map you won't be alone for long."

"Lincoln, can you let me say something?" The phone clicked loudly in her ear and all she heard was dial tone. Abby didn't realize that she was still holding the receiver until Helga came and took it from her hand.

Abby looked up at the elderly woman. "Where's Günter?"

"He is still in serving breakfast. You want that I go and get him?"

"Yes, please, I need to talk to both of you." Helga nodded and left in search of her husband as Abby reached for the phone once again. She had just finished her call when the Helga and Günter arrived.

"What is it, child?" Günter asked, not liking the look of concern on Abby's face.

"It seems that … Lincoln called me to tell me … apparently the press has discovered that I own the resort."

Günter looked at Helga and then smiled at Abby. "But that is the truth. Why would that bother us?"

"I guess it won't, but the press will," Abby said with a sigh as she stood to look out the window at the view of the mountains. "I'm gonna have to leave. Now that they know where I am, they'll be coming here by the droves."

Turning around she looked at the two of them standing side-by-side and holding hands. With a faint smile she wondered; if her parents had lived, would they be holding hands after so many years? "I didn't mean for this to happen. I show up after twenty years and I now have the entire press corps on its way." She shook her head with regret. "I'm sorry this happened."

"Abby, don't be sorry, my child," Helga said as she walked over to her with her arms opened. "We got to spend time with you—and that, my dear, is priceless. Just please, promise me that you will not wait twenty years to come back."

Returning the loving embrace, Abby smiled. "I won't. Buck and I will visit often. My lieutenant will be phoning soon, I'm sure. Tell her I'll call her back, then come and find me."

Abby noted with great concern that Sarah still hadn't returned by the time she got back to her cabin. Trying her best not to think about where she might have gone and what she was doing, Abby busied herself with her packing.

Standing in the living room looking out over the lake, she heard footsteps and hoped it was Sarah. She tried not to show her disappointment when Günter came down the driveway.

"Your Lieutenant Banks is on the phone," he said. "She is waiting for you."

"Great," Abby muttered.

"Things are not good?"

"No, things are not good, in fact they're going downhill fast," she said under her breath as she hurried for the phone.

☯

"Detective," Banks answered gruffly as Abby took her call. "I will assume you've heard about the headlines in this morning's paper, so I won't get into it. How long will it take you to get back here?"

"I can be there for tomorrow morning's briefing," she answered, looking down at her watch.

"Not good enough. The upstairs brass needs to do a press release to try to head some of this off. We need you here before the six o'clock news."

"But it will take me …"

"This isn't open for debate. Get back into the city and in my office, now!"

"I still have to pack …"

"Am I not making myself clear here, detective? 'Now' means now!"

"Yes, ma'am," she answered curtly. Abby hung up the phone and turned to see a disappointed Günter standing outside the front door.

"You are leaving?"

"Yeah."

Günter nodded. "What about Sarah?"

Abby's heart stopped. *What about Sarah?*

"She's not back yet?" Abby asked as she looked in the direction of Sarah's cabin.

"I don't believe so." Günter could see the despair on her face and it broke his heart.

She reached up and ran her hand nervously through her long dark hair. She didn't have much time.

"You must have a number or something for her in the office, don't you?"

"I'm sure we do. I'll look for you."

"Thanks," Abby said as she headed back to her cabin.

☯

The Jeep was loaded and the cabin was empty but Sarah had yet to return. One last time, Abby walked through the trees that had been the only thing to separate them and walked up onto Sarah's deck.

"Where are you?" she groaned as she paced back and forth. Looking down at her watch for the hundredth time, Abby knew she had to go. Peering inside Sarah's cabin, she saw some papers left on her table. Not wanting to leave without some kind of note, the detective entered the cabin and walked over to the paper. Ignoring the few words scribbled on it, she turned the paper over and tried to write out a note.

Sarah,

I got called back into the city. I waited as long as I could, but I had to go. Sarah, this time spent with you has been the happiest of my life and I can't thank you enough for that, but it has ended too quickly. Please call me as soon as you can, my cell 555-541-6776 and home 555-

Abby lifted her head when she heard Buck's howl. *Sarah?* Leaving the note unfinished, she hurried outside but Sarah's driveway was empty. Buck's howl turned to an irritated bark and she could hear voices trying to soothe the animal.

Hurrying back through the trees, she was surprised to see a man with a camera and another man with a microphone trying to get a look into her cabin. "Hey, you! What do you think you're doing?" she said angrily, startling the two men.

"Detective Stanfield."

Annoyance darkened her features. "Get out of here," she ordered.

"Would you care to comment on the murder of Lisa Reanichi?"

"You're on private property and you're trespassing. Now leave." She walked right up to the man with the microphone. He had been at the courthouse that day. He had seen what she could do with her fists and he wanted no part of it.

"All right, we'll leave—but are you sure you wouldn't like to apologize to Billy Ward?"

"Apologize." Abby's face turned red with anger. "Are you suicidal?"

"It's obvious now that you and the entire police department were prosecuting the wrong man. An innocent man whose life has been destroyed by your witch hunt."

It took everything she had to keep her temper in check, but she did it. Standing with one hand on her hip, she turned and spoke a foreign word to her dog. Buck instantly responded with a full snarl of his massive teeth. Both men heeded the warning and turned to leave.

"We'll be waiting for you at the front gates," the man with the microphone said over his shoulder as they quickly departed. "By the way, nice place you have here, Miss Stanfield. Just how does one afford a resort on a detective's salary, especially one of this size?"

"Buck … *morté!*" The large dog leaped from the deck on Abby's command, snarling and snapping at the two departing reporters. She called her dog back, opening the door to her Jeep. He jumped in and took his seat next to her. Pulling up in front of the lodge, Abby caught sight of the mounting press corps just outside the gate. Günter and Helga were waiting inside for her and she could see their mood was abnormally somber.

"We wish you didn't have to go, dear." Helga said.

"I know. Günter." She opened her arms to the elderly man.

"Sarah still isn't back …" She turned back as if to look at the still empty cabin. Then she remembered. "The note. I never got a chance to finish it. I don't have time …"

"It's okay, dear, I will explain it to her."

"But there were so many …"

Helga reached out and placed a hand on her arm. "I will sit her down and explain it to her," Helga said. Abby blushed as Helga gave her a wink. "I went to the reservation file for her number." Helga pressed a piece of paper into her hand.

"You better get going, my dear," Günter said turning away from the window. "Why don't you take the back fire-road, so you can avoid the press? Here's the key to the gate. Just leave it in the lock. I'll go by later and pick it up."

"Oh, that is a great idea, my dear husband," Helga said as she turned back to Abby, "You will bypass all of them and they will never know it."

Abby nodded as she took the key and said her final good-byes. Twenty minutes later, she bounced out of an old unused fire-road and onto the blacktop. No one saw her as she turned her Jeep toward the city. She had missed them all, including Sarah, who had just arrived back at the resort, horrified to see the mob of reporters already there.

CHAPTER 17

"You're still on medical leave—your suspension has not been revoked," Lieutenant Banks stated firmly.

"Then what the hell am I doing here?" Abby stood in front of her commander's desk in exasperation.

"When the news of another murder hit the papers, all eyes turned to look at Ward. But when word got out that we had him under surveillance, all hell broke loose. The press has been having a field day at our expense."

"Any idea how they found out about the surveillance?"

"No, but I will. It wasn't public knowledge. In the meantime, Ward's lawyer has informed us that his client is contemplating a lawsuit and our legal department needs some answers before this gets aired out on the news and in the papers."

"A lawsuit? I thought he said he wasn't going to sue?" Abby shook her head in disbelief.

"This isn't about the incident outside the court room. This is about the entire case. His lawyer's comment is that …" Lieutenant Banks paused, pulling her glasses off to look Abby in the eye. "He says you set him up and that you fabricated evidence."

"What? You can't be serious! So you didn't call me back here to work on the case or to work on the new murder?"

Lieutenant Banks shook her head. "No. Look, all I can say is there appear to be a few malfeasances in this case. And if that is …"

"Okay, just hang on. Are you trying to say we set him up? What about all the evidence at his house? He did it. You know it and I know it." Abby was starting to understand why Lincoln had been so upset with her. It wasn't the secret she had held back from him, but the fear of what a lawsuit could do to him professionally and financially. "So now what?"

"You need to go upstairs and sign over your notes. The legal department wants to get started."

"I can work on this but I can't work on the case, is that it?" Abby said bitterly.

"In a nutshell, yes," Lieutenant Banks said. "But, I can't stop you from doing whatever you want to do from your own home and on your own time. You've got the prelim paper work?"

"Yes."

"Then I'll arrange for Lincoln to have copies of everything."

"Thanks," Abby said sincerely. "But Linc doesn't appear to want to talk to me right now."

"Give him time, Abby. It hasn't been fun around here and he's been taking the brunt of it. Now get going. They're waiting for you upstairs."

☯

The sunlight had all but faded by the time Abby came out of the stationhouse. She was bothered by the fact that she hadn't heard from Sarah, but she hoped there was a message waiting for her at home. Buck appeared to be sleeping next to the Jeep, but she knew better. With a click of her teeth, her faithful guard dog was on his feet and ready for her next command, but as she approached he lazily stretched out with a big yawn.

"Oh, that's convincing, you big ham." His tail wagged and he howled a soft reply. The stress of the day and the long drive weighed heavily on her shoulders as she made her way out of town. The canyon she lived in was about a thirty-minute drive away. Once she started up the winding road, it was easy to forget how close the city was. The moment Abby turned into her driveway and her large tires crunched over the gravel, Buck's tail began to thump loudly against his seat.

She pulled open the door into her home and the stale air hit her full force. Dropping her bags where she stood, she started in the kitchen and opened every window and sliding glass door in the converted farmhouse. Three stories high, the open-style house was forty feet from the floor to the refurbished beams of the ceiling. The main floor held the kitchen, one of the two bathrooms, the dining room, and the spare bedroom. The stairs angled around the inner hub of the home. Their first stop was the open landing living room. The stairs carried on upward to the next small landing, which only had room for her desk and computer, before turning and heading up to their final destination—her bedroom. Standing next to her dresser, her bathroom was to her left and to her right she could look down to the open kitchen below.

Soon a gentle wind blew easily through the house as Abby stood listening to the numerous messages left on her answering machine. Most were of no importance, or could be returned tomorrow. A few were from reporters looking for an interview but none were from Sarah, and that bothered her as she headed up the stairs to unpack.

Why hasn't Sarah called? The question turned over and over in her mind as she busied herself unpacking. Several times she passed a phone, since there was one on each landing, but it just sat silently, refusing to be intimidated into ringing.

Only after everything was in its place did Abby realize just how hungry she was. Leaning over and looking into her empty fridge, she pondered her options for dinner. "Hmmm, something with mustard or salad dressing seems to be the only thing …"

The phone warbled and she rushed to answer it. Sarah's smiling eyes were vivid in her memory as she reached for the phone.

"Hello."

"Welcome home, Abby, I've missed you," the voice said.

"Fuck you!" she growled into the phone.

CHAPTER 18

Sarah sat alone in her cabin staring at the unfinished note Abby had left. Just like that, the emotional dilemma she had been tormented with had been resolved, without her input. So why did she feel like someone had kicked her hard in the chest?

She scanned the phone number scrawled out in Abby's handwriting. It seemed to be calling out to her, but Sarah hadn't budged since returning from Dexton. She had waited there as long as she could, but there had been no response to the wire she had sent to her parents. Wandering around the small town, she had passed a convenience store and spotted the dark headlines screaming from the newspapers.

> **Cops Witch Hunt the Innocent**—*Police surveillance proves Billy Ward's innocence ...*
>
> **The Cop Worth Millions**— *Detective Abby Stanfield has been hiding out at her multi-million-dollar resort ...*

Rushing inside, Sarah purchased both newspapers and quickly perused the front-page stories. Each word she read repeated loudly in her head as she recalled Abby's words. Some of the information printed in the stories was not quite the way the tall detective had told it, and some of what she had told wasn't there at all, but the bones of the stories were the truth.

Looking up from the papers, Sarah's mouth went dry. How could she possibly explain to Abby how her name was attached to the headlines?

☯

"What do you want, Billy?" Abby sneered into the phone as she glanced down at her watch.

"Now, Abby, is that any way to treat …"

"What do you want, Billy?" It took everything in her power not to hang up the phone.

"What do I want …? Oh, how I've waited to hear you say that."

Abby swallowed the bile rising in her throat as Billy pondered the question.

"I want you." His previously playful voice changed and darkened. "I want you to pay for what you've done to me."

"For what *I've* done to *you*? Are you kidding me?"

"You took it all away from me, Abby. Everything. People are looking at me like I'm some kind of animal. The press is hounding my every move …"

Abby's temper cut him off. "You're a murdering psychopathic bastard whose mind is so twisted you have no idea how sick you are."

"I am not sick!" Billy screamed into the phone.

Abby paused for a moment as she realized she was pushing his buttons. "You're sick, Billy, and you belong in a gas chamber or back inside a mental ward."

"It's not going to happen, Abby. I'm smarter than you and you know it."

"Are you? I don't think so. You've been lucky … well your luck is about to run out. You're sloppy, Billy." Looking down at her watch again, Abby calculated the time.

"I'm not sloppy, Abby, that's why you've never caught me." Billy became calmer, his voice soothing as he attempted to get control. "You've tried to destroy my life, my freedom—but no more. You had your chance. Now it's mine. A whole new game, but with different players this time, Abby … think you can save them?" he laughed and the phone went dead.

Abby looked down at the handset as the line came alive with a dial tone. Walking over to her sliding glass door, Abby looked over the flickering lights of the city. Billy Ward was still playing a game and a little voice inside her head told her she wasn't going to like it very much.

☯

It had been a long sleepless night but it was finally over. She had not heard from Sarah and she had no idea why. Now, with a cup of coffee in her hand, Abby stood on her deck and watched the gray skies turn orange with the rising sun. Turning away, she padded barefoot back inside for more coffee.

As she entered the kitchen, the phone rang and she grabbed it before it rang again.

"Hello," she said, hoping to hear Sarah's voice.

"Abby, Lieutenant Banks. I hate to call you at home, but we have a problem."

"Now what?" Abby asked as she walked outside and took a seat in one of her deck chairs.

"Someone with pertinent information is talking to the press. This morning's lead story," Abby could hear the rustle of paper before Banks spoke again, "goes into detail about facts of the case that were never released."

"Shit," said Abby as she closed her eyes and ran her fingers through her hair.

"You do realize that with this information leaked, we have next to nothing to go on. Everyone knows what we have and what we don't have. We lost most of it already."

"I know that, lieutenant."

"Abby." The way that her boss said her name told the detective there was more, but she wasn't sure if she wanted to hear it.

"It also goes on to say that your last name isn't Stanfield, and that you had to change it because of something in your past."

"Son of a—" Abby jumped to her feet. Her privacy had been invaded and the secrets of her life were being exposed after so many years.

"Abby, is there something …"

"Lieutenant," Abby paused, unsure of what to say, but she took a deep breath and plowed forward. "My parents were murdered when I was very young. The people around me decided it might be best to change my name and send me away. They thought I'd be safer that way. All right? That's all anyone needs to know. If they want more I'll gladly give you my lawyer's number." Abby sat back down in the chair, unsure of what would happen next.

"Abby, I'm sorry."

"This isn't anyone's fault. They're just trying to sell newspapers," Abby said once she got herself under control.

"When will you be in?" Banks said to change the subject.

"If I'm not working, does it matter?"

"No—I'll see you when you get here." And with that Lieutenant Banks hung up.

Abby put down the phone and collapsed into a chair. Her life was coming apart and she had no idea how to stop it. Only then did she realize she hadn't told her lieutenant about Billy's call. Looking down at the phone still sitting on the kitchen counter, she knew why she didn't want to. Her mind was too occupied with why Sarah hadn't called. The little voice in her head whispered and she heard it loud and clear. "I have her number," she said aloud. Taking the open stairs two at a time, Abby reached her bedroom and went to her dresser. Picking through what she had emptied out of her pockets last night, she found the crumpled paper Helga had given her. Flopping down on her bed, she reached across to her phone and dialed the number. She didn't realized how nervous she was until she felt the moisture of her hand against the receiver.

On the second ring, a recorded voice broke onto the line. "I'm sorry, the number you have called is not in service. Please try the number again or call your operator for assistance." Abby hung up the phone and tried once more but she got the recording again. Looking at the time on the clock next to her bed, Abby dialed the resort. She wasn't surprised to reach the answering machine, knowing Günter and Helga would be preparing breakfast at the restaurant. She left them a message to let them know that she had arrived home safe. Then she asked if Sarah was still there, and if she was could they tell her to call her. With that she said her good-byes and hung up. Grabbing what she needed for the day, Abby headed out the back door.

"Sorry, Buck, duty calls." The big dog just wagged his tail. "You have to stay here today." At the word *stay*, Buck's fluffy tail drooped but not his happy face.

He gave her a departing bark as she closed the gate behind her. "We'll play tonight, I promise." Buck sat down and watched his owner disappear down the driveway. Abby never heard his lonesome howl as her Jeep hit the blacktop.

☯

Lincoln was bent over a stack of files and didn't even look up as she stood next to his desk. Waiting, she finally cleared her throat to get his attention. He looked up at her and then dropped his head back down.

"What? Aren't you even going to talk to me?"

"What would you like me to say?" he asked quietly.

"Hi … Hello, I don't know, something, anything."

"Fine," he looked up at her. "Hi, Hello … Can I borrow a mill or two?" If his words didn't show his animosity, his icy stare did.

"Lincoln, that's not fair. At least give me a chance to explain."

Throwing his pen to his desk, he leaned back in his chair and folded his fingers over his stomach. "All right, go ahead."

Abby did just that. She explained the death of her parents, the responsibility of her inheritance, and the reasons why her uncle had sent her off to school with a new name. The black detective listened intently to the explanation but showed no real emotion. When Abby was finished, she looked at her partner in hopes of finding peace between them.

Lincoln sat silent, pondering what Abby had told him. Finally, after long agonizing minutes, he looked at her.

"How many times have I fired my weapon in the line of duty?" he asked solemnly.

"Once," Abby answered, confused by his question.

Lincoln nodded in agreement and then stood up to look her in the eye. "And that once was to save your life."

"Yes."

"But you couldn't trust me enough to keep your secret." His eyes darkened as he pushed past the stunned and silent woman. Abby watched him as he walked purposefully into the file room and, as she turned to head upstairs, she knew in the pit of her stomach—he was right.

☯

Her day did not improve. All she seemed to be able to think about was Sarah; where she was, what she was doing, and why she hadn't called. The cell phone attached to her hip had remained silent and that was starting to eat at her. The pending lawsuit should have been the most important thing on her mind, but she couldn't seem to get past her memories of a pair of emerald green eyes and a sparkling smile.

Buried in a mountain of endless paperwork, Abby had no idea of the time until the offices around her grew silent and still. It was late by the time she pulled into her driveway. She had made two stops on her way home. The first was to collect the pile of mail that had been waiting for her at the post office and the second was to pick up a few groceries.

Buck howled a greeting as she stacked her mail onto her cast and then reached for one of the bags of food with her good hand.

"Hello yourself," she said as she made her way to the door. It took several seconds before she negotiated the handle and walked into her silent home. Her eyes went immediately to her answering machine and she noticed excitedly that the red light was blinking.

She put her bag of groceries on the counter, and pressed the play button as she absently started to thumb her way through her mail.

The first message was from another reporter who wanted an interview or at least a statement about the possible innocence of Billy Ward. Abby ignored it and waited for the next voice as she continued sorting.

The next message was from Helga and Abby turned to listen just as a piece of mail caught her attention.

"Abby dear, it's Helga. Good to hear from you and glad you arrived safely."

Reaching across the stack in front of her, she lifted out a familiar looking postcard.

"Most of those reporters and TV people have left here now, so things are getting back to normal. I guess they heard that you are no longer here," Helga continued.

It took Abby a second to realize it was the same postcard she had mailed to Lieutenant Banks. *How did it manage to be delivered here?* she thought as she listened to Helga rambling on.

"I hope you've had a chance to talk to Sarah." Abby heard Helga's words clearly as she flipped over the postcard and saw the writing on the back. Her stomach churned. *This* was not the postcard she had sent to Lieutenant Banks.

The message from Helga continued, "I never got a chance to talk to her, dear, before she left with the man who paid her bill."

Abby tore her eyes from the block letters written on the postcard to look at the answering machine. Fear sliced through her as she looked back down at the postcard. There was only one person who could have sent it to her and his message was very clear.

DID YOU ENJOY SARAH'S COMPANY AT THE LAKE, ABBY?
I KNOW I WILL!

CHAPTER 19

Abby struggled to keep herself calm as she dialed Helga's number. Over and over she kept telling herself that the man Sarah left with could have been anyone.

"Hello," the voice on the other end answered.

"Helga, it's Abby."

"Hi dear, how are you? I didn't expect …"

Abby cut her off. "Helga, I need to know about the person Sarah left with."

"A nice fellow, quiet though."

Abby closed her eyes and prayed. "What did he look like?"

"He was small and quiet. I couldn't see his face because he wore a pair of sunglasses and one of those ball hats."

Please no—please no, God no, was all Abby could think. "Did he … did he say anything to you?" The woman in her was anxious and fearful, but the officer in her forced her to remain calm.

"Let me think, ummm … he said something about how nice the lodge and resort were, I recall that."

"Think hard, Helga." Abby's voice was starting to sound strained.

"I don't think so."

"How was Sarah? Did she seem okay to you? Did she say anything?"

"She seemed fine, dear."

"Helga," Abby didn't want to ask the question but she knew she had to. "Helga—could it have been Billy? Billy Ward?"

The detective's mind was racing with the thought of Sarah in the hands of a murderer like Billy Ward.

The phone went silent and Abby knew the elderly woman had been taken aback by the question. "Abby, you don't think …"

"No, I don't want to think it, but I have to. Could it have been Billy Ward?"

"Oh my … I never thought, no … yes, I don't know … maybe."

Abby thought she was going to be physically ill. Her legs felt weak as images of Billy's past victims flashed through her mind.

"How did he pay?"

"What?" Helga was confused and frightened now.

"The man, how did he pay the bill?"

"By credit card."

Too obviously a traceable mistake on his part, she thought. "I need the number, the number off the card." *If Billy has Sarah* … Abby couldn't even finish the thought.

"It's in the office."

"Okay, call me back on my cell …" Abby stopped in mid-sentence when she looked at the cell phone on the counter. "Helga, did you give Sarah my number?"

"I never really had a chance to talk to her, but she did say she got your note."

"Helga, please hurry. I need that credit card number. Call me back at home here."

She paced her kitchen for only a few seconds before she decided what to do. Reaching for the phone, she quickly punched in a number and waited for it to ring.

On the third ring, a female voice answered it, "Hello."

"Carla, it's Abby. I need to talk to Lincoln."

"Hi, Abby," said Carla as she looked at her husband to see if he wanted to talk to her—Lincoln shook his head no.

"I need to talk to him."

"He … ah," she hesitated, not wanting to be in the middle of the fight between her husband and his partner. They were a good team and she hated to see them like this. She looked over once more at her husband who was staring unmoving at the TV.

"Carla, it's an emergency," Abby pleaded. "Tell him I think Billy has taken Sarah."

"He what? Oh my God! Your friend from the resort?" Carla cried. Lincoln saw the change come over his wife's face and got up quickly to reach for the phone.

"Abby?"

"I think Billy has Sarah."

"What?"

"I just got a postcard from him, the same postcard I mailed to Lieutenant Banks." Abby barely took a breath. "He wrote on the back – 'Did you enjoy Sarah's company at the lake, Abby? I know I will!' I phoned Helga because I thought Sarah was still at the resort, but apparently she left with some guy who paid her bill. Helga said it could have been him."

"Jesus Christ, Abby," said Lincoln. "Do you have a number for Sarah?"

"Yes, but it's no longer in service."

Lincoln's detective mind was working. "How was the bill paid?"

"By credit card. Helga is going to phone me with the number."

"Abby …" Lincoln didn't want to finish.

"If he hurts her in any way," Abby said through clenched teeth, "I swear to you, I'll kill him!"

"One thing at a time, Abby. We don't even know if it's him yet. She could be at home watching TV."

"How did he get away from the surveillance team—again?"

"I, ah … they haven't had Billy under surveillance for weeks," he finally admitted reluctantly.

"What?"

"The brass pulled them off, said it was a waste of time."

"Shit!" Abby said loudly into the phone. "Do you think we can get a warrant for the farm house?"

"Not a chance. We couldn't get permission to search Billy's garbage can right now, but it doesn't matter, he's not at his place anymore. He'd been staying at a motel out on Route 15. Are you heading into the station?"

"Not yet, I'm waiting for Helga to phone me back. My cell phone doesn't work in the canyon."

"Okay, I'll meet you at the station," Lincoln said as he strapped on his gun and reached for his coat.

"Wait, Linc … there's something else you better know."

"What?"

"He called me yesterday."

"He what?" Lincoln couldn't believe how brazen Billy had become. A highly intelligent psychotic with no morals was an extremely dangerous mix.

"He called me at my house. He told me that he wants me to pay for what I've done to him."

"That cocky son of a bitch."

"I don't know how he did it, but somehow he knew how long to time the call. I couldn't get a trace …"

"I do," Lincoln said as he pulled on his coat. "During one of his background checks, I found out he worked for the phone company for a few years before they fired him."

"Phone company? Then that could mean he might be listening …" Abby pulled the receiver away from her ear and looked at it, wondering if Billy had bugged her own home phone. "Lincoln, I'll see you at the station."

Abby held on to the receiver and, as she examined the phone, she wondered if anyone else had been listening to her phone calls. No longer trusting it, she hung up the phone, reached for her keys and cell phone and was out the door.

"Buck, you gotta stay boy, look after the place okay?" The big husky wagged his tail and sat down to watch his master drive away.

Abby pulled her Jeep in at the first payphone she came to and quickly dialed Helga's number. At the first attempt the line was busy, but the second try rang through. Helga had the credit card number and Abby quickly wrote it down.

"I keep thinking that I should have done something," Helga said anxiously.

"There wasn't anything for you do to."

"But Abby …"

"Helga, trust us." She hung up the phone and, with a spray of rocks from the Jeep's tires she took off in the direction of the police station. *There wasn't anything you could have done, Helga, because I should have done something!*

☯

Lincoln was on the phone when Abby came through the doors. Her pale color and worried eyes told him all he needed to know. Abby still had no idea where Sarah was.

He put his hand over the mouthpiece of the phone. "I phoned Banks and she's on her way down here."

"Great, she's gonna go ballistic when she sees me," Abby said as she flipped through her Rolodex.

"I think she has more important things to be concerned about, Abby," he said quietly. "Abby?"

With her ear to the phone, she turned to face the man who knew her best. Lincoln looked her in the eyes and he saw what he had never seen before. "You really are in love with her?"

There was nothing for her to say as they stared at each other.

"I thought maybe she was just one more who'd fallen for those bedroom eyes of yours." He'd never seen her like this. "Jeez," was all he could say under his breath. Abby's eyes were on her empty desk as she spoke to whoever answered the phone.

"Okay people, what do we have and where are we looking?" Lieutenant Banks said loudly to all as she burst into her squad room. She stopped just inside the doors, "Where the hell is everybody?"

"I didn't know who else you wanted to call in on this," Lincoln said to his commander. "I mean, technically, we don't even have a case yet."

"Is this woman missing or not?" She looked from Lincoln to Abby for answers.

"Well, officially, no," Lincoln answered.

"Then what the hell …"

Putting the phone to her shoulder, Abby reached inside her leather jacket and pulled out the postcard. Lincoln quickly glanced over it before he handed it to Lieutenant Banks.

"No, I need it now," Abby said calmly into her phone, before turning her attention to her partner and boss. "It was in my mail, but I'm not sure when I got it."

"It's the same as the one you sent me?"

Abby nodded.

"Open mail, so forget finger prints. How many places sell this postcard?"

"I have no idea," Abby answered.

Banks tossed the postcard at Lincoln. "Find out," she told him. The black detective reached for the phone and went to work.

Within half an hour, the squad room was alive with activity as every detective worked to find the missing Sarah. Several times Lincoln looked over at Abby only to see her watching the ticking clock on the wall. He couldn't image what was going through her mind.

"Yes, I'm here," Abby said quickly into her phone. "Okay," she repeated back the number. "And the name?"

Lincoln watched his partner as she slowly hung up her phone. "Well?" he asked impatiently as Lieutenant Banks came out of her office.

"The credit card is issued to W. D. W., Inc.," Abby said, barely getting the letters out of her dried mouth. "William Daniel Ward."

Lincoln did his best to try to keep Abby's mind occupied, but it wasn't easy. She, more than anyone, knew what Billy Ward was capable of. In all the years they had been partners, he had never seen Abby so tightly strung and so emotional as in this case. She had always been quiet, almost reserved, her mind working a step ahead of everyone else's. With her somber and composed attitude, almost everyone had thought her a cold, hard-assed bitch, but Lincoln had known better. Passionate about her job, she cared deeply for those around her. But she never let it get to her until Billy Ward came along.

Now as he sat across from her, he could only watch as she worked the case the best way she knew how. She was making calls and taking notes, her eyes fixed on the pad she was scribbling on. Lincoln went to speak to Lieutenant Banks and when he got back, Abby's chair was empty. Looking around the room, she was nowhere to be seen. Leaning over her desk, he glanced down at the notepad she'd been writing on, but all it revealed was a sketch—of a pair of eyes and the name 'Sarah,' traced over and over again.

"Abby," he called out and all heads looked up from what they were doing. "Did anyone see where Abby went?" Lincoln looked back over his shoulder to his boss and he saw the concern on her face.

When no one answered him, he pushed through the doors and went down the hall to the front desk of the station.

"Did you see Detective Stanfield?" he asked the night clerk, but she shook her head. Looking left and right, he spotted the stairs leading to the roof. Taking the steps three at a time, he burst through the door and immediately saw the silhouette of his partner kneeling at the edge of the roof. Her long hair was waving in the night wind as she pounded her cast against the metal edge of the barrier that ran the perimeter of the roof.

"Abby," he shouted as he approached her, but she barely looked at him. "What the hell are you doing?"

"I've … got … to … get … this … cast … off," she said with each whack.

"I don't think you should be doing that," he said as he came up behind her. She showed no sign of hearing him as she continued to break away at the fiberglass cast.

"I've got to get this off," she growled as she clawed at it, her voice raw with emotion.

"Abby." He reached out for her, but she pulled away.

"You don't understand. I have to … I have to do something." Her voice cracked and Lincoln knew his partner was on the brink.

"Abby, stop it." Lincoln grabbed at her cast before she could strike it again. "Stop it, Abby," he said with compassion as he reached to wrap his powerful arms around her. Abby refused to be coddled and he held tight as she fought against him. Abby was strong, but her strength was waning and soon she gave in. He said nothing at first and just held her. Her cries were soft and silent but Lincoln heard them and it broke his heart.

"We'll find her, Abby. I swear," he said softly into her hair. There was no reply, not a sound for a very long time. And when she'd recovered enough to pull away from Lincoln's embrace, she wiped away the tears that she couldn't hide.

"I'm sorry, Linc," she said quietly.

"Why? You're human, Abby, just like the rest of us."

"Can't prove it," she said, trying to make a joke of it.

"I can now," Lincoln said softly. "I've seen you through a lot of things, Abby, but I've never seen you like this. She must be pretty special to have broken through that tough ass persona you hide behind."

"She is special. She's … she has a fire about her, a spark of life like no one I've seen." Abby's face came alive as she envisioned Sarah's bright smile and shining eyes. "There was … there is," she corrected herself quickly, "there's just something about her." Abby took her eyes off the city lights. "She makes me feel alive, Linc—alive, and excited about life. No one has ever done that to me before. I can't stop thinking about her, and if Billy …" Abby's face twisted in torment as she looked at her partner for help.

"Abby, I can't imagine what you're feeling right now, but you need to focus on Sarah, not on Billy. We'll find her. Just stay positive." It wasn't that much of a comfort to her, but he didn't know what else to say.

☯

They worked through the night but they had very little to go on. There was no point in dusting the postcard for prints; even if they had found Billy's on it, it wouldn't have proven a thing. The card was sold at every corner store and gas station within one hundred miles of the resort.

Lincoln waited for Billy's credit card company to fax over his last few statements to see if that information would help, but something told him it was a false lead. They had chased him for so long, they knew he wouldn't leave a loose end like that.

The new task force team that had been put together to investigate the latest murder joined them, but so far there was nothing. Abby was starting to act like a caged animal, pacing the floor, ready to pounce on anyone or anything. Lieutenant Banks strongly suggested that Lincoln take Abby to the hospital to have her cast looked at. At the very least, it would get them out of the squad room. The argument that ensued was quickly lost and they left, leaving their fellow officers to find a break in the case.

The car ride over to the hospital was quiet as Abby kept to herself, looking out the window.

"Linc, what's the name of the motel Billy was staying at?" Abby asked, finally breaking the silence between them.

"Forget it. Why would he take her to some place as public as a motel? And how could he get her in there without anyone seeing him? Even if he muted her, it would still be too risky. Anybody might see him or hear him. He's not that stupid."

With pursed and angry lips, she turned to look back out the window as they pulled into the hospital parking lot. "Maybe we aren't that smart."

☯

With the exception of the growing light outside the windows, not much had changed when they returned from the hospital, minus one cast. Everyone was deeply absorbed in looking for Sarah.

As she sat back down at her desk, Abby's cell phone warbled.

"Stanfield," she said quickly.

"Hello, Abby." Billy's smooth voice stopped the detective's heart in mid-beat. Lincoln immediately saw the change in Abby face.

"You bastard," she snarled into the phone. Lincoln grabbed for his phone to start a trace.

"What the fuck are you doing, Billy? She has nothing to do with this."

"Doesn't she? I think she does. She's someone you care about—and that, my dear Abby, is enough for me."

"Billy, I swear, if you hurt her ..."

"What, Abby? Tell me. What would you do?" he laughed as he goaded her.

"I will kill you," Abby stated calmly.

"Somehow I knew you would say that!" His insane laughter echoed loudly through her phone as she turned and looked at Lincoln. The black detective motioned for her to pull the conversation out longer.

"Just leave her out of this, Billy. Let's keep this between you and me."

"But it isn't just between you and me any more, is it, Abby? You keep bringing more and more people into this."

"Then let her go, Billy, and take me instead. That is what you want, isn't it?"

Dozens of eyes shifted nervously around the squad room at Abby's challenge. Lieutenant Banks came quickly out of her office shaking her head at Abby. "Don't," she mouthed, but Abby turned her gaze back to her partner.

"That isn't what I want anymore, Abby."

"Then what? What do you want?"

"You know what I want, Abby. I already told you," Billy said.

"Tell me again, I don't remember."

"Don't do that. Don't patronize me." Abby could hear the anger growing in his voice.

"But you said it was a game to you, Billy. I'm just trying to play by the rules. Tell me. What are the rules?" She challenged him, hoping to pull his mind off the ticking clock.

"There are no rules! You destroyed my life and now I am going to destroy yours," he screamed at her.

"That wasn't my doing, Billy, that was yours and you know it. I've never murdered anyone but you have."

"It's not going to happen, Abby. You tried to prove it but you couldn't. You couldn't stop me then and you can't stop me now."

"You want me, Billy, name the place and I'll be there," Abby said as Lieutenant Banks shot a glare at her. The look didn't stop her. "Just tell me where Sarah is."

"No, not yet." Billy started to laugh. "But I will when I'm done with her." The phone line went dead.

Looking at her partner, Abby said, "Tell me you got that. Tell me we have his location."

"It's a cell phone. She's trying to do a grid search, and someone else is getting me the number." Lincoln spoke into the phone. "Okay, hang on. He's on the east side somewhere near Liberty Square."

"Let's go, people," Lieutenant Banks ordered. "I want it on the radio and I want it now. All cars moving in that direction. Get a description of any vehicle he has access to. Let's go, move it." The room erupted into a sea of activity as all the detectives headed for their vehicles in search of a madman. Within moments, the only ones left in the room were Abby, Lieutenant Banks, Lincoln, who was still on the phone, and a few other detectives.

"Don't play games with this psycho, Abby. You're not going to use yourself as bait."

"What if that's the only way to get Sarah back? How many months have we spent trying to get him only to come up with nothing but a body count that keeps rising?"

"That isn't the point," Lieutenant Banks said as she glanced over at Lincoln.

"Yes, it is the point. He has a friend of mine, and I'm not going to just sit here while he does what he …" Abby couldn't finish the sentence, but it didn't stop her mind from finishing the thought.

"This has become too personal between the two of you. It has to stop."

"And what would be your suggestion?" Abby asked.

"He is waging a personal vendetta against you. We have to find out why."

Abby's gaze fell to the floor. "I know why," she said quietly to herself before Lincoln loudly interrupted.

"Okay, go ahead," he said as he clicked the end of his pen and wrote down the cell phone number he had been waiting for. His hand paused as he looked down at what he had written. "That can't be right."

He paused while the voice on the other end spoke. "But that's not possible," he said, looking up at Abby and Lieutenant Banks.

"Check it again! I don't care, check it again!"

"Lincoln, what's the problem?" Lieutenant Banks asked.

"You're sure. Okay," he said into the phone before he hung it up. "The phone Billy called from was a cell phone."

"We knew that," Abby said, confused by her partner's behavior.

Lincoln looked directly into Abby's face. "Your cell phone."

"What?" she asked in confusion as she looked at her phone sitting on her desk.

"The call came from your cell phone."

"How's that possible, detective?" Lieutenant Banks asked as she reached over and picked up Abby's cell phone.

Abby picked up the receiver of her desk phone. She said nothing as she punched in a series of numbers. The phone in her ear rang but the one in her lieutenant's hand did not.

"Surprise," Billy's voice cooed on the other end.

"You son of a … you want to play a game Billy? Well, I don't," and Abby hung up the phone.

"Abby?" Lincoln said.

"What? I'm not going to play this on his terms. The only way is to turn it in our favor. Which means we have to keep him on his toes and not let him think too much. When he's angry, that's when he'll fuck up."

"That's a pretty big gamble, detective."

"If anyone has any other suggestions, I'm open to them." She waited but neither of them spoke.

"How the hell did he get my cell phone?" Abby searched her memory, but couldn't come up with an answer.

"Does it matter?"

"No." She looked at her partner. "But that could be why I haven't heard from Sarah. She would have called my number and got him instead." Her face drained of what little color it had.

Lincoln thought about this for moment. "Why wouldn't she have tried you at home?"

"Helga never got a chance to give her my home number, all she had was my cell. Which would have lead her to Billy."

Abby's mind was a whirl of unanswered questions. Pulling her vision into focus, she looked up at her partner. "Pinpointing a cell phone's location takes too long, but we can get a grid on it." As if on cue, the cell phone now sitting on the desk rang.

"First, we need to find out what number this is, and how he switched it. Get back on the phone, Linc and do a back trace." Abby picked up the phone, paused to collect herself and then answered it.

"What, Billy?"

"Don't ever do that again!" His temper was raging.

"Do what?" Her voice was calm. "This?" And she hung up again.

Abby looked at the clock on the wall and an idea lightened her features. The cell phone in her hand rang but she ignored it. "It's six," she said abruptly.

"Yeah, so?" Lincoln said.

"Liberty Square's clock. I heard it chiming in the background. We need cars down there—a lot of cars! Making a lot of noise. Because I can hear through the phone. Don't you see, I'll be able to hear them." It was a risky move, but no more than what she was about to do as she opened the cell phone and then closed it, silencing the ringing once more.

"I know what you're thinking. You want a perimeter of sirens." Lieutenant Banks turned on her heels and headed for her office.

"You lost me," Lincoln said as he put his hand up and spoke into the phone, "I need a back trace on …" and he read off Abby's cell phone number. "Call me back with all numbers." Returning the receiver to the phone cradle, Lincoln turned back to his partner just as her cell phone rang again.

"As the police cars get closer to Liberty Square, they will systematically warble their sirens and I should be able to hear them on Billy's phone. The different sirens will tell me which direction." Abby flipped open her ringing phone and then closed it again.

"We're set, Abby," Lieutenant Banks called from her office. "It's in your hands now." The speakers in the squad room crackled to life.

The cell phone rang again and this time she answered it. "What, Billy?" she said sarcastically, hoping to infuriating him further as her voice filled the room via the PA speakers.

"I know what you're doing, Abby, and it isn't going to work," Billy said calmly.

"Oh do you? What's that?" she asked as she gave her lieutenant the thumbs up; she had heard the first siren faintly in the background. The commander spoke into her phone, while she watched and waited for Abby's reaction.

"You're trying to make me angry," Billy said calmly as Abby looked at her lieutenant, then shook her head. No siren sounds.

"Why would I do that, Billy?"

"Because you think I will make a mistake." Abby gave a thumbs-up, hearing the siren through Billy's phone.

"A mistake, Billy?"

The lieutenant and Lincoln continued to watch and listen but Abby shook her head, then suddenly nodded.

"You said it yourself, Billy, you don't make mistakes."

"I don't. Anything you've found—I've left it for you."

Abby's eyes opened wide and Lieutenant Banks heard another hit even before Abby shook her head. Speaking into the phone, the lieutenant began to narrow the field in the search for Billy Ward.

Using the distant sounds of the sirens, and the different tones the sirens made, Abby brought the marked and unmarked police cars in closer to Billy's location.

"But you have made mistakes, Billy, lots of them."

"I don't make mistakes, Abby."

"Don't you? I think you do. Wasn't that your thumbprint on that pop can we found?"

"You think that was a mistake?" Billy's laughter grated on Abby as she tried not to think about what he could have already done with Sarah. "That was no mistake. That was just a can I picked up when I was at a corner store. My lawyer explained that," Billy rambled on, his words barely registering as Abby strained to hear the short sounds of the sirens closing in. "Because I went shopping, does that make me a murderer?"

"We both know you're a murderer, don't we? Bi …" The siren blast was so loud Abby almost dropped her phone. Lieutenant Banks quickly gave orders over the phone.

"Hey, what is this?" Billy's voice changed as he saw the unmarked police car driving up beside him. "What the hell? You set me up, you bitch! You goddamn bitch! This is not how you play the game. Fuck you, Abby, *fuck you*—the blood is on your hands, too," he screamed into the phone just before it clicked off.

Throwing her cell phone to her desk, she and Lincoln ran into Lieutenant Banks' office. "Tell me we got him?" Abby pleaded. Banks held up her hand and Lincoln and Abby could only wait as the dispatcher relayed the information through the phone to the waiting lieutenant.

"We've got him," Lieutenant Banks said.

Lincoln put an arm around Abby's shoulder. "We got him."

Abby showed no sign of relief as she waited for news from her commander. "Yes, but is Sarah with him?"

"He's what?" Lieutenant Banks said in disbelief into the phone. "Is she there … is she in the van?"

Abby heard the little voice in her head the moment she saw the change in the lieutenant's features.

"Read him his rights and bring him in."

"What?" was the only word Abby could manage.

"His van's empty," Lieutenant Banks said, her voice ringing with disappointment as she looked at Lincoln in warning.

Abby closed her eyes, hoping to hide her frustration and fear, but when she opened them again she saw the look that had been exchanged between her boss and her partner.

"What?"

Lieutenant Banks hesitated, but finally answered her. "He's covered in blood."

CHAPTER 20

Billy sat calmly inside an interrogation room, his foot up on the table, his hands and clothing covered in dark red blood and a broad smile plastered on his face. His blue eyes sparkled with life as he gleefully watched his reflection in the glass, knowing he was being watched.

The officer who had brought him in stated that Billy had been very co-operative, almost helpful. When questioned about Sarah, he just smiled at the glass and asked, "Sarah who?" Numerous times, they asked him if he wanted his lawyer but he said no, that he had done nothing wrong.

Abby couldn't stop looking at the blood; the very thought that it could belong to Sarah was more than she could stand and she had to be led away to another room. Lincoln sat with her but they exchanged few words.

"Abby, we don't know that it's Sarah's blood," Lincoln said quietly, but Abby said nothing. It was like someone was sucking the air from out of her.

"He's playing a game. I'm sure she's all right."

Abby met his optimism with an icy stare. "Ah, yes, Billy has such a good history with women," she said.

"I'm just trying to stay positive, that's all."

"I know," she mumbled as she picked at a burn mark on the tabletop. Abby jumped to her feet the moment the door opened and Lieutenant Banks walked in.

"Just give me two minutes with him and I'll get some answers," she growled.

"As much as I would like to, you know I can't."

Abby looked at her commander but then noted the older woman's expression. "What is it? What's wrong?"

"We've got to kick him loose. We've got nothing to hold him on," Lieutenant Banks said in disgust.

"What do you mean, 'nothing to hold him on? ' That sick son of a bitch has Sarah and you want to let him go?"

"Look, Abby, I don't want to let him go but what do we have? He paid her bill and he mailed a postcard, neither of which is a crime. It's just a postcard."

Abby threw up her arms in disbelief. "This is insane! We know he has her and we have to let him go? What about the blood? He is a serial murdering rapist and he is covered in blood. That must count for something."

"Alleged. If he actually had a record of any of it we could hold him, but he doesn't," Lieutenant Banks said in a tired voice. "Either way, it's not human blood. We can hold him for twenty-four hours, but that's it."

Abby had been leaning against the wall, her arms crossed defiantly across her chest. "Not human?"

"It's animal blood."

"Animal blood?" Abby looked perplexed as Lieutenant Banks flipped open a file folder.

"Yes, we just got the preliminary back."

Abby looked at Lincoln, but the detective only shrugged his shoulders. "What's his explanation?"

"We haven't asked him."

"Well, why don't we?" Abby pushed off from the wall and headed for the door.

"Keep it professional, detective, not personal. You're not even supposed to be wearing that badge yet." Lieutenant Banks said as she stepped in front of a very determined Abby.

"It's been personal for a very long time," Abby said as she moved past her boss and walked out into the hall.

"Don't let her do anything stupid, Lincoln."

"Oh, like I can control her," Lincoln said as he followed Lieutenant Banks out of the room.

Detective Stanfield rapped on the interrogation room door before she walked in. She nodded in greeting to the two officers before she turned her attentions to a smiling Billy Ward.

"Looking good, Abby. Your little rest at Gold Creek did you wonders."

She ignored him as she pulled out a chair. Lincoln came in behind her, followed closely by Lieutenant Banks.

"Oh, I've got everyone's attention. This must be important."

"Where's Sarah?"

He turned and smiled at her question.

"How are old Günter and Helga? Such a delightful couple."

"Where is Sarah?" Abby kept her tone level, not wanting him to know how desperately she wanted the information.

"Hmmm, I'm not sure. It's a free country. I'm sure she could be anywhere."

Refusing to rise to his baiting, Abby looked down at the dried blood on his hands. "Where did the blood come from?"

"Oh this," he turned his hands over and opened his palms. "I had a small accident."

Abby put her elbows on the table and looked across at him. "It's not your blood, Billy, so where did it come from?"

"You got your cast off. How does the hand feel?" His question was so polite she had to force herself to remain calm. Rising from the table, she pushed her chair back, but left her hands resting on the back of it as she leaned down toward him.

"Where is the blood from, Billy?"

The smile slowly slid from his face and he looked up at Abby. "I told you, I had an accident. Sometime last night."

"What kind of accident?" Lincoln asked.

"I think I hit something with my car," Billy said slowly tilting his head.

"You got all that blood from hitting *something*? Come on, Billy, you can do better than that."

"What can I say, it was a bloody mess. I think it was a dog, a really big dog. Might even have been a wolf."

Abby's heart thumped as she felt the air escape her lungs. Lincoln saw the change come over his partner before he realized what Billy had said.

"Yeah, I didn't even see him, poor bugger. I nailed him full force with my car."

Abby drew herself up to her full height but Lincoln grabbed her before she could get any closer to Billy.

"Abby, you don't know." He felt her power under his grip. "Abby," he growled as he held her. "Get him out of here!" Lincoln hollered to the two other officers as he pushed Abby up against the wall.

"What, what did I do? It was an accident, I didn't even see him." The laughter that followed echoed in Abby's head.

The prisoner was hustled out of the room as Lincoln fought to hold Abby back. Pushing her hard into the wall, he struggled to get her to look at him. "Abby, you don't know."

"Get off of me!" she pushed with everything she had and Lincoln couldn't hold her.

"Abby … wait!" He raced to catch up to her as she ran through the station and out into the parking lot.

"We'll take my car. It's faster than your Jeep."

They tore out of the parking lot and headed toward Abby's canyon home, lights flashing and sirens wailing. Silently, she rocked back and forth, her eyes glued to the road in front of her. She tried not to think about what was waiting for her, or worse, what wasn't waiting for her. Abby closed her eyes and envisioned Buck's happy wagging tail, accompanied by his playful howls, as he waited for her to come home. All she could hope for was that he was there waiting for her now.

They raced past Liberty Square and Abby barely looked at the clock that had told her where Billy had been. Somewhere in the back of her head, she knew now why he had been out here. Soon they were alone on the winding road to her house. Lincoln slowed down on the last sharp corner before Abby's driveway.

A heartbroken sob broke from Abby's chest as she saw a mound of silver and black fur lying in her driveway.

"Stop! Stop the car," she cried as she clawed at the door handle. Lincoln barely got the vehicle stopped before she was scrambling out the door. Lincoln's chest ached as he watched his partner stagger toward her beloved pet. He knew as he climbed from the car that the still form cradled in Abby's arms was Buck.

Rocking back and forth, Abby held on to her dear departed pet. The blood from his broken and battered body had matted his thick fur; she was oblivious to it. Her Buck was gone, taken cruelly by a sadistic mad man, but she didn't want to think about him now. She didn't want to think about what he might have already done to Sarah or where he might have left *her* bloody and broken body.

"I'm sorry Buck, I'm so sorry," Abby sobbed into his fur. Buck had been there for her; a faithful companion who's life had revolved around his owner. Like a shadow, he had always been with her, lying at her feet as she read a book or walking by her side as she hiked the many canyon trails. Buck had been her lifeline when the job had pulled her down into the bowels of hell. Without condition, he had been there and she had always thought he would be.

Lincoln had no idea what to say to his grieving partner, so he knelt down next to her and placed a caring hand on her back.

"I … I gotta take him home, Linc." Abby voice was almost child-like as she continued to rock back and forth. "I need to take my big boy home. We'll find a place and put him to rest, somewhere in the sun." She struggled to stand under the weight of the massive dog but when Lincoln offered to help, she refused.

He went back and got the car and followed slowly behind her as she walked down the driveway one last time with her dog. Pointing out a place, Abby sat under a cedar tree with Buck. Keeping one eye on his partner and one on the job at hand, Lincoln quickly dug a grave with the folding shovel he kept in the trunk. Carefully, Abby laid her faithful companion into the ground, spoke a few silent words and then said goodbye before she took the shovel and covered him.

CHAPTER 21

The lieutenant was in mid-sentence with Assistant District Attorney Ronald de Barr when she heard the heightened buzz of her squad room suddenly silenced. Banks knew Abby had returned. She was about to excuse herself from the ADA when she saw the dark-haired detective sit down at her desk. No one said a word to Abby as she pulled out a pad and picked up her phone; they were too taken aback by her disheveled appearance and her abnormally quiet demeanor.

"Excuse me," Lieutenant Banks said to the assistant DA as she stepped to the doorway and called Abby and Lincoln. The two detectives reported to her office and Lincoln closed the door behind them.

The lieutenant looked at both her detectives and tried to think of something to say but no words seemed appropriate. "Abby, I'm sorry, I am truly sorry."

Abby looked at her boss. "Not half as sorry as I am," she said. Her words seemed so empty and emotionless that Lieutenant Banks was taken off guard.

"Look, you know as well as I do, we have nothing to hold him on," de Barr said as he clicked his briefcase shut.

"What about what he did to my dog?" Abby said calmly as she leaned back against the window frame with her arms crossed.

"Like he said, it was an accident. He's smart, detective. Smart enough to know the difference between what we know and what we can prove. I've gone over everything that you have on him and there is nothing there."

"That's just great. We bust our butts to find him, we know he killed Abby's dog and we know that he was the last one to see Sarah, and you have the balls to stand there and tell us there is nothing you can do?" Lincoln towered over de Barr, but the ADA didn't blink.

"Detective Quinn, that's enough," Lieutenant Banks ordered.

Looking to his boss and commander, Lincoln put himself in check. "Correct me if I'm wrong, but I remember something about twenty-four hours right? Then let's keep him here and maybe we can find something to charge him with."

"That is pretty weak, detective." de Barr turned to Lieutenant Banks. "Mary, I can shuffle papers the best I can, but when he screams for his lawyer, we're done."

"Fine—Ronny." She hated it when he used her first name.

"On another note, I was under the impression that she was on leave." He turned to look at Abby but she refused to acknowledge him.

"Detective Stanfield is back under my supervision."

"I wasn't aware that you had that authority, Mary," de Barr said.

"I'll deal with the brass, you deal with finding something to charge Ward with."

"All right, but keep *her* away from him. We have enough lawsuits to deal with. Understood?"

"You do your job and I'll do mine. Now excuse us, we all have work to do."

"Fine." With a wave of his hand the diminutive ADA was gone.

"All right," Lieutenant Banks said as she turned to her two detectives. "We have … sixteen hours, let's find something."

Lincoln and Abby nodded and headed for the door.

"A moment please, Abby." The detective stopped as the lieutenant spoke. "Abby, I can't imagine what you are feeling right now …"

"Nothing. I feel nothing," Abby said as she turned to face Lieutenant Banks. Her boss saw the telltale pain in her eyes. "Billy said he wanted to take away something that I loved. He has."

Banks reached up and put a hand on Abby's shoulder. "We will find Sarah."

"I hope for his sake that we do." Abby started to leave but the lieutenant stopped her.

"Abby, take a minute. Go and wash up, change your clothes and get a fresh perspective … please."

Abby hesitated, but then nodded and walked out the door and out of the squad room.

The next time Banks looked out, Abby had cleaned up and was sitting at her desk with clean clothes, her hair in a ponytail through her hat, her eyes on a notepad and her ear to a phone.

☯

It took time, but slowly they started to put bits and pieces together. Only after several calls to Abby's cell phone company did a supervisor finally admit that their phones could be reprogrammed easily. After a careful explanation of obstruction charges, the supervisor finally agreed to do the background checks on the calls made to and from Abby's real cell phone and the phone she now possessed.

Oblivious to their surroundings, Abby and Lincoln were engrossed in their work when another detective dropped off a fax on Lincoln's desk.

"What's that?" Abby asked.

"The printout of Billy's credit card," Lincoln said slowly as he glanced over the paper. Abby watched and waited, noticing his eyes flicker on something.

"What?"

Lincoln reached under his desk and pulled out a phone book.

"What," Abby asked impatiently again. "What's on it?"

"Walt's florist," he said as he found the number and reached for his phone. Abby sat up straighter in her desk as she waited to hear the result of Lincoln's questions. He asked for a manager, identified himself and then asked about a purchase made three days ago.

"They're looking it up," he said to his partner.

"What else is on there?" she asked, holding her hand out for the paper. Quickly she scanned over the few purchases Billy had made on his credit card. There appeared to be nothing out of the ordinary until she flipped over the page. There, printed clearly on the top of the page, was a name she recognized: Flanagan's General Store.

Getting the phone number, Abby dialed and waited. One ring … two rings … three …

"Fla … Flanagan's," the familiar voice stuttered.

"Sean, it's Abby Stanfield."

"Hi, Ab … Abby."

"Sean, do you remember a while back I purchased a postcard with the Gold Creek Lodge on the front of it?"

"Yes ma … ma'am, that's one of my favorites. We se … sell a lot of them."

"Yes, I know Sean, but what I want you to try to recall is someone who bought one a while ago and then came back into the store about three days ago. Do you remember?"

"Hmmm, not really." Abby could hear the true regret in his voice.

"It looks like he purchased a few things and then put it on a credit card. He's a short man … about five feet five inches or so, dark hair." When there seemed to be no recognition, she made one last suggestion that she didn't want to. "He may have been with that friend of mine—Sarah."

"Oh wait … I … I recall now, he was w … wearing a baseball hat."

"Yes, Sean. That sounds like him. What else do you remember?" It took everything she had to hide the emotions tearing her up inside.

"I re … remember Sarah, cause I always liked her. She came here a lot to u … use the phone. Her and that man, didn't co … come in together, bu … but I think they knew ea … each other."

Lincoln had been listening to the soft sounds of elevator music while he was on hold and, as Abby's demeanor changed, he turned his attention to her side of the conversation.

"They knew each other? Are you sure?" This information unsettled her. "Sean … this is very important. I need to know what he said to her."

"I … I didn't hear what they said, o … over by the postcard dis … display, bu … but that is when I remembered him from before. He … he was very par … particular about which post card he wa … wanted to purchase."

"Okay, but what did he say to Sarah?" Abby looked over at Lincoln, the two communicating with their eyes.

"I … I don't thi … think he said anything to … to her, but she ma … made a comment to … to him about what he wa … was buying."

"Why, what did he buy Sean?"

"Som … some duct tape, a roll of rope an … and a box cutter." Sean listed the tools of Billy's trade, as Abby felt her stomach heave.

"Sh … she asked him wh … what he was going to … to do with all of it and he said he … he had a fe … few loose ends to ti … tie up."

Abby fought to control herself as she said her goodbyes to Sean. She hadn't realized that Lincoln was also off the phone until he knelt down beside her desk.

"What? What did Sean say?"

"Billy purchased duct tape, rope and a box cutter. Everything he would need to continue where he left off." Abby took a moment before she turned to the silent man beside her. "Sean seemed to think that they knew each other but that doesn't make sense."

"Knew each other?"

"Do I need to ask what he bought at Walt's?" She knew the answer before Lincoln even had a chance to say it.

"A dieffenbachia plant."

The hands on the clock kept moving and the precious time that they had to hold Billy Ward was slipping through their fingers. The van he had been driving had been gone over with a fine-tooth comb but nothing of value had been found. He had obviously switched vehicles at one point because there was no evidence of the van being the vehicle that had killed Buck.

The assistant DA looked over Billy's credit card report, but de Barr told them what they already knew. It wasn't against the law to buy a plant or to purchase tape, rope and a small knife. There was no evidence that a crime had been committed.

Looking up at the clock, Abby turned to Lincoln. "We have six hours left and I can't think of anything else to do."

Lincoln looked up from the papers on his desk and, for the first time since he had met her, he saw a glimpse of defeat on her face.

"We're missing something … I just don't know what." Abby closed her eyes and dropped her heavy head into her hands. "Man, do I want a cigarette."

Ignoring her request, Lincoln thought for a moment before he had an idea. "Maybe we need to try this from a different angle."

"Different angle?"

"Yeah, instead of looking for her through Billy, why not treat her like any other missing person?"

The idea sparked some life into Abby and she pulled her hand away from her face.

"You do remember how to do a missing persons report, don't you? You know, last seen, vehicle they drive, where they work, who their friends are. Do a check of her credit cards and see if she used it after leaving Gold Creek. Or maybe she phoned a friend or a family member?"

Abby got up and walked over to one of the detectives typing away on a computer.

"Floyd?" she questioned as she pulled up a chair.

"Just tell me where you want to start."

"I'm not sure," Abby asked as she ran her fingers through her hair.

"Where does this Sarah live?"

"Ah … ummm," Somewhat taken aback, Abby thought about it for a moment. "I don't actually know."

"Okay, not a problem, how about her full name?" Floyd asked, his fingers poised and ready for an answer.

"Sarah Jolene McMurphy," she said, recalling with vivid clarity the innocent face with those emerald green eyes. Lincoln glanced over and caught a small smile lifting the corners of Abby's mouth. "She was born on the east coast but she grew up in Montana."

Leaning over, she watched with interest as Floyd searched the national database for Sarah.

"That isn't much to go on, Abby. Anything else?"

"The outside world wasn't part of our conversations." The detective realized for the first time just how little she knew about Sarah. Abby recalled with slight embarrassment that most of their conversations had revolved around her and her life.

"Wait, she drove a black Honda Prelude, license number ah … Bravo Kilo Delta six three … two four," Abby said reciting the plate from memory.

"All right," Floyd said as he tapped in the information.

"Here we go," Floyd said. "Oh—that's no help. The car is registered to a car rental company."

"What?" Abby asked as she leaned in to look at the computer screen.

"Yup, you want their phone number?"

Abby was a little confused by this new information. "Yeah, can you print out all of that?"

"Sure," he said as he hit two keys. "On its way."

Taking the information, she returned to her desk.

"It was a vacation resort. Why wouldn't she have a rental car?" Lincoln said as he watched Abby dial the number.

"Why wouldn't she tell me? Yes, I need to get some information about a car that was rented from your company." Abby told the person on the other end who she was and what she was looking for.

"Yes, okay, when was it returned? It was returned to your office … when?" Lincoln watched as Abby face changed with each piece of information she was being given. "I'll hold." She placed her hand over the receiver. "She is getting me Sarah's address, seems the car was returned two days ago but it wasn't her who returned it, it was *some guy*. She remembers because it was rented to a woman and the guy that returned it gave her the creeps."

"Billy?" Lincoln said.

"Well, he does have a tendency to give you the creeps, does he not?" Sudden movement out of the corner of Abby's eye caught her attention.

Lieutenant Banks came out of her office. "What's going on?" Abby asked.

"Billy's lawyer is here—we have to kick him free." The lieutenant was clearly not happy with what had to be done.

"Do we have anything?" Lieutenant Banks asked as she headed to the door but both Lincoln and Abby shook their heads.

"Damn it," Lieutenant Banks said with a sigh, "We tried people. Okay, I need two volunteers to shadow Ward—off the clock until I can get it approved, of course." Numerous hands shot up and she picked two on her way out the door. Lincoln saw the look on Abby's face as she tightly gripped the phone in her hand. Seeing the predicament, he held out his hand, "Gimme the phone. I'll get the info, you go with Banks."

"Thanks," she said and handed him the receiver. She was out the door before he had it to his ear.

A young female voice came on the line and Lincoln quickly identified himself. Not seeming to care who she gave the information to, she rattled off the address and name of the woman who had rented the car.

Lincoln wrote down the name and address, and then stared at it as he hung up the phone. He made the young girl repeat it twice but he knew the name wasn't going to change. Ripping the paper off the pad, he folded it up and tucked it in his pocket. With a slow sinking feeling in the pit of his stomach, Lincoln walked over to the newspapers spread over the table next to the coffeemaker. Moving one of them to the side, he found what he had been looking for—the picture of a pretty young redhead and her name below the byline. S. J. Murphy. Lincoln thought he was going to be physically ill when he realized that he would have to tell Abby that—not only was Sarah a reporter, but she was *the* reporter—the leak.

CHAPTER 22

Lincoln sat at his desk, his mind swirling with information he didn't want to think about. If Sarah was the reporter, then …

The phone on his desk rang loudly in the all-but-empty squad room.

"Homicide," he said routinely.

"Detective Quinn or Detective Stanfield, please."

"This is Detective Quinn, how can I help you?" The voice was familiar but he couldn't quite place it.

"I'm sorry to bother you, detective. This is Frank Stempler … Traci's father," the man said painfully, identifying himself as one of the parents of Billy Ward's third victim.

"Yes, Mister Stempler, what can I do for you?" Lincoln recalled the quiet mountain of a man weeping openly in court over the release of the man who had brutal murdered his little girl.

"Frank, please call me Frank," he asked solemnly.

"If you will call me Lincoln."

"Fine," Frank paused for a moment, "I was talking to some of the other parents and we understand that you have Billy Ward back in custody. Is that true?"

For a split second, Lincoln actually considered lying to him in hopes of sparing him any further pain but it just wasn't in him. "Yes, we did."

"So does that mean you have arrested him … you did?" Frank's tone changed. "You mean you had him and let him go again?"

"Unfortunately, yes. We didn't have anything to hold him on. Until we find evidence to prove that it was Billy th …"

"You know, detective, someone doesn't have to tell me it's raining when my head is getting wet and they don't have to prove that it is water. I just know." The anger and frustration was showing through the large man's quiet demeanor and Lincoln didn't blame him a bit.

"I wish it was that simple, Frank, but it's not. We have a legal system that relies on checks and balances, procedures to follow and laws to uphold. It may not always seem fair, but it is the most just system we have."

"Just and fair. Those are nice words to use when it's not your little girl. You don't have children, do you, detective?"

"No, I don't," Lincoln said sadly.

"I don't either … anymore." There was a long pause. "But I do have friends, detective, friends with connections who know how to get things done." The phone clicked quietly in his ear.

The day was going downhill, and it wasn't even past morning rush hour yet. Replacing the phone on the cradle, Lincoln sighed deeply as he dropped his tired head into his hands. Rubbing his face with both hands, he felt the coarse stubble on his chin and thought that a quick shave and a wash would do him good. Reaching into the bottom drawer of his desk, he grabbed the toiletry bag that he kept for emergencies just like this but as he was about to leave the squad room, Abby and Lieutenant Banks came through the door.

"Well that's it, he's back out in society," Lieutenant Banks stated in disgust. "Let's hope that this time we can keep tabs on him. Where are you going?" she asked, seeing the shaving kit in Lincoln's hand.

"I thought I'd go and clean up. We've been here for thirty-six hours."

"My point exactly. You and Abby need to get out of here and take a break."

"What?" Abby had just taken her seat but she jumped back up in protest.

"You need a break. Both of you. Go. Get some sleep and come back at it fresh."

"I'll sleep here." Abby pointed over her shoulder to the back room where there were several cots set up.

"No, you won't." The lieutenant stood firmly with both hands on her hips.

"But there are things we need to be doing now, not eight hours from now. I can't just leave," Abby pleaded.

"I realize you don't want to, and I realize just how personal this is for you. For that reason alone you shouldn't be involved with this, but you are … and you still will be after you've taken a break."

"Lieutenant …"

"Detective, don't make me repeat it, because if I do, it won't be a request. I don't want either of you back here until …" she looked at her watch, "after six, understood?"

Abby said nothing but reached around to grab her leather jacket and then stopped. "I don't want to go home."

"Come home with me. Carla wouldn't want it any other way," Lincoln said, fully understanding why she didn't want to return to an empty house. Abby nodded and headed for the doors. Lincoln turned around to follow her, feeling the weight of the folded paper and the torn front page of the newspaper in his pocket.

☯

Carla was not surprised to see Abby climb out of her husband's car. The partners had had their problems over the years and, just like a good marriage, they fixed them and moved on. So she knew the rough patch they had hit would only be temporary. They were close but it never bothered her. Oh, it helped that Abby was gay, but they were both too professional to allow a relationship to interfere with their partnership. She knew about Sarah, and Lincoln had phoned her about Buck, but he had neglected to tell her how everything was taking its toll on Abby. Carla smiled in greeting even though her heart broke at the sight of Abby's pale complexion and deeply sunken eyes.

"There's food on the table, towels in the bathroom, and the blinds are drawn in both bedrooms."

"Thanks, dear," Lincoln said as he kissed the top of her head and walked into the kitchen.

Abby smiled, but it was easy to see that it wasn't genuine. "I'm just going to grab a shower. I'm not really hungry." Abby turned to head for the spare room.

"I don't think so, Abby. Get your butt over here and eat something, you'll feel better."

"I'm not that …"

"Eat!" Lincoln ordered as he pointed to the table.

She didn't have the strength or the will to fight him, so she turned around. Nibbling at her food and sipping at her coffee, Abby made no attempt at any small talk.

"Abby," Carla said softly, "I'm sorry to hear about Buck."

Abby's coffee cup paused in mid-air as she sought the refuge of the view out the window. "Yeah, me too," she mumbled just under her breath. "You know he helped … he saved Sarah's life while we were at the resort." She put her cup down and swirled around the dark liquid inside of it.

"Abby, do you want to tell us about Sarah?" Lincoln knew his question may not be appropriate, but he needed answers to the questions weighing so heavily in his pocket. He looked from the somber stare of his partner to the disbelieving glare from his wife.

Abby held the cup in her hand and looked down into its depths as if searching for Sarah. Neither Carla nor Lincoln thought that Abby was going to answer him, but in a low even tone, she did.

"Where would you like me to start? She has the brightest eyes of anyone I've ever seen, they just sparkle with life. And this perfect smile that crinkles her nose … and an infectious laugh. She's small, but when she's around everything around her diminishes in comparison …" She relived a moment in her mind that brought a hint of a smile.

When Abby stopped talking, Lincoln felt the paper in his pocket and he knew this was the time to tell her. But he just couldn't bring himself to do it.

"From the moment I met her," Abby recalled the engaging smile on her face when she held up the beer and the bottle opener, "all I wanted to do was wrap my arms around her and keep her safe. She reminded me of what it's like to be alive—I mean really alive. No one has ever done that to me, no one." She looked at her partner for help. "No matter what, we have got to find her Linc."

"We will, Abby." He wasn't sure of that, but he didn't know what else to say as he watched her get up and go to the spare room.

☯

Her sleep was fitful and tormented as she tossed and turned against the demons of her memories. Abby had realized how different her sleep had been since she'd met Sarah. The nightmares hadn't ceased, but they had become bearable. But now her subconscious was pulling her out of the darkness and into a reality that wasn't any better than her nightmares.

Sitting on the edge of her bed, she struggled to button up her shirt. Her hand, though free from the fiberglass, ached as she tried to use it. Maybe she should go home for a change of clothes. *Home*. The thought crashed against her chest at the ache that word now provoked. What was home without Buck? Her restored farmhouse would be so empty. Why would she want to go home?

Pushing the thought from her mind, Abby finished getting dressed and went out in search of her partner. Walking down the hall, she found Carla in the kitchen but not Lincoln.

"Where's your husband?" Abby asked as she looked outside to see the driveway empty. "He better not have left without me!"

"Don't worry, he didn't. You were still sleeping, so he said he had to check out something and that he'd be right back."

"Did he say what? Thanks," she said as she took the offered coffee cup.

"No, but he said he would be back." Abby nodded as her eyes fell on the phone and she thought about calling to see if anything had changed, but she knew in her gut that if it had someone would have called them.

"Carla ... about not telling you and Lincoln about the resort—I hope you realize it was nothing against you. It was just ... it was ..." Abby searched to find the words she felt her friends deserved, but Carla stopped the struggle.

"Abby, the past is the past and sometimes the reasons don't matter as much now as they did then. You just have to live your life the best way you know how."

"Meaningful words to live by," Abby said after a moment of pause.

"Yes, they are," Carla responded.

"Good morning," Lincoln said as he walked into the kitchen.

Abby spun around to face him, "Where did you go?"

"I wanted to check out a few things."

"Such as?"

Lincoln looked at her for a moment, then reached into his pocket and pulled out a three-by-five picture he had obtained from the newspaper. "Is this Sarah?"

Abby felt her heart lurch at the sight of the woman she had fallen in love with. She could hear the small giggle that normally accompanied that bright smile and those emerald eyes. With an unsteady hand she reached out for the photograph as Carla looked at her husband for an explanation.

"I guess it is," Lincoln said as he watched Abby's reaction.

"Where did ... where did you get this?" Abby asked

Looking into her dark eyes, Lincoln wondered if he could tell her.

"Abby, can you just trust me with this one?"

"Where did you get the picture?" She wanted him to answer her.

"Please, just give me a day to check a few things out. Please." Lincoln watched and waited, but he knew by the obstinate look on her face that Abby was not going to wait for an answer. "I don't want to muddy the investigation with irrelevant information."

Her brow furrowed even more. "Fine, I can appreciate that, but just tell me where you got the picture."

"No."

"What do you mean no? Why … why not?"

"Because. And you're going to have to live with that. Now let's go," he said as he gave Carla a quick kiss goodbye and headed for the door.

"What do you know about this picture?"

"Not much more than I did yesterday. Now that's the end of it!" Lincoln said as he held open the door.

"I don't think so." Abby said as she stomped out past him.

☯

Lieutenant Banks observed the two walking into the squad room still nattering at each other.

"Is there a problem?" she asked as she walked over to them.

"No, not really." Lincoln said hoping his partner would say the same. He wanted to look into this on his own, without the department and without Abby.

Abby remained silent, but her eyes bored a hole through Lincoln's forehead.

"Abby?"

"No, nothing, lieutenant," Abby said as she turned and walked away.

"She okay?" Banks asked the moment she was out of earshot.

Lincoln debated his answer. "Depends, lieutenant. How do you mean that?"

"Cut the song and dance, Lincoln. Is she fit enough to be here?"

"She's a professional. She wouldn't be here if she wasn't."

"She better be. I put my neck on the line by having her back here," Lieutenant Banks mumbled. "She's your partner, so keep an eye on her."

"That's what I do," Lincoln said as his lieutenant walked away. He turned his attention to Abby, who was walking back towards him. "That's what I do."

☯

With no real new clues or information go on, Abby and Lincoln split up to work from different angles. Abby spent some time with the new team investigating the murders. The detectives were grateful for her input and experience; they knew the cases well, but no one knew them like she did. This gave Lincoln the time he needed to investigate Sarah.

He hunted and searched, finding several small stories and articles Sarah had written, but nothing with the importance of what she had written on Abby. He couldn't help starting to like Sarah, in spite of her byline. He had to keep reminding himself that if what he was finding was true, Sarah hadn't been at the resort by accident. But what did that have to do with her knowing Billy?

Lincoln looked across his desk at Abby's dark head as she rested it on her desk. For the millionth time that day, he felt the heaviness of the newspaper in his pocket. With a silent sigh, he looked out the window. Another day was not far off, and that meant another day of waiting around.

The phone on his desk lit up before it rang. He wasn't sure if he even wanted to answer it.

"Homicide, Detective Quinn," he said without emotion and without thought.

"Yes, I'm looking for a Detective Lincoln, I'm sorry I don't know his last name."

"That would be me, Lincoln Quinn, what can I do for you?" he asked as he stretched out in his chair.

"My name is Sarah, and I'm a friend of Abby's," the young voice said politely.

"Sarah?" Lincoln felt like he had been kicked in the stomach as Abby's head shot up off her desk.

"Yes," she said hesitantly. "I've tried her cell phone." Sarah didn't want to think about all the messages she had left and why Abby hadn't returned any of them. "I know she's busy but … but I need to speak to her. She told me so much about you. I knew you would be the one to get a message to her."

"Lincoln?" Abby's question was barely a whisper as she looked at her partner.

"Hello?" Sarah was more than a little confused by Lincoln's reaction and she wondered just how much Abby had told her partner.

"You said your name was Sarah," Lincoln kept his eyes on Abby, who was looking to him for answers.

"Yes, I need to get a message to her."

Abby grabbed for the phone. "Sarah."

She heard the desperation in her voice and it concerned her. "Abby? I've left you so many messages and you didn't return them … I thought that maybe … Abby, please talk to me."

"Sarah, where are you? Are you okay?"

Taken aback by the urgent pleas, Sarah felt guilt and relief flood through her.

"Abby." The feelings Sarah had kept pent up made her voice break and the anxious detective could barely understand her. "Abby, what you read … I didn't know …"

"I don't care. Just tell me where you are." Abby looked desperately at her partner, who was busy trying to get a trace on the call. "Sarah, I can't understand you … what? Where are you? Just tell me where you are." Abby was almost screaming into the phone.

"I don't … know the … city that well, but I …" Through the broken sobs, Abby strained to hear what Sarah was saying. Faintly in the background, Abby heard a voice approaching.

"Hi," Sarah said but not to Abby. "I know you said I shouldn't call her at work but …"

Abby heard a man's voice.

"Who is that? Who are you talking to?" Abby felt her blood run cold when she recognized the owner of the voice in the room with Sarah.

"Mr. Daniels, why are you getting …" Sarah's voice was abruptly cut off.

"Give me that! Who is this?" Billy demanded into the phone. "Who is this?"

Abby looked around, searching for an answer, any answer as long as it wasn't her voice.

"Abby?" he waited for a response but Abby refused to give him one. "Abby, is that you?"

"What are you doing?" Abby heard Sarah's questioning voice in the background and she pleaded with her eyes for Lincoln to find her a location.

"I know it's you, Abby, so you might as well answer me, because I am going to hang up and that will be the last time you ever hear from your precious Sarah."

Startled by his threat, Sarah questioned her boss and editor who had set her up in this hotel. He had told her she had to hide out until things cooled down and he got her another job, but now she wondered who she was hiding from. "Mr. Daniels, I would like to talk to my friend, please. Mr. Daniels, give me the phone." Sarah demanded loudly.

"I don't think so," Billy said.

On the other end of the phone, Abby heard the sickening sound of flesh hitting flesh and a sharp cry of pain. She responded instantly, "Goddamn it, Billy, let her go!" Her voice was so loud and angry that she attracted the attention of everyone in the squad room. Ignoring the eyes upon her, Abby strained to hear every sound at the other end of the phone and physically winced when she heard a thump followed by a low moan.

"Sarah! Billy!"

He screamed back at her. "You don't tell me what to do any more, Abby. I'm in control now, *me*, not you! I'm calling the shots. I'm pointing the finger at you and there is nothing you can do about it. You can't save her and you couldn't save them, and it's all on your head, Abby. And when you are left with nothing, you will spend your days thinking of me!" The line went dead.

Abby jumped to her feet so fast, her chair toppled backwards, loudly clanging to the floor. She stood there helpless, looking over her desk to her partner when Lieutenant Banks walked in the door. "What the hell is going on?" she demanded as she stood in the doorway.

"We got him! We got him!" Lincoln yelled as he hung up the phone, waving a piece of paper. "The Webster Arms Motel. Let's go!"

Banks looked from Abby to Lincoln, "Wait. Where are you going?"

"We found Sarah," Lincoln said as he rushed to the door.

"We're sure?" Lieutenant Banks questioned.

"Positive." He hollered back over his shoulder.

"Then go … and take back-up!"

The parking lot was a buzz of activity as Lincoln and Abby left with a handful of other officers. The first call for uniformed backup had already gone out over the radio, but that did nothing to calm Abby's nerves. Sarah was alone with Billy and he was out of control. The things he was capable of flashed through her mind as Lincoln sped through the city at a breakneck speed.

"Jesus Christ, Lincoln, we had this address how long ago?" She braced her body with an outstretched right hand against the dash as they skidded around a corner and into the flow of traffic. Horns honked as tires smoked, and Lincoln gunned his car through an empty parking lot.

"Not now, Abby," he yelled as he floored the accelerator. The car swung back out onto the street, fishtailing back and forth. Seconds turned into minutes as Lincoln wove his way through the morning traffic.

The two stories of the Webster Arms Motel were built next to the main highway almost thirty years previously when Route 15 was the main road out of the city. Its rooms were still clean and cheap and that was what attracted its transient cliental. What galled Abby the most, though, was that she passed it every day on the way to her house.

Lincoln powered his car onto the highway on-ramp. "How do you want to run this?" he yelled.

"I'll take the front with Decker and Hassle," Abby said, naming two of the other detectives following not far behind them in their own car. "You take Johnson and Webber around back. The uniforms should be there, so they can do a perimeter. Kill the siren. There it is." She pointed ahead to the white building on the right side of the road.

Abby did a double take as they went past an alley. Someone was standing leaning up against a brick wall. They locked eyes. "Son of a bitch, that's him!" Abby hollered as Billy broke into a run. "Back it up … back it up!" Instinctively, she reached for the door handle.

"Hang on." Lincoln slammed on the brakes and shoved the transmission into reverse as he smoked the tires. Abby reached for the radio and advised the other detectives of their situation as the unmarked sedan bounced its way down the pothole-ridden alley. Billy was scampering from side to side and they were closing the gap on him when he disappeared through a gated walkway that led to the Webster Arms premises. The car screeched to a stop and Abby jumped out. "Take the front, take the front," she shouted, pointing as she drew her weapon and charged through the gate. Lincoln took off down the alley, with one hand on the wheel and the other on the radio.

With her gun in the air, Abby made her way down the narrow passageway Billy had taken. She could hear his running footsteps but she couldn't see him in the litter-clogged corridor. The two commercial buildings were barely shoulder width apart, and their towering height choked off what little light there was from above.

"Stop, police! Give it up, Billy!" she yelled, knowing full well he would never stop unless forced to. Moving with all the speed her caution would allow, Abby darted and dodged her way down the passageway. She stopped when she heard the stutter of his steps and the sound of a rusty hinge. Moving silently forward, she spotted him just as he went through a door. Out of habit, she reached down to her waist for her radio, only to realize she hadn't grabbed it out of the car. Everything that she had ever been taught told her to wait for her partner, not to go on without back up, but she knew she had to; Sarah's life depended on it. Looking at the metal door and then down the empty passageway, Abby's thoughts went back to one of her instructors at the academy. *Never get emotionally involved in a case, because your heart will take you places your brain would refuse to go.*

"Too late now," she said aloud to no one. She pushed against the door with her shoulder and went in low with her finger on the trigger. All she could hear was the sound of Billy's footsteps climbing a metal staircase. Crouched down with her back against the door, she leaned in to see him running up the stairs. Looking back down the empty passageway, she realized it was up to her—follow Billy or let him get away again. Grabbing a piece of broken drywall, she marked a large 'A' on the door and an arrow pointing up. She hoped it was enough for someone to follow as she headed up the stairs. Keeping as close to the walls as possible, she took the stairs two at a time. Her heart was beating loudly in her ears, but it didn't drown out the gasping breath coming from the floors above her. Peering up though the spiral, she could see they were almost out of stairs.

"Give it up, Billy. You're out of breath and out of options."

"Shows how little … you know," he said as he threw his small body against the door leading to the roof. The catch gave way and the stairwell flooded in bright sunlight. Abby cursed under her breath as it clanged shut again. She had hoped that he had run himself into a dead-end.

She reached the threshold herself and paused. Going through any door was always a high risk, but a roof door was the worst. The person on the other side had every advantage; they had the light at their back, the room to maneuver for an attack, and the ability to hide or run while their pursuer waited to come through.

Double-checking her weapon, Abby took a deep breath before she launched herself against the door. Keeping low, she tucked and rolled against her shoulder, coming up on one knee on the gravel roof. Quickly she scanned the area with her weapon ready until she spotted Billy jumping onto the next roof. Her height and long legs gave her the advantage and she quickly covered the ground between them. Billy looked over his shoulder only once before he jumped to the next roof. That was the last Abby saw of him as he disappeared from sight.

As she jumped onto the roof herself, Abby realized it was the Webster Arms. The large expanse was a series of peaks and valleys in the style of the rest of the motel. She should have been able to see Billy easily, but she couldn't. There was no sign of him anywhere. The doorway into the building hadn't been out of her sight, so there was no way that he could have gone down that way. Cautiously, she moved to the closest edge and peeked over the side.

Nothing.

Where the hell did he go? She thought as she moved carefully to peer over the other edge. Again, there was no sign of him, but there was plenty of activity going on below. Police cars littered the parking lot as uniformed officers and detectives scurried back and forth. The sound of footsteps on gravel alerted her and she spun round with her gun ready, to see two detectives jumping onto the motel rooftop.

"You okay, Stanfield?"

"Yeah."

"Where is he?" Detective Webber asked, his gun drawn and pointing to the sky.

"I don't know. He was right here … and then he was gone." Abby clicked the safety on her weapon but still held it as she and the other detectives scanned the roof. "I've got to go."

"We'll keep looking, but I don't think we'll find him," Detective Webber said. "The motel is just too damn big."

Abby couldn't believe she'd lost him, but she didn't have the time to dwell on it as she quickly made her way over to the door leading into the Webster Arms—hoping and praying to find Sarah alive.

☯

A dozen people congregating outside one of the rooms told her where she needed to go.

"Sorry, miss," a uniform held up his hand to stop her from continuing.

"Detective," she said, quickly reaching for the badge in her back pocket.

"She's okay, Paul," a voice from the group spoke out as Abby pushed past them. "Come on, you guys, back up. Let's section this off …"

The commands continued but Abby no longer heard them as she stopped in front of the painted white door. She quickly looked away when she saw smeared blood next to the door handle. *It isn't hers! It isn't hers!*

She took one last breath, listened to one last heartbeat, and whispered one last prayer before she opened the door with the toe of her boot and walked in.

"Sarah!" she called out into the dim light of the motel room. As her eyes adjusted she could see evidence that someone had been living there. The large bed was made but the cover was crumpled badly. There were papers spread out all over the small round table and the kitchenette was stocked for use. Abby stepped farther into the room, just as Lincoln emerged from the bathroom.

"Abby," Lincoln said as he held up his empty gloved hands. "She's not here."

"But …" Abby's heart sank as she looked around and realized reluctantly that he was right. *Sarah, where are you?* Her heart ached.

"I think she was here, and not that long ago, but she isn't here now."

It was only then that Abby started to notice things in the room that she knew belonged to Sarah; her clothes in the doorless closet, her jacket on the back of one of the chairs at the table.

"I heard we lost Ward on the roof."

"One minute he was right there and then … gone," Abby said, nodding as she glanced back at the blood smears on the door. She looked at Lincoln in question. "What about that?"

"I'm not sure, but it's fresh. There's more here on the doorjamb next to the bathroom. Here." He handed her a pair of latex gloves, which she absently snapped on. Walking over to the bathroom, her eyes went immediately to the handprint in blood on the wall. She stepped back to look at the bloody print on the wall. Something about the handprint didn't make sense to her as she studied it. She opened her own hand and realized what made it look so different.

Lincoln was talking to the manager outside on the deck, when he saw Abby moving around by the back wall. He came back into the room. "What's the matter?" he asked his partner.

"This doesn't make sense," Abby pointed to the print.

"Doesn't make sense how?"

"Look at it," she said as she knelt down and turned her hand around. "It's upside down."

Lincoln tilted his head, trying to right the image in his mind. "How do you get a print upside down on the wall?"

"Billy's small but he's not a midget. We need more light in here." Rising to her feet, she walked over to the window and pulled back the heavy thick curtain. When she turned around to face Lincoln, both detectives stopped in their tracks. The afternoon sun revealed what the shadows had been hiding. The wall next to the bed and closet was speckled with blood.

It took everything Abby had to remain positive and professional as she watched Lincoln move closer to the wall. Pulling out a small pocketknife, he examined the blood with the end of his knife. "It's recent."

Lincoln carefully picked up the phone. Abby was still studying the print on the wall, but turned as he passed her with the phone in his hand.

"Abby." Lincoln drew her attention to the handset. Walking over, she bent down and looked closer at the dried blood and hair. Her mind replayed the last sounds of her phone conversation with Billy and Sarah and the dull thud she had heard. Obviously, Billy had used the handset as a weapon.

The image was unbearable, so she returned to the prints on the wall and floor. Tilting and turning her head, she finally came up with a scenario for the bloody print.

"Lincoln."

The detective walked over as Abby knelt down with her back to the closet. Holding her right hand inches away from the print on the wall, she then placed her left hand just next to the stain on the carpet.

"He had blood on his hands when he pushed himself to stand up." she said as she demonstrated.

Lincoln watched as Abby turned around and looked at the closet behind her. With one massive push, she moved all the clothes to one side of the closet, revealing a crude door cut into the drywall. Two clear bloody handprints showed where the door had been pushed back into place.

"Webber!" Abby called out. Lincoln scooped the clothes out of the way as Abby pried at the opening. "We're coming, Sarah," she said just under her breath.

"Webber, we need flashlights in here!" Lincoln called over his shoulder just as the door fell into Abby's hands.

"Let me go first."

"Forget it," Abby said as she peeked her head into the opening. "It's some kind of passageway. I don't know—it's hard to see. Sarah!" Abby listened but she heard nothing.

"Just wait, Webber's bringing flashlights." At that moment the detective arrived with two large flashlights and he held out one to Abby.

Pulling her gun out, she climbed slowly through the opening and into a narrow corridor with Lincoln right behind her. Panning their lights over the area, they lit up the pipes and electrical lines that ran the height and length of the motel. Abby moved off to her right, while Lincoln moved slowly to his left. He had gone only two steps when he spotted peepholes into the room they had just exited.

"Looks like Billy had a hobby we didn't know about." Lincoln flashed his light on the wall to show Abby and, as he did, he saw a light bulb with a string attached. "Here we go." He pulled the string and the entire area filled with light.

"Son of a …" Lincoln's words fell away. "Abby, you need to see this." He directed her toward the wall and Abby's jaw dropped. An entire section of the corridor wall was covered in papers, clippings and photos of Abby. There were shots of her at work, playing with Buck, and even a few of her with Sarah at the resort. There were articles, mostly new, but some old and faded, of past cases that had brought Abby some unwanted media attention.

"Holy shit," she said slowly as she glanced over the wall that chronicled most of her life.

"This guy is really sick," Lincoln said as he continued to look over the wall.

"Yes, he is," she said as she looked over the picture of her graduation from the police academy.

Abby was frozen in front of the pictures. *Where the hell did he get all these?* That was the foremost thought in her mind until she spotted something that bothered her even more. Reaching up, she pulled a photo from the wall.

"This thing goes on forever," Lincoln hollered back over his shoulder as Abby heard a distinctive *smack*.

"What was that?" she asked as she slid the black and white photo into her pocket.

Lincoln stopped and faced her, shrugging his shoulders. "I'm not sure?"

Thud.

They stood still, listening, but the only sound they could hear was the noise of water in the pipes.

"Sarah!" Abby called out as she again heard the distinctive sound of flesh hitting flesh, followed quickly by another *thud*. Abby knew she was close. "Lincoln … down here. Lincoln," Abby called out as she pointed to the back wall. Coming in closer, he at last heard the noises coming from the other side. Panning their bright lights over the wall, Lincoln saw the hole before Abby did.

"Here." Moving toward another hole cut in the drywall, Lincoln turned to his partner, "Ready," he mouthed silently.

At his nod, the pair burst through the cut piece of drywall and scanned the room with their guns and their flashlights. A beam of light shone brightly on Billy Ward just as he turned and looked at them, his crystal blue eyes wild and wide. He was standing over an unconscious Sarah, holding her upright by a handful of hair. He sneered at Abby as the flashlight beam caught the edge of a knife held firmly in his hand.

"Too late," Billy said, and they could do nothing but watch as he slashed at Sarah's exposed throat. Abby screamed at what she saw, as Billy dropped Sarah to the ground and made a dash for the door on the other side of the room. Lincoln got through the opening first, with Abby pushing him from behind. Stumbling to his feet, he glanced down at Sarah's bloodied and beaten body, but he couldn't tell if she was alive or not.

"Go … go!" Abby yelled at Lincoln as she scrambled over on her knees to Sarah's side.

Abby's hand immediately went to the blood pulsating from her neck. "Sarah! Oh God … please, Sarah, stay with me … come on." She leaned back and yelled. "I need help, somebody! Help me!"

Lincoln grabbed his radio as he took off after Billy. "We need an ambulance *now* … around back, Webber … we're around the back side of the motel. Billy is heading toward … " Lincoln's voice faded away.

"Sarah," Abby pleaded, not realizing she was crying as her tears mixed with Sarah's blood on her face. "I love you, Sarah … please don't die … please. Oh God!" Her hands shook as she tried to stop the steady flow of dark blood oozing from the gash in Sarah's throat. Everything seemed to be covered with blood as Abby looked around the dark room. She pressed down hard with her good hand and hoped for the best.

"Someone help me!" she cried out as she knelt over the motionless Sarah. "Help me! Johansson! Webber! Someone … anyone!" She knew she had to do something or Sarah was going to bleed to death. "Hang on Sarah, please just hang on," she said as she attempted to wipe away the blood from Sarah's face with her free hand. It was then that Abby saw the damage that Billy had done with his fist. Sarah's eyes were swollen; her lips were split and swollen; there were several deep lacerations to her chin and cheeks. It was more than Abby could handle.

"I'm so sorry, Sarah, I should have warned you. I should have … please, just hang on." Abby closed her eyes and felt the faint beat of Sarah's heart at her fingertips. "Just listen to my voice, Sarah, just listen to my voice," she pleaded. "We'll get through this, I promise." She felt the warmth of the small body against her, but there were no other signs of life coming from Sarah's still form.

Abby looked up as she heard footsteps coming toward her. Lincoln pushed through the door, followed quickly by two emergency medical technicians and a number of other officers.

"Is she alive?" he asked desperately, searching Abby's face for the answer.

"I don't know. I think so." Abby said quietly as if she was afraid that the frail existence in her hands would be shattered if she spoke too loud.

The EMTs went to work. They radioed the hospital, informing them of their impending arrival and the patient's need for emergency surgery. They told Abby that she was keeping Sarah alive by pressing her fingers on Sarah's carotid artery. Abby was surprised when no one attempted to take over. 'No, no, you stay right where you are," the EMT said as he prepared to transfer Sarah onto the stretcher. "You did the right thing, but if you take your hand off now, it would be all for nothing."

Abby looked at Lincoln for guidance. "She'll be fine, Abby, don't worry about anything. I'll meet you at the hospital."

"What about Billy?"

"We lost him, Abby. He seems to know this motel better than the manager, who had forgotten these rooms were even here. Seems they closed them down in the late eighties and haven't used them since."

"Well, Billy's obviously been using them," Abby said as they lifted Sarah gently onto the stretcher.

"We'll get him, Abby, we have him now. We have witnesses; we have evidence … more than enough to take him down now."

"We have to find him," she said as she looked down at Sarah. There wasn't much that was recognizable as they came out into the daylight. Sarah's young innocent face had disappeared beneath the blood and swelling. Abby leaned down and brushed back a few stray strands of hair with her free hand. "And God help him when I do."

CHAPTER 23

It was more than a few hours before Lincoln could get away from the scene to make it to the hospital. He had called several times, but the only thing he could find out was that Sarah was in surgery. Making his way through the maze of halls, Lincoln finally found the surgical waiting room and his partner.

Abby was all alone sitting in an orange plastic chair, her elbows on her knees and her eyes directed, unfocused, on the floor. Her denim shirt and her faded Levi's were covered with blood, but she paid them no attention as she compulsively rubbed her hands together, back and forth. It was hard to see her face behind her long hair, but Lincoln had already seen that pain and he didn't want to see it again.

She ignored him as he walked up to her, continuing to rub her hands.

"Abby?" he said quietly. There was no response and he was unsure if she had heard him. Kneeling down, he looked up into her eyes as she lifted her sad gaze to his.

"Hi."

"Have you heard anything?"

"They said it could take awhile, but they said she had a chance … a small chance." Abby lifted her head as the tears started to roll down her face. "I should've shot him. I should have killed him. But we had to give him a chance. I could have shot him in the passageway this morning, but I didn't." Looking back at her good hand, she tried to rub away what was no longer there. "It's her blood you know … her blood on my hands." She pressed harder with her thumb. "Her blood and there is nothing I can do to change it—I can't turn back time—"

Lincoln rose up just enough to wrap his arms around his friend as she sobbed out. "It's my fault. If … if I hadn't gotten involved with her … none of this would have happened."

Releasing her from his embrace, he took her by both shoulders and looked her in the eyes once more. "Abby, don't say that. You can't keep second-guessing yourself. You couldn't have known what he was going to do."

"No, but I knew what he was capable of. And now she is lying in there fighting for her life. Because of me. Lincoln, she had no idea what she was getting into."

Yes, she did, Lincoln thought as he once again felt the weight of the news in his pocket.

"They asked me about her family when we brought her in. I didn't know what to say. I know that they are in Europe, but I don't know how to reach them. And what do I say to them?"

"Her family ..." He hadn't thought about that and he realized then, that he had no choice but to tell her who Sarah really was. He had to ... but could he?

"You know we talked about family, she and I, but I didn't tell her everything. I couldn't. And now ... " Abby stood up and walked over to the window. *But what if I had told her everything?*

He gave her a few minutes, but he wondered if it was for her sake or for his own.

"Abby, maybe there was a good reason that you didn't tell her everything." Lincoln reached into his pocket and pulled out the folded papers. "I don't know how to tell you this," he said uncomfortably.

"Tell me what?" Abby turned to face him and, when he saw her standing there covered in the blood of the woman she loved, he had to remind himself that it was that same woman who had exposed her to the world. The pain and stress were etched deep into Abby's face, her dark eyes saddened by all that had been brought down on her. Lincoln felt he couldn't do it, but he loved her too much not to.

"There couldn't be a worse time to tell you this ... and maybe I should wait." He looked back over her shoulder to the doors leading to the operating rooms. *If Sarah died, did Abby still have to know?* He shook the thought from his mind.

"What?" Abby could see the struggle on his face and wondered what could be bothering him so much. "Linc, talk to me."

"Abby, when things weren't adding up, I had to find my own answers ... for me *and* for you."

"And?" Lincoln lifted the folded papers and held them out for Abby.

When her hand touched them, Linc held on for a moment longer. "The only reason I am telling you now is because I don't want this coming from someone else." Abby pulled the folded papers and newsprint from his hand.

She opened the papers, her lips pursed in a thin line as she flipped through each headline. But it wasn't the words that leapt off the page at her; it was the small picture of Sarah beside each headline. Sarah's face but with a different name.

"Abby, Sarah is a reporter. She was the leak."

"What? No, you're wrong! She couldn't have …" A rush of mixed emotions overwhelmed her. It seemed so unreal, so untrue.

The doors from the operating room opened with a hiss and an older man in sweat-stained hospital greens walked slowly through them. He headed towards Abby and Lincoln.

"Oh God," Abby whispered as she looked at the man. "Doctor?"

"She's alive. Extremely lucky but, thanks to you, she *is* alive." He saw the instant relief on her face.

"Can I see her?"

"She won't be awake for a long time."

"I don't care. I just want to see her."

"Okay, slow down here, detective. She's far from out of the woods."

"I know that, but she is alive and she is a fighter," Abby said.

"Fighter or not, she's lost a lot of blood. Whoever did this to her used a thin razor knife, like a box-cutter, and it broke off in her neck, which is the other reason she is still alive. The arteries were not completely severed, so that gave her a chance. Her jaw was broken, but that's minor compared to her other injuries. We found a lot of that paste substance you mentioned in her mouth and throat, but that's also minor. Several bones in her face have been shattered and will need further surgery. I'll get in touch with a plastic surgeon friend of mine once she makes it past the next forty-eight hours. The next battle after that will be against infection, but I don't think we need to get into that right now."

"But she's alive," Abby said a little more tentatively.

"Yes, she is."

"Whatever she needs, she gets. Money is no object; anything."

"I assure you, whatever she needs, she will get—with or without your financial assistance, detective. Our first priority here is the patient—not the bill."

"I didn't mean to imply …"

"It's quite all right, I understand where you're coming from. Money is not an issue now, but it will be in the future."

"When can I see her, Doctor?"

The surgeon could see the care and concern in Abby's features. "I'll send someone up for you when she gets settled into the ICU."

"Thanks, Doctor," Lincoln said with his hand extended.

"I just stitched her back together, so let's see where it goes from there. I don't want you two to get your hopes up too high. She has a long road ahead and she isn't even on it yet."

"I understand that, Doctor … I'm sorry I didn't get your name."

"Doctor Marcot."

"Thank you, Dr. Marcot," Abby said sincerely as she watched him disappear back behind the surgery doors.

☯

Reluctantly, Lincoln had to leave. He was due back at the crime scene. Abby could tell he wanted to talk, but she wasn't sure if she was ready yet. With a promise to keep him informed, she gave him a hug.

"Abby … about Sarah?" he asked cautiously.

"It's not her!" Abby stated firmly.

"Yes it is, Abby, you just don't want to admit it right now."

"You're wrong, Linc."

"I'm not, Abby," said Lincoln as he looked over at the folded papers. "I wish I was, but I'm not."

He watched her for a moment, unsure of where her mind was, but he knew his partner well enough to see her anger growing.

Jaw set, she looked at the ceiling as she ran her hands through her hair. "Goddamn it!" With her hands on her hips, she made her way over to the window. "All my life I've worked to keep my private life private, doing my best to honor my parent's memory by keeping the past where it belongs—in the past. And now it's out there for everyone to read with their morning coffee. And you're telling me it was Sarah who did it." Abby grew quiet as she looked outside.

Lincoln came up behind her. "Yes."

Abby stood silent for a long moment before she turned to him. There were lies and half-truths that needed to be clarified, but Abby just couldn't bring herself to do it now. "Who knows about this?"

"Right now it's between you and me, but it won't be for long."

She looked at her partner and closest friend. "It's not that I don't believe you. It's just … I can't believe it—because if I do, that means that everything we had was a lie."

"I wish there was another explanation …"

Abby held up her hand to stop him.

"I don't want to talk about it anymore, okay? Just give me … just give me some time."

"Okay, but right now I've got to go. Are you all right?"

"I'll be better once I know she's out of the woods."

Lincoln put a hand on her shoulder. "Abby, I'm sorry to be the one to tell you."

"Just … let it be. I need some time with this."

☯

The time in the waiting room seemed to last forever, so Abby busied herself by trying to locate Sarah's parents. She didn't have a lot to go on, but she had the resources and she put them to work. Time ticked by slowly as she made call after call, but she continued to come up empty handed. There was no sign of a Phillip or Maggie McMurphy anywhere, and she was sure they were the names Sarah had mentioned—but she had said so many things. For a brief moment, she thought about changing the search to Murphy, but if she did that it would mean … *It was her, and she was the reporter. Was it all a lie? I don't believe that! I remember the look in her eyes. But I also remember the torment she was going through—that would mean … If she was the reporter, then what did she know? I lied to her—hell, I've lied to everyone—but that doesn't change how I feel about them. The only ones who knew the truth …*

The thought of family brought a whispered name back to her, but she refused to acknowledge it. She hadn't talked to her uncle in so long, she wasn't sure what she would say now or how she would tell him about what had happened.

With nothing else to do, she did the only things she could: she paced and she waited. And she tormented herself with the past. As time ticked by, she kept glancing over at the folded newspapers, thinking. *That's Sarah's picture, but …* and she waited. She didn't want to believe what Lincoln had told her, and something in her heart wouldn't let her believe that Sarah's love wasn't real, no matter whose name was under the headlines. Slowly, Abby walked over to the newspapers and sat down. With growing anxiety, she reached for the paper and she started to read what had been written about her.

☯

A young nurse finally came down the hall, "Are you Detective Stanfield?" the nurse asked.

"Yes."

"This way, please." The nurse motioned down the hallway. "I just want to prepare you for what you're going to see. She will be hard to recognize because of her injuries, but keep in mind that it is your friend under all those wires and tubes."

"I understand, but you don't have to worry. Being a cop, I've seen a lot, believe me."

The nurse stopped at the ICU desk and picked up a metal chart. "I'm sure that's true, but when it's someone you know, it makes a big difference. She's right back here." She pointed with the chart to a dimly lit room, with a large sliding glass door.

Abby stopped outside the glass door and looked inside. The nurse had been right—it was different when it was someone you knew. Sarah's small and fragile body was almost hidden from sight beneath the tubes and wires. The stark white bandages contrasted sharply against the bruised and battered skin that she could see. A large tube went into Sarah's mouth and down her damaged throat. A valve was rising and falling with each labored breath. From the respirator, Abby looked over to the monitor as it beeped and flashed with different numbers, reading off Sarah's vitals.

The nurse put down her chart and came back to stand next to the visibly shaken detective.

"Oh my God," Abby whispered, unable to take her eyes off Sarah. "It doesn't even … " Words failed her. "Now what?"

"That depends on her. She has to want to fight to stay alive after everything she's been through. Well, that was a tremendous ordeal—quite a shock to her body. And she lost a lot of blood with that gash to her neck. I understand you saw it." Abby nodded. "It just missed her windpipe, which was good, but the soft tissue damage is quite extensive. I know this isn't what you wanted to hear, but at this point there's no sense in sugarcoating it."

Abby stared through the glass. "Will she make it?"

"The next forty-eight hours will be the toughest. After that," the nurse turned to look at the young woman in the bed, "her broken bones will heal, as will the cuts to her face and body, but the psychological damage could be extensive. The human body can be quite fragile but it's also quite resilient. She's a fighter, we can tell that already. And as for her vocal chords … that we won't know for a while."

"Vocal chords? Her voice?" Abby asked, her gaze moving from Sarah's battered body to the nurse standing next to her. "Because of that paste?"

"Paste? I don't know anything about a paste. I was referring to the damage from the actual trauma in that area. We won't know more until she wakes up. One thing at a time, one hour at a time. That's how her life will be measured for the next little while."

They both turned to look at Sarah.

"I'm sorry, I wish I could stay here with you longer but I need to get back to work."

"Thank you," Abby whispered.

"You're welcome. Just call me if you need anything. My name is Robin."

"What … what do you think her chances are?" Abby asked as she watched the rise and fall of Sarah's respirator.

"I'm sorry, I can't say. I'm not a doctor," Robin said with a weak smile.

Robin turned back to look at Sarah's small figure on the bed. "I've seen people survive worse, but to be honest with you … I don't know how."

☯

Abby watched from behind the glass for a long time before she finally found the courage to enter the hospital room. The moment she opened the door, she heard the beeps and the rhythmic hiss of the respirator and saw the constant flashes of light, all of which told her that Sarah was alive.

Beep … beep

Moving closer, she studied the deep red and purple molten bruises around Sarah's face that contrasted so sharply with the pristine white of the thick bandage around her neck.

Beep … beep

Sarah's face had been glued and stitched back together. Twisted lines of dried black blood crisscrossed her face where the skin had been split open by Billy's fist, and her swollen encrusted lips were wrapped around the plastic tube filling her lungs with air.

Beep … beep

Was this really her Sarah? Where was that innocent face, that infectious smile? Abby had to tell herself that somewhere behind those eyelids that were swollen shut was a pair of dancing emerald eyes. And she had to keep telling herself that.

Beep … beep

Abby brought up her hand to try to stop a sob as it rose from her chest. Billy did this. She knew that, just as she'd known it with all the others before. The fires of hell were burning brightly in her mind as she thought about his past and what he had already done to her life.

Beep … beep

Walking quietly forward, Abby pulled over a chair and sat down next to Sarah. Reaching through the bars of the bed, she collected Sarah's small hand into hers. *There are so many things I want to say to you, please … don't leave me.*

Beep … beep

With her emotions in check, she silently promised herself not to miss the second chance she had been given. *I love you Sarah, and one day I will look you in the eyes and tell you.*

☯

The medical staff wouldn't let her stay long in the room with Sarah, at least not for now, they said. So Abby found an uncomfortable set of chairs just down the hall within sight of Sarah's room. The nurses had tried several times to get her to sleep in one of the beds provided, but Abby refused when she realized that she wouldn't be able to actually see Sarah from them.

She went back to trying to locate Sarah's family, but she was still coming up with nothing. There was no evidence of there being a Phillip or Maggie McMurphy anywhere. The voice in the back of her head was growing louder and she knew that she couldn't ignore it any longer. Regardless of what had happened—of who she was or what she had done—Sarah needed her family with her. But if Lincoln was right, what did that mean?

With a heavy and bitter heart, Abby changed her search from Phillip and Maggie McMurphy to Phillip and Maggie Murphy. It was one of the hardest things she had ever done, but it was necessary. Within hours, she had located Sarah's parents. Reluctantly she left her name and number and was assured that someone would be in touch.

Leaning back in one of the chairs, with her head resting against the wall, Abby thought about what that information meant. Was Sarah really that reporter and, if so, did that mean their entire relationship was a lie?

No way, she thought immediately. *But if she didn't write the articles then who did? Someone had told them things that only a few people knew.*

Abby heard the approached of soft-soled shoes.

"Abby?" She opened her eyes to see Robin, the young nurse.

"There's a call for you at the desk. You can take it in there if you want." The nurse pointed to a small room that contained a sofa and phone.

"Thanks, Robin," Abby said.

The small light on the side of the phone lit up and Abby reached for the receiver. "Detective Stanfield."

"Abby, it's Lincoln." She smiled at the sound of the familiar voice. "How is she?"

"Hanging in there."

"Somehow I knew she would be a fighter."

"Just give her a chance, okay?" she said as she rubbed her face and her tired eyes. "Any sign of Billy?"

"No, but we have everyone looking. Abby, the reason I called is that you've gotten a number of calls from a Bartholomew Van Murien. He won't say what it's about."

"Did he leave a number?" Abby asked as she reached for the pad next to the phone.

Lincoln dictated the number to her as she quickly scratched it down. "Thanks, Linc."

"Who is he, Abby?"

"He's Phillip Murphy's lawyer. I've been trying to get hold of her parents but so far all I've been hitting is brick walls."

Lincoln heard the name before Abby realized that she had spoken it. He held his tongue, but only for a moment. "Phillip Murphy?"

"Please don't start," Abby said. "All it proves is that she changed her name and …" She stopped talking when she heard her own words and how they sounded aloud. The evidence was there, but she still didn't want to look at it or accept it.

"Abby, I did some more background research on Sarah. I didn't want to, I just thought maybe if I found …"

"Lincoln, I don't want to go into this right now, all right?" She was too tired to get into another disagreement with him.

"I understand and I respect that Abby, but there are a few things I think you should know about Sarah."

"Is this something I want to hear?"

"I think you might want to, yes. Did you know that she's been estranged from her folks for quite a while, since her first year of college?"

"I knew she hadn't talked to them in a while, but I didn't think it was that bad." Curiosity furrowed her forehead.

"Best as I could find out, they paid for her first year at NYU and then … nothing. No tuition, no allowance, nothing; she was on her own. She changed over to a city college and finished her degree waiting on tables and cleaning toilets. It took her six years but she did it, by herself."

"Any chance that it was a 'fly on your own' thing?"

"I don't think so. Close as I can tell, they haven't spoken since. She scratched and clawed to finish school without anyone's help." Abby leaned back in the sofa and looked down the hall where Sarah was scratching and clawing just to stay alive.

"Thanks, Lincoln," she said.

"No problem, kiddo." They spoke a few more minutes longer and then she hung up to call Phillip Murphy's lawyer.

Bartholomew Van Murien sounded just like his name; old, rich and stuck up. He was very reluctant to give Abby the number where Sarah's parents could be reached, but she professionally persuaded him and he relented. It was an overseas number, so she contacted the operator to have it charged to the police department. She had no idea what the time was in Valencia, Spain, but she didn't care.

"Hello," a groggy male voice answered the phone.

"Yes, is this Phillip Murphy?"

"What the hell time is it? Who is this?" He was waking up and none too happy about it as Abby heard a female voice in the background, "Phillip, who is it, dear?"

"My name is Abby Stanfield, I am a detective for the city …"

"Are you calling from the United States?" he growled.

"Yes sir, my name is Abby Sta …"

"I don't care who you are. It's … 4:23 in the morning here," he said, cutting her off again.

The female voice in the background clearly spoke again. "It's someone from home. Who is it, Phillip?"

"I realize that, sir. I'm calling about your daughter, Sar …" Abby tried a different approach.

"I don't have a daughter!" the man said and hung up. Abby sat for a moment in shock, looking at the receiver in her hand.

"What the …" She called the operator to put her through again. It took almost fifteen minutes before she heard the sound of the phone ringing again. This time she heard a female voice answer.

"Hello," Abby immediately pictured a small, soft-spoken woman who had been raised in a rich affluent, upper class society.

"Is this Maggie—Maggie Murphy?"

"Yes, yes it is. Who is calling please?" Abby wondered if she was keeping her voice low so as not to alert her husband.

"My name is Abby Stanfield, I am a homicide detective and I'm calling about your daughter, Sarah. She was attacked …"

"I'm sorry, we don't have a daughter." Her words were spoken but Abby didn't believe them.

"Mrs. Murphy, whatever happened between you and your child is your business, but Sarah is in the hospital fighting for her …"

"Who are you again?" she asked, cutting Abby off before she could finish.

"My name is Abby Stanfield and I am with the …"

"Are you her lover?" The question caught Abby off guard, but as she thought about it for a second, she realized it shouldn't have.

"This has nothing to do with … Sarah was brutality attacked and is in the hospital in critical condition." Abby couldn't believe how cold Maggie Murphy sounded.

"Was she attacked because she was gay?"

"What? No!" Abby was astounded at the comment. "The man who attacked her is a serial killer. Sarah is lucky to be alive. Don't you understand that?"

"Are you gay?"

"Are you even listening to me?" Abby hadn't realized how loud she had become until she looked up and saw Robin closing the door to the room.

"Are you gay, detective?" Maggie asked unmoving.

"Your daughter is in Sisters of Grace hospital, she is currently on life support and we are unsure if she will make it through the next forty-eight hours. She had her throat slit." Abby waited but there was no sound of care or concern on the other end.

"Please answer the question, detective. Are you gay?"

Abby rolled her eyes to the ceiling as she shook her head in disbelief. *How could this cold and uncaring woman be the mother of someone as warm and loving as Sarah?*

"Yes, Maggie, I am …" Abby was not surprised when the line went dead.

She sat alone for a long time in the small room. The pain and rejection Sarah must have felt over her parents' desertion was something Abby couldn't get her mind around. To be told by someone who was supposed to love you unconditionally that you no longer existed to them must be devastating. Abby was certain that she now knew why Sarah had lost all contact with her parents. In the silence of the small room, Abby wondered what her parents' response would have been. Would they have shunned and forsaken her? Would they have closed their lives to her, cast her off like vermin? She missed her parents. She missed not having them there when she was growing up. With a sad smile she recalled her mother's laughter and her father's caring touch and she knew in her heart, that their love had been without conditions. She constantly told herself that they would have been proud of her. And they would have loved Sarah.

Walking down the hall, she stopped next to the glass that separated her from Sarah. She watched the rise and fall of Sarah's chest and the rhythmic pulsing of her heart monitor.

"I love you, Sarah Murphy. Unconditionally. Without prejudice. Without hesitation." She lifted her hand to the glass and whispered, "I should have told you." *I should have told you everything.*

☯

She heard Lincoln's voice in her dreams as he asked for her. At least she thought so, until she heard his heavy steps on the hard hospital floor. Sitting up, she rubbed the sleep from her eyes as she tried to smile at her partner. But in the next moment, she was awake and knew something was wrong. Her eyes darted to Sarah, but she could see the young redhead resting in her medicated stupor.

Looking back at her partner, she realized what had struck her as odd about him. Lincoln always prided himself on his attire. His suits and ties were always the latest styles, and always neat and pressed without exception. Now his beige suit was soiled and wrinkled, his tie loose around his sweat-stained neck. As he got closer, she saw sadness in his eyes and a distinctive smell about him that she couldn't immediately place.

"Lincoln?" she said as he stopped in front of her.

He didn't know what to say as he tugged at his tie for the umpteenth time. He had hoped on the way here that he would find the words, but there weren't any. There was no easy way to tell her.

"Abby," he started. "Abby, there was a fire …"

Smoke … that was it. She recognized the smell. "Where have you been?"

"Abby …" he took her hand and looked in her eyes. "Abby, there was a fire. Your house is gone."

"Gone? What do you mean gone?" She couldn't fathom what he was saying.

"They called me when they couldn't reach you. It was all ablaze by the time I got there."

"My house is … gone?" She said in disbelief. Not her house. The home she had worked so hard on.

"I'm sorry, Abby. I was hoping to save some of it, but the fire … Abby, there's nothing left."

Abby was quiet and somber as she sat blinking back the tears. Lifting her head, she looked past Lincoln to Sarah's still form in the bed and she recalled Billy's words to her. *When you are left with nothing, you'll think of me!*

"He burned down my house, my home." She looked at Lincoln for answers but the man with the heavy heart could find none. "He said he was going to take it all away and that is what he has done." The tears came without her knowledge. "He killed my dog, tried to kill my girlfriend, he almost cost me my job, and now … and now he has taken my home." She pulled her hand from his and stood on shaky legs.

"There is nothing left for him to take … is there?" She turned back to Lincoln.

Lincoln stood up and walked towards her. "Abby. We're afraid he might be coming after you." He was close enough now to see the color change in her eyes. The brown turned black as she pulled her courage from beyond her sorrow.

"Bring it on! I'm ready for him! If he wants to come after me, I'll be waiting for him!"

"No, you won't be!" Lincoln fired back loud enough to get a dirty look from the nurse at her station. "That isn't open for discussion … period. Banks wanted you under protection. I knew you would never go for that, but she reminded me that this is not your choice. Abby, I've been there beside you the whole way but this time, I agree with her. Stay here; be with Sarah. She needs you."

There was a long drawn out silence as she looked from her partner to the floor.

"Okay." She said it so quietly that Lincoln barely heard it.

He was surprised at how easily she agreed as he put his hand on her shoulder. "We have him now, with everything we found concerning Sarah and the arson investigations at your house. There's no question now. All we have to do is find him and he'll never see the light of day without bars again." He could feel her trembling and he knew their decision was right; it was time for Abby to step away.

Lifting her head, she looked at him. "I can't believe my house is gone. Just like that, gone."

With an arm around her shoulder, he guided her to one of the chairs. "I'm sorry, Abby."

She said nothing as she took a seat.

"Anything you need, just say the word," he offered. "Anything."

"I'm gonna need a place to stay. Can you find me something?" She wiped her nose with the back of her hand, then tried to smile when he handed her a handkerchief. "Maybe a house or something. I don't know. I'm not sure I care."

"Hey." He turned her head to look her in the eyes. "If you start thinking like that, then he has won. You have to care. I know it's hard right now but look to the future." He looked back over his shoulder at Sarah before turning back to her. "Look to the future for both of you."

Abby rose and walked over to look at Sarah through the glass. Lincoln was a step behind her. "You love her, Abby, I've seen it in your eyes. And no matter what happened or how it happened, I'm sure she loves you, too. You'll get past this if you want to."

"I read the stories in the paper," she said softly as she watched the slow rise and fall of Sarah's chest. "There is no way she wrote all that."

"You sure?"

"No, but there was stuff there she didn't know. At least I didn't tell her."

☯

Beep … beep.

Something was wrong; she could hear it but she didn't know what it was. Pulling herself from a deep sleep, Abby opened her eyes to an angel in white in front of her.

Beep … beep

She looked at the machine that showed Sarah's rhythmic heartbeat. The steady rhythm had changed. *Sarah?*

Beep … … beep

Abby hadn't intended to fall asleep but her exhaustion had caught up with her. Suddenly an alarm went off and she jumped to her feet as a red light started flashing.

Beep … … beep

Abby looked from Sarah to her monitor.

Beep … … beep

Almost instantly the room filled with nurses, all bustling about, tweaking buttons and checking machines.

Beep … … beep

"I'm sorry, you're going to have to leave." A nurse took Abby by the arm and directed her to the door.

Beep … … … beep

"You need to leave. Now!" the nurse ordered.

Beep … … … beep

"What's going on?" she asked in near panic as she saw the numbers on the heart monitor dropping quickly.

Beep … … … beep

The nurse ignored her questions and returned to her patient. A doctor appeared at Sarah's bedside. Alarms and buzzers were now filling the entire ICU area as Abby watched Sarah's fight for life. "Sarah—don't you give up!"

Beep … … … beep

Another nurse came down the hallway and tried to take Abby to the next room but the detective refused to leave.

"What is going on? Tell me," she demanded loudly, knowing the answer, but refusing to acknowledge it.

The nurses directed her to the other side of the glass. "Your friend's heart has been under a lot of strain and we …" Abby looked up as the small bleeps on the screen turned to a straight line and a steady tone. Sarah's strained heart had stopped.

"Oh God, no." She put her hand up to the glass and watched in agonizing dread. The nurses were calling Sarah's name, telling her to fight, as the doctor prepared the paddles on the crash cart. They had unhooked her from the respirator and were doing manual artificial respiration with a bag and mask.

Abby blinked and jumped as the electric shock jolted Sarah right off the bed.

She knew what the straight line on the monitor meant as she listened to the doctor call out names of medications and the amounts he wanted administered. They put the paddles to Sarah's chest again. Abby winced when she watched Sarah's small body jerk with electricity.

"Come on, Sarah, fight!" Abby banged on the glass.

"Clear!" the doctor said as he released more electricity into Sarah's chest. One more time Abby's eyes darted around the room, looking from the machines to the faces of the medical staff, but there was no sign of life in Sarah's small body.

"Again!" the doctor ordered as Abby prayed. Everyone knew what to do as they fought to bring Sarah back; everyone except the terrified woman on the other side of the glass. Abby felt utterly helpless.

"Clear!" Sarah's body jerked again as all eyes turned to the heart monitor. They waited and then … *Beep.*

The lone sound stilled the room as everyone stared at Sarah's monitor. "Come on," the doctor urged, echoing Abby's own whispered words.

Beep … … … *beep.*

The room filled with excitement as the doctor shouted out instructions and the team rushed to carry them out. It seemed to Abby like organized chaos.

Sarah had pulled through and that was all that mattered to Abby. Closing her tear-filled eyes, she said a silent prayer to anyone who was listening.

"Doctor, her neck." The nurse's words sent a wave of fear through Abby as she looked at Sarah's still body. There was a growing patch of blood soaking through Sarah's neck bandage.

"She's blown her stitches." The urgency in the doctor's voice brought Abby a sense of fear she had never known. "She's bleeding out. We need to get her back up to surgery STAT!"

The last Abby saw of Sarah was her pale white face and the bright red blood flowing from her neck into a pool on the rolling gurney.

PART 2

CHAPTER 24

Abby looked down at the railing of the bridge. Her fingernail followed the grain of the wood as her thoughts toiled in the past. It all seemed so long ago, like a nightmare in the distance, but Abby knew in was no dream. Her house was gone, her dog was gone, and Sarah was—

Raised voices pulled Abby back into the present and focused her mind back on Billy's mutilated body and the ever-present ache in her chest. It was some sort of commotion over by the bridge that had brought her back from her memories. Detective Webber and Lincoln were standing inches from each other. Then Abby saw her partner take a swing at Webber's face. "What the …"

All hell broke loose as several officers tried to hold back the two angry detectives. Abby raced to her partner's side, ready to back him regardless of the situation.

"What's going on?" Lieutenant Banks ordered but no one offered her an explanation. "Detectives?" Lieutenant Banks demanded.

Lincoln turned to Abby and grabbed her by the arm. "What're you doing? Let go of me!" Abby demanded as Lincoln forcefully pulled her from the crime scene. "What the hell was that all about? Hello. Are you not talking to me?" She looked from her partner back to the scene. She could see they had rolled the body over and Lieutenant Banks was crouched down, looking at something behind Billy Ward's back.

"Abby, we need to get you out of here."

"What? Why?"

Lincoln could see Lieutenant Banks and Detective Webber heading in their direction.

"Lincoln, what's going on?"

"Abby, wait there," Banks called, holding up her hand. "Lincoln, I need a word."

Abby's brow furrowed as she watched them, unsure of what was going on. Her attention was drawn to the mortician as he laid out a body bag next to Billy's corpse.

"That's bullshit," Lincoln said, his voice rising. Abby looked over as her commander broke from the pack and headed towards her.

"Lieutenant?" Abby questioned.

"Detective." The official title from her commander unnerved her as she looked at her approaching partner.

"What's going on?" She looked from one to the other.

"Abby, I realize this isn't the time or place for this, but I've no choice."

"I'm not stupid, I know I can't be a part of the investigation …"

"That's not it, Abby," Lincoln said.

"I'm off the case. I'm on leave. What else would you like me to do?" She opened her hands as she offered the question.

"Abby, I'm going to need your gun and shield." Lieutenant Banks held out her hand.

"What?" She looked at Lincoln in disbelief. "Why?"

"For reasons I can't go into at this time."

Abby saw the reason as it crossed their faces, one at a time. "You think I did this?" Abby looked from one to another. "You can't be serious. I'm a suspect?"

"Abby," Lieutenant Banks cautioned.

"What? If that's not it, then what?" No one spoke. "Tell me. Am I a goddamn suspect?" she demanded.

"Yes," Lieutenant Banks responded flatly.

She looked around the crime scene at the faces of her fellow officers, and she knew she was more than just a suspect; they had already convicted her

"I didn't do this," she said quietly. "I didn't kill him. This can't be happening. So now what? Are you taking me in?"

"No, you're free to go, Abby," her lieutenant stated.

"For now?" she responded sarcastically, but Banks ignored it. The reality of the situation started to sink in. "Should I call my lawyer?"

She looked at Lincoln who had remained silent. "Lincoln?"

"Abby, I don't care what anyone says or what evidence they have …"

"Lincoln," his boss warned.

Abby saw in his eyes that he, at least, believed her. "I needed to call Nathan anyway, before he reads this in the papers. You want 'em …" she pulled out her precious gold shield, then she un-holstered her gun and handed them to her commander. "You got 'em."

"Abby," the distress of the situation came through the lieutenant's voice.

"You know where I'll be," Abby said to her partner.

"Abby, it is *not* personal," Lieutenant Banks said as the defeated detective pushed her way between her commander and her partner.

Abby stopped and looked back. "You're wrong, lieutenant. It's always been personal."

☯

It was late as Abby made her way down the long and silent hallway. Or maybe it was early—it didn't matter. Her head was filled with Billy's voice. His laughter rang loud and clear as did his final words to her. *When you're left with nothing ... when you're left with nothing.* That's what he had done. With his death, he had taken the last thing she had—her job and reputation.

"Good morning, Abby."

"Mornin', Robin." The nurse smiled but as she looked over Abby's haggard appearance, she knew the time away from the hospital hadn't done the quiet detective any good.

"How's she doing?" Abby paused at the desk and looked atwards Sarah's room.

"See for yourself. Her doctor was just here."

Moving quickly, Abby stopped just inside the sliding glass door. The wave of silence overwhelmed her. Sarah's heart monitor and respirator were gone!

"Go ahead," Robin said, urging the woman forward.

Moving slowly, she stopped at Sarah's bedside. With a careful hand she reached out to touch Sarah's face for the first time since the savage attack that had almost taken her life. The swelling grossly distorted her features and the dark bruises seemed to be richer in color, but there was improvement in the cuts that marred her pale face.

As gently as she could, Abby ran the backs of her fingers over Sarah's cheek and lightly brushed back her hair off her forehead. Hot tears ran unheeded down her face.

"I knew you could do it. I knew you wouldn't give up," she whispered to the silent woman of her heart. "She should wake up soon ... right?" she asked the young nurse standing in the doorway.

"When her body and mind are ready, she'll come out of it."

Abby leaned her head against the cool metal bars of the bed and watched Sarah's breathing. The movement was so simple and easy but it filled her heart with a warm sense of relief.

Abby softly read aloud to Sarah from a book of poetry. Looking up from the pages, she was surprised to see Lincoln standing at the glass. She closed the book, gave Sarah a small kiss on her forehead, and went out to see him.

"What? Are you here to arrest me?" she asked sarcastically.

Lincoln chose to ignore her touchiness. "I came to see how you're doing."

"Fine, thank you," she answered bitterly.

"And how is she?" He nodded toward Sarah.

"She has a name, Lincoln."

Lincoln held out his hands in self-defense, "Look, Abby, I didn't come here to start anything, all right? I came because I'm concerned. Billy's death must …"

"Not here! I don't ever want to hear his name uttered in her presence—*ever*."

"Look, maybe I should just go."

He turned to leave but Abby reached out to stop him. "Lincoln … I'm sorry." Abby took a moment and swallowed her anger. "You didn't deserve that."

"And you didn't deserve any of what he did." The comment stopped her in her tracks and it gave Lincoln a chance to get a good look at his partner. "You're looking better."

A small smile broke across her face. "I've a reason to." Abby turned and looked at Sarah.

"How *is* Sarah doing?" he asked.

"They took her off of the monitor and the respirator this morning."

"That's good."

"Yes, it is." They stood outside the glass door looking in on the patient. Abby could tell by Lincoln's body language just how uncomfortable he was. "Lincoln, what's wrong?"

"What?" he asked.

"Something's bothering you. What's up? If it's about what happened, I understand. Well, I don't understand—but Banks didn't have a choice. Obviously something was found—on him or near him—and it pointed a finger at me."

"I can't tell you anything, Abby, you know that."

"Yeah, I do—and I respect that—but let's not let this come between us. Okay, big guy?" He liked it when she called him that. "I mean, under the circumstances, I'd be looking at me, too."

He looked back at Sarah. "I'm off the case, too."

"Ah, Linc, that's not right."

"Sure it is and we both know it, but …"

"But?" she looked at him in question.

"Abby, we have to at least let Banks know Sarah was the reporter."

"Didn't we have this argument in the parking lot already?"

He held up his hand to stop her response. "I know. You don't think it was her, but regardless, it's her name in black and white."

"It wasn't her," she pleaded with him. "It can't be her." She heard her own words and she knew she was trying to convince herself just as much as she was trying to convince him. "It can't be her, Lincoln, don't you understand?" Abby ran her fingers through her hair and then looked back at Sarah. "It can't be her. Because if it is, then where does that leave us?" She bowed her head.

"Abby, you have to think about this. I know you don't want to but you have to. If it wasn't Sarah, then who? Who else could it have been? Abby, you're one of the best cops I've ever known and I'd trust your instincts over evidence any day. If you think she didn't do it, then that's what I think, too. But …" he held up one finger, "you have to ask yourself. If she didn't write those stories, then who did?"

"The only person who knows more about this case than you and I. Billy."

"But how could he …"

"You said it yourself, she thought she was working for him. Why couldn't the paper think she was the one filing the stories?" Abby looked at her partner. "We need to find out how they were receiving the articles."

"I'll look into it."

Abby looked at Sarah's still form lying on the hospital bed, and Lincoln could see the conflict in her face and the pain in her eyes. "But what if I *am* wrong, Lincoln?" she whispered.

"Listen to your heart, Abby," he said softly, "and to that annoying little voice in your head."

She reached up and touched the glass, tracing Sarah's face with her finger.

"Excuse me, are you Detective Quinn?" Robin interrupted.

Lincoln turned and smiled at the nurse. "Yes," he said.

"There's a phone call for you at the desk," Robin gestured back to the nurses' station. He excused himself and the nurse watched him go with interest.

"*That's* your partner?" she asked Abby.

"Yes," she said proudly before she turned to see the look on Robin's face. "He's happily married to a woman who would kick your ass for what you're thinking," she added as she left Robin to daydream.

Lincoln's call seemed to be taking a while, which gave her a chance to think. Looking down at Sarah's battered body and the thick bandage around her neck, Abby had a hard time separating what she knew from what she felt. She didn't want to believe Sarah could have fed information to the papers, but could it really have been Billy?

Abby was so deep in thought that she didn't notice Lincoln's return until he cleared his throat. The moment she turned to face him, she knew something was wrong.

"What's up? Lincoln?"

He said nothing at first. "Abby … I …" He looked up at his partner but quickly turned his gaze to Sarah.

She followed his eyes. "What? Is it something about Sarah?"

"No. Abby, that was Banks. She wants … ah, Abby, they want you to come in voluntarily for questioning," Lincoln finally said.

"Voluntarily, huh?" She had been expecting this, but it didn't soften the blow.

Abby stood up and gently brushed a lock of red hair off Sarah's forehead. "I have to go, Sarah," she said quietly.

Lincoln watched Abby hover over Sarah as she pulled up the bedding and smoothed away the wrinkles. He wondered how much more she could take as she leaned down to place a kiss on Sarah's pale cheek.

"She still seems too small in this bed," Abby whispered to no one but herself. "I've got to go, Sarah—just for a bit, okay? I'll be back soon, I promise."

With a heavy sigh she turned around and faced her partner. "Do you need to cuff me?"

"What? No. This is voluntary remember," he said.

"Is it?" Abby asked as he slid the glass door shut behind them.

The small private hospital room was now empty, except for Sarah. Her small body lay motionless until her fingers started to move, searching for the warm hand that had left.

CHAPTER 25

"But where were you last night?" Webber asked for the second time.

"I've told you."

"Then tell me again, but this time, how about the truth?"

"That was the truth," Abby snapped back.

"Are you sure? I've heard that you have a problem with the truth!"

"Fuck you, Webber!"

"That's enough, Abby! Back off a little there, detective," Lieutenant Banks warned.

Abby was tired and more than a little frustrated at being at the wrong end of an interrogation, and it was starting to show. Lincoln was nowhere to be seen, but Lieutenant Banks was there leaning against the wall listening to Webber and Ames question Abby.

"It's okay, lieutenant, they're just trying to do their job. Not well, but they're trying."

Webber glared at her.

"I was at the hospital until around ten o'clock, then I went home."

"You went straight home?"

"Yes, straight home. Well, to my new place."

"Straight there?"

"Yes. Actually no, I stopped off at a corner store and purchased some groceries."

"With your credit card?" Detective Ames asked.

"I guess so, I don't remember." Abby looked from Ames to Webber and then to her commander. "How did you know that? You've run my credit card already?"

"Just the last twenty-four hours," Lieutenant Banks answered.

"Great. Maybe it's time for me to call my lawyer."

"That is up to you, Abby. This ends whenever you say," Lieutenant Banks stated.

"Let's just get on with it." She waved her hand.

"You got groceries?" Ames questioned.

"Yes, I said that."

"Okay, why the grocery store on forty-first? That's out of your way if you're coming from the hospital."

"I was tired when I left the hospital. That's why I left. I was halfway to my house when I remembered I no longer had a house in the canyon. Billy burnt it down, remember?"

"Allegedly," Webber interjected.

"Whatever! I turned around, stopped at the first grocery store I found, bought my things, and then headed for my new place."

"So you went there by mistake?" Webber's tone dripped with sarcasm.

"Yes, I guess so, in a matter of speaking."

"For no other reason?"

"No. What difference does it make where I bought a few groceries?"

"Because it's only two blocks from the motel where Billy Ward had been living."

"How the hell was I supposed to know that? Huh?" She was tired and her irritability was showing. "If I'd known where he was, I would've brought him in, but I didn't."

"But you didn't. Instead you brutally beat and castrated him, then threw his body over the side of the footbridge," said Webber, throwing a picture of Billy's battered body at her.

"That's a pile of crap, Webber! We all know there was no evidence of his body going over that bridge. How incompetent are you?"

"I'm not the one under suspicion. You are. You have no alibi and everyone knows you wanted to kill him."

"I didn't know I'd be needing an alibi."

"But you did want to kill him?" Webber continued.

"I didn't say that."

"But you did."

"Yeah, I wanted to kill him. But I didn't!"

There was a rap on the door and a young uniformed officer handed Lieutenant Banks a file folder. Everyone watched and waited as she perused the documents inside.

"Gentlemen, give us a few moments, please." Lieutenant Banks locked eyes with Abby but said nothing until they were alone. Pulling up a chair, she sat down and tossed the file onto the table.

"Off the record—just you and I—where were you last night?" Banks asked in a hushed tone.

"Off the record." Abby looked at the large two-way mirror, knowing there were more than a few people watching them. Leaning closer to her boss, Abby whispered, "I told you. I went from the hospital, to the grocery store and then home, where Lincoln called me." She leaned back in her chair and crossed her arms.

Lieutenant Banks mulled over many questions and their possible answers in her mind, but her eyes kept returning to the file folder on the table.

"Abby, as your boss and as your friend, I'm greatly aware of everything you've been through. I can't fathom it, but I know. There isn't a person in this building who would blame you for wanting to go after him …"

"Lieutenant, I didn't kill him!" Abby stated flatly.

After a long moment of hesitation, Lieutenant Banks reached for the file folder on the table. "Then how do you explain how they found your fingerprints on the …"

The door to the room burst open, "Lieutenant, that evidence hasn't …"

"Get the hell out of my interrogation room, de Barr!" Lieutenant Banks ordered.

The assistant DA froze at the command, his face registering his shock at being dismissed so summarily. "Might I remind you, lieutenant, that …"

"No, I'll remind you! This is my squad room so I suggest you shut up and get out!" The lieutenant pointed at the door.

"I am the assistant …"

"I don't give a shit! Get out!" Her steely stare silenced him. Ronald de Barr was not accustomed to being told what to do, but nevertheless, it was her interrogation room and he knew it as he turned in a huff and left.

Abby couldn't hide her smirk. "That won't go over well upstairs." She pointed her thumb at the closed door.

"Abby, this is serious!"

"You think I don't know that?" she shot back.

"Then you also know we don't have a lot of time and I'm risking my neck here." Banks pushed the file towards Abby. "When we arrived at Ward's motel room there was a significant amount of blood …"

Abby was quickly scanning the documents in the file. "Blood and Billy seem to go hand in hand."

"This was his blood and quite a bit of it."

"So whoever killed him did it there," Abby said flipping through the papers in the file. Then she read what her lieutenant was getting at.

"Abby, we found your prints on the knife."

The door to the interrogation room opened and Lieutenant Banks turned around in annoyance as Detectives Webber and Ames walked in.

Webber looked smugly at Abby. "And it's all we need according to the DA. Abby Stanfield, you're under arrest for the murder of William Daniel Ward."

☯

Abby was read her rights, handcuffed, printed, and photographed before she called her lawyer. Finally alone with her thoughts in a cell, Abby paced and pondered the discovery of her fingerprints. She had read the reports for herself and there was no doubt, they were hers—on the knife that had killed Billy. But how?

As Abby lay down on the metal bed, the realization hit home—Billy was dead! It was finally over.

Looking up at the empty bunk above her, she tried to settle the rush of thoughts and memories in her mind. Billy was dead, Sarah was lying unconscious in the hospital, and she was locked up on murder charges because they had found her fingerprints at the scene of Billy's death. She had no job, no home, her beloved dog was gone, and her life and reputation were in complete shambles.

The ordeal of the day had exhausted her. As she draped an arm across her face to block out the dull light, she felt great relief knowing Billy was gone. The tension in her body unwound, as the memories in her mind slowed down and Abby finally fell asleep.

It wasn't a restful sleep: it never was, as visions from her past tiptoed through her subconscious.

☯

Nathan Holoman came down the stairs into the dark recesses of the police station. It had been a long time since he had been anywhere near a set of holding cells, but circumstances required it. Once, he'd been the state's leading defender, but he'd decided life was too precious to spend all of it inside a courtroom. But when Abby had called, he had come running.

It had been a long time since he had heard from her—too long, he realized now. Life had got in the way and they hadn't spoken in many years. Nathan often wondered if it had been on purpose or by accident.

Stopping, he signed the admit book and then continued to his client. Peering into the dark shadows of her cell, he saw her on her bunk.

"Abby," he called, but there was no sign that she heard him. He watched her sleeping as he impatiently waited for the matron with the key. "Come on, woman. Open this door!" The overweight matron glared at him but said nothing.

Nathan had one hand on the bars and the other on his briefcase as he waited for the cell door to open. A low moan came from the bunk.

"Abby! Abby, wake up!" Thc moment the door clicked, he pushed his way into the cell. With his large but gentle hand, he reached out and touched her shoulder. "Abby, wake up."

Her eyes flashed open and she quickly looked at her surroundings and at the man sitting on her bed. The relief was instant as she wrapped her arms around him.

"Nate," she whispered into his broad shoulder. Closing her eyes, she reveled in the comfort his strong embrace offered. It was easy to feel, beneath the expensive suit the firm figure of an athlete who may have passed his prime but had not given up his sports.

"It's okay, dear," he said as he held her. "It's over," he whispered into her hair.

It had been a long time since he had held her like this and it brought back memories. "I wish you'd called me sooner, Abby. There might've been more that I could've done." She pulled out of his embrace and looked into his dark brown eyes.

"Like what? You're a lawyer, Nate, not a miracle worker." She took a deep cleansing breath and ran her fingers through her hair.

"Well, let's see if I can miraculously get you out of this cell."

☯

There was a quick rap on the door of the interrogation room before the door opened and Lieutenant Banks walked in. A bright smile lit up her face when she saw Nathan.

"Nathan Holoman, I heard you were down here."

"Mary," he dipped his head to her.

Abby was surprised to see the reaction from her normally impassive boss.

"So money does buy the best, doesn't it?" Mary Banks teased Nathan with a suspiciously coy wink.

"It can," said Nathan as he walked around to stand behind Abby's chair. "But it wasn't money that got me down here. Was it?"

Abby looked up from her thoughts. "Lieutenant Banks, I believe you already know my uncle."

CHAPTER 26

When Sarah struggled to open her eyes, the world, as she knew it had changed forever. The dark shadows and foggy thoughts that had been her most recent life were now awash in bright stark colors. A silence rang in her ears as she tried to remember where she was and why she was there. Her entire body ached, but it was pleasantly distant. She knew there was discomfort but she didn't really feel it, until she tried to move. A wave of pain instantly overwhelmed her, threatening to engulf her back into the darkness. Suddenly, the most basic needs seemed impossible as she fought for a breath.

"Hey—hey, Sarah, it's okay—relax." The voice was soothing, but the face was unfamiliar. "Look at me, Sarah. Come on. Look at me. Focus—focus, that's it."

She didn't want to look at anything. She just wanted to breathe. Trying to do so was like drowning, an experience she knew very well. Fighting the rising panic, she looked at the young woman standing next to her bed.

"Sarah, look in my eyes. Look at me. Hi, my name is Robin," the nurse said with a comforting smile. "That's it; breathe slow—in and out. See, you can breathe—but it has to be slowly," Robin said encouragingly.

Robin was right, she was breathing.

"Do you know where you are?" Moving only her eyes, Sarah looked around the room, but recognized nothing other than that it was a hospital. Robin watched her face for a sign of the horror she had been through, but all she got was a blank stare—until Sarah tried to move her lips.

She wanted to say *no*, but it felt like someone was trying to rip her lips from her face.

"Shhh, shhh, no talking for right now, okay? You have some pretty bad cuts."

The confusion on Sarah's face was easy to see, even through all the swelling and stitches. "You'll be okay, Sarah, but for now close your eyes and get some rest," Robin said softly as Sarah's face relaxed. It didn't take long for the young woman to slip back into the peace of her medicated slumber.

☯

Much later, Sarah's eyes opened again.

"Good afternoon," Robin offered with her usual smile. "Feeling a little better?"

Sarah knew better than to try to answer. The fog in her mind had cleared enough to recall last time.

Robin picked up Sarah's arm and searched for her patient's pulse. She looked at Sarah and saw the thousands of questions she wanted to ask.

"You do know where you are?" Robin could tell by the look in her eyes that she did.

"Do you know why?" The uncertainty showed. "You don't remember, do you?" Robin waited and saw the anguish in Sarah's pain filled eyes. "You were attacked." She watched for a response but there was none. Robin looked over at the tray to confirm that the syringe filled with sedative was near. Some of the patients she had cared for over the years had reacted badly when the realization of their new life hit home.

"He was a bad man, Sarah. He's not here. You're safe now, Sarah," Robin assured her over and over, but Sarah wasn't listening.

Her memories and fears flashed in her swollen black eyes. *I remember … I remember a room—I remember pain.* Sarah attempted to move her left hand but she couldn't and she looked at make sure it was still there. It was. *So why can't I move it? Or even feel it?*

"You need to rest now, Sarah. Things will look better in the morning."

Slowly, with fierce determination, Sarah started to raise her right hand in search of her face.

"No, no, that's not a good idea," Robin said as she reached.

Sarah's eyes searched the room, but she didn't see what she was looking for.

"What is it? You want something?"

With a thick dry tongue, she did her best to moisten her swollen lips. "M … " but the simple letter was more than her sore lips and throat could handle.

"What is it … a mmm …" Robin looked around the room to see if she could understand her patient, and then it came to her. "A mirror?"

Sarah's eyes told her she had hit it on the button.

"Sorry, dear, there are no mirrors in here." The nurse saw the determination grow in Sarah's eyes. The injuries to her throat were life threatening, but the scars to her face would be life altering, especially if she saw them now. "Sorry, Sarah … you're just going to have to wait," Robin told her. "Things will look better in a few more days, I promise." Robin reached for the needle. Popping off the protective cover, she injected the sedative into the IV tube. "You need to rest." Robin smiled down at her as the medication began to work.

Sarah looked into the nurse's eyes, searching for the truth. *It's always in the eyes*, she thought as she felt herself starting to drift. *Who said that?* Sarah's mind began to wander into a field of tall green grass.

"You rest and when you wake up, I'll be here." Robin's words came through the fog, but as she began to float away the words found a connection to a memory. High, snow-covered mountains, a lake, as words floated into her mind … *take all the time in the world. When you're ready, I'll be here.*

Abby … it was Abby … where was Abby? The question was there in her mind, but the powerful drug took her away.

☯

"Docket number 022765, the People verses Abigail Stanfield." The judge looked up at the detective's name. As far as he was concerned, Abby should have just shot the bugger and then dumped his miserable body in the ocean.

Judge Howard M. Porter locked eyes with Abby. "Detective," he said almost in question.

"Your Honor." Though handcuffed, Abby nodded with respect to the judge.

Porter then turned his attention to the sharply dressed distinguished gentleman to her right. He was more than a little startled to realize Abby's lawyer was none other than the infamous Nathan Holoman.

"Councilor, I haven't seen you in a courtroom for a long time. I was under the impression you had retired?"

"I had, Your Honor, but when my client called me about this grave injustice … well, I had to come to see what my esteemed colleagues were up to."

The exchange going on between the accused and her lawyer and the judge visibly upset Assistant DA de Barr. "Excuse me, Your Honor, but this isn't a high school reunion. Miss Stanfield is charged with a heinous and violent crime. She isn't here as an officer of the law."

"And your point, Mr. de Barr?" the judge asked in annoyance.

de Barr opened and closed his mouth.

"All right then, let's carry on," the judge said with a wave of his hand.

Flipping through some of the files, de Barr pulled out a sheet and read the charges. Nate leaned over and whispered something to Abby just as she saw Lincoln enter the courtroom. He gave her a wink and a thumbs up before she turned her attention back to the proceedings.

"How do you plea, Miss Stanfield?"

"Not guilty, Your Honor," Abby said, loud and clear.

"Very well … trial is set for," he flipped through his book and exchanged some murmured conversation with his clerk, "the last week of September." He looked for any opposition; there was none. "Good."

Nathan stood with a legal pad in his hands, "As far as bail goes, Your Honor, I asked that … " He was rudely cut off by Ronald de Barr.

"Your Honor, due to the viciousness of the crime and the financial resources of the accused, the people are asking that the accused be remanded without bail," the assistant DA interjected quickly.

"No bail?" Nathan's voice rose in protest. "Your Honor, my client is a member of this city's police force, not to mention a respected and valued resident of the community that she lives in."

"Miss Stanfield *was* a member of this city's police force but was forced to surrender her badge due to her involvement in this case. She also no longer has a permanent residence within the city. The people will show that not only did Miss Stanfield murder and torture Mr. Ward, but she became obsessed with trying to prove him guilty of crimes he did not commit. I will prove she used her financial resources as well as those of the department to further manipulate the case against …"

"Enough, Mr. de Barr. I'm not trying this case right now, we're discussing bail. Council approach." He waved both of them forward as he covered the microphone at the front of his bench.

"Ronald, you can't be serious. You honestly believe Abby is a threat to society or a flight risk?"

"I do. I've seen what she was capable of, how brutally the victim was murdered."

"Your Honor, she hasn't been found guilty of anything and they are already punishing her. Abby has deep roots in this community. Her life is here."

"Correction, Your Honor, her life *was* here. She no longer has a home here, nor a job or family. She has money, power, and resources. I mean, hey, she got Nathan Holoman out of retirement."

"Ronald, that's enough," the judge scolded.

"Your Honor, just because my client is financially secure does not necessarily make her a flight risk. She isn't about to run out of town on the first bus."

"Really?" de Barr said mockingly to Nathan as he produced a file folder from behind his back. "Then what do you call this?" He opened the file and a plane ticket fell out onto the Judge's bench. Porter picked it up, and then quickly held up his hand to silence Nathan's argument as he turned the ticket around.

"First class to Buenos Aires," the judge read.

"Where did you get that?" Nathan asked.

"It was found in Miss Stanfield's vehicle," de Barr pompously answered.

Porter remained silent as he examined the ticket. "Recess for ten minutes." He slammed his gavel down and quickly departed.

Assistant DA de Barr turned to gloat but Nathan was already heading back to a confused Abby. Lincoln had made his way up to the front of the gallery and headed through the gates. Abby looked from one to the other, wanting to hear what they both had to say.

"What the hell's going on? They aren't going to grant me bail because I've got money? What kind of bullshit is that?"

"It's more complicated than that. Abby, whether or not you did this is not my immediate nor professional concern, but if you intend to leave the country I need to know, and I need to know now."

"What? No!" Her voice raised beyond a hush. "That's nuts; why would I run? Besides, where am I going to run to?" she asked in disbelief.

"Argentina," Nate answered without a blink of his eye. "Buenos Aires to be exact."

"What?" This time it was Lincoln who responded in question.

"de Barr just dumped a first class plane ticket on Porter's desk."

Abby looked around the courtroom in disbelief. "What? From where? It's not mine."

"They found it in your Jeep." Nathan wrung his hands before he turned back to Abby, "I won't ask again."

"You won't have to. I didn't buy any ticket! I'll put up whatever they want, everything I still own."

"That may not be enough, Abby," Nate said. "That airline ticket really hurt us."

"I didn't buy any plane ticket. Why would I?"

"Okay, okay." He reached for his briefcase and started to flip through the numerous files inside.

Abby turned back to Lincoln, "Did you see her?"

"Yeah, but only for a moment. She's awake but is pretty out of it."

Abby closed her eyes.

"On a different note, I got to talk to Brian Malfessto, the editor of the paper, and he has agreed to send me copies of the original articles."

"Have you looked at them yet?" Nathan asked as he looked over at Lincoln.

"I haven't had a chance to." He turned his attention back to Abby. "Abby, I've been thinking."

"About?" she asked.

"A call I got a while back from Frank Stempler." He saw the query on Nathan's face and hurried to explain. "He was the father of one of the girls Ward murdered."

"What kind of call?" Abby asked.

"Somehow he found out we had Ward in custody."

"How did he find that out? That wasn't public knowledge," Abby's eyes darkened as she frowned.

"I don't know."

"Is Stempler a person of interest, or could he be a suspect?" Nathan asked.

"Well, he's was definitely angry enough …" Lincoln's voice trailed off as he saw the door to the judge's chambers open.

"All rise," the bailiff said and Lincoln quickly returned to his seat in the gallery.

The courtroom shuffled and rustled as Judge Porter took his seat.

"The circumstances of this case greatly concern me. I know Detective Stanfield from her appearances in my courtroom and I've always believed her to be a highly regarded detective and an upstanding citizen." Abby heard the '*but*' even before Porter spoke it. "But the law's there for the protection of the people—all of the people. Unfortunately," he shifted uncomfortably in his chair, "with the evidence presented, I do believe there's an issue of flight. Bail is denied." The gavel came down hard as the entire gallery erupted with the noise of the departing reporters.

Abby turned to her uncle. "Nate?"

“I’ll do what I can, Abby,” he said as the officers of the court came to collect her.

Lincoln felt helpless. He turned to look at Nate for answers, but the lawyer was too busy looking for the judge. In all the commotion, Porter had left for the privacy of his chambers.

“Wait here, I’ll be right back,” Nate snapped his briefcase shut and headed for Porter’s chambers.

Lincoln paced the courtroom, feeling lost and alone with nothing to do. He kept his eyes on the clock as the minutes ticked by; five … ten … fifteen … twenty–two minutes later, Nathan opened the door to the empty courtroom. Lincoln jumped to his feet the moment he saw the lawyer.

“Well?” he asked.

“The ticket was purchased with cash … two days before the murder.”

CHAPTER 27

In the distance Abby heard muffled, hollow voices as she woke from her slumber. The bed she was lying on was hard and, as she turned to look at the four gray walls around her, she hoped with a falling spirit that she was only dreaming.

"Lights out in ten minutes," a distant loudspeaker intoned, informing her she was not dreaming. She was in prison—or rather, in segregation—and probably would be for a long while. The warden had granted her special conditions, but only temporarily. Sooner or later they would have to release her into the general population, out into the overcrowded crush of inmates—some of whom she had sent there herself.

With a heartfelt sigh, she looked around at her new home. Abby knew she was farther away from Sarah now than she had ever been, and there was little chance of her predicament changing anytime soon. Sarah … all she wanted to do was talk to Sarah, but how could she now? And if she could, what would she say? *I miss you, I love you … and, oh by the way, did you write all those stories about me in the paper? And what else do you know about me?*

She climbed off her bed and stood at the bars with her hands hanging into the corridor.

"Lights out in five minutes," the loudspeaker warned.

Nate had told her that they would be meeting the assistant DA and Lieutenant Banks as soon as possible. That was when she would find out what they had on her, what evidence had been found that connected her to Billy's death.

The machinery that locked down the prison was old and, as Abby closed her eyes, she felt it come to life. Her entire cot vibrated as metal slammed loudly against metal. The sound echoed off the thick walls as the lights finally went out.

In the darkness, she lay awake for hours, remembering with vivid clarity the height of the Gold Creek Mountains, the blue of Lake Alouette, and the emerald green of Sarah's eyes. But when she finally fell asleep, those were not the images that tossed her into turmoil. Her old familiar demons played with her conscience; the past toyed with the shadows in her mind. The death of her parents crept out from her subconscious. The guilt of what she knew and what she had kept from those that she loved. Time would never heal that wound, no matter what her uncle had told her.

When Abby sat bolt upright in bed, her skin was glistening with sweat and her breathing came in gasping gulps as she realized that what had happened then was coming into the light and there was nothing she could do to stop it.

☯

Lieutenant Banks averted her eyes when they brought Abby into the room wearing her bright orange jumpsuit and shackles. Her long dark hair hung listlessly around her pale face, darkening the bags under her eyes.

"Can we take those off, please?" Nathan asked the guard politely.

"Sorry, sir, but she's here on murder charges and policy states …"

"Take them off," Banks stated with authority. The guard looked from the prisoner to her lawyer, then to the lieutenant before he stopped at the assistant DA, who gave a quick nod.

"It's your necks," he stated as he unlocked the chains. The room stayed silent until the guard was gone. The moment the door closed, Abby stood up and walked over to the window.

Lieutenant Banks came up next to her and placed a hand on her shoulder. "How are you?"

Abby slid her a sideways glare. "How do you think I am?"

"Fair enough." Leaving Abby to herself, Mary walked back to the table, but kept half an eye on the stoic woman brooding by the window.

"All right, let's get this going," de Barr stated as he opened his brief-case. "Fingerprints." He threw down the file Abby had looked at earlier.

"Abby?" Nathan inquired of his client, but she refused to join them at the table.

Nate picked up his copy and reached over to hand Abby the other, but she silently declined. Placing her copy on the table, he turned his attention to the one in his hand. Nathan made a few notations and then looked at de Barr. "What else?"

"We have the murder weapon in our possession."

"Fine, I want it tested at an independent lab. What else?"

"We have numerous, and I do mean numerous, witnesses," de Barr looked over his glasses at Abby, " including several police officers, who heard the accused threaten to kill the victim."

"Are you kidding me?" Abby snarled.

"Abby," Nathan warned.

"Ronald, I don't believe you need to use the term *accused* in here, we all know Abby," Lieutenant Banks stated. "And I've a hard time swallowing Billy as a victim."

"He *is* dead, lieutenant," de Barr attempted to stand his ground against Mary Banks. "And I have several witnesses who heard Abby threaten to kill him."

"You and I know that wouldn't bear weight in court. We all make comments without ever thinking of following through with them," Nathan answered dismissively.

"Yes, well one of those threats came right after your client physically attacked Mr. Ward in front of witnesses, including several television cameras." He handed Nathan a number of sheets of paper bound together. "This is a list of those present during that altercation, together with their addresses. We also have her Jeep down at the crime lab."

"You have my Jeep?" Abby said from the back of the room but Nate held up his hand.

Abby stayed silent as Lieutenant Banks watched her every move. The dark-haired detective tried to remain aloof, but the lieutenant could tell that she wanted to be at the table.

Could she have really done it? The question had haunted Lieutenant Banks since she had seen Abby being taken away in handcuffs at the station. Looking at Abby's hands, Lieutenant Banks studied the scars left by her attack on Ward. *Could she have done it?* Lieutenant Banks' mind kept repeating the question over and over again.

"And finally, we have Billy Ward's own accusation," de Barr said.

The lieutenant watched as Abby turned to see what de Barr was referring to.

Slowly, enjoying the dramatic effect, de Barr pulled a large manila envelope from his briefcase. Opening it up, he shook out the contents into his waiting hand.

Even from her perch on the windowsill, Abby could see a large color photo of the naked back of a human body. Nate reached for the picture and pulled it in front of him as Abby walked up behind him. It was Billy, and it had been taken at the crime scene.

"A dying man's last word," de Barr said contentedly.

Looking down at the picture, Abby finally saw what everyone else had seen the night they had found Ward's body. His hands had been secured behind him with zip-ties, but he had still been able to scratch out one last message. Abby's name carved was backwards into the flesh of his back.

Billy himself had named his killer.

"Well then, Councilor, would you like to confer with your client before we discuss a plea-bargain …"

"No goddamn way!" Abby jumped to her feet.

"Abby," Nate commanded.

"Forget it, Nate, there will be no plea-bargaining here! Not now and not ever." Her brown eyes were a blaze of fury as she glared at de Barr. As a detective, she had always loathed the way he would plead down every case she had brought him and now she hated him for it.

"This is a capital one murder charge you're facing, Abby, not a shop-lifting charge."

All eyes turned to Abby as she stepped forward to face her accuser.

"Abby," Nate warned again.

Her physical presence alone overwhelmed de Barr as she glared down into the startled face of the assistant DA. "You will no longer call me Abby. Call me 'the accused'—or Miss Stanfield—but you will *no longer* refer to me as Abby."

The room remained still until de Barr broke the stare. He shuffled a few papers in his briefcase, hoping the others couldn't see his hands shaking, and Abby quietly returned to her seat on the windowsill.

"I would like a moment alone with my client please," Nathan requested.

When they were alone, Nathan turned to his niece, "Abby, you can't do that kind of thing, it only undermines …"

"Nate, cut the crap. They have a strong case against me, I know that and you know that. But I won't cower and grovel to the likes of Ronald de Barr."

"Fine, if you want to be pig-headed and stubborn, that's your birth-right, but at least listen to what they have to say. Maybe we can make a deal …"

"Forget it." She crossed her arms and looked out to the view.

"Abby, you should at least listen. If there's a chance that maybe …" His voice died out as he realized just how much like her father she was. The strong family resemblance went further than their dark eyes and their jet-black hair. Abby's jaw was set and her mind was made up, and Nate knew there wasn't much he could do to change it.

"Nate, we both know what happens with plea-bargains and deals, don't we?" she said pulling him from his memories of his fallen brother.

The comment took him by surprise. "Abby, look …"

"No," she said, quietly but firmly. "You work for me and the decisions are mine this time."

He closed his mouth. She was right. It was her case and her life. All he could do was advise her. "Yes, Abby, I work for you, but I'm also family and I'm here to look out for you. And if that means protecting you from yourself then that's what I'm going to do."

"That's fine. Just promise me, no deals."

Reluctantly, he agreed as she turned back to look out at her view.

She remained silent and Nathan was about to return to his seat when he heard her. "I don't want to go to court," she said, very softly, in a voice that reminded him of a child long ago. *I am not going to drag my life out of the shadows and into the light—and I will not do that to Sarah!*

"I'll do what I can."

"No, I mean … I will *not* go to court," she stated firmly. *I will not put Sarah through a trial.*

"But …"

"Uncle Nathan, I will not be dragged through messy and public court proceedings, and neither will anyone else. Got that? I will not go to court," she reiterated once more and the elderly councilor threw up his hands.

"You tell me what you want me to do, Abby, and I will do it. But, the only things that will keep you out of court are to plea-bargain or plead guilty." He looked at her and was stunned. "You're not serious—are you? Abby, you can't be?"

"Do you think I did it?"

"That's not the point."

"Isn't it?"

There was a knock on the door and Lieutenant Banks stuck her head in. "Can we come back in?"

"No," Nathan stated firmly.

"We're finished, come back in," Abby said as she locked eyes with her lawyer. Her mind was made up.

Banks came through the door, quickly followed by de Barr, who immediately unlocked his briefcase on the table.

"Okay, since there isn't going to be any plea-bargaining, I guess we'll see you both in court." He pulled several thick documents out of his briefcase and slid them over to Nathan.

"Before we do that," Abby began.

"Abby, wait," Nathan said. He held up his hand as he scanned the papers he had been handed. He felt the muscles in his chest tighten as he read the words for the first time and then looked up at his niece.

"Nate." Abby's eyes held the stare and the conviction of what she was going to do, but the look on his face caused her to pause.

"Abby, they're seeking the death penalty."

☯

"Are you kidding me?" Lincoln was not one to lose his temper easily, but the headlines of the morning's newspaper he held were grim.

"It's not my decision; it comes from the DA's office," Lieutenant Banks said in her own defense.

"I know that, lieutenant, but I can't believe you're turning your back on her."

"Lincoln, calm down. I'm not turning my back on her, I'm doing my job. The evidence against her is staggering."

"I don't care. We're not going to gas one of our own, that's crazy. Half of this department already has her convicted and now the upstairs brass want her in the gas chamber. How about innocent until proven guilty? How about trying to figure out who really did this? Because I know her and she didn't do it." Lincoln angrily paced.

"The evidence says otherwise."

"So you believe she did it?" Lincoln turned and looked Banks in the eye.

"I believe what the evidence tells me," she answered.

"You have a gut instinct; what does that tell you?"

Lieutenant Banks paused. "It tells me that she's more than capable …"

"Do you think she did it?" Lincoln demanded.

Leaning back in her chair, Banks recalled all the times that Abby had been there, in her office. "No," she finally said.

"So what are we going to do about it?"

Lieutenant Banks took a deep breath but said nothing.

"She didn't kill Billy Ward." Lincoln's face was solid as a stone as he reached into his pocket. "I bet my badge on it." He slammed his gold shield down on the desk and turned to walk out the door.

"Quinn," Lieutenant Banks came around her desk after him. "Lincoln," she said firmly. "I'm not accepting your resignation. Your leaving won't help her or her case." She lifted his hand and placed his badge into it. "Take this."

Lincoln looked down at the gold shield in his hand. "Lieutenant, I love this badge and I've worked my ass off for it, but to be honest with you now," he looked her in the eyes, "I trust my partner more than I trust this badge."

He laid his gold shield and gun on his desk as he silently left the squad room.

CHAPTER 28

Abby was lying in her solitude, bouncing a racquetball off the ceiling, when a guard came to her cell.

"You have a visitor," he said unemotionally.

"Who?" It was not the scheduled visiting time.

"I don't know," the guard said as he held out the handcuffs.

Abby followed the guard down the hall and through several gates and long wide corridors. Once they reached one of the visiting rooms, she was searched. When the guards were satisfied that she wasn't carrying anything, the door was buzzed open and she was let in.

Looking quickly down all the cubicles, she was surprised to see Lincoln sitting waiting for her on the other side of the glass. A broad smile filled her face as she reached for the phone.

"Hey, what are you doing here?" Though her smile was real, he could see the sadness in her eyes.

"Why didn't you just book an interrogation room? I hate this phone crap." Her eyes narrowed as she looked at her partner.

"Lincoln, what's wrong?" Then her mind went off in its own direction. *Sarah!*

He knew instantly where her thoughts had gone. "Sarah's fine, I assure you. Still medicated but improving."

Abby ran her fingers through her hair. "Don't do that to me. All right then, what?"

Without a word, he stuck the newspaper up against the glass. Abby's eyes followed the bold headlines, but she refused to read the accompanying story.

"You think they'd find another picture of me," Abby said mockingly; the picture showed her in the halls of the courthouse throwing the infamous punch.

Dropping the newspaper, Lincoln stared at her in disbelief. "This isn't funny, Abby. They're looking to gas you."

Her smile faded and her face took on a much more serious look. "What would you like me to do, Linc? Get mad, get angry, sit in a corner and cry about it? Which one of those things is gonna help me?" She looked at her partner and the truth of the matter reflected in the pain of her eyes.

She was right and it frustrated him more. "I can't just sit here and do nothing," Lincoln said.

"I'm not expecting you to. Go back to work and come up with some evidence that doesn't point to me."

Lincoln's dark eyes fell to the counter. "Abby, I'd love to but …" With his finger, he followed the deep grooves someone had cut into the counter.

"I know, I know—you're not on the case anymore. Lincoln, I don't want you doing anything that might jeopardize your career. What about the articles? Have you had a chance to look at them yet?"

"Yeah, nothing there. What you read was what was sent."

"So much for that idea. What about Frank Stempler? Any connections within the department?"

"None that I've been able to find. He's a loans manager, no record, not even a disturbance call."

Abby raised an eyebrow. "Loans manager, as in high interest rates and broken legs?"

"No, at a bank. Suit and tie type."

"Oh," she said with an air of disappointment. A silence fell between them.

"Did you know they're going to be calling me as a witness for the prosecution? That's not right," Lincoln said.

"Yes it is and you know it. That's part of your job. I realize that it isn't personal. It's just something you have to do. Just tell the truth, don't embellish it."

"Abby, I know that, but it doesn't mean …"

"Lincoln Quinn, look at me. Promise me you won't do anything that'll put your job on the line." Abby didn't notice that Lincoln seemed to be more interested in the initials carved into the counter than in making her any promises. "I think me being your partner has done that enough."

He looked her in the eyes. "You're the best partner I've ever had and I've no regrets. Not one."

"All right, let's not get too serious here. I don't think I can handle it," she said with a smile, but Lincoln knew there was a grain of truth in what she said.

"Lincoln, promise me you won't do anything to jeopardize your job." She leaned forward, closer to the glass.

He almost smiled. "I promise. So what's the plan then?"

"I don't know. I've been racking my brain in here trying to come up with something. I mean, come on, I wasn't the only one who wanted the bastard dead." She looked at her partner for suggestions.

"Well, Stempler wasn't the only parent upset that Billy Ward was still out there walking free," Lincoln offered.

"Yes, but do any of them have the connections to set me up like this? It has to be someone who knows about fingerprints. I mean some of the evidence they have, they almost have *me* convinced."

"You've seen it?" Lincoln asked.

"Yeah and it's not looking good. They even have my Jeep as evidence. That's how they figure I moved the body."

"I read the report. It's clean, not a thing in it," Lincoln said as he shot a glance at the guard. "No blood, no fibers, nothing."

"Bet that pissed off de Barr," she muttered.

Lincoln smiled and nodded. Abby sat silently for a moment, her mind working on something that had caught her attention. Lincoln had seen her do this many times and he knew he should be patient, but he couldn't. "What?"

"What if it's one of us?" she asked solemnly.

"One of us? You mean someone from inside the department?"

"I don't know, Linc … they would have access to all the information they needed as well as my personal file."

"That's a stretch, Abby, but I'll see what I can sniff out." He looked down at his watch. "I'm heading to the hospital."

Her demeanor quickly softened. Lincoln knew her well enough to know she had been trying hard to put up a brave front. "Have you talked to her yet?" Abby asked.

"No, she hasn't been alert enough to do much of anything."

"Would you mind giving this to her?" Abby held up a letter.

"Sure."

☯

Sarah was awake. Her mind was clear; she knew who she was, where she was, and why she was there—but they still refused to let her look in a mirror, which frightened her.

William Daniels. How could she have known he was Billy Ward? The thought sent a deep shiver down her spine. He had played her like a pawn and she had fallen for it. When the job offer came, she didn't think about how they had picked her. All she knew was that she was going to be working on assignment for one of the nation's larger newspapers. It was a chance to break into the big time, a chance to get her first front-page story—that first big headline about a female cop with a big attitude problem. A female detective, Daniels had said, who no one could get near enough to talk to; but he was certain Sarah could.

Billy had been right. She had got close to Abby. Then she had broken the cardinal rule—she had fallen in love with her. Been drawn into those dark eyes and the mysteries that haunted them. The story was there, or part of it, but she couldn't do it. She couldn't betray Abby's trust.

She refused to give William Daniels any information, and he had been so angry with her, but she had stood her ground. Then she had gone to Dexton, to try to find an alternative means to pay for her stay at the resort. That was when she saw the newspapers with her name under the headline.

Where had he found the information? She didn't know then, but she had a good idea now. He was Billy Ward, he was the murderer and he knew the case even better than Abby did. He had written those stories, not Sarah. But could she convince Abby of that?

Staring up at the ceiling, Sarah's thoughts tumbled in all directions as she tapped her left fingertip against her numb thumb. The paralysis was a direct result of the knife wound to her throat, or so her doctor had told her. Though he couldn't be certain, he was confident the feeling would return once she started physiotherapy.

"Sarah, you have a visitor," the nurse said, interrupting her thoughts. Sarah dropped her eyes from the ceiling and looked at the tall black stranger in the doorway. She had no recollection of this good-looking man, but his smile seemed pleasant and friendly enough. Nonetheless, she was wary.

Lincoln saw the fear in her face as he stepped farther into the room. He kept his eyes on hers, not wanting her to see him looking over her injuries. "Hi, Sarah."

She watched him take a seat next to her bed.

"You don't know who I am, do you? My name is Lincoln Quinn. I'm Abby's partner." The moment he said his name, he saw the sparkle in her eyes as she looked for the dry erase board Robin had brought her. With a shaky hand, she wrote out the word *where*.

"Where?" He looked up from the board with an apprehensive look. "Where is Abby? Well, she's ..."

Sarah started to write again and Lincoln watched as the letters formed the words *mad at me*.

"No, no dear, she isn't mad at you, far from it. She held you until they took you into surgery. She was here night and day—by your side." He looked down at her and was mesmerized by the green of her eyes surrounded by the vibrant colors of her blackened and bruised cheekbones. "Sarah, I've known Abby for a long time and I can say without a doubt—she is definitely not mad at you."

Sarah closed her eyes and Lincoln could see the relief in her body and in her face. "As a matter of fact," he reached into his jacket pocket and pulled out the envelope he had been given, "she asked me to deliver this to you." Helpfully, he pulled the letter from the envelope and offered it to her.

Sarah took the paper and held it for a moment before she brought it up to read. She recognized Abby's handwriting and she felt a deep ache in her heart as she read her words.

Sarah,
I'm sorry I can't be there for you, when you need me the most. You fought to stay alive against all the odds and you proved them wrong by proving me right. I told them you were a fighter!
Just know I'm there with you every step of the way.
With all my heart,
Abby

Sarah looked up at Lincoln with a question and he knew what it was before she circled the word *where* several times.

"I knew I was gonna have to answer this question, and I was sure that when you asked it I'd have a good way of telling you, but then I realized there's no good way of telling you. The man that attacked you—Billy Ward—was found murdered in the park. And, ah—well, they've arrested Abby for it."

An undistinguishable sound came from Sarah's throat as her eyes blinked rapidly in disbelief.

"Sarah?" Lincoln's voice rose in concern. "Robin!" he hollered loudly for the nurse as he watched helplessly. Sarah's face grew redder and redder as she fought for a breath. "Sarah, what's wrong?" A moment later, he heard Robin's quick steps as she came down the hall. "She can't breathe!" he said as the nurse looked from her patient to the detective and then to Sarah again.

"What the hell happened?" Robin demanded as she came around the side of the bed. "Sarah, look at me, slow down—you have to relax—

breath slow and deep," she said in a soothing calm voice. "Easy, Sarah—slow. That's a girl."

Once Sarah was breathing easier, Robin turned her attention to the visibly shaking Lincoln. "What happened?" she asked as she tried to soothe her patient.

"She wanted to know where Abby was. I didn't want to tell her—I'm sorry, Sarah, I didn't mean to upset you," Lincoln said with concern. He turned back to Robin. "I thought she was choking."

"She was."

"Because of the wound to her throat?"

"Partly, but he did something to her larynx and because of it her throat is still swollen and painful." Robin held Sarah's hand in support.

"Yeah, that's what Ward did. He made this paste from the sap of a dieffenbachia plant and injected it into his victim's throat. It was a painful and dangerous way to keep them quiet. Sarah is lucky to be alive," Lincoln said.

"Yes, she is, and the swelling will go down and her wounds will heal."

Robin was happy to see Sarah's breathing beginning to relax as she reached for her dry-erase board again. Robin and Lincoln watched her write out *don't feel lucky*.

"You're alive, Sarah, and that's more than Ward's other victims." Lincoln said. Sarah knew that was the truth but it didn't make it any easier for her to swallow.

Now that her patient had calmed back down, Robin left the room.

Sarah tapped her board and Lincoln looked down to see what she had written.

Don't remember paste.

"He must have given it to you after he found you on the phone talking to Abby."

Don't remember.

"That would be a good thing," Lincoln said with a smile.

Sarah circled the word *where* several times again.

"She's in the Twin Pines Women's Facility. I guess I don't have to say she's not very happy. She'd rather be here."

Sarah paused for a moment and thought about what it must be like for Abby to be behind bars.

Lincoln watched her with interest, seeing the care and concern deep in her eyes as she reached for her pen and started to write something out. He noticed Sarah's left hand remained motionless, by her side.

Tapping on the board she got his attention again, *Locked up—Bail?*

"They won't give her bail."

Why, she wrote quickly.

"Well, partly because …" he stopped when he remembered what she didn't know. "Let me fill you in a little. The first night you were here, someone—and I use that term loosely—someone burnt down Abby's house. Everything was reduced to ash. Gone." A small moan of anguish came from Sarah as her eyes widened. Lincoln could see the shimmer of tears gathering as she put down her pen and closed her eyes. *Abby, this is so unfair,* Sarah thought.

Lincoln bowed his head in silence, unsure of what to say next. "I think most of it's starting to hit home with her now. She's been more concerned about you and your well being than her own. But I'll give her credit; she's managed to keep your identity a secret. No one in the department has put your name to the name on the articles. She even has you booked into the hospital as McMurphy."

Sarah opened her eyes and the tears that had been welling up flowed down her face. Lincoln reached over, pulled a tissue from a box and handed it to her. She gently dabbed her black eyes but it made no difference to the misery on her face.

"Sarah?" Lincoln questioned softly.

She opened her eyes and reached for the pen. *Didn't write the articles.*

"I don't think she ever believed you did. And I can honestly say I don't believe you wrote them either."

But I lied to her, Sarah wrote.

"Sarah, she understands. You thought you were doing your job. She knows that better than anyone."

But I didn't write, Lincoln didn't even let her finish. He reached over and stopped her hand in mid stroke.

"It's not an issue, Sarah, believe me. I think it's the furthest thing from her mind."

Sarah lay still for a long quiet moment and Lincoln wondered what was going on inside her head. He was sure she was thinking about Abby—he could see it in her eyes. Then those eyes closed and he considered leaving; she had to be tired. But Sarah picked up her pen and began to write again.

I hurt her. How do I make up for that? She wrote slowly on her board.

Lincoln looked at the words. "I think the best thing for you to do for her is to get better. Let Abby worry about Abby. She's pretty tough, you know. She can handle it."

Not as tough as you think, she wrote.

He noticed her writing was getting slower and her eyelids appeared to be getting heavier. "I know."

Tell her …

Lincoln patted her hand. "I know what to say. You rest now, and if you need anything—call me at home or on my cell." He pulled his wallet from his pocket and flipped through it. "We were told to make sure that you had …" Lincoln turned back to Sarah, but her eyes were closed and this time he knew she was asleep, "anything you wanted," he finished softly. He placed a card with his phone numbers on the bedside table and then he quietly tiptoed out of the room.

Holoman and Associates was still one of the most prestigious law firms in the city, even though its best attorney and namesake had all but retired years ago. Many high-powered defendants with shady connections had tried to get Nathan to represent them, but he had refused them all. It was well known before he retired that, when it came to the law, Nathan Holoman was brilliant, ruthless and, above all, selective about his clients. He cherished his name and his honor above all else.

His large corner office had remained his even though some of his young associates had salivated over the rich mahogany desk, the walls of law books, and the built-in bar across from the breath-taking view of the city below and the ocean beyond. But Nathan had refused to give up the room he had so loved. Many victories had been celebrated in this office, and he hoped that his niece's was going to be another.

Nathan had pulled out every file they had given him and spread them across the large table he had set up in the middle of the room. He was busy poring over the evidence files when his secretary buzzed him.

"Mr. Holoman—sorry to bother you—but there's a Lincoln Quinn here to see you."

"It's okay, Beth. Send him in." Nathan placed his thin reading glasses onto his head and stood up to greet his visitor.

Lincoln nodded his thanks to the secretary as he held out his hand to Nathan.

"Lincoln. Good to see you." The two shared a firm handshake before Nathan directed Lincoln to a chair.

"I have to say, I was a little surprised to get your call this afternoon, Nathan."

"I'm not going to beat around the bush here, Lincoln." Nathan unbuttoned one cuff and started to roll up his sleeve. "You handed in your badge this morning."

"I … ah, how the hell do you know that?" Lincoln stared at Nathan in disbelief. "I haven't told anyone. Shit, not even my wife knows yet."

"Look, I don't care why you quit—it's none of my business—but I wouldn't be who I am today if I didn't ask questions." Nathan sat down in his chair again. "That's if you're at liberty to say."

"Oh, I've got liberty to say. I think its bullshit what they're doing to Abby. They never even looked for another suspect. Then I find out this morning they're already warming up the gas chamber! It's crap, all of it."

Nathan observed the tall detective with interest as Lincoln let go of some of his anger. "She put how many years into that department and this is how they treat her? Yes, her life was consumed with trying to put Ward away, but for a reason. That son of a bitch was guilty and everyone knew it! But did anyone do anything about it? No! They sat on their hands and quoted the Bill of Rights after every body we found." Lincoln rose from his seat and paced the room. "Abby worked harder than anyone else to find the evidence that broke the case wide open and, when he got off, she felt like she had let everyone down: the victims, their families, the police department—everyone. You should've been here, Nate. It would have torn out your heart to see what she put herself through after that." Lincoln's anger petered out and his voice returned to normal.

"I wish I had been there, but she didn't call me. Actually, before this, we haven't had much contact over the years—by her choice, not mine. I look after the family's assets and keep an eye on the numbers, but that's about it." Nate rose to his feet and walked over to his bar. "Can I offer you a drink, Lincoln?"

"No, I shouldn't, I'm … what the hell, I'm no longer on duty, am I? Scotch, if you have it."

"I only have the best," Nate said as he poured Lincoln a glass.

"You know, most people would never guess that the two of you are related," Lincoln said as he accepted the glass offered to him. "But looking at you and knowing her, I see the family resemblance."

"It's in the eyes," Nate said with a broad smile. "They came from my father."

Looking down at the dark amber liquid in his glass, Lincoln seemed to pay little attention to Nate's philosophies. "So where's the name Holoman come from?"

Nathan had taken his drink over to his desk and had lifted a framed photograph up for a closer look. "Our mother remarried and I took my stepfather's name. I've missed him over the years, my brother, I mean. He was my best friend and his death was so tragic and such a shock. It was hard on all of us." Nate studied the photograph for a moment and then held it out to Lincoln.

As he took it, Lincoln watched the distinguished lawyer drain his glass in one gulp. *Another family trait*, he thought as he looked down at the picture. The black and white photograph was of a group of people standing around on a wooden dock. Squinting into the photo, Lincoln immediately recognized the scenery and a few of the people.

"This is Gold Creek … and that's Günter and Helga." He pointed to the younger looking Scandinavian couple.

"You know them?"

"Yes, Abby sent my wife and me to Gold Creek for our honeymoon. Of course, we didn't know she owned the place," he said as he looked back down at the picture.

"Don't blame her. That was my idea. Considering the circumstance and her age, I thought it better to keep her name and financial background under wraps. That picture was taken the summer they died." Lincoln noticed the gangly-looking black-haired girl standing off to one side.

Nathan grew quiet, but looked Lincoln in the eyes. "What do you know?"

"Just the basics. Her parents died in a boating accident and you sent her away. She doesn't talk about it."

"It all seems like a lifetime ago." Nathan turned his back on Lincoln and looked out the window behind his desk. "Abby was traumatized by the whole thing and she didn't speak for a long time after that. I sent her to the best doctors. They said she had post-traumatic stress disorder. It was a lot for a young girl to handle, so I did what I thought was best. I changed her name and sent her off to school. I thought it'd do her good to be away from all that would remind her of what had happened. I often wonder if that was the best thing for me to do."

"She didn't turn out all that bad, now did she?" Lincoln said with a hint of a smile.

Nathan paused before he answered. "Hmmm—let me see. She has a problem with authority, difficulty making any kind of commitment in a relationship, except with her dog. The only real friend she has is her partner, her temper is notorious and let's not forget the kicker—she's in jail on murder charges." Nathan came around from behind his high back leather chair and took a seat at his desk. "So, you tell me; did she turn out okay?"

"She's a good person, Nate."

"I know she is, but unfortunately all that matters from here on in is what I can get a jury to believe or not to believe. Reasonable doubt is all I need. And I'm going to need the best around me to keep her out of the gas chamber. Lincoln, how would you like to come and work for me?"

The question took Lincoln by surprise. "Work for you? I'm not a lawyer."

"No, but you'd make a great investigator."

"I, ah, I'm going to need some time to think about it. I mean, are you sure?"

"I wouldn't have made the offer if I wasn't," Nathan said firmly. "I'll double your salary."

"Nate, it's not the money I'm concerned about, though the offer is tantalizing."

"Then what's the problem?" Nathan was unaccustomed to being turned down.

"My name is at the top of the list for the prosecution. How will that look?"

"For starters, I'd think having you working for me on Abby's behalf would make Ronald de Barr look like an idiot."

A smile spread across Lincoln's face. "When do I start?"

CHAPTER 29

The hours dragged by without incident and without variation. The hands on Abby's watch barely moved as she continued to throw her small rubber ball against the wall. Her thoughts rambled between Sarah, and Lincoln. And, for the first time in years, she actually thought about her uncle, the tall well-dressed man who looked so much like her father.

She loved him, but when she was younger she had hated him. He had the same dark eyes and the same dark hair, but he wasn't her father. She recalled his face was so pale that far-off day as his soft voice tried desperately to help her understand what had happened. The explosion. The fire. The screaming. Nathan Holoman had powerful friends and he used each and every one of them when he collected his niece and flew her away from it all, away from the resort and away from the only life she had ever known.

It would be a long time before Abigail would speak of that day, and then it would only be to her doctors. He had changed her name, he had changed her surroundings, but no matter what he did, he couldn't change her memories—and he couldn't take away her pain.

The walls and the echoing silence that surrounded her reminded Abby of where she was now. She was no longer in the protection of her school; she was in prison, charged with murder in the first degree. A murder flawlessly planned and perfectly executed and it all pointed to her.

Looking down at the racquetball in her left hand, she repeatedly squeezed the soft rubber, working the dexterity back into her injured hand. Tighter and tighter she gripped, wallowing in the pain that made her feel alive.

After all these years, her memories still haunted her, gnawing at her until she could almost physically feel the pain of the past. And, adding to the remorse and responsibility for what had happened then, was the guilt over what had happened to Sarah. *How can I ever face you?*

The hours in solitude made the days crawl. Her mind played to her guilt as the pain of reality drew her farther and farther into depression. Everything was gone, and every time she thought about Sarah, an overwhelming sense of remorse engulfed her. Whether or not Sarah had been *that* reporter no longer seemed to be important; it didn't matter in the grander scheme of her life. What did matter was that she loved Sarah. But because of her, Sarah's life would never be the same. She wondered with each passing hour how she would be able to live with that.

Lincoln was sitting at his table writing on a large yellow note pad when the phone rang.

"Hello," he answered.

"Lincoln, its Lieutenant Banks," the female voice identified herself.

"Lieutenant?"

"We need to talk, but not at the station. Do you know the underground parking lot on 34th and Washington?"

"Yeah," he said slowly.

"Meet me there in half an hour, just you and me."

"But what … why?"

"Lincoln, just meet me there—and don't say a word to anyone."

The sharp knock on his door took Nathan by surprise. He wasn't aware of anyone else in the building.

"Nate?" The door opened slightly and Lincoln stuck his head in.

"Lincoln," Nathan said in surprise. "Why so early?"

"I've got something," Lincoln said as he stepped into the office, carrying a large manila envelope.

"What's that?" The lawyer's tone changed to match the seriousness of Lincoln's.

"Information we both need to look at." He crossed the room and held out the envelope for Nathan. The lawyer took it and looked inside before he dumped the contents on his desk. Several papers came out along with a videocassette.

"What is this?" he asked as he picked up some of the papers. "Where'd you get this?"

"I can't say," Lincoln answered. "I didn't take it. It was given to me by a friend."

"A friend in the department. I won't ask," Nathan commented as he picked up the videotape.

"Yes, that might be a good idea." Lincoln took a seat. His heart was racing, as it had been all morning, and it was only ten minutes to seven.

"What's on this?" Nathan asked as he walked over and opened a cabinet to reveal a TV and a VCR.

"I haven't seen it, but it's supposed to be from an ATM camera that's positioned across the street from the Hasty Motel."

Nathan stopped at the mention of the motel where Billy Ward had been tortured and mortally wounded. "How reliable is your source?"

"Very," Lincoln answered somberly.

Nathan said nothing as he pushed the cartridge into the VCR and then turned on the TV. Within seconds, the screen came up with a grainy black and white picture. The dim light made it difficult to see, but the entrance to the hotel across the street from the camera was clear to see. Down in the corner of the screen, the date and time clicked past in seconds. It read 10:17pm.

In stop-action imagery, a Jeep turned into the Hasty Motel. It sat in the parking lot for a moment with its lights on and wipers going, but no one got out. Then the headlights went off and a figure emerged from the vehicle, the collar of their jacket pulled up against the rain. Raising the remote, Nate froze the screen with a clear view of the person standing next to the Jeep.

Nate walked up closer to the TV screen, "It's her, isn't it?" he asked without turning around.

Lincoln stared at the indistinct black and white image and said nothing.

CHAPTER 30

"Sarah?" a voice said.

Sarah opened her eyes and looked around the brightly lit hospital room, until her gaze fell on a white-haired doctor standing at the foot of her bed.

"Sarah McMurphy?" he asked with a smile. She reached for her dry erase board but then decided not to bring attention to her correct name. Abby's influence and Lincoln's presence had kept the reporters and the questions at bay, and for now that was okay with her.

"Hello, my name is Doctor Greene."

She started to say something, but the doctor held up his finger. "No, no, stick to writing for a while longer. No sense putting any strain on that throat yet. Now, can I take a closer look here?" He gestured towards her left hand. "Can you move your hand?" Sarah looked down, lifted her hand and wiggled her fingers.

"Very good," he said as he noticed the slight dip in her wrist. "Touch your thumb to all four fingers?" Once more she looked down and slowly touched her thumb to her first finger, her second finger, her third finger, and finally her pinky finger.

"Excellent. Now do it with your eyes closed?" He watched her reaction and knew she couldn't. "It's okay, dear, let me take a look." Dr. Greene picked up her hand and ran his pen down the inside of her forearm. "Can you feel that?" Sarah answered with a slight nod.

Holding the tips of her fingers, he ran his pen down her thumb and along her arm. "Can you feel that?" The fear in her eyes told him the answer.

"It's okay, that's normal for your type of injury. See, when you were attacked, the knife cut through some of the nerve roots at C6 as well as the SCM, or rather the sternocleidomastoid muscle and ... well, never mind all the technical jargon. The bottom line is that with therapy, it'll improve. I promise," he said with a reassuring wink.

Sarah reached for her board and wrote, *100%?*

"One step at a time, dear," Dr. Greene said, but that didn't satisfy Sarah and she tapped her board again.

"There's a lot of damage done inside there, Sarah, and unfortunately soft tissue injuries and nerve damage take time."

Her green eyes were rimmed with dark bruises, which made her glare all the more ominous as she tapped her board hard once.

"I see you've a bit of a stubborn streak. Sarah, I can't give you an answer because I don't have an answer."

She watched him for a moment longer as if deciding whether or not he had spoken the truth before she finally put down her board.

"Now, let's take a good look at that pretty young face of yours."

Dr Greene reached over and turned on a lamp. The light was intense and it caused her to squint. "You can close your eyes, dear, if the light is too bright for you. Okay … hmmm …" Sarah listened to him hum and ha as he closely examined her face. His touch was gentle as he palpated her broken cheekbone and her nose.

"You can open your eyes now," he said as he clicked off the bright lamp. When she opened her eyes, he could see almost every question and concern she had.

"Rest assured, my dear child, there's nothing here I cannot fix, but …" he held up his finger, "you have to be willing to meet me half way. Meaning, you need to do your therapy – both the physical and psychological – religiously." Dr. Greene picked up her hand. "You've been through a lot and you still have some long hard days ahead of you."

Sarah looked down at his soft hands, the hands that would make her whole again.

"Now, is there anything you need?"

She picked up her board and wrote one, pressing word: *MIRROR*.

"Not yet, my dear." The moment he said the words Sarah underlined the word several times.

"Another day or two will make a big difference."

Sarah dropped her board onto her bed and threw back her sheets. If they weren't going to get her a mirror, then she was going to go and find one.

"No, no. You need to stay in bed." Dr. Greene said quickly, but Sarah ignored his pleas and swung her legs off the bed. "Sarah, remember what I said about meeting me half way. You're not ready." She stopped. Seeing her face pale, he lifted her legs and placed them back under the sheets. "Rule number one; listen to your doctor."

Lying back against her pillow, Sarah closed her eyes as waves of nausea swept over her. She couldn't believe that little movement had not only made her dizzy, but had left her shaking as well.

"This will relax you," he said as he injected a syringe into her IV. "Sarah, I know you're scared. You've every reason to be, but this is all normal." His smile had returned and that did make her feel better. "I know you want to look in a mirror, but it'll be better if you wait. Right now, your face is still swollen. The cuts and scrapes are still very promi nent and that's all you'll see. Give it a little more time and then you'll be able to recognize the woman in the mirror."

Sarah knew his words to be true, but she still felt an overwhelming need to see for herself.

CHAPTER 31

By lunchtime, Lincoln had verified the presence of the camera at the ATM machine across from the Hasty Motel. He drew a quick sketch of the scene and marked off the distances in his notebook. He looked from the bank across the street to the parking space where Abby had left her Jeep to the orange sticker taped to the motel room door.

What the hell were you doing here, Abby? The question hung in Lincoln's mind as he made his way over to the motel room window. Peering in, he cupped his hands around his eyes to see into the dark room. The room was messy, which was odd, because every other place of Ward's had been meticulously laid out and spotless. Lincoln could still see fingerprint dust everywhere and several large dark stains on the yellow shag carpet.

"Hey, get away from that window," a female voice screeched at him. Lincoln spun around to face a short and very round older woman, with a cigarette hanging out of her lipstick-painted mouth. Her flaming red hair obviously hadn't been combed since the invention of the brush.

"I was just looking," Lincoln said honestly.

"Well, you shouldn't be. That's been taped off by the cops," she said, the ashes falling off the end of her cigarette as she chomped on her gum.

He walked toward her, wiping the dust off his hands. "By the cops, huh? What happened here?"

"Some female cop hacked up some guy with a steak knife. Made a hell of a mess of the place, too." She gave Lincoln the once over and obviously liked what she saw. "Are you looking for a room, honey? I can get ya a room, especially if you don't mind sharing, if you know what I mean."

It took everything he had not to cringe visibly at the invitation. "No—thanks."

"Well, if I can be of *any* service, I'm the manager here. So anything you want, you just give ol' Dot a holler. That's me, Dot," she said as she pointed at her chest. Her pudgy finger disappeared into the thin polyester blouse covering her enormous breasts.

Lincoln nodded and smiled. "Did you know the guy?" he asked as an afterthought.

"Yeah. He was that slime from the papers. You know, Billy Ward, the one they called the Sadistic Slasher. Freaky, huh?" Dot fished around her shirt pocket for her smokes. "He was a weird little one, that's for sure. Kinda creepy and sleazy."

"Why do you say that?" Lincoln asked as he crossed his arms.

Dot lit her cigarette and took a long drag on it as she eyed him. "You a cop?"

"Who me?" He laughed and answered her honestly, "No."

"Reporter?"

"No, just a man with a morbid curiosity. I was at my bank across the street and … well, you know."

"Too bad, I was hoping to make a few bucks out of it." She watched and waited, but the handsome black man in the suit didn't bite.

"Sorry," he said with a shrug of his shoulders.

"Ah, that's all right," she said with a wave of her hand. "I was just hoping to make enough money to pay his last month's rent. Owner's gonna get mad at me 'cause of this. It's gonna cost a fortune to have that place cleaned and the carpets replaced."

Lincoln was wondering how expensive yellow shag carpet could be when her comment jiggled something in his head. "His last month's rent?"

"Yeah, Wacko Willie hadn't paid this month's rent."

"Wacko Willie?"

"That's what all the regulars called him, Wacko Willie."

"Really? Just how long had Wacko Willie been staying here?"

"Let me think, a good three, four months anyhow," she said as she looked at the sky to count the days. "Yeah, that's about right … four months."

"Did you tell anyone else this?"

Dot eyed him suspiciously. "If you're not a cop, then you're a private dick?"

Lincoln quickly weighed his options and decided the truth might get him farther. "All right, you got me. I'm new at this," he said, hoping to snow her just a little. "I just got my investigator's license and I'm trying to impress my new boss."

"Well, why didn't you say so, honey? I'd love to help you out. Between you and me, I think he had it coming; he was a real strange one."

"Between you and me, she didn't do it. So why do you say he was a strange one?"

"Whatever, I'm sure she had her reasons," Dot said as she looked patiently over at Lincoln. "I can't quite remember what we thought was strange, but I know it was strange."

Lincoln turned his back, pulled out his wallet and removed two bills from it, then returned his wallet to his pocket before he turned back to her.

"Will this help your memory?" he asked, waving the two bills in front of her.

"Not only will it help it, it'll rewrite it honey. Just tell me what you need and that's what I'll remember," she said with a wide smile as she reached for the money.

Lincoln pulled it from her reach, "That's not what I need, Dot. I need the truth. Do you even remember the truth?"

"Of course I do," she said in a hurt tone. "He kept strange hours, like he never worked."

"He didn't work, that isn't strange," Lincoln said disappointedly.

"Okay, how about the fact that he never took anything in or out of his room?" Dot looked at Lincoln for a response, but he had no idea what to say. "Nothing. Not laundry, not garbage. Nothing in or out," Dot listed the items off on her fingers as Lincoln's brow furrowed with each item. "We never once saw him bring in any groceries, no food, nothing, nada … not even a pizza box. What do you make of that, Mister Investigator Man?"

"That's strange," Lincoln said as he walked over to the window again. Though his vision was limited, he still couldn't see any sign of anything personal. Dot was right, there was no sign of clothing or evidence of food.

"Did he ever have any visitors?" he asked as he returned to where Dot was standing.

"Nope, well, other than that police woman."

"So you saw her here?"

"Saw her? Heard her! Christ, half the complex heard her kick in the door."

"Did you tell the detectives that?" He could see that the door had been forced open as he handed Dot her money.

"Nope," she said as she folded up the bills and then shoved them down deep into her visible cleavage. "They never asked."

Lincoln wheeled his car into the prison parking lot and cursed silently to himself for being late. Nate said to meet him there fifteen minutes ago and he hated to keep people waiting. He quickly signed in, attached his visitor's pass, and then hustled down the hallway toward the interview rooms.

"Sorry I'm late, Nate," he said as he opened the door. The lawyer lifted his head and waved off the apology.

"Don't worry about it. How did you make out?"

Lincoln quickly filled him in on his discussion with Dot, the manager, and the information he had obtained from the bank.

"How did you do with forensics?" Lincoln asked as he pulled out a chair to sit down.

Nathan never got a chance to answer because Abby, in her bright orange jumpsuit, shuffled past the window towards them.

"I hate to see her like this," Lincoln muttered, knowing by the look on Nate's face he wasn't the only one.

They could see the physical toll that prison was having on her, but it wasn't just in her appearance. It was also in the way she was holding herself. Her shoulders slumped and her feet shuffled. It was easy to see she just didn't care.

The guard escorted her to her chair and undid her cuffs. No one said a word as Abby settled herself and the guard left the room. As she glanced from one to the other, her instincts told her something was up. "So how are my two favorite men?"

Nathan motioned for Lincoln to start and he obliged. "Let's see. Concerned, confused, angry … where would you like me to start?"

Her features changed instantly. "What're you talking about?"

Nathan tossed out a still copy of the grainy black and white photo from the ATM camera. "This."

Abby reached for the picture and studied it before she flipped it back on the table. "I've no idea what this is!"

"This, my dear, is a still we got off a videotape. A tape the police retrieved from the ATM camera that was across from the Hasty Motel."

"And the significance of that is what?" She looked at them for answer. "It's not me."

"Isn't it? Would you like us to bring in the entire video tape?" Nathan snapped back at her.

"There are witnesses who will state you kicked in his door at around 10:30 the night he was murdered, and that's the motel where there was a camera across the street that took your picture coming and going on the very night you told me you were home in bed!" Lincoln uncharacteristically slammed his hand on the table.

"Abby?" Nathan said quietly. She didn't respond but he knew that she had heard him. Lincoln reached for his tie, yanked it loose, and then fumbled to unbutton his top button, as Abby pushed her chair back and dropped her head into her hands. "Abby, did you go and see him that night?"

"No."

Lincoln jumped to his feet so fast, his chair toppled over behind him.

"Abby, talk to me. Talk to us." There was no response. She sat silent and unmoving.

"Do you want me to leave so you can talk to your uncle?" Lincoln looked at Nathan for help but the older man was at a loss as well.

Lincoln crouched down next to her. "You've got to help us here, kiddo."

She finally lifted her head up and shook her hair off her pale face. Lincoln reached over and placed a hand on her forearm. "Abby, pictures don't lie."

"But I do, isn't that what you're implying?"

The intense stares from both of them were more than she could handle. "I didn't go and see him, all right?" Standing up, she walked over to the corner of the room and stood with her back to them. It was a long quiet moment before she turned to them and said. "I didn't. That …" She pointed to the picture on the table. "It's not me."

They looked from her dispirited face to the photo.

"If I can't get the two of you—one who knows me better than anyone and the other my only living relative—if I can't get the two of you to believe my innocence, then how in the hell am I going to convince a jury?"

Without saying a word, Lincoln picked up the picture for the hundredth time and studied the grainy image.

"The tape came from where?" she asked him.

"There's a bank across the street from the motel. It's from their ATM camera," Lincoln said.

"Could it be a fake?"

"No, the tape is real," Lincoln said before he turned to Abby, "After we saw the tape, I went to the bank and to the motel and both verified that someone fitting your description kicked in Ward's door at around 10:30."

"It may've been somebody but it sure as hell wasn't me."

"Then who?" Nathan asked but neither of them answered.

"Well, sitting in here my mind goes in directions it shouldn't. One minute I'm thinking the entire department is conspiring against me, and now some camera at a bank has a picture …" Abby stopped talking.

"What is it?" Lincoln said.

"What bank is it?" Her eyes searched the floor as her mind worked around a piece of information.

"It's a … Great Pacific Trust," Lincoln read off a stack of papers. "Why?"

"What bank does Frank Stempler work for?"

Everyone froze at the thought.

"Shit, I don't know. Hang on." Lincoln quickly flipped through his small notebook. "Son of a bitch." He looked at his partner. "Great Pacific Trust."

☯

They spent the hour going over points of the case, but Abby was only half listening. She would come and sit at the table, but after several minutes would get up and start pacing, only to stop and go back to leaning against the wall. She reminded Lincoln of a caged animal, unsure of what to do behind bars.

Several times Nathan and Lincoln exchanged glances over her lack of interest but said nothing. Finally Nate gave Lincoln a nod towards the door and the investigator quickly understood.

"Nate, I need a break here," Lincoln stood up. "Anyone want a coffee or anything?"

"Yeah, sure," Nate said.

"Abby?"

"Huh?" She looked up from the table.

"I'm going for coffee, you want anything?" He waited for her usual snippy comeback, but there wasn't one.

"Coffee would be nice, please."

Nate waited for the door to close and for the room to still before he put down his glasses and looked at his niece.

"Talk to me," he said, meaning as an uncle and not as a lawyer.

Abby looked up in surprise. "About what?"

"I'm here to defend you on a first degree murder case and you seem more interested in the finish on the table than in what Lincoln and I are discussing."

She looked at her uncle but said nothing.

"For the love of God, child, are you even listening to me? We're it; we're the only family left. But if you don't start giving us some answers, I'll be the only one left. Get your head in the game, Abby!"

"It is," she responded but not in the way he wanted. Nate was looking for her to fight, to stand up and yell back, but she didn't.

"I don't think it is. I think you're ready to give up." Nathan reached over and closed his briefcase as if to emphasis his point.

"Give up—is that what you think? That I've given up?" She fired back at him. "How the hell can I give up—I've nothing left *to* give up!" Nate wanted a reaction and he was finally getting one. "Everything I had is gone! My job, my reputation, everything I owned! He burnt down my house, he killed my dog, and he even tried to kill …" Her voice cracked and she quickly stood up from the table, unable to finish.

Nathan followed her and placed a hand on her arm. "Yes, Abby, he tried, but he failed. Sarah is alive."

"She almost died because of me."

"Not because of you, because of Billy. Because of you, she's still alive," Nathan tried to remind her, but Abby's mind was on a different track.

"Maybe it's better this way. If she stays away from me, maybe she can put all this behind her and try to forget the whole thing happened," Abby said, her voice dripping with self-pity.

"I don't think that's the case here." Nathan's voice was soothing and calm, a sharp contrast to the erratic emotions displayed by Abby. "That is the furthest thing from her mind. Sarah is not going to forget what happened and she certainly isn't going to forget you."

"If she was smart she would. What he did to her because of me …" Abby couldn't finish the statement.

"What he has done in the past, he can never do again," Nate said. "That alone should ease your mind."

"Ease my … I'm in jail for his murder!" Abby's head snapped around, her dark eyes black with fury. "Ease my mind! What the hell do you know about easing my mind? Your answer to everything is just to pack up and move it. Forget about the consequences, to hell with your responsibilities. Just get away and let someone else pick up the pieces."

"Abby that's not fair," Nathan fired back, his own temper rising. "This has nothing to do with the past. I did what I thought was best."

"Nothing to do with the past! Are you fucking kidding me …" Her voice rose as she struggled with her words.

"I'm sorry about what happened; but there was nothing more I could do."

"I know, Nate, I've heard all of this before and its bullshit. There was a lot you could have fuckin' done, but you didn't. Instead, you picked me up, you shipped me off, and then you left me to deal with it all by myself. By myself! How old was I? I didn't know what to do. I just did what the doctors told me to do, and look where it left me!"

"You can't put all of that on my shoulders, Abby," Nate argued.

"Can't I? Why not? Maybe it's time for the world to know what happened!" she shouted.

"What happened then has nothing to do with this now." His voice had become as loud as hers.

"I was a child!"

"And I did what I thought was best!"

"*You* ran away …"

"And you think there's something I can do to change it now? Goddamn it, Abby—be reasonable!"

"I can't. My entire fucking life is now being played out in the press. I don't see your name in there anywhere!"

Coming down the hall, Lincoln heard their voices at the same time the guard on duty did. Looking through the window, they heard Abby holler something at Nathan, then pick up one of the chairs and toss it against the back wall. The noise sent Lincoln and the guard rushing into the room just as Nathan slapped Abby across the face. She instantly retaliated with the back of her hand to her uncle's nose. The room erupted into chaos. The guard went after Abby as Lincoln called out to her, but her angry eyes were locked on her uncle's and she didn't see the guard until he grabbed her and slammed her up against the wall. Instinct sent Lincoln to her defense, but Nathan held him back. Without thinking, Abby reacted, driving her elbow into the guard's nose just as his backup came through the door.

"Abby, don't fight them! Abby!" Lincoln yelled as three guards took her to the floor. Lincoln tried to take another step forward, but Nathan pulled him back out of the way. The lawyer knew how desperately Lincoln wanted to help his partner, but he also knew they couldn't get involved. Lincoln looked at Nathan, who appeared to be as frustrated and upset as Abby and Lincoln combined.

"Abby, please … don't. Just go with them," Nathan pleaded with his niece as he watched her struggling with the guard.

"Abby, stop!" Lincoln's command finally got through to her and she stopped resisting. Her lip was split and her nose was bloodied. She glared at her uncle while she was shackled. Neither of them said a word until Abby pulled her focus from Nathan and turned it to Lincoln. "Get me another lawyer," she snarled to Lincoln as she spat a mouthful of blood to the ground.

"That's enough out of you, Stanfield," one of the guards said as they hauled her from the room. Lincoln attempted to follow, but was stopped by the guard with the bleeding nose.

Lincoln stood helplessly in the doorway and watched them drag her down the hall. He turned his attention to Nathan, who was sitting at the table with his head in his hands.

"What the hell was that about?" Lincoln demanded as he noted the rising welt across Nathan's cheek. "You realize they're going to toss her into solitary?" Lincoln said as he threw up his hands.

"Calm down, Lincoln, they're not going to throw her into solitary confinement."

"You want to bet? She hit a guard, Nate, they're not going to invite her for tea. Shit!" Lincoln put his hands on his hips. "Care to tell me what started this?" Lincoln asked as he knelt down to collect the scattered papers.

Nathan said nothing. The silence between them was broken when Lincoln's cell phone rang in his pocket.

"You're not supposed to have that in here," Nathan said.

Lincoln ignored him. "Quinn," he answered curtly. "Yes, what? Right now. No, tell her to calm down, we'll be right there." He flipped his phone closed. "The cops are at the hospital to see Sarah."

"You go; I'll be right behind you. I need to settle a few things here before I can leave. Just don't let her say anything until I get there," Nate said as he quickly scooped up papers.

"Why don't I stay and you go? She needs a lawyer," Lincoln said in surprise.

"You're capable and you think like a cop, so you know what they're after. I can't leave here until I know Abby is going to be okay."

☯

Lincoln rode up the elevator, looking at his fuzzy reflection in the doors. He straightened his tie and patted down his hair. *What a day*, he thought as the elevator doors opened. Stepping from the elevator, he spotted Detectives Webber and Ames standing in conversation with a nurse just outside Sarah's door. None of them saw him as he approached them.

"I don't care who you are, her doctor stated that you're not to see her." Lincoln recognized the nurse, but he didn't know her name.

"You can't stop us," Webber said, about to push past the nurse.

"I'm sorry, officers," she said, blocking their path.

"You heard her, guys. If the doc says 'no go', then you 'no go' near her," Lincoln said stepping in front of Sarah's door.

"Quinn, what are you doing here?" Ames said in surprise as the nurse left in search of one of Sarah's doctors.

"I now work for the lawyer representing Miss Murphy and he has advised his client not to talk to you until he's present *and* her doctor has okayed it."

"Miss Murphy, huh?" Webber reached into his pocket and pulled out his notebook. "Thanks, Quinn, that pretty much tells us that she *is* the reporter who leaked the story."

Lincoln's features didn't change even though he was swearing at himself inside.

"Funny, she's registered under the name McMurphy. I wonder why that is? She isn't hiding anything is she?"

"No," Lincoln answered with an icy stare.

"Then why's she here under Sarah McMurphy?" Webber said, trying to taunt Lincoln.

"She's not hiding. In all the confusion it was just never corrected," he answered calmly, refusing to jump at the bait.

"Which is it then, Quinn, Murphy or McMurphy?"

Lincoln had walked right into their trap and he knew it. If he lied now, they could nail him with obstruction. He looked at Detective Ames but he knew there was little the rookie could do.

"So Abby was the leak after all," Webber said triumphantly.

"How the hell do you figure that?" Lincoln said in disbelief.

"Abby *was* sleeping with her. We're busting our asses trying to clean up the Ward mess you two left for us while she's spilling her guts to a little split-tail reporter."

Webber kept pushing, taunting Lincoln, but Abby's partner didn't have her temper. He knew what Webber was trying to do and he did not intend to play his game. Lincoln would have loved to carry on the conversation, but he saw the nurse coming down the hallway with a very annoyed looking Dr. Marcot.

"Officers," the doctor said in a disapproving tone, "there seems to be some confusion here." He looked from Webber to Ames. "I think you've forgotten you're in a hospital, not a police station. A hospital is for sick people, and when they are sick, they are *my* responsibility. My understanding is that you've already been informed that Miss McMurphy is not up to visitors yet, and that," he pointed his finger at Detective Webber, "includes you!"

"Actually, doctor, I believe the confusion is on your part, because the lady in there isn't Sarah McMurphy, but rather Sarah Murphy, and she is a very important witness in our ..."

"Detective, I don't care if that is Sarah the Duchess of York in there. Her name isn't my problem, her health is! When she's ready for visitors, I'll have someone contact your boss. Until then, get out." Dr. Marcot pointed to the elevators.

Webber said nothing but there was a long pause before he turned and left with Detective Ames.

Dr. Marcot offered his hand to Lincoln. "I'm sorry to rush off but I'm needed downstairs. If you'll excuse me, Robin is in with Sarah and she'll fill you in."

Confused by the doctor's comment, Lincoln pushed open Sarah's door to see Robin sitting quietly with her.

Robin rose to meet him at the door. "Lincoln," she said in relief.

Lincoln looked over the nurse's shoulder at Sarah. "Is Sarah all right?"

"She's under heavy sedation again," Robin said.

"Why, what happened?"

"She got out of bed this afternoon."

"What's wrong with that? I'd think that'd be a good thing." he said.

"She got to the bathroom by herself and looked in the mirror. She wasn't ready for that, at least not that way and not by herself. We had no choice but to sedate her."

Lincoln sighed. "So now what?"

"She had taken three steps forward but now, unfortunately, she's taken four steps back," the nurse said with regret. "The psychological effect could be devastating, especially on one who was so pretty and so young."

Lincoln moved closer to Sarah and a large flower arrangement caught his attention.

"They're from your boss," said Robin.

"Nate?"

"No," Robin shook her head. "Lieutenant Banks. She was here to see Sarah."

"Well, I'll be." Lincoln suddenly felt small for some of the comments he had made to his lieutenant and some of the thoughts he had kept to himself.

"How is Sarah now?" he asked Robin.

"Out like a light for now. She should sleep 'til morning," Robin said. "Medically she is healing quite well, all things considered."

Lincoln looked down at Sarah and he had to agree. The swelling was starting to subside, and the colors around her eyes weren't as vivid. The thick bandage that had been around her neck since he had met her had been replaced by a large dressing on just one side of her neck. Unfortunately, her head now tilted slightly to the side and the corner of her mouth had a sad droop to it, but he could still see the beauty beyond the wounds.

"She does look better," he said quietly.

"That's because we saw her at her worse. Sarah on the other hand, only knows what she looked like before the attack."

"Now what?"

"Abby's paying for the best, Lincoln, but it's in Sarah's hands now. We'll know more when she wakes up."

Lincoln sighed deeply as he thought about the day that both Sarah and Abby had been through.

"You okay?" Robin asked him when she saw his features twist and change.

"It seems so simple, but there's nothing I can do. I run back and forth between them, knowing that what they both need is each other." Reluctantly Lincoln followed Robin out of the room. He looked down at his watch. It was getting late. "Robin," Lincoln paused. "How do I help her?"

"I can't answer that, Lincoln, I'm not a doctor."

"I know that, Robin, but sometimes the soldiers know more than the generals."

She thought about the question. "She's alone right now, Lincoln, and she needs someone to tell her it's going to be okay."

CHAPTER 32

On shaking unsteady legs, Sarah made her way across the fluffy clouds of gray and white. Each step was a struggle, a challenge to make it to her final destination, which was an oasis in the distance: a palm tree leaning over a small, still pond, framed by white billowy clouds and vivid green grass. The shimmering haze of her sedative made her surroundings soft and blurry and she could barely make out the light in the distance. A light that would shine on the shadows of the secrets they had kept from her.

The fluffy clouds became painted white walls, as her hand reached out for support against the bathroom door. The metal handle felt cold as she pushed it down and opened the door. There it was; the oasis she had been looking for. She shuffled into the bathroom and placed her hands on the counter.

One deep breath cleared her mind, two deep breaths gave her nerve, and, on the third breath, she closed her eyes and turned on the bathroom light.

An image from the shadows appeared in the mirror in front of her, the broken mirror, *she thought. She gazed unmoving into familiar green eyes, but they were all she recognized. The green was vivid next to the bright red blood inside her eyes. The cracks in the mirror distorted the face she had once known so well, the face she had known all her life.*

Not my face. My face doesn't have cracks in it, *she thought. But it* was *her face, with purple and brown bruises that looked like depressed shadows. Her high left cheekbone was now sunken from sight, and muscle and nerve damage pulled down the corner of her mouth. One crack of the mirror fell across the bridge of her nose and then appeared to grow wider and deeper as it meandered down her cheek, to the edge of her jaw.*

My jaw … not *my* jaw. *She tried to open her mouth but was unable to do so. Her mouth was sealed shut.*

Who is this person? This isn't me! *With an unsteady hand, she reached out to the broken image in the mirror. She got as far as she could reach, but she couldn't touch the distorted likeness she saw. Bringing her hand back, she looked down at her fingers before she brought them up to touch her face.*

These are my hands, my fingers, but this isn't my face. This is someone else, not me … not my face? *Then she felt the thick scabs surrounding the glue and stitches that crisscrossed over her skin. With an unsure touch, she fingered her lips and pushed on the droopy corner of her mouth. Then she noticed the bright white bandage across her throat. And it all came back.*

Oh my God, it is me. *The realization tore at her mind.* That is my face. That is me. It was him!

He wasn't an editor, he was a killer. And he drove his fist into her face, over and over again. He was Billy—Billy Ward—and he brought his hand back once more, but this time it held a knife. Billy smiled at her as he slashed down at her throat.

"No!"

It wasn't a scream, it was more a stifled gurgle, but it woke Lincoln with such a start he forgot for a moment where he was.

"Son of a bitch," Lincoln muttered as he clambered out of his chair to be at Sarah's side. She was sitting up in bed, her eyes wide with fear as she tried to scream away her demons. Her voice was raw and hoarse as her small body shook with tremors of hysteria.

"Sarah," he said soothingly as he reached out for her but she quickly turned away. Ignoring her protests, he wrapped his arms around her and held her tightly. Her barely audible cries of fear ceased as she gasped for breath.

"Shhh, you're okay, Sarah, it's all over," he repeated. Very faintly he thought he heard her whisper, "No."

"I'm not going to let you go," he said. And he didn't.

After a long silence, Lincoln reached for the light over the bed, thinking Sarah was asleep.

The moment the florescent light started to hum, her haggard voice pleaded through her wired jaw. "No, please, off." She buried her head in Lincoln's chest even after he shut off the light.

In the dim gray of the room, he held her and said nothing as he rocked back and forth. He had no idea of the time, or of how long they stayed like that, but it didn't matter. She eventually stopped crying and, as his own eyes drooped, Lincoln realized she had finally stopped shaking.

Sometime in the early morning hours, the shadows in the room faded as the sun rose outside. Lincoln knew he had dozed off, but he still held Sarah in his arms and was fearful to move. He did his best to stretch out the stiffness in his body and as he turned he saw her eyes were open.

"Good morning." He was met with silence.

"How about some water? It'll feel good on your throat." He reached for her cup of ice chips, but when he offered it to her, she pulled her face away.

"Come on, take a sip," he said, but she continued to refuse, so he returned the cup to the nightstand.

The few words she had spoken had hurt her more than physically. It was painful to speak, but even more painful to listen. She could hear the difference in her voice and she didn't like what she could hear. So if she never spoke again, if she never looked in another mirror, then she could pretend it had never happened.

It never happened, it was only a nightmare, was all she thought as she lay with her back to Lincoln.

"Sarah." So many things came to his mind, so many encouraging words, but they all sounded hollow. He reached out and gently started to rub her back. "Sarah, don't do this. Don't pull away; you're a fighter, a survivor."

There was no response and he felt helplessly frustrated as he tried desperately to reach her. "When you were brought in here, you were so weak and had lost so much blood. Abby held you until they took you for surgery." Lincoln saw her eyes searching the wall at the mention of Abby's name.

"She was here by your side for every moment, until they forced her to go home." Lincoln stopped when he thought about that night—the night Ward was murdered. *How different our lives would be if Abby had stayed here.*

"Sarah, she'd be here now if she could, but she can't," he pleaded. "Come on, Sarah, look at me, talk to me."

Without a word, she reached down on the bed and struggled to pick up her notepad with her bad hand. Finally she reached for it with her other hand. She tore the page off, and handed it to him.

Lincoln hesitated a moment before he took the offered paper, and then read the words written by a shaking hand.

You can clip an eagle's wings, but you cannot strip its pride,
For its spirit will soar, beyond the mountains tall and wide.
I can't offer you your freedom, but I can remind you of our time,
To give you love inside your heart and peace inside your mind.
Trust is what I ask from you for I cannot be there to say,
To tell you that I love you and I do so more each day.

"Prophetic words, Sarah; for Abby, or for you?"

"When … you leave … give it … to Abby." Her words were slow and forced, and barely more than a hoarse whisper.

"I'm not leaving. Not until you look me in the face and tell me to go," he said daringly. "I know you think things are bad right now, but they've improved so much already. They're only going to get better." He looked down at her left hand as she flexed and relaxed her fist. "Give yourself time to heal and mend. What you saw …"

"Was horrendous," she finished for him.

"It only looks bad because you still have stitches. When Dr. Greene is …"

"Lea—ve." Her rough and gravelly voice broke under the strain of her demand.

Lincoln's shoulders sagged in defeat. "All right, all right, I'm leaving." He got off the bed, folded up the poem for Abby and put it in his pocket.

"I'll be back later." But there was no response.

☯

Lincoln was hard at work in his small office, his face buried in the medical examiner's report, when there was a knock on the door.

"You're going to make me look bad, coming in before me," Nate said as he stood in the doorway, but the look on Lincoln's face stemmed his teasing. "Long night or did you find something?"

"Both," Lincoln said with a sigh as he leaned back in his chair.

"Talk to me." Nathan came in and closed the door behind him.

"I'm torn, Nate. I need to be working on Abby's case," he said.

"You don't have to be in the office, Lincoln. If the work's out in the field, then that's where you should be."

"That isn't it. It was leaving the hospital this morning, leaving Sarah alone like that." He sat up and ran his fingers through his short-cropped hair.

"How's she doing?"

"Not very good." Lincoln looked at Nathan. "How's Abby doing?"

"I'd have to say not much better." Nathan responded. "So tell me, what can I do to help? What does Sarah need?"

"I wish I knew. She's speaking now, but so far she hasn't said much more than *leave* and *get out*. She's not eating, she's not sleeping—sound familiar?"

Nathan reluctantly nodded.

"And I know Webber will be coming back, but I don't honestly think there's anything for Sarah to tell him. Thankfully, the doctor's more concerned about Sarah's health than about her talking to that ass. The poor kid is alone in that hospital."

The words echoed in Nathan's memory and it caused him to pause, but only for a moment. "Tell you what, I'll look after Sarah today and you look after my niece's well-being."

"I'm not sure how Sarah will react to another stranger," Lincoln said honestly.

"We're not strangers; I met her father once," Nathan revealed. "He's a real piece of work, a self-centered pompous ass if you ask me. From what you and Abby have told me about Sarah's relationship with her parents, it doesn't surprise me that they've abandoned their own child. Leave her to me." He stood up and grabbed the door handle. "Did you find something in the ME's report?"

"Yeah," Lincoln said as he shifted through the files on his desk. "Ward's hands were bound with plastic zip-ties." He looked up at Nathan. "You know what they are?"

"Yes, they're what electricians and mechanics use to secure wires together and sometimes the cops use them as handcuffs."

"That's right. But what's strange is that from the position of the nodular ends, his hands were bound together when they were in front of him, not behind him."

Nathan paused for a moment. "He was found with his hands tied behind him?"

"Ah-huh," Lincoln lifted several papers, searching for something else. "And there was Demerol in his blood stream as well as cocaine and morphine—loads of it."

"So he was higher than a kite when he died." Nathan's brow pulled into a familiar crease. Lincoln caught the expression; it reminded him of his partner.

"Yeah, he would've been flying all right. He probably didn't feel a thing."

"I don't know, I think any man getting his dick cut off would feel it no matter how high he was."

"True," Lincoln said in agreement.

"Well, keep on it, Linc, there might be something there," Nathan said as he opened the door. "In the meantime, I'll phone Mary and see if she can call off Webber."

It had been a long time since Nathan had been in a hospital; the last one he was in looked nothing like this. He stopped at the nurses' desk and introduced himself. "How is our little patient?"

"Not much to tell. She hasn't spoken to a soul since Lincoln left. Her IV has been taken out, but unless she starts to drink something, it'll have to go back in," a nurse said.

"And her voice?" Nathan asked.

"The doctor doesn't think there is any permanent damage but time will tell. The biggest problem we're having besides her not eating is that she doesn't want to see anyone or be seen by anyone. It's actually quite normal with an injury like hers, but still. Dr. Greene is due here soon and I'm hoping she'll talk to him."

"And if she doesn't?"

"She's going to have to deal with nurses and doctors sooner or later. Unfortunately, we don't have the time or manpower to coddle every patient. She's already getting special treatment but we have to draw the line somewhere."

Nathan looked at the head nurse. "So what are her options?"

"Sarah's going to need special care and attention. This isn't a private hospital, Mr. Holoman. We just don't have the resources to give her the care she needs or deserves."

"Understood," Nathan said. "Can I see her?"

"Sure, that's her door over there. She prefers the lights to be left off, and don't expect any conversation, pleasant or otherwise. Just duck if she throws anything."

"Got it," he said as he headed towards Sarah's room.

Nathan stopped just outside her door. He could face almost anyone and anything, but there was something about young women in hospital rooms that completely unnerved him. But this time it was different. At least that was what he kept telling himself as he entered the room.

There was no light on but he could see her petite outline in the bed. If she heard him or the opening door, she didn't make it known. His mouth got very dry; he tried to blame the hospital air, but he knew it was more than that.

"Sarah," Nathan said as he stopped just inside the door. He didn't want to cause her any alarm. "You don't know me. My name is Nathan Holoman." There was no response as he looked over the small figure lying so still, with her back to him.

With a sense of déjà vu, he thought about a much younger Abby. He had to remind himself this was Sarah, not Abby.

He walked over and pulled the one chair closer to the bed. He watched her back, but she made no movement or sound to show she had heard him.

"Sarah?" For the first time, he wondered if she was even awake. In the dim light of the room and with her back turned to him, it was impossible to tell if she was sleeping or not.

"The nurses are concerned about your not eating." He looked over at the selection of drinks on her tray that he was sure she hadn't touched. "You need to eat something or they're going to have to put your IV back in." There was no response, not even a grumble or a mumble.

"Sarah, I feel like I already know you." He kept his voice low and soft. "I know right now you feel lost and alone, but I assure you, you're not. Anything you want is yours; all you've to do is ask." Again he was met only with silence. Realizing it was fruitless to continue, he returned his chair to the small table and sat down. Pulling his laptop computer out of his briefcase, he started to work.

The sounds of a busy hospital could be heard just outside the door, but in the room the only noise was the soft clicking of Nathan's keyboard. It was an unlikely place for him to work, but he had learned long ago, you take what you're given and you do your best with it. Hours went by but he paid them little attention as he worked diligently on Abby's case.

Nathan's fingers froze above the keyboard. Had he imagined it or had he heard her speak? "Sarah?" he questioned softly and then held his breath to listen for a response.

"Go … away." The voice was weak and raspy, the words spoken between clenched teeth, but he understood.

"No, I don't think so."

He waited patiently and a long time passed before he heard her speak again. "Why are you here?"

"I'm here as your legal advisor, but I'm also here as your friend." He watched her back and waited, but she didn't move. "I'd like to be your friend, Sarah, I'd like to get to know you if you'll let me." There was a long pause, but he knew that she was listening and thinking.

"Why?" she croaked out the question.

"Why would I like to be your friend? Well, like I said earlier, I've heard so much about you—and since you're the woman who has captured my niece's heart, I thought I should get to know you."

"Niece." Nathan barely heard her throaty voice. "Abby's your niece?" Sarah turned just enough so she could get a look at him.

He offered his best smile and backed it up with a polite nod, "Yes, that headstrong woman is my niece."

"You're Uncle Nate." She whispered it in such a way that it was hard to tell if it was a question or a statement, or just the pain of trying to speak.

"Yes, my dear, but please don't let all the bad things she says about me sway your opinion."

"I thought you were dead," she said. She watched his expression with interest and then she rolled back over.

"Why doesn't that surprise me?" he said with the slightest of chuckles. "Well, at least she mentioned me to you, that's more than she does to most."

"How is she?"

Nathan took a moment before he answered. "I wish I could say she's doing well, but the truth of the matter is, she's not. People like Abby don't do well behind bars."

Sarah closed her eyes and her mind went to an image of Abby standing in the mountain meadow, the tall grass and her long black hair blowing in the breeze. Her dark eyes were relaxing in the afternoon sun and there was a teasing smile spread lazily over her lips. It seemed like a lifetime ago and Sarah felt the ache pull at her from different memories. She had loved Abby, but she had lied to her and now … now she never wanted to face her again.

Nathan was more than aware of the subtle change in the room. He could almost sense the despair and heartbreak radiating from the young woman lying so still in her bed. He stood up and walked over to her. "Sarah?"

He looked down at his hands, at the lines and the wrinkles that aged them, and he recalled another time. "I made a lot of mistakes with Abby when she was younger. I didn't know what to do." He paused for a moment and then wrung his hands together as if hoping to remove the guilt he carried. "I feel like I've been given a second chance with her, to maybe right some of the wrongs. If helping you through this time in any way helps her, then … then the truth of it is, it helps me."

He wasn't sure if Sarah was even listening, but in some ways it didn't matter. He said what needed to be said.

"I miss her," she said in a hoarse whisper.

Nathan reached out to touch her shoulder and then thought better of it. "She misses you too."

That was the end of their conversation and no matter what else Nathan said, there was no response from the bed. He tried to get her to talk but she wouldn't. He tried to get her to drink but she wouldn't. The nurses came and went and with each visit he could see their growing concern.

He had no idea how late in the day it was until Lincoln stuck his head in the door. "How's she doing?" he whispered.

Nathan closed up his laptop and motioned Lincoln into the room.

"She's not eating and she's not really talking," Nathan said in a low whisper. There had been little to no movement on the bed in quite a while and he was sure that she was asleep. "I now know what you meant when you said that you were torn."

Lincoln walked over to the bed and sat down on the edge of it. "Sarah, it's Lincoln." He put a hand on her shoulder but she said nothing to him.

"Sarah, you have to eat something, please," Lincoln pleaded.

There was a knock on the door and Dr. Greene stuck his head in. "I understand my patient is starting to talk."

Lincoln looked at Sarah's back. "A little."

The doctor picked up the chart and looked over several different sheets. "Sarah, it's Dr. Greene, dear."

"Go away," she muttered gruffly through her wired jaw. She was tired of the constant care that kept interrupting her, the sudden arrival of all her new so-called friends.

"Now, now, I'm one of the good guys, remember?"

He was answered only by silence. "Sarah, I know that what you saw in the mirror frightened you, but I promise it'll get better. Right now you're healing and the stitches with the bruises make it look worse than it is."

You didn't see what I saw, doctor, and there is no way in hell anyone else is going to either.

Lincoln was impressed by the doctor's bedside manner but, obviously, Sarah was not.

"Everything you're feeling right now is normal. Your body has gone through a traumatic experience. You're weak and feeling disoriented, but as we decrease your medication you'll feel better. I won't lie to you, there will be several more surgeries and then …"

No more, I am not going to be someone's charity case! With that thought, Sarah turned to face the doctor. "There'll be no surgery," she said clearly through clenched teeth. "Get out."

Her reaction startled them, but the doctor recovered quickly. "But, my dear, you don't understand. Most of what you saw yesterday was in your mind. You weren't properly prepared." He tried to explain, but Lincoln could see the steely determination in Sarah's eyes as she rolled back over.

Dr. Greene looked at Lincoln and then Nathan. "Can we talk outside?"

Lincoln whispered to Sarah, "I'll be right back." He expected no response and he didn't get one.

Dr. Greene and Nathan were waiting for him in the hallway.

"So now what?" Lincoln asked.

"Tell me, has she talked to either of you?"

"A few words here and there, and the odd sentence that usually ends with 'Go away'. So, no, not really," Lincoln said as he looked at his boss.

"About the same with me, one or two word answers at best," said Nathan.

"Has she mentioned anything about hurting herself or anything that might warrant a suicide watch?" Dr. Greene asked cautiously.

"What? No," Lincoln said in disbelief. "Why?"

"She's showing all the signs of someone who's given up, and once further medical treatment is refused, well …" He looked down at her chart and reached for a pen in his pocket, "I hate to do this but I think its time to transfer her upstairs."

"Upstairs?" Nathan wasn't sure if he liked the sound of that.

"Psychiatric ward," Dr. Greene stated without looking up from Sarah's charts.

"Wait," Lincoln said as he reached out and stopped the doctor before his pen could touch paper. "Just like that you sign her off and send her on her way?"

"I don't think that's a good idea," Nathan said quickly.

"She needs round the clock attention, gentlemen, and once she has refused treatment down here, the only choice we have is to commit her. If not, there's nothing to stop her from walking out the front doors and there'll be nothing we can do about it."

"I highly doubt someone in her condition is gonna jump out of bed and leave. Especially since part of her problem is that she doesn't want anyone to see her," Lincoln observed.

"I'm sorry, but we have to look at what's best for the patient …"

"If you're so concerned about what's good for the patient, then I think you need to hear what we're trying to tell you, doctor."

"You're a lawyer. You know as well as I do, once she refuses treatment, there isn't much we can do, unless we commit her," the doctor stated.

"But is that necessary? I mean, so quickly? Give her some time. Right now she isn't thinking clearly, but I think once we can get her to understand …" Lincoln stopped when he realized what he had just said.

"Exactly my point," the doctor said reluctantly. "Does she have any immediate family we can appeal to?"

"Apparently not," Lincoln said.

"Then in the best interest of the patient …" The doctor clicked his pen and was ready to sign.

"Dr Greene, I assure you, you're about to make a big mistake," Nathan stated.

"If you have another suggestion, I'm open to it." Doctor Greene looked at Nathan and then to Lincoln. "If she was my only patient it would be different, but I'm only here as a favor. I'm sorry, I'll let Dr. Marcot know of my opinion," he said.

"You're not going to commit that young woman. Not while I still have a dollar in my pocket and a law degree on my wall." Nathan stated firmly.

"What about a private facility?" Lincoln asked.

"That would be ideal, but the waiting list to get into them is long, and Sarah doesn't have the time to wait. The longer she goes without help, the harder it will be to pull her back."

"What if we moved her to my home?" Nathan's suggestion took them by surprise.

"She needs around the clock care, not just a place to stay."

"Then that's what she'll have. How do I arrange it?" Nathan was a man of money and one who didn't waste time. Whether it was Abby's money or his money, it didn't matter to him as long as Sarah got what she needed and Abby was at ease with the decision.

"I'll get one of the nurses to help you with that." Dr. Greene said before he left.

Lincoln turned to Nathan in surprise. "Are you sure about this? I mean …"

"I'll be there for her. We'll be there for her if I have to move my entire office home. If that's what it takes to keep her out of the psychiatric ward and on the road to recovery, then that is what I'm prepared to do. Lincoln, it's rare in a man's life that he gets a chance to make up for his past mistakes." He looked back at Sarah's door, thinking about another little girl who had needed him, a little girl that he had sent away. "I'm not making this mistake again."

Just like that, the wheels started turning to get Sarah out of the hospital and to get her the help she needed.

On Lincoln's suggestion, Nathan went upstairs to the ICU and made a proposition to Robin. The young nurse was hesitant at first, but the offer was too good to refuse and she put in for an extended leave of absence. Within an hour everything was arranged with one notable omission; nobody knew how to tell Sarah what had been decided on her behalf.

☯

Lincoln quietly entered Sarah's hospital room, followed by Nathan. He went to sit on the bed while Nathan stood silently at the foot of it. "Sarah, its Lincoln and Nathan." They were answered only by silence. Lincoln looked around the dimly lit room and decided anything had to be better for her than staying there.

"Sarah, the last thing I promised Abby before she left you in ICU, was that you would get the best money could buy. No expense was too great," Lincoln said to the silent Sarah.

"No surgery," she said firmly as she faced the wall. Her voice was still extremely raspy and hoarse, but at least she was talking.

"Is it the money? Is that why you don't want the surgery?" Nathan finally asked, "Because rest assured, my dear, money isn't a problem."

Sarah said nothing.

"Sarah," Lincoln said with no idea of how she was going to respond to this, "we're getting you out of here."

They waited, but there was no answer or reaction to his statement.

"Sarah, did you hear me?"

It was obvious that she did when she moved nervously in the bed. "Why?"

Lincoln looked at Nathan to answer. "Tell her the truth," the lawyer said.

"Because," Lincoln paused. "Because if you stay here, they're going to commit you."

After several long, silent seconds, Sarah rolled over and faced Lincoln.

"I'm not crazy," she said slowly in her hoarse whisper.

"I know," Lincoln said. With Sarah's attention on Lincoln, Nathan got his first chance to get a good look at the damage Billy Ward had done to her. It angered him more than he thought possible as he looked at the rows of stitches, the dark bruising around her eyes, and the white bandage around her neck.

"I know that, but the doctors don't have much of a choice if you keep refusing to eat," Lincoln repeated.

"I'm not hungry," she answered him as she stared into his eyes. *I just want everyone to go away.*

"It's not just that, Sarah."

"We thought it'd be easier if you came and stayed with me." Nathan's words broke the stare between them, and she looked at the lawyer as if she had forgotten he was even there. "I've arranged to have Robin, the nurse from ICU, be there for your medical needs."

"Why?" she said simply. "Why are you doing this?"

"Because I love my niece, and she loves you … and that's all the reason I need."

She may have loved me before, but she won't love me now. Sarah looked at him. "What if I don't want to go?"

"Unfortunately, my dear, that's not an option." Sarah held his gaze and she saw the color change in his stubborn eyes. She'd looked into eyes like his many times before. Sarah knew the decision was final.

☯

The next morning, Sarah and Robin arrived at Nathan's seaside mansion by ambulance. The small staff at the house had strict orders to leave them alone. Robin was given her own room, right next to Sarah's. The young nurse couldn't believe how fate had shone upon her. Her student loans were paid in full, and she was now making double what she had at the hospital. *All this to look after one of her favorite patients.* How lucky was she?

True to his word, Nathan had Beth, his private secretary, pack up all the files that pertained to his niece's case and ship them to his home. That morning another desk arrived along with two portable chalkboards and a large table that he soon covered with papers and files. Two hours later, Beth arrived to finish setting up his office. Nathan then explained the situation and that the second floor north wing was off limits to everyone, with no exceptions.

Lincoln came in shortly after, carrying two large boxes of his own files and notes. Once Nate showed him his desk, the two settled down and went to work.

"I got the second set of photos from the ME and I sweet-talked Johansson for another set from the crime scene at the park. And a set from both motels." Lincoln picked through the different sets of pictures until he found the one he was looking for. "This is from the ME and it does confirm the zip-ties were put on when his hands were in front of him," Lincoln said as he rolled up his sleeves. "So I figure, they tied him up and put his hands behind him. The question is: why."

"Is there any way we can check to see where these ties came from?"

"No, they're a dime a dozen at any hardware or automotive store."

"What else is there?" Nathan asked as he started to pick through the photos one by one. "What is this?" he asked as he peered closer at the collection of pictures in his hands.

"Let me see … oh, that's what Abby and I found at the Webster Arms. It was in a corridor he had been using between the rooms."

"Good God," Nathan said under his breath as he took the photos over to his desk for a closer inspection of the montage Billy Ward had made of Abby. "He was stalking her." His knees felt weak as he sat down.

"Yeah," Lincoln looked up and saw Nathan's face had paled considerably. "Nate? What's wrong?"

"That bastard was at her graduation?" He looked up at Lincoln. "She didn't even tell *me* when she went into the academy, but he knew."

Beth rapped on the door and then stuck her head in. "Nate, Ronald de Barr is on the phone for you."

Nathan nodded as he reached for the phone. "Mr. de Barr, to what do I owe the pleasure?" he asked professionally.

"Cut the shit, Nathan. You're tampering with a witness and Judge Porter is about to find out about it," de Barr whined into the phone.

"Tampering with a witness? How do you figure that?" Nathan asked confidently as he leaned back in his chair and looked at Lincoln.

"Two detectives tried to get a statement from Sarah Murphy, the girl at the hospital, and Lincoln, who's now working for you, stopped them."

"Actually, my understanding of the events is more along the line that it was a nurse who stopped them, and a doctor who ordered them out of the hospital. Lincoln had nothing to do with it."

"Don't play games with me, Nathan."

"Believe me, Ronald, if I was going to play games, it wouldn't be with you," Nathan said coldly.

"Well, I just phoned the hospital and it seems Miss Murphy is no longer there. She left in an ambulance this morning. You wouldn't happen to know anything about that would you?"

"Hmmm, Miss Murphy … you wouldn't mean Miss McMurphy would you?"

"Murphy, McMurphy, what's the difference? You know who I mean," de Barr said.

"What's the difference? You're an assistant DA and you don't know the difference a name can make? That's first year law school," Nathan said.

"You're forcing me to take this to the judge, Nathan. Don't make me get a warrant," de Barr threatened.

"You do that, Ronald. You ask Judge Porter for a warrant." Nathan's tone changed, "But you'd better make damn sure you've got the right name on it," Nathan growled before he slammed down the phone.

"Was that a good idea?" Lincoln said.

"Sarah is going to have to talk to them sooner or later, but if I can buy her some time by playing a few name games, then I will. It also wouldn't hurt us if I can get him to run to Porter with this, because it'll make him look like an incompetent ass."

"You know, when I was a cop, I hated lawyers like you," Lincoln said with a grin.

"That's okay, young man, because when I was a trial attorney, I hated cops like you."

☯

Lincoln was getting ready to leave for the day, but he wanted to stop in and see how Sarah was doing. He had been up a few times but she had always been asleep. Taking the carpeted stairs two at a time, he turned left and went down the hall until he came to her door.

He knocked softly before he entered. Robin looked up from her paperwork and smiled at him. She put her finger to her lips and then pointed for him to talk with her out in the hall.

"She's still asleep," she said in a hushed tone.

"Is that normal?"

"Yes, the move was stressful on her, but thankfully I didn't have to medicate her."

"She's doing okay, then?" he asked, trying to see into the room. All he could see inside the room Nathan had selected, were the rich warm colors of the dark, high-polished wood that decorated the entire mansion. He saw no sign of Sarah.

"The curtains are drawn and the lights are as low as they can go," Robin said. Lincoln leaned in just enough to see Sarah's sleeping figure in the middle of a large bed. If she had looked small and vulnerable in a hospital bed, this one made her appear doubly so.

"I see the IV is back," he said nodding toward the stainless steel rack that held Sarah's much needed fluids.

"It was a condition of transport; but on a good note," she pointed to a tall glass sitting on a nearby dresser, "I got her to eat today. Well, sip actually," Robin said with a proud smile.

"I knew you'd get her to do it," Lincoln said.

"Speaking of which, I can't thank you enough for giving me this opportunity, Lincoln. You've no idea how hard I've had to work to get through nursing school. And to have all of my student loans paid off, just like that!"

"Actually, Robin, I do know how hard you worked. That's part of why I suggested you. Sarah needs someone who can talk to her on her own level, not someone who floated through school on someone else's money. Besides, Abby liked you and that's enough for me."

CHAPTER 33

Lincoln stood on the small bridge and he looked down at the water rushing below him. He was not wearing his usual pressed suit and oxford shoes; he had on jeans, a sweatshirt, and a pair of black rubber boots. With the ME report in his hand, he studied the scene where they had found Billy Ward's body. Whoever killed him had been smart enough to do it without leaving a trail, but murder was not clever and it definitely was not clean. Murder was messy … unless it had been planned and calculated.

Coming down off the bridge, he followed the path to where they'd found Ward. There was nothing left to indicate what had happened there; no marks, no footprints, no signs left behind by anyone. He slid off his backpack and put the ME reports inside. He then pulled out a large flashlight before zipping up the pack and slinging it on his back. Lincoln checked the light against his hand and then headed upstream.

An idea had come to him in the middle of the night and, as the morning sun broke through the gray skies, he went in search of the explanation of how a body could have arrived without leaving a trace.

☯

Nathan had sent Beth to the courthouse to pick up some papers, so there was no one to stop Robin when she knocked on Nathan's door. The elderly lawyer looked up from his desk and motioned her in. He took off his glassed and smiled

"Hi, Robin, how are you this afternoon?" he asked.

"I'm good, thank you," she said. "I wanted you to know Dr. Greene just left."

Nathan's smile faded into concern. "How did it go? I was going to come up but I thought the less people around the better."

"I gave her a sedative before he even showed up, so she's sleeping. I know he was careful, but I could see taking those stitches out had to be painful. And I don't necessarily mean physical pain." Robin wandered into the room and looked around.

"What did he say?" Nathan asked as he came around and sat on the edge of his desk.

"He seemed to be pleased, but every time he mentioned any further surgeries … well, let me say, I've heard better language."

"How's the therapy going for her throat and neck? Is there anything else I can do or get for her?"

"Not really, Mr. Holoman. You've got the best medical care and equipment outside of a hospital. You've got her one of the best plastic surgeons, you've hired physical therapists, and you've had that crisis councilor here. So, unfortunately, she has everything—except the desire."

"Desire?"

"To improve, Mr. Holoman. To get any better."

"Robin, please call me Nathan. You make me feel like an old man every time you call me Mr. Holoman," he said with a smile. "We are living under the same roof after all." Walking over to one of the bookshelves lining the walls, he ran his hand over the leather bindings. "Robin, there has to be a way to get Sarah past this …"

"Unfortunately, her little jaunt to the bathroom at the hospital was the worst thing that could've happened. Now that's the only image she has of herself, and until we can change that, there isn't much she is going to want to do," Robin said.

"Can we just give her a mirror and show her it isn't as bad as she remembers?"

Robin shook her head. "Unfortunately, it isn't that easy. The damage has been done, and she has to find it inside of her to undo it."

What a mess, Nathan thought as he ran his hand over his face. "There has to be something that will motivate her."

"Nathan, you and I both know who could, but there's nothing we can do about that."

"Yes, I know." Nathan walked over to one of the shelves that held a framed picture of Abby. He picked up the frame and looked down at his niece. "So it's up to us."

"Yes, it is," said Robin. "The doctor took her IV out, so she's free to roam … if she had any desire to leave her room."

"Has she even been out of bed?" Nathan asked.

"Just a little. She's still weak, and I know her whole left side has been severely damaged, but now that the stitches are out of her neck the healing process can begin."

Nathan put down Abby's picture but continued to look at it on the shelf. "At least the physical part, right?" he said in a low heartfelt tone that Robin heard clearly.

CHAPTER 34

When she first opened her eyes, Sarah didn't know where she was, but she knew it was no longer the hospital. Looking around the room, she glanced at the expensive furnishings, and recalled that she was in the home of Nathan Holoman, Abby's lawyer and uncle. *Abby.* The name, the vision, the memories. It was the first thought she had when she woke and the last one before she fell asleep.

"Good morning." She turned to her right to see Lincoln's smiling face. "Did you have a nice sleep?"

Instinctively, she pulled her face back into the shadows, shielding him from most of her fresh scars.

"Here," Lincoln said as he held out a glass with a straw in it. She wanted to refuse it, but her thirst forced her to accept his offer.

"Thanks," her lips said, but no sound emerged.

"I see your stitches came out."

He didn't have to remind her; she could still feel the sting where the thin silk had been. Sarah lifted a hand and gently touched the thin scab at the corner of her mouth. She could feel her lips, but she couldn't feel the corner of her mouth that still drooped. Both the doctor and Robin had offered her a mirror, but she no longer had the desire to see what had been done to her. She had seen enough.

"Robin told me the doctor was happy with the results, especially with your neck." She looked at him but said nothing. "It's not as bad as you think. The bruises are still fading and the swelling is almost gone …"

"But the scars remain," she said quietly, cutting off his words as she looked at the curtain covered window. "Can we change the subject please?"

Lincoln noted how clear her words were becoming even though her jaw was wired shut. There was still a rasp to her hoarse voice and he wondered how long that would last. "All right, what would you like to talk about?" he said.

Sarah kept her gaze on the window.

"Do you want the curtains opened?" Lincoln stood up." Maybe some …"

"No," she answered clearly and firmly.

"All right."

She hadn't meant to snap at him, but … "Where did Robin go?" she asked.

It was an attempt at polite conversation and Lincoln was more than a little pleased to respond. "She had some personal errands to do, so I said I'd come up and sit with you until your therapist arrives."

The room fell silent again.

"Where's Nathan?"

"He went to meet with Abby," Lincoln said.

The moment he said Abby's name, Sarah's eyes drifted downward and she began to pick at the threads of the comforter. Even in the dim light, Lincoln could see the shimmer of tears gathering in her eyes.

"Sarah," he said with a mix of concern and care.

When she moved her head, the tears spilled over and ran down her face. She did her best to ignore them and to ignore him, but as she reached up to brush them away, Lincoln came over and sat down on the bed.

"Hey, what's all this?"

Sarah said nothing, but she brought her hand up to cover her mouth and to hold her sore jaw. Her tough exterior crumbled as the tears continued to fall.

Lincoln reached out to her. The offer of compassion was more than she could ignore, and she turned to him and to his open arms. He wasn't sure what the tears were for, but it didn't matter. Sarah needed someone she could lean on and he was happy to be there for her.

After a while the tears stopped, but she made no attempt to leave his embrace.

"I miss her so much," she finally said. "We didn't know each other for that long, but I can't image my life without her in it."

It was the longest sentence she had ever said to him, and he knew it had come right from her heart.

"I think it's mutual."

She pulled out of his arms and moved shyly away as she sat up a little straighter in her bed. "Then why haven't I heard from her?" It was the hardest question she had ever asked, and she wasn't sure she wanted to know what the real answer was.

"You haven't heard from her because she …"

Sarah cut him off, "Because she doesn't want to see me. I lied to her Lincoln, I lied to her and to myself and, because of my own vanity, I put myself into Billy's hands."

"What—wait, you have this all wrong! Listen to me. This was *not* your fault. Do you hear me? You survived when no one else did. Billy set you up, but what he didn't count on was the two of you falling in love. You were the best thing to happen to Abby."

Sarah heard him but she couldn't look at him. "You said it, I *was* the best thing."

"Sarah, stop. You *are* the best thing in Abby's life. You came along when she really needed someone. Whether she wants to admit it or not, she was vulnerable—you both needed each other."

Looking down at her left hand, Sarah rubbed at her numb thumb. "I guess in some ways, you're right. The time we spent together at Gold Creek seems so long ago now, a lifetime ago."

"In some ways it *was* a lifetime ago, Sarah. The Abby that came back from there wasn't the Abby that left here."

Sarah turned and looked him in the face, "That's a good thing, right?" she asked through her clenched teeth.

"It was the best thing. I'd never seen her so happy, until she couldn't find you." Lincoln looked at her and he wondered if he was ever going to see those emerald eyes in the daylight.

"Couldn't find me?" her voice crackled with concern as her brow furrowed in question.

"We knew Ward was after you before you did. I thought Abby was going to level the city before she found you." Lincoln watched her reaction but was puzzled by it.

"What? What is it?" he asked.

"I didn't realize it was him," Sarah said finally.

"You thought he was your boss."

"Yes," she said with a slight hesitation. "I didn't give him any information on Abby … or the case."

"I know that, Sarah, without a doubt I know that." Lincoln got off Sarah's bed. "It was Billy. All along, it was him. He knew just how to play Abby, what buttons to push to get a response." He walked over to the table and picked up several sheets of paper and then threw them back down. He took a long, slow breath to calm his rising anger, but it didn't do him much good. "He promised her that he'd take away everything she had, and he almost succeeded. He got her badge, he almost killed you, he burnt down her house, killed her dog, and now she has lost her freedom." Lincoln looked over at Sarah. He could see pain on her face.

"Sarah?"

Her eyes shimmered again as she stared at him in disbelief.

"Buck … he killed Buck?" she whispered with her hand over her mouth.

Lincoln grimaced and swore at himself. "I'm sorry, I forgot you didn't know."

"Oh my God. Poor Abby." Sarah felt an ache in her chest for the big friendly dog that had saved her life. "He was like her child, you know." She looked at him and he nodded in agreement.

"Yeah, I know. It was devastating to see. I helped her bury him. He was a great dog." Lincoln recalled the sound of Abby's sobs. "A really great dog."

"I just can't believe it … Buck's dead. What happened?" she asked.

Lincoln quickly went over what had happened and how Ward had played the system to his benefit and to Abby's detriment.

"So she thought it was my blood?" Sarah asked without looking at Lincoln.

"Yes," Lincoln answered.

Sarah reached over for her glass and took a drink from the straw. "I hope the poem I wrote for her has helped." She saw a strange look cross Lincoln's face.

"What?" she asked as she put down her glass.

"She, ah … " Lincoln bit down gently on his tongue as he tried to think of a good way to explain why the poem was still in his jacket pocket.

"She's angry with me, isn't she?"

"What? No," he said quickly. "Abby is …" He stopped to think about what word would best describe his highly-strung partner. "I think with everything that's happened, she's just mad, period." He could see that his explanation had not eased her mind. "The last time we saw her—Nathan and I—things got out of hand. There was a confrontation between her and Nate."

"Out of hand? What do you mean a confrontation?"

"There were some heated words between them and Abby slapped Nate and then took a swing at one of the guards and broke his nose. So they tossed her into solitary to cool off."

"Solitary? I thought they only had that in prisons?"

"Our city's pre-trial is pretty much like a prison. And when they get someone in there with a hot head and an attitude, they don't mess around. They can't afford to. Anyhow, I guess the stress of it all just pushed her past it. She and Nathan started yelling at each other and the next thing you know Abby's in shackles, yelling at her lawyer, and there's a guard with his nose …"

"They had her in shackles," Sarah said quietly.

"Yes," he said as he turned and looked at her. Lincoln could see Sarah's energy was waning and the emotions of the morning were taking their toll.

"She'll be okay," he said. "She's got you."

"And I've got her," Sarah said so softly that he didn't know if he was supposed to have heard her or not. "We're just not together."

She lay back on her pillow and he turned to sit back down at the table. "But why me, Lincoln?" she asked after a long pause. "Why her?"

"I don't know." Lincoln's attention was diverted by the sound of tires screeching outside Sarah's window. Crossing the room, he pulled back the curtain. Lincoln didn't see Sarah cringe at the bright light because his attention was on the Mercedes Benz racing down the driveway.

"What is it?" Sarah asked when she saw the concern on his face.

"It's Nathan," Lincoln said.

"But I thought you said he was going to meet Abby."

"He was," Lincoln said as he turned back from the window.

"Lincoln?" she asked as she heard a car door slam.

"I don't know." He turned to leave. "I'll be right back."

Sarah said nothing as she watched the concerned man leave the room. He left the door open, so she easily heard his footsteps as he rushed to find out what had happened.

Lincoln had just about reached the top of the grand staircase, when the front door flew open and Nathan stormed in. The normally distinguished gentleman looked more than a little ragged as he grabbed the solid wood door and slammed it behind him. Even in her room, Sarah felt the concussion of his actions.

"Nate?" Lincoln questioned as he looked down at Nathan standing at the front door.

"That stubborn, pigheaded … " He tossed his briefcase to the floor and threw his hands in the air. Lincoln didn't have to guess who he was referring to.

"That obstinate niece of mine," Nathan hollered as he stood in the main foyer. "She's refused to see me. The message I got was that I'm no longer her attorney and that she'll be representing herself!"

Lincoln stopped short at the bottom of the stairs. "She can't do that. Can she?"

"You know as well as I do that she can and she did." It was the first time Lincoln had seen Nathan rattled. "The judge will recommend co-council, but it's her right to represent herself if she wants!"

"I'll go talk to her," Lincoln said. "She's just mad at you right now."

"Son, that child has been mad at me for twenty years and you aren't going to change it."

"I know Abby. Give her some time to cool down and she'll be thinking with a clearer head."

"She's had nothing but time to think. Oh, she is so … so stubborn!"

"Yes, she is, but something tells me it's a family failing," Lincoln said with a hint of humor. He took a step past Nathan. "I'll head down …"

"Don't bother. She has stated clearly that she wants no visitors. Period."

Lincoln stopped. "No visitors? She can't mean that."

"That's what I thought, too, but the request came straight from Abby. She not only fired me, she no longer wants to see anyone."

"Anyone?" a small raspy voice said and both men looked up in surprise.

"Sarah?" they said together. Nathan's voice registered his shock at the sight of the young woman out of bed. Lincoln's voice was filled with concern at her appearance. Sarah clutched tightly to the handrail with her right hand. Her head tilted slightly forward and to the right, a consequence of the knife cutting through the thick muscles of her neck. Abby was forgotten as the two men raced up the stairs. Lincoln's young legs got him there sooner, but Nate wasn't far behind.

"You shouldn't be out of bed by yourself," Lincoln said as he scooped up her small frame without asking. Sarah's face was pale and covered by a thin sheen of perspiration. She was trembling and Lincoln was unsure if it was because of what she'd done, what she'd heard, or from the constant discomfort she must be in. He carried her back to her bedroom as Nathan walked beside them.

Nathan looked at her and tried to work out what had changed. In the light of her bedroom he saw that her stitches had been removed.

The only bandage left was the thin white gauze along the left side of her neck.

"I want to know what's going on," she said weakly.

"Then we'll keep you informed," Lincoln said as he knelt one knee on the bed and then lowered her down.

"What's going on here?" Robin said as she came in the door and was surprised to see everyone hovering around. "Are you okay?" she asked Sarah as she put down her purchases and came over to the bed. "You are awfully pale." Robin picked up her wrist and immediately began to calculate her patient's pulse.

"Sarah decided to go for a walk," Lincoln said as he stood up and crossed his arms.

"She what?" Robin looked at Lincoln and then turned her attention to Sarah. "Yesterday you're hiding from the world and today you're going out walking?" She lifted the comforter and Sarah slowly climbed back into her bed. "You can't be doing that. Your body isn't ready for you to try stuff like that on your own. Everything in moderation."

Lincoln looked from the patient to the nurse and, though he was greatly concerned for Sarah's well-being, he had to smile. She was already asleep, missing most of Robin's lecture. He was just about to comment when the cell phone in his pocket rang. Quickly, he left the room to answer it so as not to wake her.

"Quinn," he said and then he went silent as the person on the other end spoke. "What … when?" The serious tone of his voice rose. "Shit."

Not liking what he heard, Nathan met Lincoln in the hallway as he was closing his cell phone.

"What? What's wrong?" Nathan asked.

"Abby has demanded to see the judge. She wants to change her plea!"

CHAPTER 35

Abby looked out of the small slit window of the prison van as it moved through the city. She could smell the asphalt after a light sprinkle of rain as she listened to the hustle and bustle of the streets. It made her miss her freedom all that much more.

Freedom and Sarah, and not in that order. Abby leaned back. *Sarah.* How she longed to hear Sarah's voice, to feel the smoothness of her skin, or to look for just a moment into those eyes. *Sarah, I wish you knew how sorry I am for what happened to you. It's my fault—my doing and I am going to fix it …* her thoughts trailed off.

The van came to a stop, with the cold gray of the courthouse looming in front it. She had always hated coming to court and today wasn't much different. A couple of turns later and they were pulling into the brightly lit underground stall reserved for prisoner transfers. No words were exchanged as they took her up the stairs and into one of the several holding rooms. And there she waited for her turn in court.

☯

The courtroom halls began filling up as word got out that Abby Stanfield was heading into court. The press had been having a field day with the beautiful, rich ex-detective. Her photogenic features and her quick tongue sold papers and made for ratings. The only thing more sought after was a picture of the infamous Sarah, Billy Ward's last victim, and the rumored reason for Abby's vigilante attack. The bounty for a single photograph of Sarah was growing daily, but so far no one, not even the press, could find where she had gone.

Lincoln and Nathan came to a quick stop in front of the courthouse. They had to reach Abby before she got in front of Judge Porter. There were several reporters hanging out on the front steps and the moment they saw the two men hurrying towards the door, they converged on them like locusts.

"Is Abby going to admit she killed Billy Ward?"

"Is it true that Abby Stanfield fired you, Mr. Holoman?"

"Why are you here if you're no longer representing her?"

The questions got louder and meaner but neither Nathan nor Lincoln responded. Holding out one long arm, Lincoln parted the reporters for Nathan to get through. The counselor quickly made his way into the building and away from the questioning mob. Moving swiftly through the maze of corridors and hallways, Nathan finally found his way to the segregated area where Abby would be waiting.

"Abby Stanfield," he said slightly winded to the uniformed courtroom officer. "I'm her lawyer."

The young guard sitting there looked through a large stack of messy file folders. "Sorry, pops, no go," the young man said flippantly.

"Excuse me," Nathan growled at the lack of respect, "I've a right to see my client …"

Thumbing quickly through all the papers, the young guard responded. "You might have that right, but your client isn't here. She's already been taken into the courtroom. Guess you need to get to court on time, huh, pops?"

"I guess. Thank you."

"No problem, pops."

Nathan turned, but as he did, he caught the edge of the bottom file with his finger and the entire stack of folders spilled over onto the floor in a mass of mixed paperwork.

"Holy shit, man, look what you did," the young guard said as he jumped off his chair.

"I'm sorry. How clumsy of me. You know, at my age things like that just happen." Nathan said. "Don't call me 'pops,'" he muttered under his breath as he hurried down the hallway.

☯

Lincoln waited just outside the massive wooden doors of the courtroom. Nathan was taking too long but he didn't want to go in without him. With one last look down the empty corridor, he reached for the door and walked into the stuffy, noisy courtroom. A moment later the side door opened and in shuffled Abby, in her bright orange jumpsuit and her rattling chains.

Without Nathan, he had to do something before it was too late. Lincoln whispered loudly to her, "Abby."

She ignored him but many others in the courtroom didn't.

"Come on, Abby, talk to me." He waited but she had nothing to say to him nor would she look at him.

"Don't do this," Lincoln pleaded as he noticed Nathan enter the courtroom.

"All rise," the bailiff called out as Nathan and Lincoln locked eyes. He could tell by the look on the lawyer's face that he had not had the chance to speak to his niece.

Lincoln turned around. "Abby," he hissed and received a cautioning glare from the bailiff.

"The Honorable Judge Porter presiding," the bailiff said as the judge in his black robe entered. "Please be seated," the bailiff directed.

Lincoln looked back to Nathan in panic as the elder lawyer made his way through the rows of people. "She won't listen to me," he said when Nathan squeezed in beside him.

"All right," the judge said as he peered over some of the documents on his desk.

"I understand you're now representing yourself, Miss Stanfield, is that correct?" The judge took off his glasses and looked down at the defendant's table.

"Yes, Your Honor," Abby said, standing to address the court.

"I have to advise you against that. This is a capital case."

"I know, Your Honor, but it is my right."

Judge Porter frowned down at her, "Yes, it is, but you are not a lawyer and you need a one, someone who knows the law and what the procedures are, so I will insist on at least co-council."

"That's fine, but it won't be necessary. Before we waste any more of the court's time, I'd like to render a new plea."

"Now just hold on. Are you aware of the consequences of this? You're charged with felony one murder and the prosecution is asking for the death penalty." Porter was more than concerned and he went so far as to cast a glance at Nathan, who sat helpless in the front row.

"Yes, Your Honor, I am," Abby said, standing tall with her hands bound in front of her.

"Abby," Lincoln whispered just under his breath, "for Sarah's sake, don't do this." He saw the quick downcast of Abby's eyes and he knew he had reached her.

"All right, Miss Stanfield, you have the legal right to represent yourself, but I wish you'd refer to your council."

"I just want to get this over with," she said.

With no other option, Lincoln turned to Nathan, "Get this to her."

"On the charge of murder in the first degree how do you plead ..." the judge started.

"Excuse me, Your Honor." Lincoln jumped to his feet. "I have something to say." The courtroom erupted into a buzz of surprised voices.

"Detective Quinn, take your seat," the judge ordered as he pounded his gavel.

The big man stepped over the railing separating the court from the gallery. Two of the bailiffs closest to the judge moved forward, but Porter cautioned them back. He knew Lincoln and he was not afraid of him.

"Your Honor, I need to talk to you," Lincoln said, taking several steps towards the bench.

"Detective, take your seat." Porter smacked his gavel several times. "Order in the court!"

Several people jumped to their feet; most were reporters wanting to get a better view. "I said I will have order in my courtroom!" Judge Porter demanded and two of the court officers moved towards Lincoln.

"Detective, I'm going to hold you in contempt of court. Now everyone sit down and shut up." The courtroom was out of control and Porter's words were having no effect.

"Lincoln, what the hell are you doing?" Abby demanded but he never even gave her a glance as the two officers came between him and Porter's bench.

Now or never, Lincoln thought. Ignoring Abby's pleas, he gave one of the court officers a shove. All three went down in a pile of twisting and wrestling bodies as Judge Porter continued to pound his gavel.

"I said order in this courtroom, I said order!" His face turned redder with each blow of his wooden mallet.

In all the commotion, no one noticed Nathan step over the barrier and come up behind Abby. "Don't do this, Abby, if not for you then for Sarah—she needs you," he whispered into her dark hair as he pushed a piece of paper into her hand and then quickly returned to the other side of the partition.

Several other officers had joined in the struggle, and soon they had Lincoln lying face down with his hands in cuffs. The disheveled bailiffs dragged him to his feet to face the angry judge.

"Lincoln Quinn, in all my years I've never seen anything so foolhardy as what you just did. I would've seen you in chambers," the judge snarled at Lincoln. The winded investigator said nothing as he licked at his bloody lip. His attention was on Abby who was reading what he hoped was the poem Sarah had written for her.

"That's enough, people." This time the judge's voice carried authority and the gallery began to quiet. "Five hundred dollars and a night in jail ought to cool you off. Take him out of here," the judge ordered.

Four bailiffs surrounded Lincoln as he searched past them to try to glimpse Abby's reaction as they took him through the door. With onc last look, he finally connected with her dark, haunted eyes.

"Think about Sarah," Lincoln hollered as the door closed before he had a chance to see if it had made any difference.

CHAPTER 36

The fingers of the clock next to her bed moved slowly as she looked at it for the hundredth time.

"Nathan said he'd phone," Robin said as she watched the agony of waiting on Sarah's face.

"I know," Sarah said as she fidgeted on her bed. Looking down at her sweat pants, Sarah picked at the fabric pills and then brushed away a few pieces of lint before she looked over at the clock again. Barely a minute had passed.

"Come on," Robin said as she jumped to her feet. "You're driving yourself crazy and you're making me nuts. Let's go downstairs and see what we can find on the TV."

Fear instantly took away the anxiety of waiting. "No," Sarah said and she unconsciously leaned away from the nurse and from the idea.

"Sarah, the house is empty. Nathan and Lincoln are gone and it's the staff's day off. The house is ours." Robin watched her, hoping to see some sign that she had piqued her interest.

The young patient said nothing.

"Abby is news and I can guarantee the press will be covering whatever is happening. So you can sit and drive yourself crazy or you can follow me downstairs to the TV and we can see what's going on together." She saw the want cross Sarah's face.

"Come on, it's just you and me." Robin waited.

Sarah turned to face her. "Can't you bring a TV in here?"

"What do I look like, Superman? The TV that's downstairs is bigger than you are." She watched and waited. "It's up to you … do you wanna go downstairs or do you wanna wait here?"

Looking down at the clock, Sarah didn't move but Robin knew now that she was going to. Patiently, she waited and watched Sarah struggle with the last of her inner demons before she moved to the side of the bed. With her good hand on Robin's forearm and the nurse's arm around her small waist, the two slowly made their way out of the room.

Together they stopped at the top of the stairs to give Sarah a chance to catch her breath. Looking down at the black and white tile of the entranceway below she tried to smile.

Seeing the rare sight, Robin wondered what had brought it on. "You okay?"

"Yes, I was just wondering if all rich people bought their flooring at the same place. My parent's entranceway has the same tile."

Robin looked down and smiled herself. "Beats me. The only thing black and white in my parents' house was the TV."

They made their way down the stairs, and within a few minutes, Robin was directing them into Nathan's den.

"You weren't kidding," Sarah said as she motioned towards the TV that stood taller than she did.

"No, I wasn't," replied Robin with a chuckle. She moved over to a chair and picked up the remote. With a click and a hum, the TV screen began to brighten. Robin searched through the channels looking for one of the several local stations.

"There," Sarah said as she pointed to the screen and to the reporter standing on the front steps. "Turn it up." The low muffled conversation came to life on the TV.

> *"Lincoln Quinn was also a detective on the Ward case before he resigned to work for Mr. Holoman in the defense of his old partner, Abby Stanfield." The screen flashed to a departmental picture of Abby, taken at a different time in her career.*

The TV screen split and the newscaster appeared on screen next to the on-location reporters. *"Other than the prison van that brought her here, there has been no sign of the ex-detective. I'm Nancy Deveres for KGTV outside the courthouse."*

> *"Thank you, Nancy. Abby Stanfield, the wealthy ex-detective who has been charged with the grisly murder of William Daniel Ward, has fired her high-priced lawyer …"*

Sarah turned from the TV.

"I'm sure she knows what she's doing," Robin said.

"Does she?" Sarah asked as she turned back to watch more of the newscast.

"It is speculated that Miss Stanfield may be looking to throw herself at the mercy of the court, but pleading guilty when the state is seeking the death penalty, well, that is just ..."

Sarah's lips parted as the anguish erupted from her heart. An undistinguishable sound came from her throat as she turned in panic. "Death penalty?" she said through her wired jaw.

Robin quickly came to Sarah's side. "I thought you knew. Oh, sweet Jesus, I thought you knew." Reaching for the remote, she muted the TV.

"She's pleading guilty, and they want to execute her?" Sarah's eyes were wide and white as Robin did her best to try and calm the young woman down.

"Nathan and Lincoln aren't going to let that happen ..."

"They knew and they didn't tell me." Fear and disbelief pulled at her mind as she thought about the consequences of Abby's decision. Bringing her hand up to cover her mouth, a small sob escaped through her lips. "Abby, why? Why would she plead guilty?"

It was a question Robin didn't have an answer for as the commercial ended and the news returned to outside of the courthouse.

Without a word, Robin reached over for the remote and the volume.

"... a short scuffle between Lincoln Quinn and several of the court officers. A very angry Judge Porter cited Mr. Quinn for contempt of court and fined him five hundred dollars and a night in jail. The bailiffs then took Mr. Quinn away but not before he shouted out for Sarah. Miss Stanfield silently watched the whole proceedings from behind the defendant's table.
So who is Sarah? The young woman who was brutally attacked ..."

"Sarah—Sarah look at me," Robin pleaded, but it was too late—the images were already there.

Sarah felt her world freeze as she watched her face looming larger than life on the fifty-six inch screen. A full glorious color picture—her picture—before Billy had gotten to her face. Then the photo faded away as they showed the video of Sarah being wheeled out of the motel with a blood-soaked Abby by her side, holding onto her throat. Abby's tear-stained face was ghostly pale as the paramedic rushed past the camera to the waiting ambulance. Sarah felt herself grow weak at the sight of her bloodied and battered face.

"Sarah … look at me!" Robin demanded as she attempted to block Sarah's view of the screen. "Sarah, that was the past—you survived." Robin looked into her eyes and she could see the damage had already been done. The horrified woman who had been in the hospital, the one who had seen her face in the mirror, sat unmoving and Robin had no idea what to do.

"Sarah, don't let that image back inside—it's not you. What you remember is not you!" Robin knew the only image Sarah had of herself was what she had seen in the mirror.

Sarah lifted her face and turned her eyes to stare into Robin's. There was an anger there Robin had not seen before.

"You're right, Robin. What I remember *is* no longer me." With effort, Sarah pulled herself to her feet and then left without saying another word. Robin followed behind her the whole way, until Sarah reached the top of the stairs.

"I would like to be alone, thank you," Sarah said without turning around.

"Sarah, I'd prefer …"

"*I* would prefer to be alone," Sarah replied and, with a wave of her hand, she moved slowly down the hallway and disappeared into her room.

☯

As Nathan opened the front door of his home and walked in, he saw Robin sitting on the stairs. The look on her face told him there was bad news.

"Robin?" The door remained open as he quickly crossed the foyer.

"I thought we'd made this great breakthrough, you know. I got her to come out of her room and downstairs. Progress, one step at a time," she said dismissively. "And then just like that," Robin snapped her fingers, "she takes two steps back."

Nathan dropped his briefcase and joined her on the stairs. "What happened?"

"She saw it all on TV."

"Saw what?"

"Everything—but mainly that gruesome video of them wheeling her out of the motel."

"Oh my God."

"You could say that. First she hears the news that they're seeking the death penalty and that didn't go over well. Your department! Then just as we were getting over that they broke in with Lincoln's little charade." Robin stopped and pondered the afternoon with a deep sigh. "And then the dumb bastards had to go and show that bloody … She flipped." Robin looked down at her hands as if hoping to find some answers. "I don't know what to do with her. I'm not a psychiatrist. I'm a nurse."

"You're doing just fine Robin, better than we are."

"I know. Your day wasn't much better."

"Not really. Lincoln's little charade, as you called it, was in hopes of getting Abby to at least talk to one of us."

"And?"

"She read the poem Sarah had written her and then she stood up in front of Judge Porter and requested a new bail hearing." Nathan sighed with relief.

"A new bail hearing? Is that possible?"

"No, but she had to do something. So Porter denied her request and advised her to seek new council. To which my lovely niece replied that if she had to have council then she wanted it to be family."

"Family?" Robin lifted her eyebrows. "She told everyone you're related?"

"Yes she did, which sent the reporters scurrying like the rats they are."

"Why would she do that?"

"Because, my dear," he said with a smile as he rose to his feet and looked up the stairs, "that's now the lead story. And most of the reporters should forget that Lincoln yelled out Sarah's name. Now if you'll excuse me, I need to go and talk to her." Nathan nodded his departure and started up the stairs.

☯

Knocking on the door, Nathan poked his head into the bedroom and was surprised to see Sarah seated at the table.

"Quite a day," he declared. "For both of you," he added as he closed the door.

Sarah said nothing as she kept her eyes on the table and the notepad in front of her.

"Sarah, I'm sorry. Lincoln and I decided that …"

"Who are you to decide anything for me!" Nathan was taken aback by her anger. Sarah had barely raised her voice above a whisper and now she glared at him with all the fury and frustration she was feeling. "Everyone is making decisions, and no one is asking or telling me anything!"

"I had every intention of telling you, but my mind's been on Abby."

"Abby! She's making the biggest decision of all, and she isn't thinking about anyone but herself!"

"The problem is, my dear she has too much time to think about everyone but herself. She has all but consumed herself with guilt—over everything—over you."

Seeing the impact of his condemning words, Nathan changed the subject. "But it's how she feels about you that is what did it." Nathan sat on the edge of the bed, facing Sarah. "You did what no one else could do. You got through that thick head of hers."

"How did I do that?"

"Lincoln's little distraction was designed for me to get your poem to her. We didn't know what else to do."

"And?"

Sarah looked over at him and Nathan smiled. "I've a meeting to see her tomorrow. I thought maybe you'd like to come with me."

"No," she said without hesitation.

Nathan was taken a back. "Why not?"

"Because," she answered abruptly.

"Because what?"

She fought her inner fears but she couldn't fight them all. "Because I don't want her to see me like this."

"Wait, help me out here. Abby saw you at the worst of it and that never altered her love for you."

"I don't care," she shot back.

"I think you *do* care. I think you're afraid. But you shouldn't be. Abby loves you and you love her. I won't sit here and pretend that I understand women, or lesbians, but I know when I see two people in love, and damn it Sarah, you love her and she loves you!" His tone changed and his words came out a little harsher than he intended.

"Nathan, you don't know how she would react."

"Yes, I do. She would react as she did today."

"And if she doesn't?" Sarah turned with anger in her eyes. "What if she doesn't? I couldn't handle that. I couldn't. I see the pity in everyone's eyes when they look at me, pity and fear that it could have been them."

"I think you're selling my niece short."

"You're right, Nathan. She's strong-willed and strong-minded enough to stand beside me because it's the right thing to do, because she feels she should."

"Sarah …"

"Nathan, it's been a long day and I'm extremely tired."

He was not going to give in to her argument that easily, but he saw the exhaustion on her face. "This isn't finished," he said as he stood up to leave.

"Yes, it is," she said as she crawled onto her bed and turned her back to him. "Yes, it is."

[illegible] was, but my mind [illegible]

CHAPTER 37

"Nathan, have you looked over this evidence yet?" Lincoln asked, looking up from his desk to gaze at the lawyer sitting perched on the wide windowsill.

Nathan looked over his glasses at him. "Most of it, but I haven't gotten all of it from de Barr." Nathan noticed the perplexed expression on Lincoln's face. "Why, is there something I should be looking for?"

"I'm not sure."

Nathan pulled off his glasses.

"The whole motel room thing still bugs me. I mean why the two motels? Does that bother you?"

"Lincoln, I'm a lawyer. Everything bothers me."

"Maybe I should take a trip down to the lab and see what Hyme can tell me."

"Fred Hyamensky is still working forensics?" Nathan's tone showed his surprise.

"He's in charge of the Crime Scene Unit, but he rarely leaves the lab now. I don't think he'll ever leave CSU. I think it's his dream to have his dead body analyzed in his own lab."

"Well, just remember, you're working for the other side now."

"I know." Lincoln stood up and grabbed his coat off the back of the chair. "I'm just gonna pop up and say hi to Sarah before I leave."

"She still hasn't left her room, you know," Nathan said regretfully. "It's been how many weeks? When I go in to see her, she barely acknowledges my presence. According to Robin, she hardly talks to anyone. The therapists come and go, and she does what she needs to, but not much more."

"I know, I went in a few days ago and mentioned again that we could get her in to see Abby."

"And?" Nathan asked with interest.

"I got no reply. She'll talk to me, but not a lot and definitely not about Abby."

Nathan frowned. "But she's still sending her notes and letters."

"Yes, but that's it."

"The deposition she gave de Barr didn't help either. Dr. Greene was here yesterday and he wasn't surprised by her slow recovery. He said writing out the whole experience again could be a benefit, but it could also be detrimental. Physically she's healing fine, a little slow but fine." Nathan sat down at his desk and rubbed his face with his hands. "I just don't know what else to do for her."

"I don't either. She won't let us put a phone in her room, nor does she want to look at a TV again. She just wants to hide."

"Yes, but for how long?" Nathan asked. "We've a date looming in our near future, and after that …"

"Robin has mentioned that maybe it's time for a psychiatrist." Lincoln said. "But I think what she needs is something none of us can give her."

"Abby?" Nathan answered.

Lincoln turned back to look at him but he knew there was no more to say.

☯

"Good morning," Lincoln said. "How's everyone today?" he asked as he removed his coat and left it on the back of the chair at the desk.

Sarah turned to face him, expertly keeping herself in the shadows, concealing her scars. "Hi," she said to him softly through her clenched teeth.

"I'll leave the two of you alone," Robin said, rising from her chair.

Lincoln came over and sat on the edge of the bed. "You're looking good this morning," he said honestly. As much as she tried to hide in the shadows, he could see the natural beauty coming back to her face. The scars were still red and angry looking, and her head tilted from the cut to her neck, but the real essence of Sarah was starting to return with or without her help.

"You want to go for a walk in the gardens with me today?" Lincoln asked her the same question every time that he came to see her, but Sarah's answer was always the same.

"No, thank you."

"Sarah, are you ever going to leave this room again?" he asked her.

With the edge of her fingernail, she picked at her blue jeans, refusing to look at him "Why should I? Everything I want is right here."

The honest answer took Lincoln by surprise, but he realized she was right. Everything she wanted was right at her fingertips, just as Nathan and Abby had requested.

"You don't have Abby," he said softly, and though he saw a physical reaction, Sarah said nothing.

She rarely said much of anything, but her mind was never silent. Thoughts of Abby and their precious time together kept her sane. She had a longing, one she had no idea how to deal with; an ache in her heart that filled her with doubt and fear. She and Abby had exchanged letters, even poems, but some things were never said or referred to. For Sarah, it was the dreadful memories she had. The reflection she had seen in a cracked mirror haunted her almost as much as a pair of wanting dark eyes. *But will she ever want me again?* The thought bored a hole in her mind.

"Sarah?"

Lincoln had been speaking but, as usual, she only heard pieces of what he had said.

"Are you listening to me? Come out and join us. You leave your room for your therapy, why not come down and have a meal with me and Nathan?"

"Sucking a puréed meal through a straw isn't exactly eating." Her tone hinted at some strong emotions hovering just below her calm exterior.

"Then at least let us put a phone in here. Then I can make arrangements for you to talk to Abby."

"I'm not ready." That's what Sarah said, but Lincoln wasn't sure if that was what she meant. He knew she was scared, and he was sure he knew why.

"It'd be good for her to hear your voice. I think it'd be good for both of you." He watched her as she struggled against what he knew was in her heart. *Maybe a different approach*, he thought. "She needs you, Sarah. She needs to know that you're here and you're okay."

Tightly she pressed her lips together, but he could still see the emotional quiver that refused to be hidden. Bringing her hand up, Sarah covered her mouth, "She gets my letters, she knows."

"She needs to hear it from you. She needs to hear your voice …"

"I can't," she said.

"Can't or won't?" He didn't let up. "I think it's time for you to make a decision, Sarah, before it's too late. They've a hell of a case against her, and if we lose, you're going to spend the rest of your life wishing you had this time back." Lincoln knew he was pushing, but he needed to get through to her. "She loves you Sarah. Maybe you need to ask yourself if you love her."

Fire flew from her emerald eyes, "How dare you! I do love her—don't you ever question that!" This time the snarl coming through her clenched teeth had nothing to do with her wired jaw.

"Then prove it."

The challenge was there, but quickly the fire went out and the ever-present fear returned. Lincoln saw it happen right before his eyes.

"I can't," she said with tears in her eyes as she rolled over to face the wall. "Not yet." The conversation was over.

Lincoln sat there for a long time listening to her breathing as he watched her back. He didn't understand her reluctance, but then again he wasn't Sarah. Patience was what Dr. Greene and Robin had impressed on him and Nathan, but there were times when they didn't understand, anymore than they could understand what Abby was going through.

Lincoln searched his mind for an answer. Sarah needed a gentle push, but he had no idea how to give it. Slowly rising off the bed and whispering a goodbye, he reached for his coat but his hand stopped in mid-air when a thought popped into his head. In need of an accomplice, he headed out of the room in search of Robin.

☯

Nathan's tie was loosened just below his collar as he sat across from his niece in one of the glass interview rooms. Since her little escapade with the guards, they were no longer given the seclusion of solid walls. Nothing could be heard, but everything could be seen.

"I'm just saying, Abby, they have motive and opportunity and they have the murder weapon with your prints on it."

Abby was listening to him while sitting on the back of the chair with her elbows on her knees. The change of scene from her cell had improved her disposition but not by much.

"I know that." She saw Lincoln coming down the hall. "But what do we do now?"

"We take each point they have and we destroy it any way we can." Nathan's eyes shifted to the door as it opened. "Lincoln," he said nodding in greeting.

"Nate, sorry I'm late. I was longer with Hyme than I thought I'd be."

"How is ol' Hyme?" Abby asked.

"I had a nice chat with Hyme, a very interesting chat." Lincoln pulled two files from his attaché case and handed one to each of them.

"What's this?" Nathan asked as he put his glasses on.

"It's the forensics results from Billy's apartment," Abby said as she slowly read through them. "This is what I read when they brought me in." She looked up at Lincoln.

"Not quite," he said as he reached for his own copy. "This is what was found—as far as prints went—in the motel room, on the counter, and on the knife."

"So what?" Nate questioned.

"There were only three sets of prints found, one on a glass, a partial on the counter … and the full set on the knife."

Abby looked up from her paper in question. She didn't get it, and in some ways she didn't care. Her life was a mess, Billy was dead, Buck was dead, and Sarah …

"Abby—are you with us here? Concentrate please. An entire murder scene and there are only three sets of prints. What's their argument? You wore gloves the entire time until it came to holding the knife and grabbing the counter? And according to Hyme when they started their tests on the prints, he noticed something peculiar."

Nathan pulled off his glasses. "Define peculiar?"

"He found something interesting with the talcum powder from the inside of the latex gloves," he explained.

"This is relevant because? I mean, everyone wears gloves at a crime scene, especially when they are lifting prints," Abby said.

"Yes, but Hyme brought to my attention two things," Lincoln held up two fingers. "First, the high amount of talc around the evidence, mainly the cellophane transfers and the bookbinding tape, where there should only be minute traces if any; and second, the talc comes from Jensen gloves and is chemically based."

"So," Abby asked in a confused question. "The department has used the Jensens for years."

"That's right," Lincoln turned to Nathan, "Except … the department stopped using them three years ago."

Abby leaned forward in her chair.

"They changed to a more environmentally friendly product."

Nathan watched the interchange with interest, and then with annoyance. "Okay, it sounds good, but if I don't understand it, then a jury sure won't."

Lincoln tried to explain as Abby started to pace the room. "When you take a fingerprint, you dust first with powder, and then you take transparent cellophane strips, which you lay over your print, to lift it off. The bookbinding tape is a stretchable adhesive you use to lift prints off curved surfaces, like the edge of the counter at the motel. It's mandatory that everyone wears gloves, and the gloves are provided to you from the department," Lincoln continued. "What it means is someone was there wearing old gloves while lifting Abby's fingerprints."

"Couldn't someone have just had an old pair lying around?" Nathan asked.

"Old gloves become brittle over time," Abby said and Lincoln nodded in confirmation.

"This is all interesting, but it doesn't prove anything," Nathan said.

"Okay then, how about the fact that Hyme told Webber what he had found," Lincoln kept his eyes on his partner. "And Webber told him to bury it."

"Now *that's* interesting," Nathan said.

Abby's eyes widened. "That dirty son of a bitch."

"Hyme says there's enough for him to testify that someone could've tampered with Abby's prints."

"Now that's something I can work with," Nathan stated.

"And one other thing," Lincoln reached for some papers. "In the complete autopsy—and I quote, 'the mid-shaft fracture of the left clavicle, and the majority of the bruises and lacerations covering the victims body, were caused by blunt force trauma … postmortem.'"

"Postmortem?" Abby questioned.

"Postmortem," Lincoln responded. "Who ever beat the crap out of Ward did it *after* he was dead."

Abby looked at her uncle but said nothing further as she leaned against the wall.

"And last but not least …" he pulled a picture out of his attaché case, "the murder weapon." He handed the photo to his partner. "Look familiar?"

"It's one of my kitchen knives," Abby said in shock as her uncle snatched the picture.

Nathan studied the photo. "Are you sure Abby?"

"Yes—well, as sure as I can be from a picture. How can this be good news?"

"Think about it, Abby," Lincoln looked at her and then at Nathan. Neither understood what he was trying to say. "Your house burnt down—why would you still have one of your kitchen knives? Did you have it at the hospital with you that night? Ward was the only suspect in the arson investigation. What if he took one of your knives back to his motel? That would explain your fingerprints on it."

"Feasible," Nathan said. "And arguable."

Abby's mind was swirling with all the information. "I still think Webber had something to do with this. At the very least, he hindered the investigation. He knew about evidence and he didn't do a thing to find out the truth. And if he overlooked that, what else was overlooked or pushed to the side?"

"But I can't believe Webber could've murdered Ward," Lincoln said.

"I don't think he did it. He's not smart enough for all of this. But he sure was quick to pin it on me." She slid down the wall and sat on her haunches with a tired sigh. Lincoln knew she had ended the conversation just as Sarah had done earlier.

Silence fell over the room as the two men went over the papers at the table, leaving Abby to herself. After awhile Lincoln pushed his chair back and strolled over to talk to his partner.

"How you holding up?" he asked.

Abby gave him a shrug, but kept her eyes on the cement floor.

"Tell me what you need, Abby, and I'll do my best to get it for you."

"You can't undo what's already been done." She lifted her eyes. "How's Sarah doing?"

"She's doing good, Abby. Robin says the physical therapist is pleased with her progress."

Abby lifted her head and looked Lincoln in the eyes. "But? I hear a 'but' in there."

Passing a quick glance over at Nathan, Lincoln turned back to Abby. "She won't come out of her room except for therapy. We tried to coax her out, but she wouldn't have anything to do with it."

Abby stood up and faced Lincoln. "What do you mean you tried to coax her out? She's not a frightened animal in a cave for Christ's sake!" Abby was getting annoyed.

"You have to try to understand, she holes up in her room with the curtains drawn. She'll only talk to Robin and sometimes me. She's still pissed at Nathan."

"Pissed at Nathan?" Abby looked at her uncle. "Why's she mad at you?"

Nathan threw down the file he had been looking at, "Because I didn't tell her that the State is trying to gas her girlfriend, but don't worry she's set me straight. I was informed that I need to learn to communicate—that lack of communication is half of the world's problem. People don't know how to talk anymore and they definitely don't know how to listen," Nathan said smartly as a small smirk lifted the corner of Abby's mouth. "You find this funny?"

"No," she said. "I find it reassuring. That's the Sarah I fell in love with. She said the same thing to me." She wandered back over to the wall, with the comfort of knowing that the real Sarah was alive and kicking. But the warm feeling inside soon turned to an ache. The thought of the old Sarah only brought to mind the new one. The one with all the pain, the scars, and the memories of what had been done to her.

Little else was said between them, but the two men could see Abby's mood changing and not for the better. Her smile faded and she grew quiet as she sat alone against the wall. When they addressed her, she would answer with only a yes or no.

Nathan had noticed that Lincoln had been keeping a close eye on the time. So he was not surprised when Lincoln leaned over and whispered. "Trust me with this."

"What?"

Lincoln looked over at Abby. "I need you to watch the guards."

"What are you thinking, Lincoln?" Nate questioned suspiciously.

"Hand me your cell phone."

"You can't use that in here," Nathan said as he looked in the direction of the guards.

"I know. That's why you're keeping your eyes peeled," Lincoln said.

☯

Sarah was lying on her bed doing some of the exercises her therapist had left for her. Robin had taken her book and said she would be in the garden if Sarah wanted her.

Sarah paused and, with no one watching, she reached up and traced with her finger the scar that ran over the bridge of her nose.

It's not as painful as it used to be, she thought as she felt the smooth raised skin, *but it still feels odd, like it isn't even me.* Over and over she followed the thin red ribbon down to the edge of her chin. Her hand stopped when she heard the warble of a phone.

Rising up on one elbow, she looked around to see where the noise was coming from as the phone rang again. It was coming from Lincoln's coat, still hanging on the back on a chair. "Lincoln, you … I'm not answering that," she said to no one as she flopped back down on the bed. After a few more rings, the cell phone went silent.

Reaching over to the window, she pulled back the thick curtain just enough to let in a little sunlight. She missed things she used to take for granted—the fresh smell of the outside world, the warmth of the sun on her skin—but her life, as she had known it, was over. And as she felt the scars on her face and the thick scar on her neck, she knew she never wanted to leave this room again.

The cell phone in Lincoln's coat warbled again and Sarah glared over at its intrusion. It kept ringing but she had no intention of answering it.

But what if it has something to do with Abby? That thought was enough to move her. Walking slowly over to stand next to the chair, she hesitated and then reach into the inside pocket and pulled out Lincoln's small cell phone. *What if it had been Abby … but what if it hadn't?* She looked over at the window and at the sliver of light she had allowed in. Torn between the longing ache she felt and the fear that had overgrown her life, she was in a tug-of-war of emotions. A feeling of desolation overwhelmed her as she realized how much she missed Abby. She desperately wanted to look into her eyes one more time, but she feared what she would see. People had been so kind to her since all of this had happened, but she would always see the truth in their eyes, the horror and revulsion they tried so hard to hide, and the pity that quickly followed.

The cell phone warbled again and she jumped. Sitting back down at the edge of the bed, Sarah stared at the phone.

Nathan looked at Lincoln. "She isn't answering," Lincoln said in a whisper.

"Keep trying. No one can ignore a ringing phone for long." Nathan looked past Lincoln's shoulders to see if there was anyone watching them. "Are you sure she can hear it?"

"Oh yeah," Lincoln said as he tried again. "Robin said the coat was right where I'd left it."

Nathan watched him, but Lincoln shook his head as he listened to the ringing of his phone.

"What arc you two doing?"

They turned to Abby's stern accusation, their faces showing their guilt as she rose to her feet. She waited for some kind of answer but neither of them knew what to say.

"Lincoln, you know you're not supposed to be using a cell phone in here. You two are gonna get me in more shit." She glared at her old partner.

"There's no answer anyhow," Lincoln glanced at Nathan.

"Then hang up."

Lincoln felt dejected. "You know one of these days Abby, your impatience is going to bite you in the … " The ringing suddenly stopped and Lincoln spoke quickly into the phone. "Sarah? Sarah, don't hang up," Lincoln pleaded as he kept his eyes on Abby's pale face. There was no sound on the other end.

Lincoln handed Abby the phone. The men did their best to block the guard's view as Abby slid down the wall with the cell phone to her ear.

Abby's heart was beating so loudly, she was certain Sarah would be able to hear it on the other end of the phone. "Sarah, don't hang up. I know you're there … please."

Sarah wanted to hang up, to keep the outside world out of her room. To keep it all at bay, the truth, the realities, the fear.

"Sarah?" Abby desperately whispered.

A sob broke from Sarah's heart and Abby closed her eyes at the child-like sound that came through the phone. No more words were needed as the two women connected for the first time in months.

"Abby?" At the sound of Sarah's voice Abby's heart ached and she dropped her head to her chest. There was so much she wanted to say, but she suddenly couldn't find her voice. Her mind flooded with visions of the times they had spent together. Sharing laughter and tears at the resort; the long and heart wrenching hours she had spent in the ICU. She wanted nothing more at that moment than to be able to reach out, brush back Sarah's hair, and look into her eyes.

Alone in her room, Sarah sat on the bed with tears streaming down her face. The sound of Abby's voice made her realize how long it had been since they had spoken to each other. A lifetime had passed since their evening on her deck at Gold Creek, a lifetime of pain and medication since she had looked into Abby's eyes and had seen her perfect smile.

Without a thought, Sarah sniffed and Abby instantly responded. "Sarah … are you okay?"

The sound of her concern brought a combined sob and chuckle to Sarah's lips. "I'm better than I was last time you saw me."

Another wave of strong emotion washed over Abby as she heard the difference in Sarah's voice and the tightness in her speech because of her wired jaw. "Is there anything you need?"

Sarah fought back the tears with the heel of her hand. "Anything I need? You're in jail on a murder charge and you're worried about me?"

"Yeah, so what's so wrong with that?" Abby felt a warm glow that she hadn't felt in a long time.

"There's so much I want to say to you. I just don't know where to start. We left a lot of things unsaid when you left the resort, things I … Abby, I never lied to you. I may not have told you everything I should've, but I did not lie to you."

"I know that, Sarah."

"Do you? I mean, after everything that's happened?" Sarah paused, "Abby, I'm so sorry about Buck, I can't even imagine …" She couldn't finish and neither could Abby. After a moment of silent sorrow for the dog that had meant so much to them, Sarah finally found her voice.

"This is such a mess, Abby," she said.

"I know, and I wish you hadn't been dragged into the middle of it. I'm sorry, Sarah, I'm sorry this happened to you." Abby tried to fight but she lost the battle and Sarah heard her voice break.

"You didn't do this, Abby, Billy did. He brought me into this, not you. That's the kicker isn't it … if he hadn't, I wouldn't have met you."

Abby opened her mouth and closed it again. This was the Sarah she knew, the one who could look through a disaster and see a flower blooming in the rubble. She was right, and it made it all the more unbearable for her to think about.

"But if it hadn't been for me …"

"Don't, Abby! Do you hear me? Don't! You told me once that we can never go back, we can never change the past, and you were right. We can't; what's done is done." Sarah herself was a little taken aback by her outburst and the ferocity of her statement.

Abby took a deep breath and then let it out slowly. "And what about what he did to you?" she asked quietly. "How do I deal with that?"

There was no sound on the other end of the phone, but Abby knew Sarah was crying. It tore at her heart not to be able to hold her and she felt frustration growing inside her. "He did it to hurt *me,* Sarah, and for as long as I take a breath I'll know that."

"And what could you have done differently? Nothing."

For a moment there was silence on the phone, as they each thought about what could have been and what was. "Sarah …" the truth was on the tip of Abby's tongue, but the pain of it silenced her again.

"Hey, what's going on in here?" A guard was standing in the doorway.

"Oh, shit," Lincoln muttered.

"Sarah, I gotta go. Be strong—please. I love you," Abby said quickly, but before Sarah could respond the line went dead.

☯

The gentle ocean breeze wafted the smell of roses through the garden. The crash of the waves below the tall cliffs echoed rhythmically in Robin's ears as she did her best to concentrate on the book in her lap. The wooden benches along the manicured pathways were her favorite places to sit and read, but today she just couldn't keep her eyes on the words. The moment Lincoln had left, she had had second thoughts about his plan—but by then it was too late. She prayed it wouldn't have negative repercussions. Sarah was making progress, mentally and physically, but if they pushed her too hard they could send her deeper into her depression.

Looking down at her romance novel, Robin realized she hadn't paid any attention to the words she had just read. So she started once again at the top of the page.

His passion wouldn't be denied; he wanted her and he was going to take her. "Magdalene, I must have you with me, without you … " Raoul pressed his naked chest against her outstretched hand. He could feel her fingers as they ran through his dark chest hair, causing his loins to ache and harden …

Robin's cell phone rang and she quickly answered it, ignoring Raoul and his aching loins.

"Hello," she said.

"Robin?"

"Lincoln. How'd it go?"

"Good, really good. They talked, they finally talked."

"That's great," Robin said.

"I haven't seen Abby smile like that in a long time. And at least we got Sarah to talk on the phone," Lincoln said.

Robin looked back to the house and there, in the doorway leading out to the gardens, was a shyly blinking Sarah. "You did more than that, Lincoln. A lot more than that."

CHAPTER 38

Many things changed after that day in the rose garden; those in and around the mansion saw a whole other side to Sarah. No longer did she hide out in her bedroom. She even started to join the others downstairs for her meals. Robin kept track of all Sarah's medical needs, which were shrinking by the week. Lincoln's time at the mansion was also shrinking as he spent long hours tracking down even the smallest of clues in hopes of finding new evidence. Nathan had his hands full dealing with a now cooperative but emotionally declining Abby.

The conversation between Sarah and Abby had been a catalyst of change for Sarah, bringing her the courage and strength she needed to face each day, though she still refused to face herself. However, it had the opposite effect on Abby. She had become bitter and angry over her imposed exile. The cell phone incident deprived her of her last privilege: now the only person she was allowed to see was her lawyer. With only her uncle to talk to, her world became dark and desolate. Letters came in for her daily from Sarah, but they only seemed to draw her more and more into herself and deeper into depression.

The trial date was looming and Nathan had approached Abby about getting a continuance, but she wouldn't even discuss it. That was the date that they'd been given and that was the date they'd keep.

One afternoon while going over papers, Nathan leaned back in his chair and took a long hard look at his niece. Her shiny black hair now hung limply around her pale face, and her eyes were sunken with dark circles below them. Her eyes had always held a mystery, a mystique, but as he watched her peruse a document he realized that they had lost their luster. They had lost their sparkle of life. Abby was dying in prison; mentally and physically, the guilt and isolation was killing her.

She looked up and saw her uncle's face. "What?"

Nathan pulled off his glasses. "Abby …" He looked her squarely in the eyes. "Abby … did you kill him?"

She looked down at the papers covering the table, and then at her hands. There was a long heavy pause before she spoke. "No, but I think I know who did!"

They had taken Abby back to her cell, despondent and totally exhausted. Nathan sat there long after his niece was out of sight. With his head in his hands he thought about what she had said. It was possible, but was it probable? And if so, how the hell was he going to prove it?

Sarah was exercising when she heard Lincoln's car pull into the driveway. It was still early in the afternoon and she was surprised to see him at the mansion. Resuming her therapeutic regimen, she stopped when she heard raised voices coming from the study. Grabbing a towel, she threw it around her neck and she headed out the door.

"But you're her lawyer," she heard Lincoln holler.

"And I'm also her uncle, but I still can't tell her what to do. I work for her, she's the client."

Coming down the staircase, Sarah didn't like what she heard.

"She can't drop this bombshell on us a week before trial. There's no way that I can …"

"What bombshell?" Sarah asked as she stood in the doorway to the study.

Both men stopped talking to look at her.

"What bombshell?" she said with more persistence.

Nathan threw up his hands and then gestured for Lincoln to tell her as he sat down at his desk.

"Abby thinks she's figured out who killed Ward," Lincoln said stubbornly in Nathan's direction.

"That's good news, right? I don't understand. What are you so upset about?" she looked at Lincoln and then to Nathan.

"Because of *who* she thinks it was!" Nathan spat out in disbelief.

Sarah waited but neither told her what she was waiting for. "Who?"

"She thinks Billy killed himself to frame her." Nathan's tone lacked enthusiasm.

Sarah said nothing as she walked over and took a seat in one of the overstuffed leather chairs. "Is it even possible?"

"No," Nathan said sadly. "I think she's spending too much time thinking and it's affecting her psychologically. I honestly think she may be losing her mind in there."

"And I don't," Lincoln fired back. "Ward was one crazy bastard, and he was twisted enough to do it."

"No, Lincoln, you have to be twisted enough to believe it."

"But he did have the smarts to set it up, he had the weapon from her house, he had the opportunity to put it all in motion, and God knows he had the motive. He hated Abby!"

"Lincoln, enough!" Nathan said firmly.

"But could he have?" Sarah asked hesitantly. "I mean …"

"The evidence leads the trail."

"Lincoln, it is too preposterous."

"Not if you put it all together. We know he was high on drugs and booze, so what if he starts to cut himself at the motel, just enough to bleed everywhere. He wouldn't have felt it. Then he goes to the iron bridge at the edge of the park, finishes the job—jumps into the rain-swollen river, knowing it would batter his body. The rain stops, the water recedes, leaving his corpse high and dry with no surrounding evidence." Lincoln looked from Sarah to a disbelieving Nathan. "Look, I followed that creek. The only way he got in that water is from the iron bridge. A grate just before the bridge would have stopped his body if he'd jumped any higher up. So that's the starting point."

Sarah waited as the two men stood contemplating the information.

"It's possible, Nate, trust me. But if she wants us to try to prove it, then we need to get a continuance and Abby refuses to."

This was news to Sarah. "Why would she do that?" she asked.

Nathan walked over to the window and opened it. "In all my years, I've come across a select few clients who didn't belong in jail." He took a deep breath and continued. "I don't mean because they were innocent. I'm referring to people who can't be locked up." He paused for a moment. "Sane people who have lost their minds by being behind bars." Nathan turned back to them, "Have you ever seen a wild flower that's been planted inside, away from the sun and the wind? No matter what you do for it, it dies, because it was never meant to be indoors. That's what's happening to Abby; she's dying in there."

"Then we have to get her out," Sarah pleaded. "We have to do something."

"She is doing something. She's forging through, pushing for an ending regardless of the outcome. She wants it over with."

"But doesn't she realize that pushing this through without us being totally prepared could cost her her life?" Lincoln questioned.

"I don't think she knows what's happening to her. She just knows she wants it over."

"You're scaring me, Nathan," Sarah said quietly.

"I don't mean to."

Sarah swallowed her fear and took a breath, "Can I get in to see her?"

Months ago, it was what everyone had hoped for. Now it broke Nathan's heart when he shook his head, "No, there's no way I can get you in."

"But if I can …"

"I'm sorry, Sarah; if there was a way, I would pursue it, but there just isn't."

They grew silent, lost in their own thoughts of what Abby was going through and what they could do to help her. Nathan returned to his desk. Lincoln examined the documents and pictures on the table.

"So now what?" Sarah asked the two experts who turned to look at each other for answers they didn't have.

"If Abby says she thinks Billy killed himself, then that's what I believe," Lincoln said as he sifted through some papers.

Nathan jumped up from his desk. "Do you realize what you're proposing?"

"Yes, I do, Nathan. I believe what my partner is telling me. Ward was one sick man, but he was a clever man. Clever and calculating."

"So you want me and twelve jurors to believe he started to cut off his own penis, walked down to the old iron bridge where he finished the job, then jumped into the river to make it look like someone beat him up!" Nathan paced and ranted. "You want me to make them all forget about the fingerprints, the forensic evidence … oh yeah, let's not forget that annoying little picture of Abby at the motel."

"Well, we already know there are inconsistencies with some of the forensic tests," Lincoln stated as he looked over the messy table.

"Yes, but we don't know what that means," Nathan said as he walked over to stand beside him.

"But you said you had gotten people off with less," Lincoln said.

"Reasonable doubt is reasonable doubt, but I need more information to sway a jury with this kind of evidence against her."

"What inconsistencies?" Sarah asked.

Realizing her knowledge of the case was sketchy, Lincoln and Nathan quickly filled in what information they could, as she stood looking over the evidence on the table.

The first thing she saw was a picture of Billy Ward taken when he had been arrested. It was the first time she had seen him since his attack on her and she glared disdainfully at the picture.

Unconsciously, she reached up and touched the thick scar on her neck as she recalled his voice, his sadistic laugh, and the hatred he had for Abby.

Lincoln had been watching Sarah carefully, and when her hand went to her throat, he glanced over at Nathan for his take on the gesture. Nathan's expression told him he didn't like what he had seen either.

"Sarah," Lincoln said gently but there was no response. She was in the grip of a strong mix of emotions she wasn't aware she possessed.

"You know, I was never one who believed in the justice of an eye for an eye, but I'm glad he's dead," she said as she tossed the picture down onto a stack of other photos. Trying her best to ignore the emotions pulsing through her, she glanced over the rest of the table, and pushed back several photos until she uncovered Abby's mug shot from the pile. She reached out her finger to trace Abby's face.

"She looks tired in this," she murmured.

Moving closer, Lincoln looked down at the picture, "She was. I'd just brought her from the hospital."

"I guess it wasn't a picnic for anyone," Sarah said as she looked up at Lincoln with the odd tilt of her head that was a legacy of the attack.

"She never left your side, not until she was forced to."

"And if she had just stayed …" Sarah let the comment die on her lips as her gaze fell on some of the full color photos of Billy's body at the crime scene.

Lincoln reached for the glossy prints. "Maybe you shouldn't be looking at all of this stuff."

"I want to help," she said as she moved the pictures out of his reach. "I do have a brain and I know how to use it." She stood her ground, but Lincoln could see the thin cracks showing in her emotional armor. "Now if you will excuse me, I'm going to take a quick shower and then I'll be down to help however I can." With her newly healed jaw set firm in decision, Sarah turned and left the room.

"Strong-willed women. You can love them or hate them, but you surely can't ignore them," Nathan commented.

"Don't let 'em fool you, Nate," Lincoln said as he watched Sarah make her way up the stairs. He turned back to look at his boss. "It's hard to be tough when your bottom lip's quivering. I'll be right back."

☯

"Sarah?" Lincoln tapped on her door.

"Ah … just a sec." He could hear muffled sounds and then a moment later she opened the door with an attempt at a smile. Lincoln could tell that at one time, her smile must have been as vibrant as the green of her eyes, but the scars would no longer allow the corner of her mouth to lift.

"I was just going to jump into the shower," she said as she made a gesture toward her bathroom. Glancing in the direction she had pointed, Lincoln could see the mirror that had been removed at her request still hadn't been returned.

"I just wanted to talk to you. I haven't had much of a chance to do that lately." He looked around, noticing the changes to her room. The curtains were pulled back, and the window and the door to her private deck were open to the refreshing ocean breeze.

"You don't have to babysit me anymore, Linc. I'm a big girl and I can take care of myself."

"I know that, Sarah, and I'm not here to babysit you. I'm here as a concerned friend."

"I'm okay … really," she said as she got off the bed and walked over to the window.

"Funny," he said, "from here it looks like you've been crying."

She turned to face him with all the inner strength and courage she could muster. "Is that a crime?"

"Only if you're lying about it." They locked eyes and Sarah did her best to stand her ground, but Lincoln saw through her tough façade. The harder she tried to hide it, the more her bottom lip trembled as the tears grew in her eyes.

"Sarah," he said compassionately.

But she put her arm out to stop him. "Please don't." She took several deep, cleansing breaths, until she had regained her self-control. "It's just … after what Nate said, I can't imagine what she's going through and … I wasn't aware they had so much evidence against her."

"They do. A lot of it's circumstantial but there's no denying it's an uphill climb."

Sarah knew what he was saying, and it brought another wave of emotions that threatened her steely determination. Annoyed for showing her vulnerability, she angrily brushed back a tear that had squeezed through. "And I want to help. So let me."

Her tenacity made him smile. She did her best to return it.

"Are you sure you're ready?"

Leaning back, Sarah looked out the window at the vast Pacific Ocean. "She was there for me when I needed her. By my side. Now I want to be there for her. I can't think about what my future would look like without her in it …"

"You've been there for her, Sarah. You're good for each other and you deserve to be together."

"Thanks, Lincoln, that means a lot to me."

"You're an incredible woman, Sarah, and I don't have to guess why Abby fell in love with you."

Sarah reached up on her tiptoes and pulled his head down enough to place a kiss on his cheek. As he straightened back up, he looked hard into her eyes and then he glanced over the scars on her face. He hadn't meant to, but he did it and he saw her instant reaction. Sarah's smile quickly faded and she brought up her hand to cover the side of her face as she turned away. Without a word, she headed out onto her small deck.

Silently cursing himself, Lincoln quickly followed. "Sarah, I'm sorry. I didn't mean …"

With her back to him, she held up a hand to stop his words. "It's a natural reaction and I'm learning to live with it."

He knew the words were right, but they weren't the truth. "But you don't have to learn to live with it. Dr. Greene's one of the best plastic surgeons on the west coast. He said …"

"Lincoln—stop. It's something I … it's who I am now and I have to learn to deal with it."

She still hadn't turned to face him and he knew why. "But I don't understand. You don't have to …"

"Lincoln, this is my life and my decision. I'll decide what and how I'm going to live it."

"But are you? Living it, I mean?" He didn't mean to be cruel but he thought another small push might be what she needed.

Turning around, he could see the anger and resentment burning in her eyes. "Yes, I am. Every day."

"Really? Doesn't look like it to me," he challenged. "Have you looked in a mirror lately?"

The direct and painful comment blindsided her and she reacted like an animal that bites out of fear.

"Get out!" she snarled pointing back at the opened patio door.

Lincoln stood unmoving. "Sarah, I didn't mean to …"

"How dare you!" Her eyes grew darker as her fear turned to pain. "How dare you!" she shot back angrily. "Get out of my room, Lincoln."

"No," he said as walked over to her. "You can't keep walking around avoiding your reflection."

"Don't tell me what I can and can't do. My reflection is my problem. I would think you would have enough things to deal with, without looking for more," she said as she took a step towards him.

"I do … and I will," he fired back at her. "Right after you face what you're most afraid of. The image that's in your mind."

"What would you know about what's in my mind?"

"Because that isn't what you look like anymore. You need to face the evil that your mind sees because that is the only place it really exists."

"I will face what I want to face—and I'll do what I want to do, when I want to do it. Now for the last time … get out of my room!"

"Hey … hey … hey, enough already!" Robin demanded as she came through the bedroom. "I could hear you two all the way on the other side of the house." She looked from Lincoln to Sarah. "Drop it, both of you."

"Right after he minds his own business," Sarah snarled.

"Which I'll do, once you realize what you remember isn't what the rest of us see."

"Lincoln, enough!" Robin ordered. "I think it's time for you to go." She waited and when he made no motion to leave, she pulled at his arm. "Now." Escorting him out into the hallway, she closed the door behind them and glared at him.

"What the hell are you doing?"

"I'm trying to help her," he declared.

"Help her? My understanding is your knowledge is in the field of law enforcement, not psychiatry. Sarah needs time. What you're doing is not helping her. If you push too hard, the psychological damage could be devastating. Do you not understand that?"

Lincoln looked at Robin and realized that his emotions had pushed him beyond what his brain should have told him. Running his hand through his short hair, he scratched at the back of his neck. "Oh, man, what've I done? I'm so sorry. I don't know what came over me. One minute we were just talking and then … I need to go back in there." He reached for the door handle but Robin blocked his way.

"I don't think that's a good idea. Give her some time. When she's ready, she'll look to see what there is. But a mirror will only give her one point of view. It won't show what's inside, and when the time comes for her to want to deal with that, she will. But you can't push it."

They talked for a while longer before Lincoln reluctantly left Sarah's well-being in the hands of the professional. Robin waited for him to reach the stairs before she opened the door and went in to see what kind of damage had been done.

Much to her surprise, Sarah was just coming out of the bathroom, her hair still wet from her shower.

"Hi," she said.

"You okay?" Robin asked.

Sarah stopped and looked out the window. "Would it matter how I answered that?"

"Yes, it would, but I would prefer the truth."

Sarah looked down at her hands, tracing her finger along her deadened thumb. It was such a strange feeling for her still, to see her movements, but not be able to feel them. "I'm a little screwed up right now," she finally admitted as she looked up at the view out her window. "On the one hand, everything seems to be happening so fast, I can't stop it. Hell, I can't even get it to slow down. And then on the other hand, things are going so slowly it's frustrating." Sarah reached up and touched the scar on her neck, but she didn't need to. Robin knew exactly what she was talking about.

"Maybe it's time to get you someone to talk to."

"Only if she has black hair and brown eyes," Sarah said as she strolled past Robin out to her deck. "I don't want to talk to anyone else."

The young nurse followed her and the two stood silently at the iron rail for a long time.

"I'm scared, Robin," Sarah finally whispered.

"I know you are, but it's not as bad as you think it is."

"It's not just that." She turned and faced Robin. "Yes, my appearance scares me, but not for the reasons you think. See, when I met Abby, it wasn't by accident. It was planned, but what followed wasn't." She paused for a long moment and then decided to speak the truth. "For the first time in my life I found love. I found someone who loved me for who I was … or at least, who she *thought* I was. I kept things from her and I pretended to be someone I wasn't. I didn't intend to fall in love with Abby, but I did. I so wanted to tell her that, to tell her the truth—and I was going to but …" She turned and looked over the ocean as the tears fell. "She fell in love with who she thought I was, but that wasn't me. What do I do if the real me isn't who she is in love with? I'll never know if it's me she loves or the image she remembers and is unwilling to forget."

The admission didn't surprise Robin, but Sarah's fears told her just how deep her scars really were. "I think you need to give yourself and Abby a little more credit. The woman I got to know in the hospital, the one who slept by your bedside, doesn't seem like the type that falls for just anyone. She fell in love with the real you, Sarah. What's inside is who you are, not the skin on your face."

"But how will I ever know?" she sniffed.

"Because you will be able to see it in her eyes," Robin answered.

CHAPTER 39

They pored over papers, reports, documents, lab results, photos, anything that might lead to a missed piece of evidence, but it only seemed to lead to further frustrations. They talked about the case, and they talked about Abby, but neither Sarah nor Lincoln ever talked about what had happened that afternoon in her room.

Nathan had begun the tedious work of scripting out his opening statements. If he knew about the unspoken tension between them, he showed no sign of it. His heart and his mind were on the task in front of him, and on the life of his niece.

Leaning back in his chair at his desk, Nathan heaved a heartfelt sigh and both Sarah and Lincoln looked at him.

"You okay, Nate?" Lincoln questioned with concern.

"Yes. I'm just going over everything for the opening statements. At times it seems so overwhelming but then … Abby's right; it is possible, but there's nothing here that can make it probable. It will be a hard sell for the jury. I just wish there was more."

"More? Are you kidding me?" Lincoln squawked.

"No, I'm not kidding. It's all out there somewhere. No one's clever enough to do what he would have had to do and not leave evidence behind." He tossed his glasses onto the desk.

"We can't just give up," Sarah said.

"Never—not until the jury has read a verdict. Only then is a trial over. And then we start on appeals."

"That's if we lose, and we aren't going to." Sarah stated firmly.

"What points do you have so far?" Lincoln asked.

"Let's see." Nathan reached for his glasses and then perused the tablet in front of him. "I'm going to start off by putting Billy on trial. I hate the 'discredit the victim defense' because it can blow up in your face and you can wind up just getting sympathy for the victim, but I've no choice."

"Sympathy for Billy? You're kidding right?" Sarah asked.

"No," Nathan said reluctantly.

"But after everything he did to those girls!"

"I'm going to try to sneak it in as often as I can, but Billy was never convicted. Therefore, it's inadmissible, but the prosecution is going to have to allow some of it. If not, they have no motive and that helps us." Nathan looked down at his notes. "If I guess right, de Barr will try this by a time line. He will go from opportunity; Abby left the hospital and had the time. Then the picture of her at the motel will show she was there …"

"Picture of her at the motel?" Sarah interrupted in disbelief.

"Yes, an ATM camera across the street got a video of her arriving in her Jeep. We have the video here somewhere." Lincoln looked at the shelf where they'd stored some of the evidence and then he looked down at the table. "Video's over there, but here's a couple of still photos." Lincoln handed the grainy black and white pictures to Sarah.

"Is it her?" Sarah asked examining the picture in her hands.

Neither answered the damning question. They silently went back to work as Sarah continued to study the picture.

"This isn't her," Sarah suddenly stated.

"But it could be," Nathan suggested.

"No, this is not her."

Nathan and Lincoln looked at Sarah in surprise. "What do you mean it isn't her?"

"Look." She pointed to the figure standing next to the Jeep. The two men looked at each other, but neither understood what she was trying to show them. "Her Jeep is here, isn't it?"

"Yes, after they were done with it, we had it brought here. It's parked in the garage," said Nathan.

"Follow me." Sarah rose to her feet and the men quickly followed. She led them to the large garage outside, walked over to Abby's black Jeep and stood next to the driver's door. "See," she said with her arms out.

"See what? I don't get it," Lincoln said in mild frustration.

With her back to the Jeep, Sarah measured herself against the height of the hardtop, and then held up the photo. "Who ever this is, it isn't Abby. Look for yourselves. That person comes to the same height on the Jeep that I do. What's Abby?" Sarah looked at Lincoln. "Six foot and then some?"

"Six one." Lincoln stepped forward and took the picture from Sarah's outstretched hand. "How'd we miss that? There's no way this is Abby. This person's way too short."

The early morning sky was gray and the air was cool as Sarah moved gracefully through the rose garden. The only sounds around her were those of nature as she came to the end of the pathway. Here, surrounded by roses and overlooking the ocean, Sarah took a seat on the bench to enjoy the view for a moment. It had become a morning ritual for her, coming out to the garden and doing her exercises on a small patch of grass in relative seclusion. No one was there to bother her, no one was there to push her beyond where she wanted to go, and that was just fine with her.

The case against Abby was foremost in her mind as she watched a lone sea gull play in the currents of the wind. There were times when the reality of what they were doing was too much for her, when the color photos would flash vividly in her mind and she would have to step out for a break. She would feel that they were making progress, bringing to light more discrepancies in the prosecution's case, but then Lincoln or Nathan would remind her how unpredictable a jury could be and she would feel fear waft over her once more.

She rose from her seat, walked over to the small patch of grass just above the high cliffs, and began her exercises. By the time the sun actually broke over the horizon, Sarah's skin was glistening with sweat. Now finished, she picked up her towel and a bottle of water, and returned to sit on the bench. Taking several long drinks of water, she looked over the ocean and was amused to see the sea gull was still there, happily playing with its freedom. Suddenly she was aware of a presence and she turned around as Lincoln came into view.

"If I'm bothering you, I can leave."

"No, you're fine," she said, but he could hear a slight hint of reluctance in her voice.

"Sarah, I wanted to talk to you alone before the trial starts." Lincoln said nervously, wiping his palms on his pants, and then crossing and uncrossing his arms, "I know … um …" Lincoln quickly closed the distance between them and squatted next to her. "Sarah, look at me," he pleaded softly.

Her eyes searched the skies for the sea gull, but to her disappointment it was nowhere to be seen.

"Sarah, please." He reached over and laid a gentle hand on her forearm. The contact was enough to reach her and she turned to him but kept her eyes on the ground.

"I'm sorry, from the bottom of my heart. I'm sorry. I didn't mean to hurt you and I didn't mean to upset you. I was only trying to help, and instead I did you wrong." His words were honest and sincere, but she still couldn't look him in the eye.

"Me, too," she said softly. "You're a good man and a good friend, Lincoln, and I couldn't have gotten this far without you."

He smiled at her. "Yeah, I think you would've."

"Thanks, Lincoln," she whispered.

☯

It was early Sunday evening the night before the trial and the only indication of the pending case was the rise of tension throughout the mansion. The extra staff Nathan had brought in had either been sent home or back to the office.

Reasonable doubt was all he needed and, while he wasn't feeling confident, he was definitely feeling hopeful.

"Nathan?"

The lawyer looked up at Lincoln who was standing over the table that had been covered with evidence and documents. "Are you going to need all of the pictures for tomorrow or do you just want the ones you've marked?"

"We should have them all there, just in case someone throws us a curveball." He gestured to all of the papers on the table.

"We can pack them up and take them with us," Sarah said.

"Uh, us?" Nathan looked at Lincoln.

"Yes, us," Sarah stated. "You didn't think I was going to hide out here, did you?" Seeing their reactions, she put down her pen, "Forget it. I don't care about the press anymore. They're going to find out who I am sooner or later and I don't care who sees me. I'm going to be in that courtroom tomorrow morning."

Nathan scratched his head and licked his dry lips. This was something he hadn't thought of. "Unfortunately, my dear, no, you're not," he said as gently as he could, but he saw the fire ignite in her eyes.

"Yes, I am. After all of this, damn right I'm going to be there."

"Sarah." Nathan came around his desk towards her.

"Don't you '*Sarah*' me," she fired back. "I'm strong enough. I need to be there for her."

"I'm sorry," he said, "But you can't be."

"What do you mean, 'I can't be'? Why not?" She looked from Lincoln to Nathan for an explanation.

"Sarah, you're a witness for the prosecution," Lincoln said. "You're the key to the prosecution's case, the catalyst that set Abby's rampage in motion."

"What does that have to do with me going into the courtroom?"

"You can't be in the courtroom until after you have testified."

"What?" she looked desperately from one to the other, "But you're testifying and you're going in tomorrow," she said to Lincoln.

"Yes, I am, but my name's first on the witness list. After I'm done, I can be in the courtroom."

"But then—," She stopped as the realization hit her. "Where's my name on this list?"

Lincoln looked at Nathan, and Sarah's eyes followed. "Nathan? Where am I on this list?"

"Last," the lawyer finally said.

"Last! Then that means I can't be in …" Sarah's words trailed off as she grasped the full impact of what they were saying, and she sank into her chair.

"Sarah, I'm sorry. I didn't really think you would want to be there—with the press and the people. I thought you understood." Nathan got up and walked over to her chair. Crouching down he placed his hands on hers.

"It's not fair, Nathan," she said through tears of frustration. "Why do I have to be last?" She looked into his familiar eyes. "Nathan?"

"Because …" He paused for moment. "They're going to use Billy's attack on you as Abby's motive. Your love life is about to become very public, Sarah, and for that I'm truly sorry. Especially once the press finds out who you are."

"And my father said I'd never amount to anything." She pulled her hands out of Nathan's hold. "I guess Mother's bridge club will be flapping their gums like crazy." She walked over to the open window and stood silently listening to the distant crash of the surf.

"I'm sorry, Sarah …" Nathan stopped when she held up her hand. Her entire body and soul ached as the knowledge started to sink in. She had been at the height of anticipation, thinking about seeing Abby again, but the reality of life had put an end to all of it. She wouldn't be seeing Abby tomorrow; she wouldn't be seeing her for a long time yet and there was not a thing she could do to change it.

"If there's nothing else—I think I'll go outside. I need the fresh air." Neither of the men said a word as they watched Sarah quietly leave the room.

Dressed sharply in a tailored dark suit, Abby paced the room as she waited for Nathan. The level of her nervousness surprised her, but she did her best to remain calm as she walked back and forth across the tile floor. For the first time in a long time, she instinctively reached into her pocket for a cigarette and then stopped when she recalled that she had quit.

The door opened and Nathan walked into the room.

"You're looking fresh and ready this morning," Nathan said as he pulled out a chair.

She looked at him in annoyance. "You know, for a lawyer you suck at lying."

Nathan realized the suit improved her appearance, but not her attitude. Abby's strained face showed her exhaustion.

"Did you get much sleep last night?" When she didn't answer him, he looked over at her. "Abby?"

"Where's Lincoln?"

"He can't be in here, or in the courtroom, until he's done testifying."

"Oh, yeah. Bet he's happy," she said.

Nathan went back to his papers and he didn't notice the perplexed look on her face. "Now, I don't have to remind you about courtroom etiquette, do I? Keep your emotions in check. No laughing, no smiling—unless it's appropriate. Which is never. If you have something you want to add, whisper it or write it in a note. Pay attention to what's happening and …" He looked over at her, and he realized she wasn't paying attention even now. "Keep your eye contact with the jury to a minimum, and for God's sake don't tell anyone you've been golfing with O. J. Abby, you're not even listening to me," he said impatiently.

"What?" she looked at him with an air of distraction. "I know courtroom etiquette, you don't have to tell me."

"Really? Been golfing lately?"

"What? I don't golf." She looked at him in confusion.

"Abby, pay attention. I need your mind on the game," he pleaded, but he could tell her attention was elsewhere. "Abby, your trial starts in forty-five minutes; are you aware of that?"

"Yes Nate, I am."

Nathan turned to his niece. "What's going on?"

"Why?"

"Don't bull shit me, Abby, we don't have the time."

"It's just that … well, I thought Sarah would've been with you."

"You know she can't be in here."

"I know. I was just hoping that maybe you could've pulled a few strings and … whatever." She dropped into one of the chairs.

"I wish I could."

"This is going to be hard on her. There are times when I regret having to put her through all of this."

"You don't have a choice, my dear. Don't you think it's time that you concerned yourself with your own well-being? I assure you, we've no intentions of letting anything or anyone upset her. Mind you, when the press finally figures out who she is and who her parents are, I fear things could get out of hand."

"Nate, depending on how things go, I want your word that you'll look after …"

Nathan held up his hand to stop her. "You don't even have to ask."

"Thank you," she said softly.

"There's no need."

"Yes there is, and I should've done it earlier. Uncle Nate, thank you for everything. I can't imagine what this would've been like without you." It was the first time in a long time that she referred to him as her relation, and he had to admit it felt good.

Being back in the legal trenches had also felt good, but having his niece's life and freedom in his hands was draining. He wasn't the young man he had been the last time her welfare had been in peril, but he was looking forward to being in the courtroom again. He just wished he knew what the outcome was going to be.

"Are you ready to do this?" He gathered up all his papers and slid them into his briefcase.

She hesitated for a moment. "Would it matter if I said no?"

"No, not really." Nathan stood up. "Any questions?" He paused when he saw a shadow of something cross her face.

"Abby?"

Standing tall and quiet next to the table in her expensive suit, she looked more like a model than a murder suspect. Taking the last few steps towards the door, she stopped and, much to his surprise, she reached out to give him a hug. The embrace was as real as the fear he felt in her tension-filled body. Still holding on to her, he whispered into her ear.

"It'll be okay."

Pulling back from him, she shook her head before she looked into his eyes. "And if the truth comes out?"

Holding the stare, Nathan tried not to show how he felt. "We'll deal with it—but for our sake, let's hope it doesn't."

The courtroom was packed to capacity: parents of Billy Ward's victims; lawyers and law students sitting shoulder to shoulder with reporters; and members of the public who just wanted to be there. The air was electric as people coughed and shuffled, whispering comments and speculating to each other.

Barnard and Cheryl, two lawyers from Nathan's firm, sat quietly amongst the boxes and folders filled with papers. Neither seemed to be overly concerned about the expectant atmosphere of the courtroom; they had their work to do and they were doing it. The noise level dropped considerably when the side door of the courtroom opened and Nathan and Abby came in together.

Abby sat silently observing the legal team working on her behalf, but out of the corner of her eye she noticed a familiar face and she turned in acknowledgement.

Lieutenant Banks nodded discreetly but her expression didn't change. A moment passed and she stood up and came over to the short partition separating the defendant from the public.

"Nathan," Lieutenant Banks hissed loudly.

He turned around in surprise. Seeing Banks, he jumped to his feet and went to her. Abby watched with interest as the two whispered back and forth, but try as she might she couldn't make out what was being said.

The doors to the courtroom opened and Ronald de Barr, with his entourage of legal assistants, entered like a rock star. If it hadn't been her life on the line, Abby would have found great amusement in the assistant DA's circus-like performance. With much pomp and circumstance, de Barr marched down past the rows of the gallery with his eyes firmly set on the judge's bench. When he reached the small gate in the partition, his eyes drifted over to where Lieutenant Banks was in heavy discussion with Nathan. Anger flashed on his cocky face as his glare went from his professional adversary to Abby.

Ignoring de Barr, Nathan and Banks finished their conversation and parted. Nathan's outward appearance had not changed, but Abby could sense something was wrong. Nathan took his seat and reached into his briefcase.

Abby leaned over and whispered, "What's going on?"

"I'm not sure," he said without looking at her. "Mary got wind of something yesterday and she spent the morning trying to find out what's going on, but she came up empty."

"Well, de Barr certainly didn't like the idea of the two of you talking. Did you see the look on his face?"

"Yes, I did." He pulled out several papers and scanned them quickly.

"What's that?"

"The witness list," he said concentrating on the names listed. "de Barr applied for a warrant but Mary couldn't find out what it read, only that it had something to do with a witness ... which bothers me." Nathan turned to his niece and looked her dead in the eyes. "Should it bother me?"

Before Abby could answer, the door at the front of the courtroom opened. "All rise. The Honorable Judge Porter presiding," a voice boomed as the black robed judge entered his domain.

"Ladies and gentlemen, are we ready to proceed?" the judge asked after everyone returned to their seats. He nodded to the bailiff. "Bring in the jury."

A hush fell over the room as the twelve members of the jury and the two alternates made their way into the courtroom.

"Okay, let's get this going," the judge said to the prosecution and the defense team.

"Actually, Your Honor," de Barr rose from his seat with a paper in his hand. "Before we get started, I've one small item that needs the court's attention."

"Here we go," Nathan said under his breath to Abby, without moving his lips.

"I have a warrant, Your Honor," de Barr waved the paper in his hand, "for the arrest of Nathaniel James Holoman," de Barr stated as he turned to smirk at the defendant's table.

The entire courtroom erupted as Nathan jumped to his feet. "What? That's preposterous! What's the charge?"

"Manipulation of a prosecutorial witness."

Abby started to rise out of her chair, but she felt Cheryl's hand on her forearm. "Let him handle it, Abby," she warned.

"This is an outrage," Nathan bellowed at Ronald de Barr. "I'll hit you with a slander suit that's so large, de Barr, your grandchildren won't have enough money to change their minds."

"You and your money don't scare me," de Barr challenged before Judge Porter's gavel rang out loudly.

"Gentlemen, that will be enough!" He pounded angrily. "Counselors approach the bench." All the lawyers on both sides rose. "Lead counsel only," Porter warned.

He waited for the two men to approach. "Before either of you says a word, heed my warning." The judge leaned forward with his hand over the microphone. "I *will not* let you turn this trial into a circus. Keep the cheap tricks and theatrics where they belong, not in my courtroom! Is that understood?" he demanded.

"Your Honor, it wasn't my intention to disrupt your courtroom, I was only ..."

"Oh, cut the shit and ass kissing, de Barr! It was your intention and you know it. If you want to use this trial to your own benefit that's your business, but play it to your television audience not to me." de Barr did his best to keep face, but Nathan turned his attention to the judge.

"Now let me see this warrant." The judge lifted the paper from the ADA's hand. "What are you trying to pull here?" he muttered as he looked over the legal document. "You got this on Saturday evening, so why are you serving it here, this morning, in my courtroom?"

de Barr looked from the judge to Nathan as both stared back waiting for his answer.

"I was waiting for further information, and I was unable to proceed with serving the ..."

Annoyance crossed Porter's face. "If what this says is true, Ronald, you should have done something about this a long time ago, not now. You wanted to grandstand for the jury and the press." Before de Barr could answer, Porter held up his hand. "Save it. All right ... manipulation of a prosecutorial witness, explain this."

"Your Honor, one of the key witnesses for the prosecution, who has been uncooperative to say the least, has been hiding out at the residence of Mr. Holoman."

Irritated by the accusation, Nathan looked at Porter, "He's referring to Sarah Murphy, who has only been hiding out from the press, not from the prosecution. He has had full access to her, and has spoken to her on several occasions, your Honor." Then he turned to de Barr, "You're making her sound like a criminal."

"She's a witness for the prosecution and she's living at your residence." Porter looked up from the warrant.

"The young woman is recovering from life threatening injuries, Your Honor."

"Injuries she received from the victim in this case," de Barr cut in. "And it's her girlfriend who is sitting there in the …"

"Hold it … hold it." Porter held up his hands. "I'm not doing this here. In my chambers."

The judge rose from his bench and the two lawyers followed him, both firing accusations back and forth as they made their way into Porter's chambers.

"I can't believe you're doing this, Ronald. This is petty even for you," Nathan sneered as they walked. "Manipulation of a prosecutorial witness! What a load of crap."

"You have my witness and you're filling her head with all kinds of things."

"She's a witness, and what she's a witness to isn't going to change." Nathan shook his head in disbelief. "Give the child a break. She's still recovering and she needs a place to stay."

de Barr fired back. "Then get her a hotel room."

"She's not staying in a hotel room! If you recall, that's where she was attacked."

"Gentlemen, enough," Porter warned as he removed his robe and sat down at the desk in his chambers. "Now explain this to me again, Ronald."

☯

"What's going on?" Abby hissed the moment Nathan got back to the table, but he ignored her as the judge took his seat.

Porter made quick work of telling the jury to disregard the charges mentioned by the prosecution. Then he motioned for an adjournment until the following morning. With a bang of his gavel, Porter left the courtroom. The bailiffs came over to escort Abby to a holding room and Nathan silently followed.

"What the hell is going on?" Abby asked angrily as the door closed behind Nathan.

"De Barr is putting on a show for the jury," he said as he sat down.

"Well, it worked. Did you see the looks on their faces?" Abby said.

"Yes, I did."

"So what is all this about?"

"Sarah. We have to move Sarah out of the mansion."

"What? Why? Wait, is that what this was all about?"

"In a sense, yes. By the law, he's right. She shouldn't be there while we are at trial."

"So he waited until now, that little prick," she said. "Well, he got the show that he wanted. The second you all left the courtroom, every reporter flew out of there like rats leaving a sinking ship. You realize your place is going to be crawling with them now that they know who she is and where she is?"

"Yes. I let Lincoln know when we came out of Porter's chambers, so he is on his way back to the mansion." Nathan leaned back in his chair and ran his fingers through his hair. "It was a dumb stunt on de Barr's part designed to rattle my cage and to generate more publicity, but it'll leave us with a foot in the appeals doorway."

Abby face grew somber. "You think they're gonna win, don't you?"

"I always think they're going to win. It makes me try all that much harder to prove them wrong."

"But do we have enough to prove them wrong?"

"All we need is reasonable doubt. And that, my dear, we have."

☯

Lincoln raced up to the front gates of Nathan's mansion, and was not surprised to see reporters already set up next to the driveway. He inched his way forward as the tall iron gates opened, allowing him to pull past the small mob, but not before he heard the barrage of questions.

"Is that really the daughter of Phillip Murphy in there?"

"Do you know Sarah Jane? Was she Billy Ward's last victim?"

"Did you know S. J. Murphy was the reporter who broke the story on Abby Stanfield?"

He did his best to ignore them, but the questions just kept coming. When the gate clicked shut, Lincoln roared away down the driveway. His car had barely come to a halt when the front door opened and Robin came out to greet him.

"They started arriving fifteen or twenty minutes ago. Sarah knows they're there but not why."

"Where is she?" he asked as he climbed from his car.

"In the garden, where else," she called after him.

☯

The pressures of the morning weighed heavy on Sarah's small shoulders as her fingertips brushed over the bright red scar on her neck. Even with all the work she had done in physical therapy, her head still tilted to one side and the corner of her mouth refused to smile.

"Sarah."

She turned to see Lincoln moving quickly down the pathway towards her.

"Lincoln, what's going on?" The fact he was back at the house this early concerned her. "Is Abby okay?"

He came around the edge of the rose bushes and she saw the forlorn look on his face. "Abby's fine."

"Then what are you doing here? And what's with all the reporters outside?"

"They … the reporters, and I'm sure now half the state, knows exactly who you are and where you are."

The disappointment showed clearly on her face as she tried to smile away the news. "We knew this was going to happen. You all did a great job of keeping it a secret for as long as you did, but they were going to find out eventually." She turned away from him and from the thoughts racing through her mind. "It's been a long time since I thought about being in the public eye. I always hated the whole society page stuff." She looked back at him. "Guess that's part of the reason why I never got along with my social climbing parents. Lincoln, there's something else isn't there?"

He sighed deeply, "Sarah, you can't stay at the mansion any longer."

"What?" The information was not what she was expecting. A wave of fear came over her face.

He quickly filled her in on what had transpired in the courtroom that morning.

Sarah felt her heart skip a beat at the thought of leaving her protective sanctuary. "I have to leave," she whispered in disbelief as she looked over the garden and then down at the turbulent ocean below. "After all this time—why now? Lincoln, where will I go?" she questioned over the rising sound of the surf.

"Nowhere that you don't want to." Lincoln watched the blood drain from her face. "Sarah, Nathan has no choice, but I assure you wherever you go, you won't be alone and your privacy will be protected."

"I'm sure it'll be okay," she said out loud but not to him, as her hand unconsciously came up to cover the scarred side of her face. "I'll be okay." She sat up a little straighter and pulled her hand away from her face. "I'm not going to run and hide," she said defiantly over the increasing noise.

"No one said you would, but as you could see from the front gates, the press isn't going to give up easily," Lincoln said loudly over the rising winds.

Sarah turned and looked him in the eyes, "Well, you know what … neither am I!"

He smiled at her show of spirit. "Somehow that doesn't surprise me," he hollered as a rush of thundering air burst above the cliff with the swirl of helicopter blades.

Startled by the helicopter's sudden appearance, they turned and looked directly at the photographer hanging out of the side of the open door. Reaching over with his long arms, Lincoln pulled Sarah to his side, doing his best to shield her as she held up her hand to block the camera's view. Her red hair thrashed wildly in the downwash of the rotors, the ends of it whipping against her sensitive face.

"Lincoln," she called out in a mixture of pain and fear as she turned into his protective shoulder.

"Come on," he shouted over the noise. With their heads ducked away from the camera and from the power of the helicopter's wash, they rushed along the garden pathways. Approaching the mansion, Lincoln looked up to see Robin throwing open the door.

"What the hell's going on? It sounds like *Apocalypse Now* out here."

"The press," was all Lincoln needed to say as they hurried past the nervous nurse.

"Sarah?" Lincoln motioned to the small sofa against the wall.

"I'm okay," Sarah said, but her voice was shaking almost as much as she was.

"No, you're not," Robin said as she took her wrist to check her racing pulse.

"I said I'm fine," Sarah said in a stronger voice as she pulled her wrist from Robin's hands. "Don't treat me like a child. Yes, I'm shaking—that stupid helicopter scared the shit out of me."

Lincoln knelt down in front of her and placed a caring hand on her shoulder. "You realize that was a reporter?" he asked.

"I think that was pretty obvious. I'm sure he got a couple of good shots, too."

"There must be something we can do to keep the helicopters away, isn't there?" Robin asked as she heard the noise of the intruding aircraft flying over the mansion again.

"Nothing short of inviting the president over for dinner," Lincoln commented as he looked up at the ceiling.

"They'll leave when I leave," Sarah said quietly.

Before either of them could comment, the dining room door swung open to an angry Nathan. "I knew it wouldn't take them long to get here," he said, gesturing to the ceiling.

"And with a telephoto lens, no less," Lincoln said. "She was out in the garden, and I'm sure they got a clear shot …"

"You know '*she*' is right here. I hate when you do that," Sarah said as she jumped to her feet. "I'm no longer in a drug-induced coma, so don't talk over me or around me like I'm not even here."

"We don't mean to, it's just that …" Nathan stopped. "You're right and I apologize."

"It's my life," she said as she looked from one to another. "Maybe it's time for me to make some of the decisions." The room fell silent. "Can they really make me leave Nathan?"

"Yes," he answered reluctantly. "Sarah, don't worry about it. I'll get you the best room in the best hotel in town.

"For me to hide out in? For how long, six weeks? Six months? I might as well be in prison."

She sat down, dejected, in one of the tall chairs. "Nathan, I appreciate the offer, but no. Besides, it'll still be a hotel and I'm not overly fond of them right now."

Nathan walked over to her and placed both his hands on her shoulders. "You tell us then, what do you want to do?"

Sarah looked everywhere but at Nathan.

"Sarah?" he questioned.

She lifted her eyes and looked at him. "I don't know."

At that moment, Nathan wanted nothing more than to take her in his arms and tell de Barr and Porter to go to hell, but he knew it would only make matters worse and the headlines bigger.

"Any ideas?" he looked at Robin and Lincoln.

"All I have is a one bedroom studio suite," she said apologetically.

Lincoln walked over to kneel next to Sarah, "How about you come and stay with Carla and me, for tonight anyway? All we have is a pull-out sofa in our second bedroom, but it'll get you out of the mansion and away from the press."

Sarah looked at Lincoln, "Don't you think you should ask Carla first?"

"Nah. She'll be thrilled," he said with a smile.

"Now all we have to do is figure out how to get you out of the mansion without the world's press following you." Nathan said.

"Don't worry. I have an idea," Lincoln said with a growing grin.

☯

First out of the gate was Nathan in his sports car, roaring quickly through the mob of reporters, some of who sped away in pursuit. Next out of the driveway was Lincoln, quickly followed by Robin, both taking their share of following press, now falling over each other in an attempt to decide which vehicle actually had Sarah in it. Several minutes later, Nathan's long black limousine slid slowly out of the driveway, the black tinted windows hiding the identity of the occupants in the back.

"That's it, that has to be what she's in," one of the two reporters left said as he ran to his car. "The limo and the Mercedes are the only vehicles the old man owns."

Agreeing with his colleague, the other reporter jumped into his car and they both left in pursuit.

The pair smiled with delight as they followed a safe distance behind the limo, each dreaming about the money they were going to get for the picture. Ten long nervous minutes later, Abby's black Jeep emerged slowly from the tall iron gates. Wrapped in a scarf and large dark glasses, Sarah looked left and right, but there was no one there to see her as she zoomed off with Lincoln's home address held tightly in her shaking hand.

☯

Sarah was nervous about meeting someone new, but it only took a few minutes for Carla to put her at ease. Lincoln had given his wife little notice, but it had been enough for her to buy a few groceries and to get dinner started before Sarah arrived. By the time Lincoln walked in the door, she was sitting at the table chatting with Carla and sipping tea.

"Any problems?" he asked as he approached his wife, and kissed her cheek.

"Nope, Carla had the garage door open and was waiting for me. I can't believe that it worked," Sarah said.

"I knew they'd go after anything that left the mansion, and they knew what everyone had been driving in and out of the gates, but I was sure they hadn't counted on Abby's Jeep being there."

It felt strange for Sarah to be out and away from the mansion. She hadn't realized how much security the house had given her. Carla and Lincoln had made her feel welcome, but she was far from feeling at home.

After dinner, Sarah insisted on helping with the dishes. It was something normal that never happened at Nathan's. Lincoln sat down on the sofa and without thinking turned on the TV. Before the picture even developed on the black screen, they all heard Abby's name from the set. Lincoln immediately pressed the button to change the channel.

Sarah left her dishtowel on the table and came into the living room. "Go back, please."

"I don't think …"

"Lincoln, please."

Sarah stood watching as the images of her and Lincoln in the rose garden came up on the screen. Each picture flashed before them; Lincoln with his arm around her, Sarah holding up her hand and turning her face away as her hair was tossed wildly around, the pair scurrying for the shelter of the house. Sarah lowered herself to sit next to Lincoln as an image froze on the screen. It looked like the first shot taken; Sarah's green eyes were open wide in fear and confusion, and the clear photo showed the details of each of her scars.

Lincoln and Carla waited for some response from Sarah, but she sat silently looking for the first time at her real image. When the story was over, Lincoln muted the TV.

"Sarah?"

There was a pause and she tried to master her emotions, roiling just below the surface, before she turned to smile at Lincoln. "They didn't exactly get my good side did they?"

The comment was not what he was expecting and he had no idea how to respond.

CHAPTER 40

Lying in the darkness, Sarah had no idea what the time was or how long she had slept. A distant thump pulled her from her thoughts. Pulling back her comforter, she tiptoed across the bedroom and peered out the front window. Through the dim light of early morning, she saw a small figure hurrying down the Quinns' sidewalk—to his bike.

"Paperboy," she whispered to herself in relief. She was about to go back to bed when her curiosity won over her fear. Quietly, she left her room, crossed the kitchen, opened the door and scooped up the newspaper. Taking it back into the kitchen, she sat down at the table and stared at the headlines.

The Missing Victim—Sarah's Scars

The bold print screamed at her, but she couldn't bring herself to unfold the paper to see the pictures. "I can do this," she whispered to herself as she reached out, but her hand was shaking so hard she had to stop.

Looking down at her hands, pictures flashed through her mind—images frozen in time that would be forever part of her life. Her face prior to leaving for the resort; her bloody body being wheeled out of the motel with Abby by her side; her face in the mirror. Lifting her eyes, she stared at the paper until she realized it wasn't a picture she needed to see but the truth of what she had become. "Facing evil, isn't that what Abby said?"

Pushing her chair back, Sarah headed to the small bathroom next to the garage. Flipping the lights on, she kept her eyes on the counter.

"I can do this, I can do this," she whispered to herself. "It's not that bad." But the memory of what she had seen in the hospital burned in her mind. Closing her eyes, she searched for the inner strength she knew she had and the courage that made her who she was.

"Sarah." It was Lincoln's voice calling for her.

"I'm in here," she answered him.

Lincoln had seen the newspaper on the table and the bold headlines. "Sarah," he called as he hurried fearfully towards the bathroom.

Ignoring him, she kept her eyes on the counter as she swallowed several times hoping to bring moisture back into her dry mouth. "I can do this," she said, as she took a deep breath and looked in the mirror.

Nathan nodded to the bailiff outside Abby's door. The officer said nothing but nodded in return as he stepped to the side to allow the lawyer access.

"Good morning, Abby," he said as he came through the door, but he was surprised to see her seated at the table and not in her customary position against the wall. "How'd you sleep?"

"Sleep isn't something I do well," she answered in a low tone.

Nathan turned to look at her and he knew by her smoldering expression that something was amiss. "What's wrong?"

She lifted her eyes off the table and focused on him. "You know it amazes me that you can stand there and ask that, like you have no idea what could be wrong. Is that a lawyer thing? Do you learn that shit in law school? 'Hide The Truth And Cover Your Ass 101'?"

Nathan was taken aback, "Where the hell is this coming from?"

Abby angrily bolted from her chair, but said nothing. After a tense moment she took a deep breath and walked away from him. "Why is it that even with all the money we have, we can't protect those we love?"

The bold question was more of a statement than a query and Nathan knew that as he watched her walk over to the wall. A sullen silence filled the room as Abby leaned against the wall.

"What the hell are you talking about?"

"She didn't deserve this … any of it!" Abby finally burst out.

Only then did he realize where her anger was coming from. "You heard about the helicopter?"

"Heard about it and read about it."

"You've seen the paper?"

"In full color."

Nathan ran his fingers through his hair. "Abby, we did the best we could, but we knew it wasn't going to last forever. Once they knew who she was … well, it only made her more sought after. And then yesterday de Barr gave them the address. I sent Lincoln there as fast as I could but I couldn't stop the helicopters."

He watched her close her eyes. "She looked so different," she said quietly.

"You mean the scars?" he asked.

Abby didn't answer him.

"She was scared, Abby."

"Can you blame her?"

"No."

Pushing herself away from the wall, Abby wandered over to the table. "Whatever she wants …"

"Abby," he interjected. "Money isn't an issue right now."

"I wasn't thinking of now."

Opening statements finally got under way and, as expected, de Barr started off by building up Abby as a highly decorated detective with several commendations and honors and an unblemished service record. That was, until Billy Ward. de Barr then painted a different picture of Abby; a detective out of control, one with an uncontrollable temper and a desperate need to find a serial killer.

Several times he portrayed Abby as a woman bent on vicious revenge. He built up the case against her and then he laid out all the evidence they had to prove it. When de Barr finished, Porter banged his gavel to announce the lunch recess.

Abby leaned over to her uncle and whispered in his ear, "If I was on that jury, I'd be thinking, '*Fry the out-of-control bitch.*'"

"That's enough," Nathan fired back sternly as he watched the jury file out the door. "I don't want to hear that again," he warned as the bailiff motioned for Abby to rise.

"You saw their faces, Nate. You tell me what they were thinking," she said over her shoulder.

Refusing to acknowledge her, he turned around and looked for Lincoln in the mob of departing people, but there was no sign of him anywhere. Looking back at Abby, he thought about what she had said. She was smart and she knew, just as he did that de Barr had done his job.

When the court resumed, Nathan kept his opening statements straightforward and without the dark emotions de Barr had used. He delved more into Abby's service record and her exemplary work. He explained how her cases were meticulously handled, following every last lead and loose end until there was nothing left. Until the day a young woman was brutally murdered and the case of the Sadistic Slasher was handed over to her and Detective Quinn.

Then Nathan went to work, showing how Billy Ward had taunted the police, daring them to catch him, and how he had then turned his attention and obsession onto Abby. He goaded her and the entire department after each kill, phoning Abby at home and on her cell phone, turning the investigation into something very sinister and very personal. His fixation on Abby and his desire for her attention drove him to destroy everything she loved, but it still wasn't enough for him.

Ronald de Barr was a little confused and mildly concerned at the way that Nathan was laying out the case against Abby. He too was showing how far Billy had pushed her, and it was a questionable defense, until Nathan Holoman did what he was famous for. He opened a door no one had seen. He unexpectedly accused Billy of killing himself as a final desperate ploy to destroy what remained of Abby's life.

With all his expertise, Nathan laid out their defense, balancing the evidence to show how far Billy had gone to feed his own obsession with Abby, but at the same time showing the professionalism of his client. Billy pushed, but Abby refused to play his game. Using the leniency given to opening arguments, Nathan led the jury through Billy's insane but detailed planning: the inhumane way he ended Buck's life and how he burned down Abby's home, but not before taking one of her kitchen knives to use on himself. He continued with how Billy had hired a pretty young reporter in hopes of exposing Abby's personal and private life. When that didn't work, he—Billy Ward himself—sold the stories to the press under that same reporter's name.

Abby closed her eyes when Nathan went into detail about Billy's dreadful attack on Sarah, an act that was only perpetrated for one reason; to get back at Abby. And when that didn't work, how he ended his own life in one last attempt to take away Abby's freedom and possibly her life.

"When this case is over, the evidence will show that it was Abby Stanfield who was the victim here, and that Billy Ward insanely took his own life in one final attempt to destroy hers. And as you can see ladies and gentlemen of the jury, he almost succeeded. But with your help and understanding of the facts and evidence in this case, you can send a message to him in hell; his plan didn't work." Finally, Nathan sat down.

Abby leaned over to him, "You convinced me," she whispered, "I knew I *didn't* do it."

Nathan and Cheryl walked out the doors of the empty courtroom together speaking in low hushed tones. Nathan looked up with surprise to see Lincoln sitting on one of the benches waiting for him.

"Lincoln," he said in a concerned tone. "I'll see you back at the office, Cheryl."

"All right." She nodded in greeting to Lincoln and then left the two men alone.

"How did it go?" Lincoln asked as he stood up.

"The scales of justice sway back and forth, my friend," Nathan said as he clapped a hand on Lincoln's shoulder. "It's best just to be patient. There're twelve jurors and we just need one."

"I know that," Lincoln answered. "But which way are they swaying right now?"

"The evidence is in the prosecution's favor, but that'll change once we get into the heart of the case and to old Hyme's testimony. It's going to be tight," Nathan said as they walked side by side through the marble hallways of the courthouse. "So what brings you here? I thought you would be busy with paperwork."

"Well," Lincoln hesitated enough to cause Nathan to stop. "Did you see the paper this morning?"

"Didn't everyone? Even Abby got her hands on one."

"She wasn't the only one," Lincoln said sympathetically. "Sarah saw it too."

"Why didn't you tell me earlier?"

"Because it wasn't the only thing she saw this morning."

☯

Locking eyes with her reflection, Sarah stared into the familiar green eyes as Lincoln came into the bathroom.

Slowly, she reached up to her image in the mirror and then stopped. Turning her hand around, she brought her fingertips towards the bridge of her nose and the jagged scar that ran across it. As she had done so many times before, she traced the smooth tender skin, but this time she watched as she did. Gently, she followed the scar over and over again as she moved closer and closer to the mirror.

"It's me, isn't it?" she said softly to Lincoln.

He had no idea what to answer, so he told the truth, "Yes, Sarah, it's you."

Licking her lips, she felt the sagging corner of her mouth. "You know, I still remember the sound of those first punches." She brought her finger down and played with the scar at the corner of her mouth. "Not the pain so much, just the sound. I wanted to scream, but nothing came out."

"That was because of the dieffenbachia paste," Lincoln said.

Turning her head slowly from side to side, she examined the damage left behind by a madman. A sunken cheek, several small jagged lines that had been opened by his fists and a drooping lip. "I don't remember much after that, but I recall him laughing." Sarah brought her face around and then lifted her chin at an angle to get a better view of her neck.

"I do remember him holding me up by my hair as he waited, but I didn't know for what." She tenderly ran her fingers along the red scar on her neck as her eyes drifted away from what she saw. "He told me that he wanted her to watch me die. I didn't realize then he was referring to Abby." Sarah lifted her eyes and looked at Lincoln. "He wanted her to see me die."

"But you didn't. You never gave him that satisfaction. You fought to stay alive. You won, Sarah. You beat him."

"I did, didn't I?" She stood there for a moment and then closed the distance between them, accepting the offer of Lincoln's arms around her. Laying her head against his chest, she closed her eyes and whispered, "I want it to be over. I want my life back."

"I wish I could do that for you, turn back time and make all this go away, but I can't."

"I know that. I have to live with what has happened." She pulled out of his caring embrace and looked up at him. Lincoln saw something different in her eyes. "I have to live with what has happened, but I don't have to live with the scars."

"Sarah?" he asked unsure of what she meant.

"I think maybe," she turned and looked at her reflection in the mirror, "I'd like to see Dr. Greene now."

CHAPTER 41

It wasn't often that Nathan used his name and wealth to move and manipulate things, but when something was important to him—like his niece—he was relentless. When Sarah decided to have the plastic surgery he did everything in his power to make it happen, and to make it happen quickly. The first obstacle was arranging for Sarah to see Dr. Greene, but that wasn't as hard as trying to book the surgical time. But he did it. Sarah was booked for her plastic surgery under a different name at a different hospital.

Nathan couldn't have been happier than when he finally got to bring his niece some good news. Abby was happy for the first time in a long time—and it was she who came up with the answer for Sarah's housing problem. Gold Creek. It was perfect; away from the trial and away from the press. Judge Porter could put a gag order on her whereabouts so Sarah would be left alone to heal. Nathan couldn't wait to tell her. It was a good way to start the day and, in his mind, a good omen at the start of the trial.

Lincoln was called as de Barr's first witness, and reluctantly he took the witness stand. It didn't take de Barr long to realize he wasn't going to be helpful. With permission from the judge, the ADA treated Lincoln as a hostile witness and slowly de Barr extracted the information he was looking for. As Abby's partner, Lincoln confirmed her temper and her obsession with proving Billy's guilt.

By Lincoln's second day of testimony, Sarah was on her way to the hospital with Robin at her side. On Lincoln's third day, Sarah woke up once more surrounded by the white walls of a hospital room.

Robin was there by her side as Sarah's eyes opened in fear and panic.

"It's okay, Sarah, you're all right." Robin said as she leaned over Sarah's hidden face. "Do you remember where you are?"

One of her hands was attached to an IV drip; Sarah reached slowly with the other to feel her face, but Robin quickly stopped her.

"No, no, don't touch it," Robin said as she reached over and picked up a cup of water with a straw in it. "Here, this will help your throat."

Sarah took several sips of the cold water and her throat did feel better. "How long?" she asked as Robin sat down on the edge of her bed.

"Not for a while. Why don't you get some sleep, dear."

Sarah started to nod, but stopped. Though the pain was less severe than what she had already endured, her face still hurt. "Have you heard from Nathan? What's happening?"

"Of course. I talked to him yesterday when you came out of the operating room. Abby nearly drove him crazy until she knew you were okay. He stopped in on his way home last night but you were still unconscious." Robin knew it wasn't what Sarah was waiting for. "Lincoln is almost done testifying. He said de Barr has his hands full with him. Lincoln knows what to say and what not to say, and how to get around the questions he doesn't want to answer. Nathan said it makes Lincoln look like he's hiding something, but it's also making de Barr look like a bully."

Sarah leaned back and looked up at the ceiling. "That's what Nathan was hoping for."

"What to do you mean?" Robin asked.

Through the thick bandages, Sarah explained, "The jury is too busy looking at Lincoln and de Barr's battling personalities and not at the evidence the prosecution is trying to present."

"I never thought about it like that."

"Nathan explained how the law itself is boring, and evidence is even more boring, so what happens is the jury winds up paying more attention to the witnesses themselves than to what they are saying. It's not their fault, it's just human nature."

"But this is a murder trial," Robin said in disbelief. "Shouldn't they be paying attention to the evidence?"

"They should be, and most will be, but it only takes one." Sarah's words were becoming slower.

"Look, you need your rest for the helicopter ride tomorrow. I'm going to be just over here," she pointed to a chair next to a window, "reading. All right?"

"Yes," Sarah wiggled a little deeper into her bed. "How *is* Raoul doing?"

"Naked from the waist up as always," Robin said with a grin as she took her seat and opened her novel.

It was Lincoln's last day on the stand when the helicopter landed across the street from the hospital. The entire staff had been abuzz about the mysterious patient who had arrived with her own nurse and had been seen only by Dr. Greene, and the arrival of the helicopter only sped up the rumor mill. Almost everyone agreed that the patient who had received such rapid plastic surgery had to be someone who was not only rich, but also extremely famous.

It was Robin's first flight in a helicopter and it showed as she did her best to keep one medical eye on her patient and the other on the distance from the ground.

Sarah reached over and took Robin's hand and the nurse did her best to smile.

The pain in Sarah's face had eased considerably, but the dull ache was constantly there below the thin bandages. Dr. Greene had rewrapped her face this morning, and she had watched his face and his expert eyes and was relieved with his pleased reaction.

"Can I see?" she pleaded.

"Not yet; you need to be patient and give everything time to heal," he said with a nod to himself. "Maybe when I see you in a few days."

☯

Sarah was going back. Back to where it all started. But it wouldn't be the same without Abby, though she was looking forward to seeing Helga and Günter. Then with a touch of sadness, she fondly remembered who else wasn't going to be there. *Buck*.

A while later, the helicopter began descending, and she opened her eyes to see the majestic snow-capped mountains and the clear blue waters of Lake Alouette. She had a strange feeling of coming home. Looking down at the wooden docks, Sarah remembered walking down Abby's for the first time with a bottle opener in her hand.

Robin noticed a subtle change in her patient and she wondered if coming back here was a good idea.

The helicopter swung around as it approached the landing area and Sarah spotted two familiar figures coming out of the log building.

"Helga and Günter?" Robin yelled over the noise of the rotors.

Sarah didn't respond as she fought down the rising lump in her throat when she saw them standing there waiting, holding hands, just as she had remembered them. The familiarity was welcome but strangely painful as she reached to adjust the scarf around her head.

The pilot brought the machine down gently and then gave them a thumbs-up to disembark. Sarah didn't move as she looked out over the lake. Robin was concerned.

"Are you okay, Sarah?"

She only nodded.

"One step at a time, all right," Robin warned as she placed a hand on her arm. "It's been a long day already."

"I know," Sarah said as she turned to face her nurse, but suddenly she felt nervous about seeing the elderly Scandinavian couple. "I'm not sure if I can do this," she said as she watched the pilot walk over to Günter and Helga.

"Do what?" Robin asked in confusion.

Sarah dropped her eyes and looked down at her hands. Subconsciously, she rubbed at her numb thumb, something she now did whenever she was nervous.

"Sarah?" Robin reached for her hand.

"I'm afraid," she finally revealed.

"Of?"

Lifting her eyes off her hand, she looked at Robin. "Of what I'll see in their eyes."

The comment stunned Robin for a moment as she fought for the right words, knowing the wrong ones would only deepen Sarah's fears. "Sarah, look at me. There's nothing for them to see."

Keeping her eyes on the young nurse Sarah replied, "Maybe not now, but they know what's under all of these bandages."

"No, they don't. Not even you and I know what is under there now. That's what you have to keep telling yourself. What was there before is now gone."

Sarah knew Robin was right but it didn't make it any easier as she reached for the door handle. "The scars may be gone, but the images never go away," Sarah said softly under her breath.

☯

The moment Sarah's foot touched the ground she felt the tug of déjà vu. The log lodge, the smell of the pines, and the blue of the lake in the distance brought a flood of memories that pulled at her heart with an ache she wasn't sure she could endure. Introductions were made and then the small group slowly made its way towards the cabin.

"It's okay to remember, my dear," Helga whispered to Sarah, knowing where the young woman's mind was. "Just try to dwell on the good and not the bad."

"I know," Sarah whispered back as she climbed the wooden steps onto the deck.

Coming through the large sliding glass doors, Günter gestured to a large arrangement of red roses. "Two dozen, best I can count," he said as she walked over to them.

She leaned forward and took in the fragrant smell before she reached for the card.

Until I am there with you
All my love,
Abby.

Sarah reached to touch one of the soft petals of the roses before she pulled one of the stems from the display. She closed her eyes and she buried her nose deep into the flower. The room was silent as she turned and headed for one of the bedrooms.

"Thank you," she said quietly. "I think I'll lie down now."

Robin began to follow, but Sarah held up a hand. "I'll be okay," she said as she disappeared into the bedroom.

Helga looked nervously at Robin. "Did we do okay?" she whispered.

"You did great," Robin said sincerely as the three made their way outside.

"But she seemed so quiet and subdued," Günter commented with great concern as he looked back at the closed bedroom door.

"Part of that is the medication she's on; she just had surgery. But in reality, she's no longer the woman you knew. Not physically, or mentally."

Suddenly, Günter snarled something in his native tongue. Robin had no idea what he had said, but she thought she recognized Billy's name before Helga shushed him. The elderly couple exchanged a few more words before Günter stomped off the deck and up the driveway.

Unsure of what to say, Robin changed the subject. "This is a beautiful resort, Helga. I've never been out of the city before, so I was a little apprehensive about coming here. The closest hospital's so far away if there's a problem."

"It is okay, my dear, we are all here to help," Helga put an arm around Robin's shoulder. "In the old country, we had to learn to do it ourselves. I myself have helped many babies into the world," she said with great pride.

"That's good to know, Helga, but I don't think childbirth is going to be Sarah's biggest problem."

CHAPTER 42

"Well, that wasn't too bad," Abby said as she sat down at the table next to Cheryl.

"I think it went well," Nathan said of Lincoln's testimony. "Some hurt, but I think the real damage was to de Barr himself. He came off looking like a bully."

"He is thorough, but he's too busy grandstanding for the press and the jury, and that's going to help us, too," Cheryl said. "So who's next?"

"Fred Hyamensky, with the forensic evidence. Now this one we'll have to be careful with. Too many times I've seen all this science and DNA mumbo-jumbo confuse juries to the point where they don't care what the evidence says and they just choose to ignore it."

"Hyme is one of the better ones. He can put it all into laymen's terms and make them understand things they know little about," Abby said as she watched her uncle.

Nathan lifted his head and caught her eyes. "Yes, but remember, Hyme isn't on our side this time."

"But he does have the evidence that shows the different talcum powder, and that shows someone tampered with the fingerprints. Put that with the fact that Webber didn't want to investigate it further, that's something. And with the knife Billy took from my house. I mean correct me if I'm wrong, but that's some strong evidence that points to someone else."

"Yes, but …"

There was a quick rap on the door, "Is this a private party or can any old witness join in?" Lincoln said, sticking his head into the room.

"Come on in." Nathan waved as Abby quickly stood up to meet her old partner halfway. The elderly lawyer watched the two embrace and he smiled, realizing Lincoln's testimony had done nothing to damage their friendship.

"I'm sorry, Abby," Lincoln said.

"For what? You did what you had to do," she replied, "but then again you didn't have to keep saying I was hot-headed and opinionated."

"Don't forget overbearing," Lincoln said with a smile.

"Okay, I hate to break up this happy reunion, but we still have a pile of work to do," Nathan said as he peered over his glasses.

"I know," Lincoln commented as he looked at his boss, "But before we do that," he turned back to Abby, "I just talked to Robin and they arrived safely."

"That's good to hear," Nathan said as he watched Abby's features relax at the news. "I know Dr. Greene was happy with the way the surgery went."

There was a sharp knock on the door and the conversation ceased as the bailiff walked in. "Judge Porter has requested your presence in his chambers," he said.

"Now?" Nathan asked with a concerned scowl on his face.

"Now," the bailiff replied.

"I don't like the sound of that," Abby said as she looked at her uncle.

"Neither do I," Nate replied as he walked to the door. "Cheryl, you'd better come, too." He held the door open for her and they left together.

Abby wanted to hear every detail of every moment Lincoln had spent with Sarah, and that included the morning she looked in the mirror.

"It was one of the hardest things I've ever witnessed," Lincoln said, recalling the events of that morning. "But she stood there and faced it."

A smile slid across Abby's face.

"Just when you think this young little thing can't handle another blow, she surprises the hell out of you." Lincoln shook his head in disbelief.

"Oh, I know."

The door opened and Nathan walked into the room, followed by a somber looking Cheryl.

"What?" both asked at the same time as the saw the dejection in the lawyers' faces.

Nathan stood there silent for a moment and Abby's first thoughts went to Sarah.

"Nate?"

"Judge Porter was just notified. Fred Hyamensky was in an accident on the coastal highway." Nathan sat down at the table and removed his glasses. "He was driving home and something happened, they don't know what. Mechanical failure maybe, or possibly a heart attack. His car went over the embankment. They pronounced him dead at the scene."

There were no words to express the mix of feelings they experienced as they bowed their heads in silent remembrance. Hyme had been a friend and a colleague to each one of them. The city had lost one of their own and one of the best forensic pathologists around. And Abby had lost the cornerstone to her defense.

CHAPTER 43

Even through the gauze bandages, Sarah could feel the light breeze off the lake on her tender skin. Closing her eyes, she let her mind wander until she could almost hear the patter of Buck's feet or the sound of Abby's voice. It made her heart ache, but at the same time it was strangely comforting. Coming to the resort had been a good idea. No one knew who she was and it was obvious no one cared. Her bandages caused a few looks of compassion and curiosity, but soon she was forgotten as the other guests went about their business of enjoying their holidays.

Today was the day. Without waking Robin, she had left the cabin and wandered down to the end of the dock to watch the sunrise. Strangely, it was her way of being closer to Abby, and it gave her a chance to think about her future. The helicopter would be arriving some time this morning to take her back to the hospital. The last of the bandages would be coming off and she would finally get to see what she looked like. Dr. Greene and Robin had already warned her there would still be bruising and discoloration and that swelling would temporarily distort her features.

Looking down at the sun-bleached dock, she picked at a sliver of wood. Different pictures flashed through her mind. She saw her face mixed with other people's faces as she recalled with vivid clarity what she looked like before Billy Ward, and after. And she remembered that horrible day in the hospital bathroom.

It is what it is; no one can turn back time. Isn't that what Dr. Greene said? I've seen the worst and no matter what, it will be better—not perfect but better.

Still picking at the weathered dock, Sarah's eyes happened to glance down through the slats of wood to the shimmering reflection in the water below. Her curiosity got the better of her and she leaned past the edge of the dock to look at her bandaged reflection. The water was so clean and clear that she could see to the sandy bottom as she focused back on her wavering image. The first thing she noticed beyond the stark white of the bandages was the positioning of her eyes. They were once again symmetrical, evenly situated above her repaired cheekbones.

Wanting a better look, Sarah swung her body around and lay down on her stomach for a closer view. Peering into the water, she studied her face, trying to see the 'old her' and the 'new her' for the first time. She squinted and examined the skin as it wrinkled and gathered at the corner of her eyes. *My eyes, they look like … my eyes … I wonder …* Several times she turned her head to the right as far as the scar on her neck would allow her, trying to see what had changed. Looking closer into the water, she tried to wrinkle her nose, but the skin beneath the bandage was still too tight and it caused her to grimace. That too was something new for her to study, but she wanted to see what was hidden below the gauze and she reached to remove it. Carefully, she picked at the white tape holding the bandage in place.

"I don't think you're supposed to do that." Robin's voice startled her so much she almost toppled into the water.

"Holy crap, Robin, you scared me," Sarah stammered.

"You know, we have mirrors for that now," Robin said with her hands on her hips.

"I thought I saw something on the bottom of … I was just…" Sarah realized Robin wasn't buying what she was trying to sell. "I wanted to see what I look like," she said sheepishly.

"And I'm glad to hear that, but I think you'd do better to wait for the doctor and for something better than a lake to see your reflection in."

Sarah sat up and pulled her legs in to sit cross-legged. "It looks like me, but different." Not wanting to see Robin's reaction, she lifted her gaze to look at the distant mountain. She didn't feel different, but she knew she looked different; there was no changing that. *But maybe I am different. I know I am not the same person who arrived here the first time. So much has changed … so much.*

"That's not necessarily a bad thing, is it? It's still you after all."

"I know, but …" her voice trailed off when she heard the sound of a helicopter in the distance. Searching the blue skies, she spotted the tiny aircraft. "They sure make a lot of noise, don't they?" she asked, thankful that she was able to change the topic. Sarah watched as the helicopter circled to land. "There's someone in it," she pointed out to Robin as she stopped on the deck.

"I know," Robin answered loudly over the noise.

"What do you mean, *you know*?" Sarah looked from the smiling nurse to the helicopter as the passenger door opened. Squinting through the rising dust and sand, she saw a tall figure exit the chopper. "It's Lincoln," she exclaimed with delight as she ran down to meet him.

"Wow, is this the same quiet, reserved woman I saw leave my house?" Lincoln said with a laugh as Sarah's arms tightly embraced him.

"What are you doing here?"

"I thought you might want some company today," he said.

"You're coming with me?"

"Yes, ma'am," he said as he looked over his surroundings.

"How is she? How's Abby? How's the trial going?"

"Abby's doing just fine, and you know I can't discuss the trial with you," Lincoln commented as they turned and headed down the driveway towards the cabin and Robin.

"But if you're here … Lincoln, what's wrong?" Sarah asked in a serious tone.

"What makes you think something is wrong?"

"Instinct," she said as she studied his face. "Spill it. What's wrong?"

There was no avoiding answering her. Lincoln turned back around to face both Sarah and Robin. "There was a traffic accident yesterday and Fred Hyamensky was killed."

Robin had no idea who Fred Hyamensky was, but Sarah did. Her gaze fell to the cedar deck as her hand came up to her mouth. Seeing Sarah's reaction, Robin turned in confusion to Lincoln. "Who was Fred Hyamen …"

"The forensic pathologist who worked the crime scenes," Lincoln said.

"Doesn't that mean he was on the side of the prosecution?" Robin asked in confusion.

"Yes, but we were counting on his testimony to blow away half of their evidence. Look, I shouldn't be discussing this with Sarah sitting …"

"Lincoln, don't piss me off with that shit." Sarah eyes shot fire.

"I'm not trying piss you off, I'm obeying the law," Lincoln explained.

"Well, sometimes the law is stupid and needs to be bent," she snarled back uncharacteristically.

"Now you're starting to sound like Abby. The law is there to keep society structured, to protect us …"

"From who? The dangerous people, like Abby?" Sarah stood up and faced him. "I know the difference between the truth and a lie, and when the time comes for me to testify I will tell the truth, the whole truth, and nothing but the truth." Sarah squared her shoulders, pulling herself up to her full height. "Billy Ward used me, he manipulated me, and he tried to kill me. He got pleasure out of feeding me his voice-numbing concoction, so that he could beat me within an inch of my life without anyone hearing me scream. Well, they will hear me now! They will hear that all he wanted and that all he talked about was revenge against Abby. He wanted to make her pay!"

Looking up to the mountains, Sarah vented the pain and emotion that had been dormant since her attack. "When Ronald de Barr puts me on the stand, I'll tell how he bragged about the murders he had committed, and what he did to those girls when they were alive and what he did after they were dead. Those girls meant nothing to him! He didn't care who they were, only that he could torture them—that was all he talked about. Pain and torture, everything to him was pain and torture, right from his childhood in some mental hospital to his loathing of Abby. He was a sick and twisted little man who should have stayed in that hospital. He's dead, and you know what? I'm glad. He used his own life as his one last attempt to destroy Abby's. But that's not going to happen. Not while I still have a beating heart and a single breath in my lungs."

"Sarah, we're certain Billy killed himself," Lincoln offered her in support.

Sarah pulled her eyes away from the view to look at him, "But without Hyme, how can you prove it?" she asked.

CHAPTER 44

Sitting on the edge of the hospital bed, Sarah nervously swung her legs. Lincoln had done his best to calm her, but there wasn't much more he could say. He rose to his feet and crossed the sterile room to look out of the window.

"So what happens now, Lincoln? I mean with Hyme's death and the trial?"

"They'll have someone else come in and interpret his notes. They'll also have his deposition from earlier, but unfortunately *we* needed him in person. There's no way he would have put any of what we needed in his notes, not to mention what Webber said to him about doing any further investigations. It does give us some room for a retrial though."

Sarah grew silent and Lincoln could see her wheels turning. "Lincoln, what do you think her chances are?"

He sighed deeply, "I don't know. I mean a few days ago, Nathan was optimistic; we had things laid out and we had a plan. But this has taken the wind out of our sails. In some ways, pointing a finger at Ward makes us look desperate, and that isn't a good thing in the eyes of a jury."

She studied him for a moment, trying to decide if he was telling her the truth. "Lincoln, you didn't answer my question."

"Maybe I don't have an answer," he said.

Sarah looked at the floor as Lincoln looked for solace outside the window. "Then, Lincoln," she questioned, "shouldn't you be out investigating or something instead of being here babysitting me?"

Walking over to her, he took her hands in his, "Dear, I'm not babysitting you, I'm here as a friend, to support you in any way I can. Besides, we have a two day recess because of the accident."

"I still think your time would be better spent ..."

The door opened and in walked a jovial Dr. Greene. "And how's my star patient doing today?"

The conversation between Sarah and Lincoln ceased. "Nervous, scared ... a little excited too, I guess."

"You should be. This is the big day. Do you know your arrival and departure by helicopter turns this place into a gossip pit?" he said as he went over to the counter to take out a sterile tray. "Half the staff thinks you're a movie star here for a nip and tuck, the other half thinks you're in the witness relocation program. I love it," he said with a chuckle as he brought over the tray.

Everyone grinned and some of the tension was eased. "Okay," Dr. Greene said. "Are you ready?"

Seeing the fear in Sarah's eyes, Lincoln reached over and picked up her hand.

She squeezed tightly. "As ready as I can be, I guess."

With steady, skilled hands, Dr. Greene began the long process of unrolling, unwrapping and removing. For the most part, Sarah kept her eyes closed as she felt her cotton protection being taken off.

Lincoln was amazed and intrigued as Sarah's face began to emerge. As each bandage came off, he felt her shaking grip tighten on his hand as a vaguely familiar face came into view. For the first time since they had met, Lincoln started to see the woman whose picture he had carried in his pocket so long ago.

"You can open your eyes now, Sarah, it's all over," Dr. Greene said softly as he removed his gloves. Slowly, she did as he said and then he reached for her shoulders. "Now remember, there's still swelling and bruising but they will go away."

Sarah nodded but said nothing as she turned to Lincoln. His broad smile told her more than any words could.

"You look better than your pictures."

"Really?" she asked in a small voice.

"See for yourself," Dr. Greene said as he offered her a handheld mirror.

She hesitated, but finally took it. Keeping the mirror side down, she laid it across her lap and looked at her friend for support. "Lincoln, I don't think I can."

His smile faded and he grew serious, "Yes, you can."

"But what if …"

He stopped her, "But what if nothing. You've come this far … do you want to stop now? Because that's not the Sarah I've come to know."

Her eyes searched his for the strength she needed and Lincoln did his best not to fail. He held her stare and refused to let his eyes wander.

"I know you're scared Sarah, but that's normal. I see it in almost all of my patients … even the movie stars." Dr. Greene's attempt at humor broke the stare between the two friends.

Sarah looked down at the mirror in her lap. Removing her other hand from Lincoln's grasp, she put both hands around the handle of the mirror and lifted it up.

Just like her reflection this morning in the lake, the first thing she noticed was her eyes and her cheekbones. Dr. Greene was right; there was still a lot of swelling and discoloration, but the woman looking back at her was someone familiar. Raising a hand, she gently touched her cheek.

"Careful," the doctor commented.

After several long minutes of examination, she finally admitted what everyone knew. "It's me," she said keeping her eyes on her reflection.

"Yes, my dear," Dr. Greene answered as he too admired his work. "It's you. There wasn't anything there for me to change. I just had to put back the pieces, that's all."

"I told you, you look like a million bucks." Lincoln couldn't control the smile on his face.

"Thank you, doctor," Sarah said as she reached to touch the bridge of her nose. The scar was gone and her nose was back to being straight—swollen, but straight. "Thank you," she continued, but as she spoke, Sarah noticed her mouth still didn't properly form her words.

Seeing her concern, the doctor said, "There was a lot of damage to that side of your face, as I'm sure you know. I wish I could tell you it'll all heal, but I can't."

Keeping her eyes on her face, Sarah tried to smile and she saw what couldn't be fixed. The left corner of her mouth rose only slightly.

"It will improve, as will the movement in your neck, but it will take time and hard work."

"But they *will* come back?" she asked as she attempted to work a smile onto her face.

"They will improve. And there will be a couple more minor surgeries, but ..."

"But I'll never be like I was before?" She pulled her eyes from her reflection.

"Sarah, I'm sorry," the doctor finally admitted. "Maybe down the road, I mean things in the medical field are changing every day ..."

The two men in the room had no idea what to say as they cautiously watched her. After a few more glances in the mirror, she finally put it down and walked over to the window. Concerned, Lincoln followed her as the doctor picked up the tray and took it over to the counter, giving the two a little privacy.

"Sarah," Lincoln said softly and, to his surprise, she turned around with a smile.

"I'm okay," Sarah answered with rising confidence. "It's the new me and I can live with it. I'm alive. That's more than the rest of Billy's victims, isn't that what you said to me in the hospital?" With her head held high, though slightly tilted, she walked over to Dr. Greene.

"I can't thank you enough," she said, tears welling up in her eyes. "You've given me back more than just my face. You've given me back my life and for that I'm grateful. How could a 'Thank you' be enough?"

"Because, my dear," Dr. Greene said with a smile, "it just is."

☯

Sarah and Lincoln waited for the helicopter to return to pick them up.

"You don't have to come back with me. I'm sure you have things to do," Sarah said as she glanced at her reflection. It was new and it was different and it would take some time to get used to it.

Lincoln looked down at his watch without answering.

"Okay what gives? That's like the tenth time you've looked at your watch. The pilot said he'd be back at one o'clock and it's only twelve-forty-five."

"It's not that, it's just …" The cell phone in his pocket rang and she saw him smirk. He reached for the phone and then held it out to her. "I believe this is for you."

"Abby?" she questioned. Lincoln nodded toward the ringing phone.

Licking her lips, she flipped it open with a hesitant, "Hello."

"Sarah." The voice on the other end of the phone echoed through her soul.

"Abby."

"I only have a minute, but I wanted to talk to you so badly. How are you? Is it okay? Are you okay?"

"Abby." The tears ran freely as Sarah closed her eyes and recalled every inch of that beloved face.

"Sarah?" Abby questioned with concern.

"It's good, it's me … a new me, but it is me …" her voice broke.

"For the first time in my life, Sarah, I can honestly say I'm glad I had the money to do it, to do all of it. I can't take back what's happened to you, but I hope I can make it better."

"You have and more. I want to see you."

"I want to see you, too, but I've got to go. Nate snuck me in this phone and I don't want to get caught with it," she said in a rush. "Tell Linc I said thanks. Sarah, I love you—" Abby barely got the words out before the phone line went dead.

"I love you, too," Sarah whispered as she brought the phone to her chest and hugged it.

CHAPTER 45

Lincoln sat alone in the helicopter as the night sky swallowed the view except for the distant lights of the city. It had been a long day, with many emotional ups and downs, and he laid his head back against the cushioned wall. Seeing Sarah again was like a breath of fresh air, something he definitely needed after his stressful testimony. Then to be there when she saw her face again almost made him forget about Hyme and the uphill climb that lay ahead.

He was so pre-occupied that he didn't hear the chopper pilot's voice. "I'm sorry, what was that?" he said, leaning forward.

"Where you'd like to be dropped off?"

"Oh … at the hospital. That's where my car is."

"All right, we'll be there in a few minutes," the pilot said and Lincoln nodded.

Minutes later, Lincoln was standing on the helipad at the hospital waving goodbye to his ride. "Beats the hell out of driving," he muttered to himself as he turned to find his car. Walking past the hospital doors, he noticed a sign hanging in the well-lit hallway that said *Psychiatric Ward*, with an arrow pointing the direction. Lincoln's mind wandered back to the conversation he had earlier with Sarah. In all the work and background checking they had done on Ward, nothing had ever come up about him spending time in a mental hospital.

Then why would he have said that to Sarah? Lincoln thought to himself as he spotted his car. Carla was waiting with a late dinner for him, but he only picked at it in silence. An hour later he got up from the sofa, kissed her on the head and told her not to wait up as he was going to the office. With a heavy heart she watched him leave; she knew he would turn every stone until every question had an answer, one way or another.

☯

Digging deeper than he and Abby ever had, Lincoln discovered more and more of Billy Ward's past—to a point. Lincoln's small office was strewn with notes and pictures. Then slowly, with his methodically-trained mind, questions started to nag at him. He wrote them down and stuck them on his window so he could see them at any time, but the answers he was looking for just seemed to keep eluding him. When he ran out of sticky notes, he swapped to a dry erase pen, and wrote on his windows. Names of mental institutions were written up everywhere, to be crossed out one by one when their answers came back negative. Not one had ever admitted a William Daniel Ward.

Lincoln's glance fell on the videotape from the ATM camera. Slipping the tape into the VCR, he leaned against his desk as he watched it play one more time. He knew if he could find whoever it was in that Jeep, Abby would be a free woman. The tape played but he didn't need to watch it. He knew it by heart; the Jeep drove in, sat for a minute and then the person got out. Lincoln leaned forward and froze the tape.

"Who are you?" he asked the black and white image. "Someone had to have seen you. No one is that—" Lincoln snatched the tape from the machine and left.

Pulling into the Hasty Motel parking lot, Lincoln climbed from his car with the videotape in his hand. Looking across the street, he glanced at the ATM machine and the people waiting in line to use it. The camera had an unobstructed view of the motel and in daylight it made the evidence all the more disheartening.

A buzzer blared as Lincoln pushed open the single glass door. The smell of stale cigarette smoke instantly invaded his nostrils. An elderly man pulled himself away from his small color TV, but kept on eye on it as he parted the numerous strands of orange plastic beads that separated his business from his living quarters.

"What can I get for ya, buddy?" the man asked without even looking up.

"I'm looking for Dot."

"Who's askin'?"

"A friend."

"She ain't here," the man grumbled as he finally turned his unshaven face to see who was asking the questions. "And you ain't no friend of hers," he said as he checked out Lincoln's impeccable attire from head to toe.

"Do you know where I can reach her? A home number?"

"Nope. Whatcha want with her—you a cop or something'?"

"No. I'm a private investigator and I need to speak to Dot."

"About?" the man asked as he sucked at his teeth.

"That's none of ..." Lincoln stopped and thought about the tape in his possession. Maybe this guy saw something that Dot didn't. "Actually,

I work for the lawyer who is representing Abby Stanfield, the woman accused—"

"I know who you mean, that broad that hacked up that guy? Is it true that she cut off his unit? Man, that's sick."

"Yes, that's the case I'm referring to." Lincoln decided he didn't need to embellish any further. "Did you see anything that night?"

"Nah, I just started here a couple weeks back … but I heard all about it. What'cha need to know?"

"I was hoping to talk to Dot, so can you tell me when she'll be in?"

"I 'spect never."

"Excuse me?"

"Apparently she called the owner in the middle of the night, said she was leaving. Packed up and was gone by morning." The man was losing interest in Lincoln and he turned back to his TV program as he scratched at his unshaven chin.

Lincoln suddenly wondered if de Barr or Webber had found Dot. Realizing he needed this man's undivided attention, Lincoln pulled a few bills from his wallet. Snapping the money in his hand, he held it out to the grubby attendant. "Did she leave with anyone?"

"Don't think so." The man reached for the money, but Lincoln pulled it back.

"Now this is important … do you know if she talked to the cops?"

"Can't say," the man said, eyeing the bills.

"Try," Lincoln said firmly.

"Look mister, from what I know 'bout Dot, those little green backs was all she thought about. If someone offered her money, she'd say, or *do*, just about *anything*." It wasn't what Lincoln wanted to hear, but he paid the man and quickly left for some fresh air.

Once inside his car, he pulled out his cell phone and quickly dialed a familiar number. "It's Lincoln. I think we may have a problem."

Nathan looked over his cluttered desk and closed his eyes. "How's that?" Lincoln quickly filled him in.

"Dot's disappeared and I can't help but think that de Barr or Webber are behind it. What if they call her as a witness?"

"Let me phone Mary and I'll see what I can find out. In the meantime, I need you to keep on the Stempler and Reanichi angle."

"You got it," Lincoln said reluctantly as he started his car.

Time lost all meaning for Lincoln as he sunk himself further into Abby's case. Carla hadn't been happy about his absenteeism, but she wanted Abby home as much as he did. So she reluctantly saw him off to work every morning, earlier and earlier. He was growing desperate, searching for anything that might clear her, but there was nothing. Nathan couldn't find out anything about the whereabouts of Dot and that concerned them. Nothing looked worse for a defendant than when the prosecution brought out a surprise witness.

It was late in the afternoon and Lincoln sat with his back against the wall with several files laid out in front of him. He was exhausted but he refused to give up. The answers were here; he just hadn't found them yet.

Struggling to his feet, he grabbed his coffee cup and headed out of the door. He needed the break more than he needed the caffeine.

"Hey, Lincoln, coming up for air?" one of the lawyers said as he entered the lunchroom.

"Hey, Robert," Lincoln nodded as he poured the coffee. There were several people in the room. Most were either lawyers or legal assistants and they all seemed to be in deep thought as Lincoln wandered over.

"What? Did someone tell a lawyer joke and you're all trying to understand the punch line?" Lincoln said as he lifted his cup for a sip.

"Close," Robert said. "It's the riddle of the day and we're trying to figure out the answer." Lincoln had heard about the daily mind-benders that Nathan had started years ago. They got people thinking, and talking to each other when they normally wouldn't have known each others' names.

"What's the riddle?"

"Two women, same mother, same father, same birthday, same age, call each other sisters, but they are not twins."

Lincoln looked around at the circle of Ivy League brainpower and tried not to laugh. "Are you serious?" His smile disappeared when he realized they were. "Come on guys, look at the obvious. If there are two, why can't there be three?"

"Three?"

"Triplets. They're not twins, they're triplets." The room erupted into groans and moans as they realized the simplicity of the answer.

"Good job, Linc," Robert said as he patted him on the back. "We only thought about two, not three."

Lincoln chuckled. "I find it's better if you say things out loud; you can actually hear the answer. I mean, come on, three is always better than …" Lincoln's eyes widened and his mouth fell open. "Two. Holy shit! Why not three … she had no voice," he said in a rush of startling insight.

"Lincoln, are you okay?"

"She had no voice," Lincoln said as he raced from the room, ignoring those left behind.

Lincoln burst into his office searching for a file. Spotting what he was looking for, he grabbed it and quickly started to leaf through it.

"It's not here," he said as he took the file folder to his desk. Quickly, he cleared a space and laid the open folder down. Running his finger over the pages of documents, he felt the rush of adrenaline recharge his batteries. "It's not here, it's not here," he repeated as he looked up from his desk and reached for the phone.

"Lieutenant Banks, please," he said into the receiver.

The wait was long but finally he heard a familiar voice.

"Banks."

"Can we talk?" was all he said.

"Lincoln? Sure."

"I need a favor, well, two actually."

"If I can," she said without hesitation.

"I need to take a look at Webber's notes from the motel."

"From which motel?"

"The Webster Arms."

"All right—what are we looking for?" she asked.

"Something that I hope isn't there."

"Something that isn't there?" Banks questioned.

"Yes."

"Okay, and?"

"I need a search warrant … without Webber and de Barr finding out."

"Oh, you're not asking for much," she said sarcastically.

"Mary, we need this … badly." He didn't have to tell her how desperate they were.

"Okay, consider it done. I'll meet you at the motel."

"Sure, and thanks."

"Don't thank me yet," she told him. "What address do you want on the search warrant?"

"The Webster Arms."

"I know that, but which room do you want the warrant for?"

Lincoln hesitated. "I don't need it for a room; I need it for the whole motel."

CHAPTER 46

Life at the resort was everything Sarah needed to aid in her recovery. Robin, along with the visiting therapist, was there to help with her mental and physical needs, but Robin knew her duties as a nurse were almost over. She decided to phone Nathan to discuss the end of her employment. The conversation was short and to the point. She could tell he was tired and extremely busy, so she didn't keep him. When their business discussion was over, she asked about Abby and the trial.

Nathan didn't respond right away and that told her more than his words did. "Our turn's coming," he said, hoping he sounded more optimistic than he was.

"If there's anything else I can do, please don't hesitate to call. I'd like to think I'm more than just the hired help," she said with a chuckle.

"You are more, much more." They talked for a bit longer, but then Nathan said he had to go.

Now all Robin had to do was tell Sarah, and she didn't have to guess where she'd find her. Taking the road past the cabins, she branched off to a small trail that wove around the edge of the lake. Following the tall timbers, she let her fingers play through waist high grass. For a city girl, she had to admit she was going to find it hard to leave all this. The trail rose up and she came over the crest of a small hill that opened to a shaded field of rich, green grass. One morning while out for a stroll, Sarah had discovered the field at the end of the lake, and Günter had made her a bench so she could sit and enjoy the surroundings in solitude.

The tall elms and cedar trees towering over the field protected Sarah's delicate skin from the sun. The harmful rays were something she had to avoid. She went there frequently.

Sarah looked up from her book when Robin broke from the trees. The nurse lifted a hand to wave. "Hi."

"Hi yourself." Sarah's face brightened with her arrival.

"I think you've found paradise, Sarah," Robin said as she looked around the shaded clearing to the view of the lake beyond.

"It will be," Sarah commented as she too turned her attention to the view, "when Abby's here to share it with me." Robin saw the smile grow on her face. It would never be what it was, but the lopsided grin she had now was becoming her own.

"So what brings you all the way out here?" Sarah asked, pulling Robin's mind from her memories.

"Sarah," Robin stopped when she realized she had no idea how to say this. "The offer, or rather the opportunity Nathan gave me, was something out of a dream. Come and help this wonderful woman overcome a horrible incident in her life. Live in this beautiful mansion that overlooks the ocean, and then come here to this lovely place. All that and pay off my student loans, too. But it hasn't been like work to me, Sarah. It's been an experience I could never replace. I've come to look on you all as friends, and that's something I don't take lightly."

"Robin?" Sarah knew what was coming but she didn't want to hear it.

"Sarah, you don't need me anymore," Robin said as she reached for her patient's hand. "But there're lots of people in the ICU that do."

"You're leaving?"

The young nurse nodded.

"I'd love to stay; I mean, who wouldn't? But the fact is I became a nurse to help people."

"And you are, you're helping me," Sarah pleaded.

"No dear, *you're* helping you. My job here is done."

Sarah looked down at her hands. She didn't want to admit it, but she knew Robin was right.

☯

The trial was over for the day, and the courtroom was empty except for Nathan who was sitting alone at the defendant's table. The seclusion was what Nathan needed as he pulled off his glasses and pinched the bridge of his nose. It was only when he was alone that Nathan could admit to himself that the trial was not going well. The evidence the prosecution had was overwhelming, and the more he listened to himself try to sell their theory to the jury, the more he realized how pathetic it sounded. It would have been a hard sell with Hyme's help, but without him and his expertise, the whole defense was crumbling.

Nathan knew they were in trouble by the churn of his stomach and the ache in his heart. Dropping his head into his hands, he was lost in thought and never heard the door to the courtroom open. He was haunted by a recurrent thought; why hadn't he done something sooner?

"Nathan," Cheryl said softly with concern for her boss.

Startled by her presence and embarrassed by being caught off-guard, he responded quickly. "Cheryl."

"We need to talk." She sat down across from him. Studying his tired face, she offered a small smile to the man she admired and adored.

"What's up?"

"I've worked for you for a long time, almost my entire professional career. I've never seen you get so lost in a case that you can't see the answers in front of you."

"Cheryl," he said her name with a veil threat of caution.

"I'm sorry, Nate, but someone has to say something here. You have me as second chair for a reason and that isn't to sit here and say nothing. You're too close to this, it's too personal and you're not thinking clearly."

His body language changed, as did the color in his face, "I'm thinking just fine thank you, and if you're not careful …"

"What, Nate, are you going to fire me? Then fine, so be it, but I'm not going to sit here and be silent. You know me better than that. Nathan, if this was any other client you would've been pushing for a plea bargain … and I think you'd better now."

"Cheryl, I can't."

"Nathan, you have to. We needed Hyme and his testimony to make this theory of ours work, but we don't have Hyme, God rest his soul. And now we're left standing here looking like amateurs, so desperate that we're trying to prove the man murdered himself."

"We're sticking to the game plan."

"Then we're going down with a sinking ship and you know it."

"We've poked a few holes in their theory; we just have to keep at it," Nathan tried to argue, but he wasn't even convincing himself. "We only need one … and I think jurors three and seven are starting to see things differently."

Cheryl looked at him and then set her jaw. "Different enough to save your niece's life?"

He looked at her, but he couldn't hold the stare.

"Are you willing to risk it, Nate? Talk to her. Abby's smart enough to realize what's happening. Why don't you see what de Barr has to offer?"

"Because Abby is the client, Cheryl, and if she says no plea, then we have to abide by that," he said. He tried to sound hopeful but he knew his heart was not in it.

"She may be the client but you're the lawyer. Convince her. Because I'm afraid at this point if you don't, we'll be watching her last breath through a pane of glass."

He sat silent for a moment and thought about what she was saying. Cheryl watched him struggle with her words. She knew it was the truth. And so did he. Nathan rose to his feet and walked up to stand in front of Porter's bench.

"You know they offered me a judicial position years back," he ran his hand over the dark polished mahogany, "but I turned it down."

Cheryl watched him with concern before she answered. "I know that."

"Yeah," he said as he remembered his past. "Do you know why I turned it down?"

"No."

"I didn't want to stop being a lawyer. I love this," he gestured to the courtroom. "I love the intellectual challenge. I couldn't give that up." He wandered over to the witness box and stood for a moment before he walked around it and took a seat in the chair. "But do you know why I retired?"

Again she shook her head.

"Because over the years, I came to hate this. I started to hate that same legal system I once loved so. With its backlogged, backdoor bureaucracy, and its imperfect interpretations of the law—it's no longer the law of the people. Madam Justice no longer wears a blindfold; she sees the color of your skin and the size of your bank account."

"Though I applaud you, that's not always true, Nathan," Cheryl said.

"Isn't it?" He stood up and stepped down from the witness chair. "Nowadays, with the way the media is, the public gets exposed to crime and violence in the news and everywhere else. You're guilty before a trial starts, and *then* they expect you to *prove* you're *innocent.* Do you know how hard it is to change someone's mind once it has been made up—especially, if you're a minority or poor? That's not justice."

"But, Nathan," Cheryl interrupted, "Abby is neither a minority nor is she poor."

"I know that, Cheryl, but the media and the public have already decided she's guilty." He sat back down at the table and stared at the floor.

"What if she takes a Serrano/Alford plea?" she suggested.

"Pleads guilty without admitting she did it?"

"Yes. It may save her life." She watched him toy with the idea, turning it over in his mind. He rose to his feet again and started to pace in front of the bench. After several rounds of back and forth, Nathan stopped, put his hands on either side of Judge Porter's nameplate and hung his head.

"I've never given up on a case before," he said more to himself than to his associate.

"You're not giving up, Nate, you're doing the best thing for your client," she assured him.

Nathan spun around, "She isn't just my client, she's my niece! And I don't see how her spending the rest of her life in a federal prison is the best thing for her."

"Because, Nate, it's better than the alternative," Cheryl stated flatly. "Convince her to plead it. You can do it. You can save her life before it's too late."

"There's always the appeal process, and we can try a different defense."

"Do you want to take that chance? Change horses half way through the race? The second we do that, we're admitting the horse we're on is a loser."

Nathan looked up at the flag at the back of the courtroom and thought about the freedom it represented—freedom Abby would lose if he convinced her to plead. But Cheryl was right. It was better than the alternative.

There was nothing more for him to say. The stillness in the dim courtroom played with his mind as he felt the dejection heavy in his heart. The risk to Abby's life was growing with every day the jury heard more of the damning evidence.

Suddenly, the solid back doors of the courtroom flew open, startling Nathan and Cheryl. Lincoln marched his way silently towards them, stopping just shy of the wooden gate. He glared at his boss. "You son of a bitch," he growled. "You knew! You both fucking knew and you didn't tell me!"

The tension in the courtroom was palpable as the three stood listening to the echo of Lincoln's accusation.

"Lincoln?" Nathan questioned warily as Lincoln stood glaring at him.

"Goddamn it, Nathan, the two of you said nothing!" Lincoln was livid as he flung open the gate separating them. "Why! You son of … when were you going to say something? Or where you both praying no one would find out?" He was gripping several papers tightly in his hand and he slammed them to the table.

Cheryl looked nervously between the two men, confused and unsure of what to do, but Nathan made the decision for her. "Cheryl, I think maybe you should leave us."

"Nathan?" she queried.

"I'll be fine," Nathan assured her as she collected her things and quickly left them alone.

The two men eyed each other as quiet settled over the courtroom again.

"What is that?" Nathan finally asked, motioning towards the collection of papers on the desk.

"The truth of what you and Abby have been hiding," Lincoln snarled uncharacteristically.

Nathan walked over to the table. He spread out the papers, glancing over all of them at once.

"Where did you get these?" Nathan asked nervously.

"The Webster Arms Motel," Lincoln answered bitterly as he watched the elderly lawyer.

"Where?"

"The Webster Arms. We didn't look hard enough; Billy had a third room there."

"A third room?"

"A stupid riddle got me thinking. Sarah couldn't speak because of that dieffenbachia shit, so where was the plant? It wasn't on any of the evidence lists—none of his tools were. And then it hit me, if Billy had two rooms at the motel, why couldn't he have three? He had to have another place because he had to work out his plan somewhere. Someplace where he could keep his things. I got a search warrant with the help of Mary Banks and we started looking. The whole back of the motel had been closed off for years, so it gave him the perfect place to hide. Lieutenant Banks is there still collecting evidence, but I grabbed this."

"Mary is collecting the evidence?"

"Don't worry, Nathan, she didn't see this." Lincoln pushed the sheets of paper and they fanned out across the table. A single sheet of paper caught Nathan's attention and he reached for it.

"Oh my God," Nathan said in a tired voice as he slowly dropped into a chair. Peering over the top of the paper, Lincoln saw what he was holding.

"That's your signature isn't it?" Lincoln accused, but the lawyer stayed silent. "Not only were you there, Nathan, but it was your money that paid for it!" He slammed his hand down hard onto the table. "Why didn't you tell me?"

"Because it didn't seem to be important at the time."

Lincoln rolled his eyes and laughed humorlessly. "How could it *not* have been important? If Ron de Barr had gotten his hands on this …"

"But he didn't," Nathan said firmly.

"Are you sure? Because if he has it'll be the final nail in Abby's coffin!"

Nathan was desperate to change the subject. "What else did you find in the room?"

"Enough evidence to silence the prosecution, but not enough to silence me."

"Lincoln, where are you going?" Nathan asked as he watched the young man turn to leave.

"I have a few words for my ex-partner and I don't think you want to hear them," Lincoln said over his shoulder as he stormed out of the courtroom.

☯

Sarah felt a heaviness in her heart as she watched the sun rise over the mountain and spread its rays over the still waters of Lake Alouette. Robin was leaving today and Sarah felt a growing fear at the prospect. The sun climbed higher in the eastern sky as Sarah strolled back to her cabin, to where Robin was packing. The thought of her friend and nurse returning to the city filled her with apprehension.

She had been so lost in thought she hadn't heard the distant thumping of an approaching helicopter. Increasing her pace, she caught glimpses of Robin's ride through the breaks in the trees as it flew in low over the water. Through an opening in the trees, she saw someone sitting in the passenger seat next to the pilot.

Lincoln, she thought, her face brightening with a hopeful smile. Sarah started to run towards where the helicopter would be landing. It hadn't crossed her mind that Lincoln might come out with the pilot, but it did make sense.

Coming up to the lodge, she saw the tips of the rotors as they peeked out in steady rhythm past the edge of the building; the helicopter had already landed. Slowing her pace, she came around the corner and she saw the aircraft sitting in the middle of the grass. Lincoln was already opening his door, but something about his demeanor told her something was wrong. He hadn't seen her, as he climbed out. He hesitated a moment before he turned to open the back door and it was only then that she realized there was someone else with him.

Sarah stopped and so did her heart as she saw Lincoln open the door and, in the shadows, she saw Nathan in the back of the aircraft. He seemed tired and old, and even from this distance she could sense the tension between the two men. She didn't want to think of the reason.

Nathan's here, her brain screamed at her, *but Nathan shouldn't be here. He should be with Abby. He should be defending Abby at the trial.* She stood riveted to the ground as she struggled to keep her world in focus and her thoughts under control. *Nathan, why are you here?* She wanted to scream but she couldn't find her voice.

"No," Sarah whispered to herself as the potential meaning of their appearance started to sink in. *Why are they here, why aren't they with Abby? Because* … "No," she said louder, shaking her head as tears welled up in her eyes.

"Sarah," Lincoln called out, but his voice disappeared into the sounds of the helicopter's rotors winding down. Nathan said something to him and Lincoln turned to look at the front of the aircraft.

There was movement on the other side of the helicopter. Sarah saw the pilot walk past his door and her reality wavered when she saw the dark-black hair on the figure behind him.

Watching the far side of the helicopter, Sarah was certain she saw someone familiar. Someone she should have recognized. Someone who looked … *like Abby!*

Sarah's hand came to her mouth to cover her sob when Abby walked past the pilot.

The vision before her was somewhere between a mirage and a dream. Dressed in her dark Armani suit, Abby appeared elegant but exhausted. Her pale skin contrasted sharply with her black hair as it fluttered with each step she took towards Sarah.

"Abby," Sarah whispered in astonishment. She couldn't believe her eyes. *It … it isn't possible. Abby's still in jail!* But she wasn't, she was there right before Sarah's eyes.

Abby's normally stoic appearance crumbled as she stared at Sarah's small form standing like a dream only a few yards away. Feeling weak from the excitement and having been out of touch with the world for so long, she concentrated on Sarah's eyes. Each shaky step took her closer to that green. Her long legs quickly covered the distance separating them as tears silently flowed down both their faces. Sarah closed her eyes as she felt Abby's powerful arms engulf her. It was all a dream.

"Abby, tell me this is real," Sarah whispered into her chest.

"If it's not, I don't want to wake up," Abby answered as she kissed the top of Sarah's head.

Neither spoke for a moment, both trying to believe in the reality before them. "But I don't … I don't understand," Sarah said as she lifted her head and looked up into Abby's eyes. "Oh God, I've missed you," she said as a fresh batch of tears sprang to her eyes.

"Not half as much as I've missed you." Abby leaned down and gently kissed the lips that had haunted her dreams—lips that accompanied the happy memories that had kept her sane when the dark walls had started to close in. They were softer than she remembered. All she wanted was to sink into Sarah, to become so intertwined with her that they could never be separated again. Abby's senses were going wild. The fresh air, the smell of Sarah's hair, and the growing desire inside her made her pull back out of need rather than want.

Sarah's heart was beating so rapidly she could barely control her breathing as she reached up to touch Abby's cheek. "Your eyes are darker than I remember."

"And you're even more beautiful than I remember," Abby said as she reached down to brush back Sarah's bangs.

The loving gesture was almost more than Sarah could handle and tears spilled over once more. "I know a good doctor," she whispered.

"He didn't make anything that wasn't already there," Abby said with conviction. "You were a beautiful woman when I met you. You took my breath away then and you're even more breathtaking now," she said as she took Sarah's face in both hands and leaned down for another kiss.

"Abby!" Robin's shocked voice broke them apart. Abby straightened up as the young nurse approached them. Ignoring the tearstains and the blushing, excited cheeks, Robin looked from Abby to the two quiet men standing off to the side.

"I don't understand. How can you be here?"

Abby looked over Sarah's head to the men she'd come with. "I think Lincoln should answer that."

"Abigail!" Helga's voice made all heads turn as she came out of the lodge with Günter not far behind. "Abby, is that you?"

"In the flesh," Abby answered as she finally released her hold on Sarah.

Sarah stood alone watching the pale woman greet them. The scene felt unreal as she brought her hands up hugging herself.

Seeing Sarah standing by herself, Lincoln walked over and put an arm around her. "You okay?"

"Yes … no, I'm not sure; this all seems so unreal." She couldn't take her eyes off Abby. "That's her … right?"

"Yeah, it's her," he answered with a somber tone that made Sarah turn to him.

"I don't understand what's happening. How can she be here, Lincoln? What about the trial?"

"Porter threw the case out this morning." Sarah looked over at Nathan and was once again startled by his appearance. He looked as though he had aged twenty years since she had seen him last. He looked tired and drawn as he stood with sagging shoulders. "We found all the evidence we needed to prove Abby's innocence."

"But how, what evidence?" she asked in confusion.

"Part of it was you, Sarah," Lincoln offered.

"Me?" she asked as she felt Abby slide in next to her.

Robin looked over at Nathan and then at Abby. "Why don't we take this inside?"

Sarah slipped her arm around Abby's waist and it felt like the most natural thing in the world as they headed for the cabin. "I just can't believe you're here," she said leaning her head into Abby's shoulder.

"That would make two of us. I was beginning to wonder if I'd ever be outside again." Abby looked down at the grass beneath her feet. "Or ever see you again. I could get lost in those eyes of yours and never want for another thing." Sarah smiled and her cheeks reddened as her eyes drifted to the gravel pathway.

It was only then that Abby dared to glance at the scar on her neck. It looked better than she could have imagined, recalling with vivid clarity what it looked like at the motel. Wanting nothing more than to forget that day, she leaned down and kissed the top of Sarah's head again.

"I've missed that."

"We've missed a lot of things," Abby said.

Sarah glanced up and saw her dark eyes staring at the ground. "Abby?"

The dark-haired woman lifted her head and Sarah could see the pain in Abby's eyes as she looked over the large, empty deck of the cabin. Suddenly Sarah knew what had brought on the renewed shimmer of tears.

"Buck," she whispered and Abby nodded as they started up the stairs.

☯

The day had moved into evening but everyone in the cabin was oblivious to time. Food had been eaten, alcohol had been consumed, but there was still much left to be said. Sarah sat close to Abby on the sofa as Lincoln answered most of the questions, but Nathan interjected when he needed to.

"When Sarah and I were talking the other day, she said she couldn't scream because of that dieffenbachia concoction. It got me thinking. There was no dieffenbachia in any of Ward's rooms, yet we knew he bought a plant. So, Lieutenant Banks and I went back to the Webster Arms. In the closed back section of the motel where we found you, Billy had another room. It was booby-trapped to self-destruct, but thank God it didn't. It was all there—everything; the dieffenbachia paste, the cocaine and morphine, some things he had taken from Abby's house, another knife that matched the murder weapon, pictures, fingerprints, an entire box of Jensen latex gloves. He'd even kept some of the things from the other women he had murdered. But more importantly, we found his computer—with a detailed plan of how he was going to kill himself and frame Abby for it. Billy had deleted it all but we were able to recover most of it. He planned everything, from the date that he burnt down Abby's house to using the same brand of gloves and zip-ties the cops use. He even had the weather forecast mapped out so there'd be enough water in the creek to carry his drugged-up body down stream."

"Oh my God," Sarah whispered at the true depth of Billy's insanity. She leaned into Abby's comfortable embrace.

"Everything was there, Sarah," he murmured as he lifted his gaze and his dark eyes connected to Abby's. "Everything." Nothing was spoken between the old partners, but there was plenty of communication.

"It was incredible how he planned it all. He had the technology there to do anything he wanted regarding phones and cell phones. He had more books than the police academy on police procedures." Lincoln looked over at Abby. "It was obvious that he had been planning this for a long time, years even."

Sarah caught Abby's downcast look out of the corner of her eye.

"If we hadn't gone back, we probably would never have found it all." Lincoln commented before he raised his drink, but his hand stopped in mid-air as he shot a look at Abby. "And then we'd have never known the truth."

"Thank God you did," Sarah said with a smile, "because now we have Abby back where she belongs." Everyone agreed but the eye contact between Lincoln and Abby intensified.

Günter held up his glass of aquavit. "To the return of our beloved Abby, and to the men who brought her home," he began but a quick rap on the door interrupted the toast. Everyone looked up to see the pilot standing there.

"Come in, Drake," Nathan motioned.

"I don't mean to interrupt you, sir, but I just received a call on the radio. There's a medical emergency in a small town just ten minutes from here. They need to fly someone to the hospital, ASAP, and I was hoping you wouldn't mind if I took the chopper …"

"No, by all means go," Nathan waved him off.

Robin jumped to her feet, "Can I help? I'm an RN."

"Couldn't hurt," Drake responded.

"My bags are already packed," Robin said before she disappeared into her room. She returned a moment later. Sarah jumped off the sofa and gave her nurse and friend a quick hug. They knew they'd be seeing each other in a few more days for Sarah's next medical follow-up.

Lincoln jumped up. "Actually if there's room, could you take me back to the city too?"

"Lincoln, you can't leave," Sarah begged.

The pilot looked hesitantly at Lincoln. "It'll be tight quarters, man."

"Lincoln. Please … stay." Abby's tone was low as she looked at her partner and friend.

Shifting his eyes, he stared at Abby in contemplation. "Please," she said once more.

"Yes or no?" Drake said impatiently.

"Come on, Lincoln," Sarah said, not seeing the hidden communication going on. "Please … "

Lincoln couldn't resist Sarah's plea. "All right, fine. I'll stay. Go, Drake," he said and the pilot quickly departed.

"Thank you," Abby said, but Lincoln said nothing as he got up to grab another beer.

☯

With Robin's unexpected departure, the atmosphere in the cabin changed. Leaning back against Abby, Sarah started to notice that things in the room were not quite what they seemed. People were talking, but there was a level of tension just below the surface and the more she observed, the more obvious it became. Lincoln's manner towards Abby and Nathan hinted at some underlying anger. Their conversations seemed short and testy. Sarah at first blamed the stress they had all been under, but then she caught a few glares between Abby and Lincoln she didn't understand. Sarah said nothing.

Wanting out of the small cabin, Lincoln approached Helga to use their phone to call Carla. She and Günter were about to head home anyhow, Helga stated, and it signaled the end of the celebrations for the night.

"We have available cabins, I will give Lincoln the keys for everyone," Günter said as they all stood up. "You wait here."

"That's fine with me," Nathan said as he sat back down.

With everyone gone, and Nathan relaxing in the rocking chair with his eyes closed, Abby felt the log walls closing in on her. "I need to get outside—I've spent too much time inside four walls."

"I'm coming with you," Sarah whispered.

Abby smiled down at her. "I wouldn't want it any other way."

Once outside, Abby leaned her head back and took in a deep breath, "A storm's coming," she said with her eyes closed. "I can smell it in the air." She reached for Sarah's hand. "Come on." Together they went down the stairs and out onto the dock. Sitting down on the bench, Abby looked up at the outline of the vast mountains she had known and loved all her life. Dark ominous clouds were swirling over their heads.

Abby shook her head. "It all seems so unreal," she said into the night. "This morning I was heading for the gas chamber, and now here I am, under the night sky," Abby turned and looked into Sarah's eyes, "with you."

A smile lifted the corner of Sarah's mouth, and with longing in her eyes, Abby drank in the sight of her. Reaching out, she cupped Sarah's cheek and brushed her thumb over the corner of her mouth. Sarah remained silent, feeling the gentle touch electrify her as Abby traced the outline of her lips. Acutely aware of their mutual want and desire, Abby slowly leaned forward and kissed her. Like a feather in the wind, the contact between them was soft and tender as Sarah closed her eyes and melted into the kiss. She wanted more, so much more … so she was surprised when Abby pulled back. It took her a moment to recapture her breath as she opened her eyes.

"I could do that for the rest of my life," Abby whispered.

"And I'd like that very much," Sarah responded. "My dreams never felt like this, not this good. But it all seems so surreal." Sarah had to shake off her nerves as she looked at the heavens for help. "I mean, you're here with me and all I can think about is … is …"

Taking her eyes off the stars, Sarah turned to Abby.

"Is what, Sarah?"

"All the things I've never been able to say to you because I didn't want to put it in writing. All the things I want to explain to you, to your face." Sarah turned in her seat so that she could look straight at Abby. "When I came here, I came as a naïve reporter, with aspirations of headlines and bylines. I knew nothing about the real world and all of its ugliness. I came for the story but I didn't count on the woman behind the story."

"Sarah, sweetie, its okay." Abby reached out to touch her face, but Sarah stopped her.

"Please, let me finish." Sarah's throat felt dry as she licked her lips. "I never meant to hurt you …"

"No, Sarah, I'm the one who should be apologizing. I'm the one who needs to explain …" Sarah reached up and put her fingertips on Abby's lips.

"No, please," she begged. "If we're to build a relationship, it has to start on a solid foundation of trust. And that starts with the truth."

"Yes, Abby, relationships should be built on the foundations of trust and truth!" Lincoln's words startled them. They'd had no idea he was there as he started down the dock.

"Lincoln." Abby's tone completely changed and Sarah wasn't sure what to make of it.

"What?" He threw out his hands in surrender. "I'd think that after everything we've been through, the truth would be easy."

Sarah frowned curiously as she looked from Lincoln to Abby. There was a slight slur to Lincoln's words *but not enough to explain his sarcasm*, she thought as she recalled his consumption of beer. *What was he talking about?*

"I'll deal with this my way." Abby stared coldly at her old partner.

"Really," he said, challenging her as she rose to her feet. "I think Sarah deserves to know the truth, I mean after everything she's been through. Matter of fact," he stopped in front of Abby, "I think we all deserve the goddamn truth."

"Lincoln, you've been drinking," Abby stated.

"Yes, I have, though not half as much as you do."

"Lincoln, I'll deal with this … my way," she vowed.

"How, Abby? Like you did with me? I worked with you for how long and you told me nothing? You lied to me, just like you've lied to her," Lincoln pointed at Sarah.

"I never lied to her."

"You never told her the truth either," he fired back angrily.

"Excuse me, I hate when you do this! *Her* is right here and she'd like to know what the hell you two are talking about," Sarah said as she stood up, but the two ex-detectives ignored her as they glared angrily at each other.

"Lincoln, this is my business." Abby fought to stay in control.

"Abby, it stopped being just your business when all of our lives got turned upside down. He had pictures of all of us! All of us, Abby!"

Abby's mind was racing between what Lincoln was saying and what Sarah was hearing.

"Lincoln, you know nothing about this."

"I know nothing about it because you and your uncle decided I didn't need to know anything about it. And if you had your way, I'd still know nothing about it!"

"About what?" Sarah cried.

"I saw the commitment papers, Abby—with Nathan's *Goddamned* signature!"

"Lincoln, shut up!" The harsh words came out before Abby realized it. All she wanted to do was to stop what was happening, to make it all stop and go away.

"No, I want the goddamned truth, Abby, because I'm not going to shut up." He stared into her dark eyes and he saw what he had never seen before. A resemblance he couldn't believe. "You know, you and your uncle have the same eyes; they never change even when they're lying right to your face."

"You son of a …" Abby snapped and responded the only way she knew how. Lincoln barely saw the hand coming, until her open palm connected with his cheek.

"Abby!" said Sarah as she watched Lincoln wipe the blood from the corner of his mouth.

"She's trying to shut me up, but it's not going to work." He spat blood onto the dock. "Abby has a secret she's been hiding, a secret that almost got you killed."

Abby's face was a mix of rage and disbelief; her hands were shaking and adrenaline was pounding blood through her system as she glared at him. She had never imagined anything that could make her hit her best friend, but there were now many things in her life she never could have imagined. She had to stop him, but she also knew she couldn't.

"Abby! Lincoln!" An authoritative voice broke the tension and they turned to see Nathan marching down the dock. "Lincoln, you don't know the whole story."

"Then I suggest you tell us before your niece takes my head off."

"Lincoln, that's enough," Nathan said as he tried to remain calm.

"No, Nathan, it's not. Sarah has a right to know and if you aren't going to tell her, then I will." He turned to look at a bewildered and confused Sarah.

"You're right, she does," Nathan said peacefully, "but this was my idea, not Abby's."

Nathan's arrival calmed the heated scene and, with the intense standoff over, Abby stepped back, dropped her head and closed her eyes. It was out of her control, out of her hands; and once again she knew there was nothing she could do about it.

There was a moment of silence before Nathan spoke. "It was my idea right from the start. You saw it—that was my signature on those commitment papers, not hers."

"What idea and whose commitment papers? What are you guys talking about?" Sarah's frustration was mounting.

Nathan looked at his niece as she silently sat down on the bench and he saw a vulnerability he hasn't seen since she was a child. He walked over, crouched down in front of her, and took her hand. She lifted her head to look into his eyes. "I couldn't stop him …" Abby's voice faded away.

Sarah's brow furrowed as she tried to make sense of what was happening. She looked at Lincoln and wondered just what Abby was trying to stop him from doing.

"I know, sweetheart." Nathan wanted to stop her pain, to make it all go away, just like before. "I made decisions I shouldn't have, but I was doing what I thought was best." He was speaking now more to the group and less to her niece. "You have to understand, I wasn't a parent. I was a young, smug lawyer, with this big grandiose career in front of me. I didn't have time for a child; I didn't want to take the time. Never in my wildest dreams did I ever think I'd be starting a chain reaction that I couldn't control."

"Is that what this was all about, Nathan, control? You trying to control …" Lincoln began.

Anger and annoyance flared up in Nathan's eyes and he turned to Lincoln. "No, Lincoln, this isn't about control and it isn't about keeping secrets." Nathan turned back to Abby. "It was about an uncle trying to do the best for his niece, doing whatever he could to keep her safe."

Fear and confusion pulled at Sarah as she came over to Abby. The strong, proud woman she knew seemed only a shadow of her former self. "I don't understand, safe from whom?" Sarah asked.

"You have to understand—it was horrible, nothing I could ever have imagined. By the time I got here it was all over but the smoke coming from the wreckage," Nathan said sadly.

"What?" Sarah was even more confused as she looked into Abby's vacant stare. "I don't understand. What wreckage? Abby?"

Abby felt herself lifted back into the past. A distant memory called to her from the lake as she lifted her head to look over the still waters. She heard a child laugh, a giggle, and she glanced over to where a dock used to be. Where there was once a boat and her young self with her smiling and laughing parents. *"Abby … are you going to come with us?"* her mother called out to her as she waved happily at her daughter.

"Mother," Abby said softly, calling out to a memory that plagued her dreams. "They had no idea," she muttered to herself but all of them heard her.

"Abby. Abby, look at me. It's all over now." Abby heard her uncle's voice, but she couldn't see him—all she could see was her parents sitting in their boat. *"Come on, Abby, we'll go for a quick spin around the lake,"* her father said, motioning his daughter to come with them.

Tears sprang from Abby's vacant eyes. "I was supposed to be in that boat. I should've been," she said in a small scared voice as the images of flames erupted in her mind. She was a child again, a young child on a hot summer's day, as she watched her parents' boat explode in a horrific fireball. "They called to me. And I stood there and watched them."

"Oh my God. This is about your parents. You were there?" Sarah whispered at the agonizing discovery. Abby had told her they had died here at Gold Creek but she didn't know how. "You saw it happen?" Sarah asked in heartbroken disbelief. "Oh my God, you saw it happen."

"Did you know that my mother was still smiling when they exploded?" Abby said matter-of-factly as the tears spilled over. No one knew what to say as this normally strong woman came apart before their eyes.

"Abby." Sarah went to her side, but she didn't seem to notice. Rubbing her back, Sarah forgot about her anger and confusion as she looked for answers from either of the two men, but she could tell by the look on Lincoln's face that Abby's strange demeanor concerned him, too.

"Abby?" Sarah leaned over and whispered softly into her ear.

"I remember their faces—the concussion—the heat of the fire."

"Abby," Sarah whispered again.

The softly spoken sound of her name brought her back from her past. She looked around and then angrily brushed away the tears as she jumped to her feet. "I didn't know what he was planning," she said as she stood and looked out at the dark waters. "It was me that he was after—that was what he wanted; he wanted to kill me. And he almost did."

"What? Who?" Sarah was lost in confusion.

"Abby," Nathan said as she turned around to face them all. With her red-rimmed eyes and her pale complexion, this wasn't the Abby they knew, and Nathan recognized the pain she was going through. "Don't do this, Abby; it wasn't your fault."

"Wasn't it? I knew, but I didn't tell anyone. I should have, but I didn't—and look what happened. I didn't know how much he hated me." She looked at Sarah who felt her heart ache for the pain she could see in Abby's eyes. "I don't think he cared that he killed them. Because he wanted it to be me."

"Abby, I don't understand." Sarah started towards her, "Are you talking about your parents ...?" but Abby held up her hand to stop her.

Fighting to stay in control, Abby took several deep breaths, but she couldn't stop the tears anymore than she could have stopped the murders. "It was Billy. He killed them. He killed them because of me."

Sarah was certain the dock below her feet moved. "What?" Abby's words started to sink in. "Billy—Billy Ward? Oh my God," she said as her hand went to her mouth. "Oh my God," she repeated over and over as she tried to comprehend. "Why would he do that? I don't understand?" The questions tumbled out of Sarah's mouth. "Why didn't you tell me?" Her mind was spinning. "He killed your parents."

Abby looked over to where she had last seen her parents. To the dock that no longer existed but would forever burn in her mind. "He killed them because he hated me, because of me ..." Taking a deep breath, she brought her eyes back to Sarah and finally told her the truth. "Not *my* parents ... *our* parents—Billy was my brother."

Everything stilled at that moment. The air hung silent. The waters, tranquil as the full moon, reflected in Sarah's wide eyes. She knew her mouth was open, but she did nothing to close it. "He was your brother."

The information hit her like a bolt from the sky. "But how … Billy Ward was your brother?"

"Not by blood," Nathan said, "Adopted, Billy was adopted—"

"But that isn't …" Feeling her knees weaken Sarah stumbled backwards and landed flatly on the bench. Lincoln reached to assist her but she pushed his hand away, "No, don't … don't touch me," she fired at him and he pulled back his offered hand. "You knew."

"No, I didn't, I only just found out, too," he claimed.

Everything was overwhelming her, as she looked for reason in Abby's eyes. "That … that *animal* … was your brother." Sarah tried to fathom what she was saying but it made no sense to her. "That's not possible. How could that monster be related to anyone?" She wanted to cry but she wanted to scream more.

"Adopted. Sarah you have to understand …" Nathan tried but she glared at him.

"Understand … I have to understand. No, the only thing I had to do was survive, remember that—that's what you all told me, and now you want me to understand! He tried to kill me, Abby's brother …" Her mind bounced from one emotion to another. "Why? Why wouldn't you tell me?"

"Sarah, it wasn't Abby idea, it was mine. She was too young to realize what the consequences would be. I'm the one who decided to send her away, to cover all of this up. We were all so young, we had no idea …"

"She was a child then, not the woman I know now." Sarah turned her fury toward the tall, silent woman. "You could've told me."

"What would you've liked me to say? The man who almost killed you …" Abby's voice faltered, "the one who beat you senseless, was my brother. The same man who murdered all those women was my adopted brother whom my uncle had committed for killing my parents."

Sarah looked at her "You should've told me," she whispered slowly as she rose from the bench.

"We couldn't," Nathan said. "We couldn't tell you any more than Abby could tell Lincoln when she discovered he was killing those girls."

"When *did* you know?" Lincoln accused his partner.

Abby took a deep breath. She felt defeated, exhausted and spent, and she sat down and dropped her head into her hands. "After Traci Stempler—he sent me an email telling me how disappointed he was that I couldn't find him. I didn't even realize it was him; he had changed his name, and of course he was no longer the child I remembered."

Sarah looked at Nathan and the tired old lawyer sighed. "Please, let me explain." He looked at Abby but she wasn't looking at anyone. "My brother and his wife wanted a family, and when they seemingly couldn't have children they adopted William. But he wasn't the normal, happy child they had hoped for. He had some disturbing tendencies even as a toddler. Then Annie got pregnant with Abby. They tried their best to treat the two kids equally, but Billy became spiteful towards young Abby, and soon they feared for her safety." When Nathan paused, Lincoln looked over at Abby; she still had her head in her hands. He didn't know if it was because of the pain of the past or the shame of the present. Sarah was standing off to one side, listening in shocked disbelief as Nathan continued with his story.

"I wasn't around that much, but I talked to my brother enough to know that things were not good. Finally, the day came when he asked my legal advice about putting Billy into foster care. Getting him away from Abby, away from the family. Afterwards, I thought it was over, and everyone could breathe again, only it wasn't. Billy had kept in contact with Abby, he—"

"He sent me letters." Abby didn't lift her head as she spoke; she kept her eyes down and away from those she had hurt. "He sent me threats, but I never believed him, because there were times he was so nice and I missed him. Then one day out of the blue he showed up here, at Gold Creek. He had taken off from his foster family, for a visit, he said. I should have told someone," Abby's voice broke. "But I didn't and he murdered them." She swallowed several times and they waited for her to finish. "They took him away from here and he was laughing the whole time …"

Nathan took up the story. "When I arrived, I did what I thought was best. I had him committed, away from here and away from Abby, and I thought that was the end of it. I had my hands full with an orphaned niece I had no idea what to do with." Nathan reached down and placed a hand on Abby's shoulder. "I gave her everything money could buy, anything I could think of that might help, but I didn't give her the two things she needed most; my love and my time."

"You did what you could," Abby said quietly.

"I don't understand how he got out. Shouldn't he still be in an institution?" Lincoln asked as he tried to make sense of everything he had been told.

"We thought he was still hospitalized in Europe, but he was too smart for them—fooled the doctors into thinking he was sane. Apparently, he walked right out the front doors a free man. No one thought to call me or Abby."

"But maybe if we'd known who he really was, maybe we could've stopped him," Lincoln said.

Abby lifted her tearstained face to look at her ex-partner. "You think I haven't thought of that every day and night since this thing started?" She glanced fearfully over at Sarah, who had quietly taken a seat at the end of the bench. It was easy to see even in the dark the shock and pain this was causing her. Abby had no idea how to make it better.

"He was obsessed with Abby. He felt she owed him, just for being born. He hated her for taking away his family, taking away his life, but that was his own doing. He was sick and twisted even as a young boy." Nathan tried to explain, but Lincoln didn't want to hear it.

"But if we had known …"

"The only difference it would have made would have been the name we called him. Nothing else," Abby stated to her partner.

"But you should've told us," Sarah finally said quietly and all eyes turned to her. "I knew your parents had died here, but I didn't know you had seen it happen. I understand that, but you should have told us that he was your brother."

Abby stood up and walked over to Sarah. She had to make this right—but but she knew that Sarah's trust in her had been shattered. "There are a lot of things I should've done. I wish I could change that but I can't." Abby knelt down in front of Sarah. "I've spend half my life blaming myself for my parent's death—and a fortune on therapists so I can say, 'it wasn't my fault', but here I am again, wishing I could turn back time. But I can't. I can't bring back my parents, I can't bring back any of those girls—and I can't change what he did to you."

Sarah stared at her in silence, her mind a kaleidoscope of memories. "And I can't *forget* what he did to me. I'm sorry, I can't … I can't sit here and listen to this any more." Sarah stood up and Abby followed her.

"Sarah, please. Sarah!" Abby pleaded. "Sarah, I'm sorry."

She looked up at Abby with tears in her eyes. "So am I, Abby, so am I. It feels like I have been waiting a lifetime to see you again; but right now, I can't stand the sight of you!" And she walked away, leaving the three on the dock, silenced by her bitterness and understandable anger.

Nathan, feeling his age, took a seat on the bench. Lincoln licked at his split lip and Abby stood silently brooding.

The dark clouds at the end of the lake brought a chilling wind as Abby turned to face Lincoln. "I'm sorry. I wanted to tell you the truth, but I didn't know where to start or how to explain. And I'm sorry for that." She motioned to his lips.

The tall black man said nothing in response.

"Lincoln," Nathan said with a sigh. "My intentions were honorable, but I've lived in shame for what I did. I should have done more, but I can't change that now. I always feared that one day the truth would come out and everything that we had protected would be destroyed, and I knew that the more people who knew the truth, the bigger those chances were."

Lincoln looked from the elderly lawyer to Abby, "At what point would the truth have come out if I hadn't found it? When they were strapping Abby to the chair? Or would the two of you have taken it to the grave?" Lincoln turned and left them with the silence.

Looking over at his niece, Nathan felt emotionally and physically drained. "I'm sorry, Abby."

"So am I," she said as she watched the light come on in Sarah's bedroom. "So am I."

He turned around and saw what she was looking at. "Give them time, they'll get over it."

Sarah's light went out. "And what if they don't?" Abby asked. She glanced at him with tired eyes. "Can I live with myself for what I've done?"

Nathan pulled his eyes away from the cabin and looked out over the water. "You don't have a choice, Abby, it's already been done—that's the hardest part."

CHAPTER 47

Sarah cried herself to sleep and woke up several times during the night, unsure of what was real and what had been a nightmare. How could she love the woman whose lies had lead to the evil that had been forced upon her? She didn't know how, but she knew the hard part was that she did. She had heard Abby come in at some point and she had lain awake hoping for a knock on her door, but the only sound she heard was the tinkling of a glass being removed from the cupboard and the splashing of liquid filling it. She knew Abby was into the aquavit Günter had left behind. Struggling between love and anger, trust and betrayal, Sarah debated going out to talk to her, but at some point the decision was made for her when she fell back asleep.

The next time she woke up, she still felt tired, but no longer wanted to sleep. It was time to get up to face the day and hard reality. A quick peek inside the other bedroom told her Abby's bed had not been slept in.

"Old habits die hard," she muttered, thinking about Abby's sleeping patterns. It also didn't surprise her to see an empty living room and half empty glass of aquavit sitting next to the sink. Walking around the counter she stopped and looked out the front windows, but there was no sign of Abby on the deck. A frown creased her forehead when she spotted handwriting on the mirror above the fireplace.

I love you. I never meant to hurt you. Forgive me.
-A

Sarah stared at the barely legible message for a long time, chills running up her spine. She looked back at the glass by the sink and at the open bedroom door, before stepping outside.

Menacing dark clouds rolled over the mountaintops, sucking the light from sky. The air was muggy and humid as the storm hung over the entire valley. Standing at the edge of the deck, she could barely see down to the gloomy waters of the lake, and it was too dark to see the end of the dock.

"Abby," she whispered, an ominous feeling growing inside her. Something was wrong—very, very wrong. Turning around in growing panic she looked back at the cabin and then back to the eerie calm of the lake. "Abby," she said louder. Far off in the distance, the skies flashed and made her jump. Electricity raised the hair on her arms as she searched in the darkness. "Abby!" she called out but her voice was lost in the rolling thunder that rocked the entire shoreline.

Looking down at the lake, Sarah could see a sheet of rain bearing down on her. The winds churned up the waters, blowing her hair into her eyes and blinding her. She quickly went down the stairs and looked out, but the lake refused to give up any of its secrets. Panic and fear clouded her judgment as she tried to think of where Abby could have gone.

The lake water tossed in earnest now as the winds lifted the surface into whitecaps. Sarah felt the first few drops of rain and she brought her hand up to shield her eyes as a flash of lightning lit up the skies. Through the rain, she saw an empty aquavit bottle discarded on the bench.

"Abby," she called, but her voice disappeared into the wind as she fought against the intensifying gale. Picking up the empty bottle, she peered into the water. In a flash of lightning Sarah saw a dark shadow in the water that stilled her aching heart.

"Abby!" Her scream was lost in the storm as she jumped into the rolling waters and immediately vanished from sight.

☯

The cabin was dark and still when Abby tiptoed into the kitchen in search of the open bottle of aquavit on the counter. Pouring a glass, Abby tossed it back with one swallow. She left the glass next to the sink and, with the bottle in her hand, headed outside.

Taking a seat in one of the chairs on the deck, she took a drink from the bottle as she thought about her past and what it meant for her future. Her parents were gone, and the brother who had haunted and hunted her was out of her life for good.

She had feared him as a child, but as an adult she had loathed him. Yet somewhere deep inside she still felt a loss. All his life Billy had reminded her that she was everything that he was not. Her outgoing personality and athletic ability overshadowed his shy, clumsy nature. As brother and sister, they were opposites in almost every way, but their intellect was the same.

Abby's birth had brought out a side of Billy no one wanted to discuss. He had always felt he needed to be better than her in order to belong. Soon that competitiveness had become unhealthy. He turned on her, becoming mean and vengeful. She recalled, with a mixture of pain and relief, the day he left. She didn't understand what a ward of the court was; all she knew was that he wasn't going to be there to hurt her any more. But he did come back, and he hurt her more than she thought was possible. Until he hurt Sarah.

Sarah. The ache was almost unbearable, so she took another drink, hoping and trying to dull the feelings inside her, but she couldn't. She couldn't hide any more, not from them and not from herself. Over the years, she had learned to do things out of necessity, things to help her try to forget, but her mind wouldn't let her. She had become a master of concealment, hiding her emotions and feelings behind a warrior's armor, but only when she was awake. The night brought dreams she couldn't control, nightmares that would always remind her of what had happened. No matter what she did, she couldn't escape, so she built her walls higher and thicker. And nobody could hurt her if she never let anybody in.

Abby leaned back and took another drink. The nightmares that haunted her sleep had now become her reality—one she had always feared. Grabbing the bottle by the neck, Abby left the deck and headed down to the dock. Ignoring the approaching storm, she lay down on the wood and looked up at the swirling clouds.

"Same sky, same place," she sighed deeply. "Same woman." She reached for the bottle and chuckled. "Same drink." She reached out but her smile faded when she realized Buck was no longer there to pat and to hear her. Tears filled her eyes as she tilted her head back to finish the bottle. She left it sitting on the dock and went in search of more alcohol to ease her pain.

Creeping back into the cabin, she stopped outside Sarah's door. Swaying slightly, she thought about knocking, but her hand stopped in mid-air. What she was going to say? Nothing had changed; it had still been her brother and it was still her lie.

Staggering and stumbling as she turned, Abby went to the kitchen cupboard for another bottle. Being as quiet as a drunken person could, she searched the kitchen but there was nothing left for her to drink. Disappointed, she sat down on the sofa and stared down at the coffee table. She spotted a felt marker and decided to leave Sarah a note. Pulling the cap off with her teeth, she stood looking for something to write on when her eyes fell on the mirror.

Stepping back to look at the words she had written, she caught her reflection and she sneered at what she saw. Dark hair hanging around her pale face, eyes dark and bloodshot. Suddenly she thought about someone else's reflection and what she must have seen. *Sarah, what have I done to you?*

Frustrated and angry, Abby staggered back down to the end of the dock. Too many voices were churning in her head as she watched the clouds darken. Dropping her aching head into her hands, she tried to unravel the mess that was her life.

"I have no more secrets and there are no more lies, so why don't I feel any better?" She yelled into the storm. But the questions had no answers, at least none she could think of in her inebriated state. The skies crashed and thundered as she tried to no avail to make sense of her life.

"I need more to drink." She stood up and headed to the lodge.

Stepping into the building, she looked around at what was familiar and what was new. There was a wall of pictures she hadn't noticed before and she wandered over to it. She looked at picture after picture of families and couples enjoying their stay at Gold Creek. The more she looked the more she realized alcohol wouldn't cure the regret and the shame she was feeling. It was time to sober up and face what was left of her life. Leaving the wall behind, Abby made her way to the kitchen and some much needed food.

A while later, hunched over a sandwich, Abby looked out the window at the storm. Mother Nature was displaying all her power and fury as the thunder rumbled the walls and the lightning lit up the sky. Peering out into the darkness, Abby brought her cup of coffee to her mouth but froze when she saw someone out on one of the docks.

"Holy shit!" she exclaimed. "Get off the dock, you fool." She ran for the door and out into the storm. The wind whipped at her hair as she made her way down the grassy lawn toward the shoreline.

"Get off the dock, there's lightning out there," she yelled through cupped hands, but her voice couldn't be heard over the wind. Abby started to lift her arms up to wave when she realized who it was on the end of the dock.

"Sarah!" Thunder boomed all around her. "Sarah, get off the dock!" She waved but Sarah's attention was elsewhere. Abby knew she had to get to her and fast.

Large raindrops pounded the ground around her as she sprinted down the gravel driveway. "Sarah!" she yelled as the entire sky lit up over their heads. Then to her horror, she watched helplessly as Sarah dove into the blackness of Lake Alouette.

"No!" she screamed as she powered her long legs down the dock and launched herself into the water. Diving down, she searched the depths but there was nothing for her to see. She wanted to scream but she couldn't as she turned left and right, feeling and searching the cold dark waters. Every second was precious as she moved below the water's surface, but soon her lungs burned for oxygen and she had to go up for air. Abby broke the surface, but the choppy waves made it nearly impossible for her to see anything.

"Sarah," Abby screamed but all she heard was the sound of the storm. Taking a deep breath, she dove back down under the water. Moving farther away from the dock, Abby reached out into the blackness and touched something. Grabbing hold of whatever it was, she pushed to the surface, dragging her catch with her. The moment her head came out of the water, she looked down at the motionless woman in her grip. They had been here before, but this time things were different.

"Sarah!" Abby pulled the limp body higher in the water, yanking the head up as she kicked her legs towards the dock. Over and over she called out to Sarah, but there was no response. Abby felt the ground come up below her feet and she hauled her load up onto the dock through the pouring rain. The winds howled overhead as Abby climbed out and knelt down next to Sarah. Quickly she checked for a pulse on her neck, the action bringing a flash of déjà vu which she quickly shook off. Sarah's heartbeat was strong but she wasn't breathing. Abby leaned over and began to administer artificial respirations.

"Breathe, Sarah," she screamed at her between breaths. "Come on!" She pushed the air into the young woman's lungs and challenged her to come back. "Don't give up now." Abby's hands were shaking so badly she could barely pinch Sarah's nose as she continued her desperate attempt to bring her back to life. "Damn it, Sarah, don't you give up—you're a fighter. Breathe!" she demanded and suddenly, without warning, Sarah obeyed. Her mouth opened wide and a rush of water came out as she coughed and gagged.

"Sarah," Abby sobbed as she turned her over, allowing the young woman to expel all she had inhaled. Holding her and crying at the same time, Abby brushed back the wet hair out of her eyes. "Why, Sarah? What were you thinking?"

Sarah coughed violently trying to clear her lungs as she clung to Abby. After several long minutes, she finally sat up straighter and the two women knelt facing each other as the storm blew violently around them.

"What were you trying to do?" Abby asked as she kissed the top of her head.

"I was … I thought," *cough* … "I thought you'd," *cough* … "I thought you'd gone in …" She pointed to the empty bottle of aquavit sitting on the bench in the rain.

Abby's tightened her embrace. "Sarah, you jumped in the lake because you thought I had?"

Sarah nodded, shaking the rain from the end of her nose. "I couldn't find you," she answered.

"But, Sarah," Abby said in shock. "I thought you were trying to commit suicide. You jumped in the lake … Sarah, you don't know how to swim."

Sarah turned to look at her and managed a weak smile, "I … I forgot."

Abby let her tears fall as she returned the smile, "God, I love you," she whispered as a flash of lightning shot overhead. "Come on, I need to get you inside," she said as she easily scooped up the young woman in her arms.

Sarah studied the face so close to her and she could smell the strong odor of alcohol. "I saw the note on the mirror, and the empty bottle, and … well, I thought I saw something in the lake and …" she stopped talking and Abby stopped walking.

"You thought I'd had too much to drink and had fallen in?" Abby said still in shock as to what Sarah had done.

"Yes," she answered honestly. "You seem to drink a lot. Is that only when I'm around?"

Abby ignored the question and said nothing until they were inside the shelter of the cabin. "I thought you wanted to leave?" Abby said as she put the young woman on her feet.

"I did—I do. I am angry with you," Sarah said.

"Sarah, how many times can I say I'm sorry? I never meant for this to happen …"

"But it did, and you lied about why," Sarah stated simply. Her face twisted with painful memories of what she had been through and it tore at Abby's heart. "He was your brother, Abby, I just can't … I don't understand the why, or for what reasons." She was confused and she wanted answers. "Can you at least help me understand?"

Looking away from Sarah, Abby forced herself to recall another time and another place. "I don't fully understand why he did it. I was too young." Rubbing her hands together, she spoke about her past. "I knew there was something about him that scared me, and when he realized that, he used that fear." Abby swallowed. "They tried to help him, Mom and Dad did, but he seemed to resent it. The more doctors they sent him to, the more troubled he became. Until he snapped." Sarah said nothing as she listened to Abby. "I know now, what he really wanted was to hurt me. So they sent him away and he went to live with another family. And then that summer, I found him hiding in one of the cabins. I should have told someone he was there, but I was scared …"

Abby turned her attention back to Sarah. "When I think about Mom and Dad, or those women, when I look at you, I can't help but remember the boy I knew, and the man he became." For the first time, Abby reached for the scar on Sarah's neck. "He's gone now, but the memories will never go away."

"No, they won't," Sarah said as she pulled away before Abby could touch her. "They won't go away no matter how much you drink, Abby! You know, one day you will sober up, but I will be left with the scars." She was angry; her words were bitter and sharp. "I don't climb inside a bottle every time I can't face something. But you know what, Abby, the reasons why he did what he did aren't half as important to me as why you did what you did." Abby heard the resentment in her voice.

Abby hung her head. She struggled for some semblance of a response but she knew there wasn't one. "So now what? Where do we go from here?"

Sarah looked down at the floor.

"Sarah?"

"I don't know, Abby." She moved to the window and watched in silence as the wind pinged the rain into the glass. Abby knew there was more than one storm going on as she watched Sarah struggle for the words. "I've found out who I am and what I'm made of—I'm a fighter, a survivor. I'm no longer that naïve girl who arrived here looking for a story." She looked down at her numb thumb. "I don't even know if that's a good thing or a bad thing."

Looking at her, Abby had to agree she was a different woman. But that didn't change how she felt. She was in love with the woman on the inside. The one she had lied to.

"I need to sort things out in my mind, Abby …" Her words disappeared with the wind howling against the log cabin walls.

"I love you, Sarah. I know that now more than ever."

Sarah turned back to her. "The hard part is I love you, too, Abby." Her tears streamed unchecked down her face, "But sometimes love isn't enough. I have to trust you, Abby, and I don't know if I can do that."

"Look at me, Sarah, and believe this. From the first day that I met you, you changed the woman I thought I was. I do care, I do love, and I can trust! I am not that hard-hearted cop I thought I was. Yes, I told you lies and I spoke mistruths, but so did you for your own reasons."

"That's not fair, Abby."

"All's fair in love and war, Sarah, isn't that what they say? I love you and what happened to you is not fair, but I have held your lifeless body in my arms not once but twice and I know with all the truth that I can muster that I don't want to lose you. I don't want to live without you. The lies we told each other have nothing to do with how we feel. I don't care if you are a reporter, that doesn't matter." Abby reached to wipe away the tears on Sarah's face. "I can't change what has happened to you, but that doesn't alter how I feel. I fell in love with the woman inside. Please, give us a chance."

Sarah looked away as Abby pleaded for their relationship. "I can't stay here," Sarah finally choked out. "I'll be leaving with Lincoln in the morning."

Abby's mouth opened but nothing came out. The reality of what Sarah was saying hit her in the chest—hard.

"It's too much for me right now. Everything we thought we had, Abby, has been built on lies. I lied to you and you lied to me. What kind of a relationship does that give us?"

"We can start again, Sarah." Abby's head was swimming and her heart was breaking as she felt the remains of her world crumble around her. "We can build on what we have."

"What *do* we have?" Sarah tried to stay strong and determined but her voice betrayed her. "Maybe with time … maybe with time we can find what we lost, but what's left after the dust of all those lies settles?"

"Love," Abby answered honestly.

Sarah closed the distance between them and looked into Abby's eyes. Reaching up, she placed a hand on Abby's wet cheek. "I love you. I want you to know that. But I need time."

The tears overflowed as Abby struggled with her emotions. "I don't understand, but if that is what you want, I'll abide by your wishes." Abby straightened herself up and cleared her throat. "I told you once before—take all the time in the world." Abby swallowed the lump threatening to take her voice. "And when you're ready, I'll be waiting for you." Abby leaned down, kissed the top of Sarah's head, and then turned to leave the cabin. "When I first saw you that day on the dock …" Abby tried to collect herself as best as she could, "I knew you were trouble for me."

"And how is that?" Sarah asked softly through her tears.

Abby looked into her emerald green eyes. "Because you were just the right size to slip through what I had spent a lifetime building up. You need to get out of those wet clothes." She nodded towards Sarah's chest and, as the redhead glanced down at her damp attire, the door of the cabin closed softly.

☯

The storm blew out by late morning and the skies were clear and blue as Nathan's helicopter left the resort. High on a mountain, in a field of tall grass, a lone figure sat astride her black stallion. With an aching heart and a pounding head, Abby watched through shimmering tears as Sarah flew out of her life.

CHAPTER 48

Carla was washing dishes when a black Jeep pulled into their driveway. She was about to tell her husband that he had company, but decided enough time had gone by and the two friends needed to repair what had been broken. Lincoln had forgiven Nathan, but he hadn't spoken to Abby in months. He felt that her lies were far more hurtful and damaging than the lawyer's. It had taken a while, but Lincoln had returned to work at Holoman and Associates.

Out in the Jeep, Abby took several breaths before she found the courage to face what she had done. Leaving the vehicle, she headed up the walkway. Much to her surprise, the front door opened before she had a chance to knock.

"Carla?"

"Abby." Carla held her arms open and gave the dark-haired woman a much-needed hug. "How are you?"

Abby came out of the embrace and released a very audible breath. "Good days and bad days."

"He's in the study," Carla said without being asked and Abby nodded.

The door was closed, so Abby knocked first and entered. Lincoln had his head buried in his computer and didn't look up. "Did I hear someone at the door?"

Abby took several steps into the room before she answered, "Just an old friend." Her mouth was dry and her palms were sweating as she waited to see his response.

Lincoln sat up but didn't turn to face her.

"Please don't ask me to leave." She waited and he didn't. "I don't have much left in my life, at least not much that used to be there, and ah …" Abby cleared her throat as Lincoln turned to face her. She found it hard to look him in the eye, but she held on to what had brought her here. "I am trying to takes some steps to repair what I … There's no excuse for what I did. I know that now. I abused our friendship and I took advantage of the situation." She rubbed her palms on her jeans as she looked around the room. "Man, this is tougher than I thought." Lincoln remained silent, which made it even harder.

"I should have trusted you. You are more family to me than Nate is, and I ah …" Abby lost her words for a moment. It had been so much easier last night looking in the mirror, but she pushed on. "I should have told you the truth. I don't know when, but that doesn't matter, at some point I should have … told you. I was wrong and I hurt those that I love the most." Her voice started to waver and she looked out the window, but Lincoln saw the tears. "I am sorry, Lincoln. Please forgive me. I need you back in my life. I can't do it alone."

He stood up and came around his desk. "There was a lot of water under that bridge you burned. How can I know that I can trust you?"

"Because I know how much I hurt you, Lincoln. I know I handled this really badly but there just wasn't a good time to tell you. I know that sounds like a cop-out and that isn't an excuse. I was wrong; that's the bottom line. But you have to give me a chance to earn back your trust; you have to."

He stood tall and silent for what seemed like forever, and Abby waited, unsure of what to do next. He had missed her, more than she knew. Many times Carla had tried to get him to call her, but he couldn't find the words. Now here she stood before him, and he realized that it was time to put the past where it belonged.

Lincoln held open his arms. "I've missed you, Abby." He looked at her and the two friends embraced. Not much else was said for a long time as she held on to him for the strength she needed. They parted and he looked her in the eyes, and for the first time he saw they were clear and bright. "So now what? I gather from your uncle that you're not going back to the force."

"No, not at this time. I've talked to Banks and my job is there if I want it, but I don't want it right now."

"I hear you're building a new place out at Gold Creek?"

"Yeah, at the one end of the lake. There was a clearing and … ah."

He knew all too well about the clearing and what she was building there. Watching her for a moment, he dared to go where Nathan had warned him not to. "And Sarah?"

That topic was too painful and she shook her head no.

"Abby?"

"I'm not at that step yet."

And for now, Lincoln let it go.

CHAPTER 49

There was a knock on Lincoln's office door and he looked up as Nathan poked his head in. "Working hard or hardly working?" Nathan asked.

"Depends if the boss is looking," Lincoln quipped back.

"How's your case load?" Nathan asked as he leaned in with his hand on the door handle. "I'm heading out to Gold Creek. I'd like you to join me."

Lincoln looked down at the clutter on his desk. "Is there a problem?"

"No one knows her better than you, and I was hoping you could tell me," Nathan said with concern.

"Ah, what the hell." He reached for his suit jacket off the back of his chair. "I needed a break anyhow."

☯

They didn't talk much on the ride out to the resort, mainly because it was difficult to converse over the noise of a helicopter. Lincoln was looking forward to seeing Abby again. Their visits were few and far between, but not by his choice. Abby wasn't the same person any more and he never knew if it was because of the trial, the truth, or the pain of a lost love.

Sarah was gone and she had yet to resurface in Abby's life, but she had been in contact with him. She had found a job working for a small paper in Boulder, Colorado. No one knew who she was and she liked it that way. They had talked about many things in the past few months, but they had never talked about Billy and they never talked about Abby. He wanted to, but she wouldn't have it. Time had healed *his* hurt, and he knew now that Billy's kinship to Abby wouldn't have made any difference to the case or to the number of victims he had left behind. But he wasn't Sarah and he didn't have the scars that she did.

Lincoln felt a nudge and he looked over at Nathan. The elderly lawyer pointed out the window. "Can you see it?" he hollered over the roar of the rotors.

Lincoln leaned over and peered out the window. Even from this height he could see the new log home rising out of the lush green mountains. In the shade of the trees, next to a small wooden bench, Abby occupied her every waking hour building a home in hopes that Sarah would return. At first everyone thought the labor of love was a good idea; it gave her something to do besides dwell on old memories. But time moved on and Sarah hadn't returned and they wondered if she ever would.

"Quite a place," Nathan said.

"Would you expect anything less? But what happens when it's finished?"

"That is what I'm concerned about. I've tried to talk to her … but she's so stubborn and pig-headed," Nathan said loudly. "We've talked about things we've never talked about before. Her parents, Billy … but two things are still taboo. Her plans for the future …"

"And Sarah," Lincoln finished for him.

"You're the closest to them both, Lincoln. You've got to get through to one of them."

He looked at his boss, "And which one would you suggest? The stubborn, pig-headed brunette or the obstinate, inflexible redhead?"

☯

Lincoln made his way up the heavily trampled trail. He could hear the pounding of a hammer echoing over the lake and surrounding mountains. Coming over the last rise he stopped to take in Abby's creation; a beautiful log home with a high pitched roof and large windows for a spectacular view.

Abby was pounding a nail into a cedar shingle on the roof. Gone was the gaunt prison pallor, replaced by a muscular body and bronzed skin, which now glistened in sweat.

"One gear, one speed—forward and fast," he said under his breath as he started walking towards her. "Hello, the homestead," he hollered.

A bright smile filled Abby's tanned face. "Lincoln!" Quickly she scampered down the ladder.

Coming out of their embrace, he tried to look into her eyes but she quickly avoided his gaze. "Well, what'd you think?" She held her arms out in gesture.

"You've outdone yourself. I thought you did great work on your farm house, but this … this is something." Lincoln looked over at her. "You're looking well."

"The outdoors agrees with me," she said seriously.

"And obviously sobriety does, too?"

"Yeah—I haven't touched a drop since ..."

Lincoln watched her profile as she looked over her home. "Since when Abby?"

Ignoring his question, she opened a can of iced tea and took a drink. "Abby, Abby ... look at me." She did as he requested. "You can't even say her name?" He knew her well enough to see the pain before she hid it. "You're putting everything you have into this home. What happens if she doesn't come back?"

Lincoln watched her jaw muscle clench as she fought to stay in control. He reached out and grabbed her by the arm. "Abby, look at me," Lincoln asked, but she looked anywhere but at him. "Damn it, Abby, you're keeping so busy because you don't want to think about the alternative."

"What would you know?"

"I know you're hurting. You want something so bad, but you have no idea how to get it."

Abby shook her head but said nothing.

"Abby, I know you. I know how scared you are."

"Of all the things I am, Lincoln, scared is *not* one of them," she fired back.

"Aren't you? You're pushing yourself so hard so you don't have to think about her. You don't even have to think, just work and breathe." He waited but there was nothing. "Tell me I'm wrong. Tell me to go to hell. You won't, Abby, because you know I'm right."

"Go to hell, Lincoln," she said, pulling her arm out of his grasp.

"No! I'm not doing this any more. You love her, Abby, and it's killing you not being with her. Those emotional walls you've built up have been coming down since you met her and that scares the shit out of you. She's seen the real you—we all have and it scares you."

"Enough, Lincoln," she stated calmly but firmly as a darkness passed through her eyes.

"Jesus Christ, Abby!"

Abby's eyes dropped, but Lincoln never wavered. "I know you love her and you're busting your ass to build this, but you can't even say her name!" Abby tried to look away, but Lincoln stepped in front of her. "You *are* going to listen to me, even if I have to beat it into you."

She looked her partner in the eyes. "You just don't understand."

"No. I don't." He stood before her. "Make me understand. You love her and she loves you. The answer seems simple to me."

Silently, Abby stood, but Lincoln could see her struggle to keep her lower lip steady. "I gave her my word," she finally said quietly.

"What?" Lincoln responded in shock and surprise.

"I gave her my word."

"Word, what word? What kind of bullshit is that? You let the woman you love leave because you gave her your word?" He couldn't fathom what she was trying to say. "Are you telling me you are putting yourselves through all of this because of some stupid—what—honor?"

"It's not stupid, Lincoln. She told me she needed time."

Rolling his eyes to the skies, he let out a chuckle of disbelief. "Oh for the love of …" He looked back at her. "You know, I always thought as a lesbian you had it made. You're a woman, so you should be able to understand women. You of all people would know what makes a woman tick. But you're more fucked in the head than most of the guys I know."

"What the hell's that suppose to mean?"

"It means you've been pining away for her, while she's been waiting for you to get her."

Abby shook her head. "No, Lincoln, you don't understand. She said she needed time."

"No, you … arrrrgggg … you fool! You don't understand. You're not waiting for her, she is waiting for you!"

She opened her mouth to protest but then quickly closed it again.

"Abby, I never said I understood women, but I do know the rules. Sometimes, for whatever reasons, you say one thing and we're supposed to know you mean the exact opposite. When you run, it means you want us to run after you."

She listened to his words, she listened to her heart, and for the first time in months, she listened to the little voice in her head.

"Go after her, Abby. It's what you both want."

The solemn woman turned back and looked at the home she had been building. She had poured her heart and soul into keeping her mind occupied, but he was right, it hadn't worked. Everything she had done lately had been for Sarah.

Soulfully, she looked at her partner. "But I have no idea where to even find her."

Lincoln smiled. "I do."

Helga was in the kitchen pouring coffee for Nathan and Günter, when she spotted Lincoln and Abby coming down the road.

"Well, as I live and breathe," she muttered.

"What is that, my dear?" Günter looked up at his wife.

She gestured towards the front walkway, "Mohammad got the mountain to come in for lunch." All eyes turned to see Lincoln opening the door for Abby.

Nathan quickly rose and went to her with open arms. "My dear, it's so good to see you," he said.

"I don't mean to be rude, but I'm not staying." Abby didn't see the wave of disappointment looks that went across the room. "Uncle Nate, I was hoping to borrow your chopper."

"My chopper? Where are you going?"

Abby shifted her gaze to Lincoln. "Boulder, Colorado."

CHAPTER 50

"Take the quote out of the first line and put it to the end of the story, all right?" the man at the head of the table said. "Okay, where are we with the story on the closing of those hospital beds?"

"That's mine," Sarah quickly responded to her editor as she flipped through her notes. "The decrease in the number of beds is part of the new clinical service plan, at least that's what the press release says. Management says it'll save money, but the medical authorities say it'll cost lives."

"Good. You okay with contacts? If you need any, talk to Berelli, he knows everyone," he said with a gesture to an older man snoozing in his chair.

"Who's next?"

The meeting was interrupted by a sharp rap on the glass door. "What!"

"Sorry to interrupt, Mr. Gower," the receptionist held out a piece of paper. "But I just got a message for Sarah. It sounded important."

Bob Gower looked at her in annoyance. He hated having the dailies interrupted. "What's the message?"

The receptionist looked at Sarah. "Did you have a meeting scheduled for today?"

Flipping quickly through her Day Timer, Sarah shook her head, "No."

"Just give her the message," Bob Gower said impatiently.

The receptionist handed Sarah the small pink note. "They said to tell you they were waiting. I thought you had forgotten a meeting."

"No, I don't think so, but thanks," Sarah said with confusion as she took the note.

"Okay, back to business."

Sarah unfolded the note. *I'm still waiting.* She thought about the message for a moment, but then placed the neatly handwritten note down on her pad. Looking around the table at her fellow reporters, she tried to get back into the conversation but her eyes kept returning to the note. *I'm still waiting.* Waiting for what?

"Sarah?"

"Pardon?" She looked at her boss, totally unaware of what he had asked.

"Are you with us here? I don't have all the time in the world. I've a paper to put out …" His voice droned on as she felt her heart skip a beat as she picked up the message. *I'm still waiting.* Her mind went to the only place it could.

"Sarah! Where are you going?" Bob Gower demanded as she rose quickly from her chair with the note in her hand.

"I just … I have to check something …" Quickly, she reached for the door and left the meeting. Her heart was racing and she couldn't seem to catch her breath.

"Excuse me." Sarah approached the receptionist. "This message; what else did they say?"

"Nothing, they were very precise about what I wrote, but that was it."

"Did they leave a number?"

"Nope, she just told me how to write the note and left."

Sarah put her hands on the counter, "Left?" She turned and looked at the doors that lead to the elevators. "She was here?" Not waiting for an answer, Sarah rushed past the cubicles and pushed open both doors. There was no one there, as she looked left and right in the empty vestibule.

Stabbing at the down arrow for the elevator, she watched and waited, continuously tapping the pink note against her thigh. "Come on, come on, come on!" But the elevator car wasn't moving fast enough.

"Forget it," she said impatiently as she took off for the stairwell. "Please … please … please," she repeated on every step as she hurried down the stairs. There were several people milling around the lobby as she burst out of the doorway, but none were Abby. Her eyes scanned back and forth, but there was no sign of the dark-black hair. Sarah entered the revolving doors that exited the building. Banging on the glass, Sarah pushed hard—but the harder she pushed, the more resistance she got from the door. By the time she reached the sidewalk, she realized it was too late. There was no sign of Abby anywhere.

With sagging shoulders, she turned back towards her building.

Sarah took a deep breath as she squinted into the sun. *Another day and another disappointment—where are you Abby?* She looked down at the note in her hand. Crumpling the paper, she walked over to a garbage can and threw it away. With a heavy heart, she entered the revolving door and left the outside world behind. She looked through the glass to the mirrored wall inside the lobby. In the reflection she saw a world oblivious to her existence: people hustling down the sidewalk, cars impatiently threading their way through traffic, the green of the aspen trees in the park across the street … and a tall, dark-haired woman leaning against one of the stone statues.

Sarah spun around inside the tiny enclosure of the revolving door. Though her line of vision was obstructed, she knew it was Abby. With both hands she pushed harder for the doors to rotate as she tried to look past all the obstacles blocking her view. When she was finally released back out onto the sidewalk, she stood and stared at the woman across the street.

There she was. Dressed in jeans and a white shirt with a dark blazer, her long legs crossed at the ankle as she stood waiting.

"Abby?" Looking both ways for traffic, no other words or thoughts came to her mind as she quickly darted across the street.

The two studied each other silently, wallowing in the remembrance, taking in all they'd forgotten.

Looking longingly into Sarah's eyes, Abby finally found her voice. "I didn't know how much longer I was supposed to wait," she said with a sheepish grin.

Sarah choked out a sobbing laugh as she brought her hand up to cover her mouth. There was no response, but all Abby had to do was to open her arms and, without hesitation, Sarah fell into her embrace.

"Sarah, I am so sorry, I know …"

"Shhh," Sarah put her fingers to Abby's lips. "It's all been said, one way or another, by one of us or both of us."

"But I want you to know," Abby said.

"I do know. But no more secrets, Abby. You've spent your life hiding and running." Abby lifted her head to look away, but Sarah wouldn't let her. "I think it's time for you to stop."

Sarah saw the tears shimmering on the brink of falling. "I have stopped," Abby whispered as she reached into the pocket of her jeans. She pulled something out and placed it into Sarah's hand.

Sarah's face turned serious, as she looked down at the plastic token in her hand. The number ninety was inscribed on both sides. "Ninety?" she questioned.

"Days sober. I'm not hiding inside a bottle anymore." There was a long and hard silence as Sarah studied the token and took in what it meant. She clasped her fingers around it and then looked into Abby's eyes. Only then did Sarah realize what looked so different. It wasn't that the pain was gone, but the clarity of what remained. "I don't want to run and I don't want to hide, Sarah. There is so much that I have missed because I was afraid, but I have nothing to be afraid of anymore except losing you. I want you in my life." A tear spilt over and ran down Abby's cheek. "I need you in my life."

"We said a lot of things," Sarah said as she brushed back the tear.

"I'm not saying it will be easy. I'm just asking for you to give us a chance. We have something, Sarah, and I don't want to let that go. Sarah, I need for you to forgive me."

Sarah closed her eyes and wrapped her arms around the woman she loved. "I already have, Abby—I already have," she said as she melted into Abby's embrace. It was a comfortable feeling that she had missed. "I love you, Abby."

"I love you too," Abby whispered into Sarah's red hair, "Can I take you home now?"

"In your arms, I am home."

CHAPTER 51

MONTHS LATER

"Would you stop fussing? The place looks great," Abby said to Sarah as she scurried around the log home.

"I want everything to look perfect," Sarah answered over her shoulder. "Not everyone's seen the place, you know."

"It's a housewarming, Sarah, not dinner with the president."

Coming up behind her, Sarah slid her arms around Abby's waist. "I'd like to think that it's more than just a housewarming," she said as looked down at the sparkling diamond newly set on her finger.

Turning around to face her, Abby smiled down at her. "Do you like it? I mean really, because we can go and exchange it for whatever you want."

Taking Abby's face into her hands, Sarah repeated once more, "I love it."

"I'm glad," Abby said as she leaned down and kissed the side of Sarah's cheek as her hand slid farther down …

"Hey, stop that!" Sarah playfully slapped her hand away.

"No one's due here for another half-hour," Abby said in her own defense.

"I know, but I want to make sure everything is perfect. It seems so long since I've seen Lincoln and Carla. I mean, I'm not the one who hops into the helicopter and goes into the city for coffee like it's a ride to Flanagan's."

Abby shot her a playful scowl as she walked over to the window, "Come here," she said with an outstretched hand. Pulling Sarah in front of her, Abby wrapped her long arms around her and they snuggled into each other. "Are you happy?" Abby whispered into her ear.

Sarah turned around and lifted her hand to Abby's cheek. "Like in a dream," she replied. She looked into the dark eyes sparkling with the magic of love. "Are you?"

"How could I not be?" Abby said with a smile as she leaned down and kissed Sarah gently on the mouth. "They're going to be here when?" she said with a sly wink.

"Would you stop," Sarah said, blushing.

"Only if you want me to," Abby said as she dipped her head enough to look at Sarah with inviting eyes.

"Abby," Sarah giggled out the name as the dark-haired woman pulled her backward towards the sofa.

"What?" She responded with tender kisses and soft caresses as they intertwined. Moans mixed with giggles, and sighs turned to gasps of desire as Sarah found herself lying on top of Abby. Abby's eyes traveled down Sarah's face, but they stopped at the scar on her neck. With a slow hand, she reached out and fingered the fading red line. Sarah said nothing as she watching Abby's eyes.

"Does it hurt anymore?"

"No," she whispered as she watched Abby's eyes. "Don't do it," she warned softly.

Abby lifted her gaze to look at her. "Do what?"

"Don't start the *what ifs*. We both know what the therapist said." Sarah referred to the psychiatrist they were seeing to help them deal with the past. "Go forward, Abby, and leave the past where it belongs." Sarah watched her. With help, Abby's nightmares were becoming more and more infrequent, but every once in a while, Sarah still saw the pain and heard the memories. "Look to the future. We have a resort to run, and by spring Carla and Lincoln will be making you a godmother."

"Making us," Abby corrected. "What about you. What about your wishes?"

"I've got everything I could ever have wished for." The corner of Sarah's mouth lifted into a smile. "I've a home that you've built to my every whim, and I have friends around me who care," she said. Then she added, "and a diamond ring from the woman I love."

They shared a kiss, a moment in time when all else was forgotten.

There was the distant sound of a motor and the two parted. "Must be them."

Quickly they pulled on their boots and jackets, then hand-in-hand they waited as the first set of headlights from one of the resort vehicles came into view.

"Excited?"

"Of course I'm excited, it's a party," Sarah said with a twinkle in her eye.

"No, there's something more than that."

"Maybe," she answered with a mischievous grin as the vehicle came to a halt in their driveway.

"It's Nathan," Abby said into Sarah's ear. "He's looking good." The trial and the truth had taken a heavy toll on him and, at one point, Abby had been gravely concerned about his health and well-being. But looking at him now, she knew he, too, was learning to live again. With a quick wave, she turned to collect some firewood.

"Ah, Abby, he's not alone," Sarah quickly whispered. The comment caught Abby by surprise and she turned back to see Nathan helping Mary Banks to her feet.

"Well, son of a …"

"You go, Nate," Sarah said just loud enough for Abby's ears. "Does this make her Aunt Mary?"

Abby shot her a glance that was a weak attempt at a glare.

☯

The log home was bustling with company; sounds of laughter could be heard floating over the snowdrifts. Every time Abby's eyes went in search of Sarah, she found the young redhead huddled next to Carla and it didn't take a detective to know the two were up to something.

"Everyone, if I can get your attention, please," Lincoln clinked on his glass. It took several moments but the noise in the room finally hushed. "I would like to make a toast."

Out of the corner of her eye, she saw Sarah come back into the room.

"Where did you go?"

"Nowhere," she said quietly with a smile.

"I saw …"

"Shhh, they're toasting you," Sarah whispered with a nudge.

"Toasting me or roasting me," muttered Abby under her breath.

"Believe it or not, we did miss that surly attitude and the sharp wicked tongue of yours. Welcome home, Abby," Lincoln said with a raised glass and the room followed suit.

The attention was more than Abby wanted to deal with, but Sarah's arm around her waist kept her in the center of the room.

"And to Nathan Holoman, still one of the best damn lawyers out there," Lincoln continued and the room echoed his toast. "And the second best boss I've ever had."

The chuckles rippled through the room as Mary and Nathan slyly grinned at each other.

"Now before I let you all loose to continue this party, I do have one more thing I would like to add." Lincoln grew serious. "In everything that's happened over this last year, we didn't have time to honor one of our own." A different tone came over the room. "We were taught by him how to preserve a crime scene and we were lectured by him when it was forgotten." There was a mumble of agreement. "Many of our cases were won or lost because of him, so I ask you to raise your glass to one of our own: to Hyme, the best witness on the stand. May your prints be clear and your powder dry."

"To Hyme," they all said.

With the toast done, Sarah quickly excused herself, and Abby was about to follow to see what she was up to when Lincoln's somber face caught her attention. He had moved away from the center of the room and was looking out the front window.

"Hey, partner, you okay?" she asked.

His eyes remained on the moonlit snow-covered lake. "Yeah, I was just thinking about Hyme. He would've blown this case wide open."

"Linc, it's over with, let it go."

"I'm trying, Abby, but something's been bothering me. And you always told me, that when something with a case is bothering you, it's because something isn't right." Lincoln turned and looked at Abby. "Who was driving that Jeep?"

"I don't know …"

"And who did Dot hear that night?"

"Lincoln," Abby said slowly. "Let—it—go."

"Aren't you curious? I mean, why did he leave all that evidence for us to find?"

"Lincoln," she answered, "it's in the past. We got a lot of answers from his laptop but some of that stuff just wasn't recoverable. We'll never know. Let it go."

"Abby?" Sarah's searching voice came over the steady hum of the room, but Lincoln and Abby were locked in a stare.

"Doesn't it bother you?"

She had no time to respond before her girlfriend found her and ended the standoff.

"Come here, you." An excited Sarah took Abby by the hand and dragged her back into the center of the room. Looking over her shoulder, she watched Lincoln slowly join the rest of the guests.

"Wait here," Sarah asked.

"What?" Abby was confused as Sarah put up a hand. "I said, wait here—please."

Something was up and Abby knew it had been brewing most of the evening. Anxiously she watched Sarah disappear into the kitchen. Moments later Günter and Helga came out and stood next to Nathan.

"Abby."

She turned at the sound of her name and looked into Sarah's sparkling emerald eyes.

Abby smiled. "You look like you're about ready to burst," she said with a chuckle.

"I asked you earlier if you were happy, and you said you were." Sarah squirmed nervously back and forth from one foot to the other. "But I think you *could* be happier. Just wait," she stopped Abby before she could respond. "I wanted to get you something." Suddenly Sarah found herself with a large lump in her throat. "But what do you get the girl that has everything?" Sarah continued to squirm but something moved and Abby realized it wasn't just Sarah squirming as a little black nose popped out of her sweater.

"Lincoln helped me find him." Sarah lifted out the young puppy and handed the silver and black ball of fur to her. "Abby, I would like you to meet LB."

Abby reached for her new friend, "LB?" she questioned as she held the puppy over her face. He leaned down and licked at her nose.

"Little Buck—he came from a litter sired by Buck's brother."

Abby closed her misty eyes as she recalled another time and another place. And for the first time in a long time the past made her smile.